DRAGONSLAYER

How can we possibly overcome this, he thought, as awe threatened to paralyse him? It did not seem possible that human or dwarf valour could prevail against such a thing. It was just too big. They were like mice trying to overcome a grown man. Even as these thoughts surged through Felix's mind, Gotrek reached the dragon's foot.

Felix's numbed mind noted that the talons of the creature's paw were almost the size of the Slayer. If this dismayed Gotrek, he gave no sign of it. His axe flashed through a thunderous arc and bit into the dragon's leg at about the spot the ankle would have been in a human. The mighty blade parted scales and flesh. Greenish blood spurted steaming from the wound. The dragon bellowed its rage and pain once more then bent forward, its head coming down with the speed of a striking serpent, its huge jaws opening and threatening to take Gotrek in one gulp.

Felix wondered if the moment of the Slayer's doom had finally arrived.

Also from the Black Library

GOTREK & FELIX: TROLLSLAYER
by William King

GOTREK & FELIX: SKAVENSLAYER
by William King

GOTREK & FELIX: DAEMONSLAYER
by William King

SPACE WOLF
by William King

RAGNAR'S CLAW
by William King

GAUNT'S GHOSTS: FIRST & ONLY
by Dan Abnett

GAUNT'S GHOSTS: GHOSTMAKER
by Dan Abnett

HAMMERS OF ULRIC
by Dan Abnett, Nik Vincent & James Wallis

EYE OF TERROR
by Barrington J. Bayley

INTO THE MAELSTROM
edited by Marc Gascoigne & Andy Jones

REALM OF CHAOS
edited by Marc Gascoigne & Andy Jones

STATUS: DEADZONE
edited by Marc Gascoigne & Andy Jones

A WARHAMMER NOVEL

Gotrek and Felix

DRAGONSLAYER

By William King

A BLACK LIBRARY PUBLICATION

First published in Great Britain in 2000 by
Games Workshop Publishing
Willow Road, Lenton,
Nottingham, NG7 2WS, UK

10 9 8 7 6 5 4 3 2 1

Cover illustration by John Gravato

A CIP record for this book
is available from the British Library

ISBN 1 84154 122 2

Set in ITC Giovanni

Printed and bound in Great Britain by
Omnia Books Ltd., Glasgow

See the Black Library on the Internet at
http://www.blacklibrary.co.uk

Find out more about Games Workshop
and the world of Warhammer at
http://www.games-workshop.com

'As we flew back from the lost citadel of Karag Dum, I was excited by the prospect of seeing Ulrika again and by the thought of resting for a while after our adventures. Little did I realise that our perils were just beginning, and that we would soon encounter enemies both old and new, as well as one of the mightiest monsters it has ever been my misfortune to meet.'

— *My Travels With Gotrek*, Vol III
by Herr Felix Jaeger (Altdorf Press, 2505)

PROLOGUE

NIGHT OF THE SKAVEN

SOON, THOUGHT Grey Seer Thanquol, my brave warriors will attack.

Thanquol rubbed his paws together with glee. Soon all his planning and bargaining would pay off. Soon he would have his revenge on the dwarf, Gotrek Gurnisson, and his loathsome human henchman, Felix Jaeger. Soon they would regret forever that they had meddled in the plans of so mighty a sorcerer. Soon he would send them screaming and begging for mercy to their well-deserved deaths. Soon.

All around him, he heard his forces moving into position. Rank upon rank of awesome skaven warriors, the very cream of ratman soldiery, moved through the dark. Their pink eyes glittered in the gloom; their long tails lashed with suppressed killing lust; their fangs glistened with saliva. Just behind him, his monstrous bodyguard, a huge rat-ogre, the third to bear the name Boneripper, grunted with bloodlust.

The rat-ogre was bigger than any human, more than twice as tall and ten times as heavy. Its head was a terrifying combination of rat and wolf. Its red eyes burned with insane rage. Its monstrous talons were extruded from its stubby fingers. Its long, worm-like tail lashed the air furiously. This new rat-ogre, a replacement for the one slain by Felix Jaeger at the Battle of the Lonely Tower, had cost Thanquol a small fortune in warp-tokens. It was not the only thing that had cost Thanquol during his recent visit to Clan Moulder's huge burrow at Hell Pit. He had been forced to pledge more than half his personal fortune and a share in the spoils of the coming victory to the warped rulers of the clan in return for their support in this new venture. Still, thought Thanquol, it was an immaterial consideration. The rewards of his inevitable victory would more than recompense him for his outlay. Of that he was utterly certain.

He considered the force that had been rushed to this out of the way place in response to his brilliant scheming. Not only were there Stormvermin and clanrat warriors in the livery of Clan Moulder, there were rat-ogres and packs of huge rats goaded on by beastmasters as well. His army numbered almost a thousand.

With such a force Thanquol felt certain that victory was assured. Particularly since their opponents were mere humans. How could they stand against the true inheritors of the world, the progeny of the Horned Rat himself? The answer was simple: they could not. It made Thanquol's tail stiffen with pride when he contemplated the scale of the victory that would soon be his.

Thanquol sniffed the air with his long, rat-like snout. His whiskers twitched excitedly. Perhaps it was the proximity of the Chaos Wastes he sensed and the presence of a great motherlode of warpstone, the very essence of magical power. Once more he wondered at the stupidity of the Council of Thirteen's edict prohibiting skaven armies from entering those daemon-haunted lands. Surely the loss of a few skavenslaves would be more than compensated for by the vast trove of warpstone they could garner? Granted, in the past the Wastes had swallowed entire armies of ratmen whole, but surely that was no justification for the Council's timidity? Thanquol felt sure that under his leadership, or at least with his guidance from afar – for, in truth, there was no sense in risking the loss of a skaven of his towering intellect – a verminhoste would succeed in such a mission.

And there were alternatives. If he possessed the airship that those accursed dwarfs had built for Gurnisson and Jaeger, and which his doltish lackey, Lurk Snitchtongue, had so far utterly failed to capture, he could use it to prospect for warpstone in the Wastes. He lashed his tail in frustration for a moment when he considered the imbecilic incompetence of Lurk, then wrung his paws together gloatingly as he thought about the aerial vessel. There were no ends to the uses he could put the thing to once it was his.

It would swiftly transport the grey seer and his bodyguard anywhere in the Old World. It would deliver troops behind enemy lines. It would be used as a prototype to build an aerial fleet and with such an armada Thanquol, and – he loyally hastened to add – through him the Council, would conquer the world.

Of course, first he had to get his paws on the airship, which brought his attention firmly back to matters at hand. Through the spyglass he could make out the fortified mansion inhabited by the dwarf's Kislevite allies. It was typical of the fortified manor houses built by the human clans in this area. It was surrounded by a high palisade and a ditch, and within the house itself was a rugged structure of stone and logs. The windows were narrow, mere arrow slits in many cases. The doors and gates were massive and strong. It was built to resist an attack by the monstrous creatures so common here, close to the Chaos Wastes. Inside there were stables, for the humans here dearly loved their horses. Thanquol had never understood this. He thought the beasts good only for eating.

The mansion was typical in all respects except one, he noted gleefully. Outside the main building was a massive wooden tower topped with a metal platform. Save for the material from which it was built, it was identical in all respects to the docking tower Thanquol had seen at the Lonely Tower before the airship had sailed off to avoid falling into his clutches. Doubtless this was the place where the airship had stopped en route northwards into the Wastes. Refuelling or reprovisioning obviously. To Thanquol's keen mind that implied there was a limit to the vehicle's range. That was worth knowing. But why here? Why so close to the Chaos Wastes?

Briefly Thanquol considered what this might mean. Why had the dwarfs, particularly the accursed Trollslayer Gotrek Gurnisson, decided to take such a valuable device into the Wastes? If only that dullard, Lurk, had managed to find out. If only he had reported back as he had been instructed. Thanquol was not in the least surprised that he had not. It was ever his fate to be served by buffoons who lived only to spoil his ingenious plans. Thanquol often suspected that these catspaws were foisted upon him by the machinations of his devious enemies back in Skavenblight. The intricacies of skaven politics were endless and mazy, and a leader of Thanquol's genius had many jealous rivals so filled with envy that they would stop at nothing to drag him down.

Doubtless once Gurnisson was in Thanquol's clutches he could be made to reveal his mission by various cunning methods of persuasion known to the grey seer. And if he could not, Gurnisson's henchman, that wicked human Felix Jaeger, could be made to talk. Actually, thought Thanquol, he would probably be the easier of the two. It was not that Thanquol feared a confrontation with the demented one-eyed dwarf, not in the slightest. He was, he knew, in all respects fearless, and not in any way, shape or form scared of a mindlessly violent brute like Gotrek Gurnisson. He had proven this time and time again in his encounters with the Slayer. It was just that it would take less effort to make Jaeger talk.

Come to think of it though, Thanquol was forced to admit, Jaeger himself could be stupidly stubborn about such matters. Perhaps it would be easier simply to capture a few prisoners from the mansion below and interrogate them about the dwarf's purpose. Surely they must be privy to the secret. After all, how could the stunties have gone to all the trouble to build the tower down there in the midst of this forsaken steppe, and not have revealed their mission to their human allies? He must make sure that his allies captured a few of the humans for questioning. In fact, he would give the order at once.

Thanquol tittered at the thought. Whatever plan the dwarfs had, it must be an important one for them to spend so much time and effort, and to risk the airship, to implement it. Perhaps they sought gold or magical treasures in the Wastes. Knowing dwarfs as he did, Thanquol thought this was the most likely explanation. And, as soon as his incredibly brilliant plan was implemented, whatever treasures his enemies had garnered would be gripped firmly in Thanquol's mighty taloned paw.

He reviewed his scheme in his mind. So simple, yet so devious. So direct and yet so cloaked in subterfuge. So clever and yet so foolproof, as all great skaven plans must be to avoid being fouled up by witless underlings. Truly it was proof, as if any were needed, of the singular genius that was Thanquol's. Step by logical step he reviewed it.

First, they would capture the mansion. Then when the airship returned as it assuredly would, they would take the dwarfs by surprise once it docked. Before they could fly off, using superior skaven sorcery, a special spell that Thanquol had prepared for just this moment, they would immobilise the ship. Then nothing would remain for them to do except reap the rewards of victory.

Of course, there were a few things that could go wrong. Thanquol prided himself that part of his genius was his ability to deal with the unexpected. With any skaven force there was the chance that lackeys would mess things up. And there was a slight possibility that the dwarfs might destroy their airship rather than let it fall into skaven paws. Such things had happened in the past, for dwarfs were a foolishly proud and insanely stubborn race. And there was the ever-so-slight chance that they would fly back by a different route.

Thanquol shivered. All his divinatory skills told him that this was a near impossibility. He had read his own droppings having eaten only of fermented warpstone-spiced curd for thirteen whole hours, suffering the most dreadful flatulence as he proved his devotion to the Horned Rat in this approved manner. The sanctified excreta had assured him that his plan could not fail and that he would encounter the dwarfs here. Of course, as with all prophesies, there was a certain margin of error that had to be taken into account, but nevertheless Thanquol felt that his vast experience in scrying had stood him in good stead. Other, lesser seers might allow their wits to be clouded by their own desires and hopes, but he had read the signs with the rigorous impartiality that was one of the signs of his unfailing genius.

He felt sure that the accursed Gurnisson would return from the Wastes. Frankly he doubted that anything could prevent it. Thanquol could read the omens and he knew that the dwarf carried a mighty doom upon his shoulders. It was the sort of destiny that could only be overcome by the possessor of an even mightier one. Naturally Grey Seer Thanquol knew that he was such an individual. Still, it would not pay to underestimate the Slayer.

In his warpstone-induced dreams, Thanquol had seen many a strange vision as he sought signs of his enemies' whereabouts. He had seen a mighty fortress buried deep beneath a mountain, and a struggle with a daemon of truly terrifying power, a being of such surpassing and baleful might that Thanquol was loath to think about it. He pushed the thought aside. The dwarf would return, bringing the airship with him. It was his destiny to fall before the titanic intellect of Thanquol. No lesser doom could stay him.

Thanquol noticed that the Moulder clawleaders were watching him. He cursed under his breath.

'What are your instructions, Grey Seer Thanquol?' rumbled the most massive of them. 'What do you require of us?'

'My orders,' said Thanquol emphatically, 'are that you and your skaven are to proceed at once with the plan. Take the mansion and keep as many of the humans alive as possible, for questioning. Pay particular attention to preserving breeders and their runts. The manthings become particularly malleable when you threaten them.'

'We would preserve them anyway, Grey Seer Thanquol. For our experiments.'

Thanquol tilted his head to one side to consider the clawleader's words. What did the Moulder mean? Was his clan considering some new program of breeding, one that involved mutating humans? That was worth knowing. The skaven seemed to realise that he had let something slip, for he turned his back on Thanquol and lumbered down the hill to instruct his troops. Excitement filled Thanquol.

In five minutes the attack would begin.

ULRIKA MAGDOVA STOOD on the battlements of the mansion and gazed towards the distant mountains. She was a tall woman, garbed in the leather armour of a Kislevite warrior. Her hair was short and ash blonde, her face broad and oddly beautiful. Her hands played with the hilt of her sword.

Behind the mountains the aurora blazed brightly in the sky. The scintillating light of the Chaos Wastes at night illuminated the peaks from behind. They were huge saw-toothed fangs belonging to a distant monster that intended to devour the world.

At that moment, she was wondering whether the monster had swallowed Felix Jaeger and his companions. There had been no word or sign from them in weeks, and not all the divinations of the sorcerer, Max Schreiber, had succeeded in revealing anything about their fate. Ulrika wondered whether she would ever see Felix again. She wondered whether she even wanted to.

It was not that she wanted him dead. Far from it. She desired his safe return with all her heart. It was just that his presence was so... unsettling. She was more attracted to him than she should be. He was, after all, a landless adventurer from the Empire, a self-confessed criminal and revolutionary. She was the daughter and heir of a March Boyar, one of those nobles who guarded the northern boundary of Kislev from the creatures of the Chaos Wastes. It was her duty to marry according to her father's wishes, to cement alliances with neighbours, to keep the blood of her clan strong and pure.

Idiot, she told herself. Why does that even matter? It was a simple bedding down with a man you liked and wanted. You've done it before and you will do it again. It was not uncommon or disapproved of here in Kislev, where life was short and often ended in violence; where people took what pleasure they could, when they could find it. Why does the fact you slept with a landless adventurer matter at all? There is no future to it. Yet she had thought of little else since he departed. Typical of the man, really, that he should inflict such confusion on her and then depart, the gods alone knew where.

He had his reasons, she knew. Felix Jaeger was sworn to accompany the Slayer Gotrek Gurnisson on his death quest however long that took, and however much it might end in his own death. Ulrika came from a culture that respected oaths, as only a barely civilised people, who enforced their own laws with the sword, could do. Here on the marches there were none of the lawyers and written contracts so common in the Empire. Here you did what you swore to do, or brought shame on yourself and your family.

And look what that oath had done to the foolish man. It had carried him away on that great dwarf flying machine into the Chaos Wastes in search of the lost dwarf city of Karag Dum. Ulrika had wanted to beg him not to go, to stay with her, but she was too proud to speak, and she had feared that he might refuse – and that would have been a shame she was unwilling to endure.

She kept her gaze on the mountains as if by staring hard at them, she might be able to see through the rock to what lay behind. And anyway, she had no idea how he felt about her. Perhaps it was just a one-night thing for him. Men were like that, she knew. They could promise you the world in the evening, and not even have a kind word come dawn.

She smiled. She doubted that Felix would be at a loss for a kind word, or any words at all. That was what she liked about him. He was good with words in a way her dour folk were not. It was a gift she envied him, if truth be told, for she was not good at saying how she felt. And in his own strange way, she felt that Jaeger was a good man. He could fight when that was called for, but it was not his whole life, the way it was for the men around whom she had grown up.

There were times when she thought that he was not hard enough, and there had been times when he surprised her with just how cold and ruthless he could be. Certainly only a dangerous man could be an associate of Gotrek Gurnisson's. From what the dwarfs who had built the tower had told her, the Slayer was already a dark legend among his people.

She shook her head. This was getting her nowhere. She had her duties to perform. She was her father's heir, and she was needed here to ride the borders, to lead the riders, a duty she fulfilled as ably as any man, and better than most.

Footsteps sounded nearby. She turned her head to see Max Schreiber walking along the parapet towards her.

'Can't sleep?' he asked, smiling. 'I could mix you a potion.'

'Checking the sentries,' she said. 'It's my duty.'

She looked at the magician. He was tall and dark with a scholar's pallor and wide eyes. Recently he had taken to cultivating a goatee beard, which suited him. He was wearing the formal garb of a magician of his college, long flowing robes of gold over a jerkin of green, and yellow britches. An odd-looking skullcap perched on his head. A handsome man, she thought, but one who made her uneasy, and not just in the unsettling way good-looking men sometimes did. Here was one who truly stood apart from most of humanity, by virtue of the power in him, and the training that let him wield it. She did not quite trust him, which was the way she reckoned most of humanity felt about magicians in general. You always wondered about them – could they read your mind, bind you to their will with a spell, ensnare you in illusions? And you feared to say such things aloud or even to think them in their presence just in case they could, and they took offence.

Schreiber himself had never given her any reason to doubt his benevolence. It was just...

'You were wondering about the airship,' he said.

'Are you a mind reader, then?'

'No. Just a student of human nature. When I hear a young woman sigh and see that she is looking north into the Wastes, I can put two and two together. And I've seen you and Felix together. You make a good couple.'

'I think you presume too much.'

'Perhaps.' He smiled; a little sadly, she thought. 'Herr Jaeger is a lucky man.'

'What's lucky about having to cross the Chaos Wastes?'

'That's not what I meant, and you know it.'

'I am not a mind reader either, Herr Schreiber, so how can I know what you mean if you do not say it?'

'Why do you dislike me, Ulrika?'

'I don't dislike you.'

'You do not seem to approve of me.'

'It's just you are...'

'A sorcerer?'

'Yes.'

He smiled a little sadly. 'I am used to it. People do not tend to trust us or like us much either. It was not that long ago that they stopped persecuting us in the Empire.'

'They still burn witches here, sometimes. Warlocks too. I am sure some of my people here would like to do that to you.'

'I have noticed.'

'We are close to the Chaos Wastes here. People are suspicious. I would not take it personally if I were you.'

He shook his head ruefully, and his sad smile widened. Ulrika realised that, given the chance, she could actually like the man. 'I don't see how I could take being burned at the stake other than personally.'

'You have a point.'

'Thank you,' he said with a faint trace of irony. Suddenly he cocked his head to one side. He seemed to be listening.

'What is it?' Ulrika asked. She felt suddenly afraid.

'Hush! I think there is something out there.' He closed his eyes and his face went slack. She sensed the play of power around him. Through his shuttered eyelids she saw a glowing light, as if his eyeballs had become tiny suns that could shine through flesh. The muscles on his jaw tightened. He muttered words in the arcane tongue under his breath.

His eyes snapped open. She could see the light in them fading, like the embers of a dying fire. He reached out and touched her on the arm. His grip was surprisingly strong for a scholar. 'Remain calm,' he said. 'Show nothing on your face. There are things out there and we must get away from this parapet.'

'We must give the alarm.'

'We will give no alarms if we are shot by a sharpshooter,' he said softly.

'Who could hit us in this light?'

'Trust me,' he said guiding her along the parapet. 'Walk normally and then climb up the ladder into the watchtower.'

'What is going on?' Ulrika asked. The urgency in the magician's voice had communicated itself to her.

'There are skaven out there. The ratmen followers of Chaos.'

'How do you know?' she asked and then cursed herself. She already knew the answer. He was a magician. She altered the question slightly to cover her mistake. 'That they are skaven, I mean.'

'I have studied the minions of Chaos extensively,' he said, in his quiet voice. Ulrika knew that his calm tone was meant to reassure her, to keep her calm. It annoyed her slightly that he thought she would need such treatment. If he noticed he gave no sign. 'It's why the dwarfs hired me, after all.'

They had reached the ladder. 'Climb. I will follow you in a moment. As soon as you are in the tower sound the alarm bell. We don't have much time.'

Despite her mistrust of him, she never doubted that he was serious. In this, at least, she had perfect faith in Schreiber. Out of the corner of her eyes, she thought she detected a faint scuttling mass, as of quickly moving creatures coming close. As she swung out onto the ladder she had a crawling feeling between her shoulder blades. She imagined that she was being targeted with a bow or a crossbow or one of those strange sorcerous weapons Felix had told her the skaven used. She felt cold sweat start to run down her back. She was amazed by Schreiber's courage. The whole time, he stood there like a man engaged in a casual conversation, keeping up a flow of quiet chatter. Only once she was well up the ladder did he begin his own ascent.

She scampered up as quickly as she could and as soon as her feet hit the deck of the tower she reached out and grabbed the pull of the great bell. She tugged it with all her strength. The clear chiming tone rang out through the night. She knew it could be heard all across the manor, from the deepest cellars to the highest chambers.

'Awake!' she shouted. 'Enemies are without!'

No sooner had the bell's tolling started to fade than she heard a great feral roaring in the distance. She knew beyond a shadow of a doubt that the skaven were out there. Warriors were already starting to tumble from the manor house, weapons held ready. She saw her father's massive form emerge into the darkness. A partially buckled cuirass was around his chest and one of his body servants helped him adjust the straps as he roared orders to the men.

'Oleg – take your section and man the parapet. Standa – I want archers on all four walls till we see what direction the attack is coming from. Marta! Gather all the servant girls and draw water from the wells in case of fire. Get bandages and unguents ready for the wounded! Come on! Look lively!'

Ulrika was glad her father was there. He was a veteran of a thousand battles along this dangerous border. His very presence was heartening to all his followers as well as to her.

She glanced out of the watchtower and saw the horde approaching them. There were hundreds of skaven, advancing like a furry tide across the cleared ground. She wondered if her father had enough men in the manor to hold them. Somehow she doubted it. There had been reports of more and more Chaos followers coming and going through the passes. Most of the troops of riders were patrolling the border with Chaos. It had been their misfortune, or perhaps a tribute to skaven cunning, that they had been attacked when so many of their riders were abroad.

As she drew her sword, she wondered if she would ever see Felix again. Then the first wave of skaven hit the wall, and she had time to think of nothing else except fighting for her life.

ONE

THE RETURN

FELIX JAEGER LOOKED down from the bridge of the *Spirit of Grungni*. He was a tall man, blond of hair, broad of shoulder, narrow of hip. His face was tanned and worry lines radiated out from his eyes that really should not have been etched on the face of one so young. But then, as Felix would have been the first to admit, he was a man who in his time had endured more than his share of worries.

His hands were braced on the great wheel of the airship as he made a course correction, steering the mighty vessel directly towards where he believed the pass out of the Chaos Wastes should lie. His hand still hurt from the burns he had taken wielding the Hammer of Firebeard. He was grateful to be able to grasp anything at all. He had been lucky. The dwarf healing salve had helped a good deal.

His keen eyes scanned the tormented land below him, watching the arid semi-desert scroll along beneath the *Spirit of Grungni*. In the distance, he thought he could make out a rising dust cloud. He shivered. Whatever was making it, it was not friendly. Nothing here was.

He looked at the compass but he knew it was not always reliable in the Wastes. Several times he had seen the lodestone needle rotate around in a circle under the influence of evil magic. Fortunately they were now nearing the edge of the cursed land, where the oddly-coloured storm clouds did not always obscure the sky, and the stars were often visible by night and sometimes in the dim light of day. These gave him something to navigate by. Several times they had drifted far off course until they had found a star to navigate by, which had added days to their travel time.

Felix exhaled loudly. He was bone weary. He was no longer glad now that Malakai Makaisson had taught him how to fly the vessel – although it gave him something to do, and kept his mind from worrying about things he could not control.

The nose came round sluggishly, which was not surprising. The *Spirit of Grungni* was loaded to capacity and then some. The survivors of the dwarf community of Karag Dum, those who had been left alive after the last fatal confrontation with the daemonic bloodthirster and its minions, filled every cabin and spare cranny on the airship. The hold bulged with the treasures they had taken from the lost citadel. Felix wondered how Hargrim and his people would take to their new life beyond the Wastes.

The drone of the engines was loud as they struggled to drive the ship into the wind. Felix cursed, for it seemed that the very elements conspired against them on their journey out of the Wastes. He half-suspected evil magic. There were dozens of mages sworn to serve the Dark Powers down there, and it was easy to imagine one of them whistling up a wind to slow the airship down, or a storm to drive it into the ground. The *Spirit of Grungni* was protected against the direct effects of magic but there was really nothing anyone except another magician could do against such indirect methods.

Felix strove to push such thoughts aside, to think of happier things. He wondered what Ulrika was doing just now, whether she missed him, or even thought about him at all. Perhaps she had forgotten all about him. Perhaps he had just been a brief fling for her. Any such thoughts were driven from his head by the sound of loud cursing from behind him.

Gotrek Gurnisson entered the bridge of the airship and made his presence felt in no uncertain terms. He stomped around the command deck, glaring at the apprentice engineers, and casting irate glances through the crystal windows as if half-expecting to see an enemy flying towards them. Considering that a mere few days ago Gotrek had been near death from the wounds he had taken in his battle with the Bloodthirster of Khorne, the dwarf had made a remarkable recovery. He still did not look well. His massive chest was swathed in bandages. His huge red dyed crest of hair poked out of a turban of similar bandages wrapped around his head. The same cloth obscured the eyepatch that normally covered his empty left socket. One of his arms was bound in a sling but he still managed to carry his massive axe in his right hand. Considering Felix would struggle to lift the weapon with both hands, it was an impressive feat.

Actually, the fact that the Slayer was up and about at all was a testimony to the ruggedness of the dwarf physique. Felix knew that if he, or any other man, had suffered the wounds Gotrek had, he would have been bedridden for months, if he could have survived at all.

'Feeling better?' Felix asked. Gotrek's cursing had already given him an answer to that question.

'I feel as if I have been trampled on by a herd of donkeys, manling.'

'An improvement then?'

'Yes. Yesterday I felt like I had lost a head-butting contest with Snorri Nosebiter.'

'Well, you're lucky to be alive at all. That's what Borek says.'

'What's lucky about it, manling? If I had fallen in combat with that accursed daemon I would have atoned for my misdeeds, and you would be composing my death saga. As it is, I have to listen to Snorri Nosebiter snoring and boasting about how many beastmen he slew. Believe me, there are some fates that are worse than death.'

Felix raised an eyebrow. He knew the dwarf well enough now to understand when he was making a joke. Oddly enough, given the fact that his avowed purpose in life was to find a heroic death in battle, Gotrek did not sound all that sorry to still be alive. Felix suspected that he actually detected a note of sour pleasure in the Slayer's voice, though he thought it diplomatic not to point this out. Instead he said, 'But if you had fallen, none of the folk of Karag Dum would have escaped, the Hammer of Firebeard would have fallen into the hands of the Chaos worshippers, and the Great Bloodthirster would have had his revenge on the race of dwarfs. Surely that is something to be thankful for?'

'You might have a point there, manling.'

'You know I do. And we did help Borek prove his theory about the location of Karag Dum. We did find the lost city, and we did recover the sacred hammer.'

'There's no need to belabour the point.'

'And we did thwart the powers of darkness, and get a fair haul of gold and–'

'I said–'

'Felix Jaeger does have a point, Gotrek, son of Gurni,' said a deep mellow voice. Felix glanced back to see that the ancient dwarf scholar, Borek, had also entered the bridge. He was stooped almost double with age and he had to use a stick to help him walk but there was a vitality about him, and an excitement, that Felix had never seen before. He was filled with life and triumph. Their success at Karag Dum, if you could call taking part in a battle that had left most of the dwarf population of the city dead a success, had given meaning to his entire life. They had recovered Firebeard's hammer and would restore it to the dwarf people. Felix knew that Borek thought they had performed a mighty feat of valour. He himself was not so sure. Beside the scholar was his nephew, Varek, who had accompanied Felix and Gotrek and Snorri into the lost city, and had recorded their deeds. Varek's glasses glittered in the light filtering onto the command deck. He smiled at Felix and the Slayer cheerily.

As well he might, thought Felix. Not many dwarfs could claim to have survived an encounter with a daemon of Chaos.

Just behind them stood Hargrim, the son of Thangrim Firebeard, his beard dyed as black as his clothing as he mourned his father. Now his father was gone, he was the leader of the folk of Karag Dum. His face was as grim as death. His eyes were sad as only those of a dwarf who had lost father and home at the same time could be.

He noticed the look Borek gave him. It was not really a look suited to an ancient whose white beard dragged along the floor. It held an element of reverence that made Felix uncomfortable. Since his return from Karag Dum most of the dwarfs on the airship had been giving him that look. He had lifted Firebeard's hammer and invoked its power in the battle with the great daemon. Apparently he was the first and only human in history since the time of the man-god Sigmar to have performed such a feat, and they now regarded him as blessed by their gods. Felix did not feel particularly blessed. Just invoking the hammer's power had almost killed him. And fighting the daemon was a feat he hoped never to have to repeat in his life.

'Look down there!' said Felix to distract them. His keen eyes had caught sight of movement in the Wastes from the edge of the vast dust cloud. By all the gods, it was huge. If it were being made by a force of men, Felix would have suspected the presence of an army. Here in the Chaos Wastes, who knew what it signified?

As they closed with it, he could see a group of figures, made tiny by the airship's altitude, riding across the land, a massive cloud of polychromatic dust rising in their wake.

Borek peered down through his pince-nez glasses. 'What is it? Tell me! My eyes are not so good.'

'It's a trail of dust,' Gotrek said. 'There are riders down there. A lot of them.'

'I would say several hundred. Black-armoured Chaos knights. Heading south, the same direction we are.'

'Your eyes are better than mine, manling. I'll take your word for it.'

'That's the tenth party we have seen since we left Karag Dum. All heading in the same direction.' Slowly something became evident to Felix. He felt his heartbeat start to pound, and his mouth go dry. They were passing over the heart of the dust cloud now, and he could see many more figures. Thousands of them, perhaps tens of thousands. He thought he could make out the misshapen figures of beastmen, and other more disturbing things. It was apparent that the Chaos worshippers they had seen earlier were either stragglers from, or the rearguard of, a much mightier force. One that was heading directly into the lands of men.

'By Grungni, it's an army on the march,' he heard Varek say. The young dwarf had a spyglass pressed to his face and was looking through it intently. 'This is larger than the force that besieged Karag Dum. What is going on?'

'I fear the Powers of Chaos are planning a new incursion into the lands of men,' Hargrim said. 'No place will be safe for my people.'

Felix felt a thrill of fear. The last thing anybody in the human lands wanted was a full-scale invasion by the followers of the Ruinous Powers. They were numberless and powerful, and Felix suspected, after what he had seen in these Wastes, that only their constant internecine fighting kept them from sweeping away human civilisation.

'Good. I could use a decent fight,' Gotrek said.

'I would have thought you'd had enough of that recently,' Felix said sourly.

'There's never enough fighting for a Slayer, Felix Jaeger,' said Borek. 'You should know that by now.'

'Unfortunately I do.' A new worry entered Felix's mind, one he knew he had been trying to keep out all day. 'If they invade, the Chaos hordes will come through the Axebite Pass.'

'What of it, manling?'

'Ivan Straghov's mansion is right in their path.'

'Then we had best hurry on and warn them, hadn't we?'

EXCITEMENT AND TENSION filled Felix's mind. They were through the pass. The land of Kislev lay before them. In hours he would see Ulrika again. He felt more nervous than he cared to admit. As nervous as he had ever been before a battle, perhaps more so. He wondered if she would be as pleased to see him as he was going to be to see her. He wondered what she would say, what he would say, what she would be wearing. He shook his head. He knew he was behaving like a schoolboy with a crush, yet he could not help himself. It had been a long time since he had felt this way about anyone. Not since the death of Kirsten at Fort von Diehl, which seemed like years ago. It was a pity that he had to be bringing such bad tidings.

He placed the spyglass to his eye and scanned the horizon, hoping for a first glimpse of the mansion, and was rewarded with a view of what he thought was the mooring tower. Soon, he thought, soon.

'Looking forward to being back?' said a voice from beside him. Felix looked down at Varek. The young dwarf was looking at him with something uncomfortably like hero worship. Felix had no idea why. Varek had shared in all the perils of the descent into Karag Dum Felix had faced and had done his part to bring their quest to a successful conclusion. There was no reason for him to idolise Felix but it was apparent that he did.

Varek wore a leather helmet and flying goggles. Makaisson had been teaching him how to fly a gyrocopter on the return trip. He had just come back from a flight, Felix realised.

'Course young Felix is,' said Snorri Nosebiter. 'Even Snorri can see that. He's going to see his lady friend.'

Snorri winked across at Felix knowingly. It was not a reassuring sight. Even bandaged as he was, Snorri Nosebiter was the only dwarf Felix had ever met who was more terrifying than Gotrek in appearance, and the wounds he had taken at Karag Dum had not improved his looks. Like Gotrek, Snorri was a member of the Slayer cult, sworn to seek heroic death in battle. Like Gotrek his squat ape-like body was covered in tattoos. Unlike Gotrek, however, he had three nails driven directly into his shaven head. This was in place of the crest of hair that most Slayers had. Snorri was not the brightest of dwarfs but, for a Slayer, he was friendly.

Felix focussed the spyglass on the approaching manor house. There was something odd about it. At first he could not work out what, but slowly he started to put his finger on it. There were not enough people in the fields around it. In fact there was no one. There should have been serfs, carts, workhorses, soldiers, sentries, riders coming and going with messages. He ran his gaze across the horizon to make sure he was right. His heart was beating faster. His palms felt suddenly sweaty. There was a sick feeling in the pit of his stomach. This was wrong. Had the forces of Chaos already been here?

He breathed a prayer to Sigmar that nothing had happened to Ulrika, and then added one for her father and the rest of the people on the estate, but he was not sure his prayer was going to be answered. Looking closely at the mansion he could see signs of a disaster.

It looked as if the gate had been forced with a battering ram. There were signs of burning on the stone walls. Whole sections of the palisade had collapsed. It all reminded him sickeningly of the aftermath of the massacre at Fort von Diehl.

'No, not again,' he muttered.

'What is it, manling? What do you see?' Gotrek asked.

Felix did not answer. The only thing that gave him hope was the fact that he could not see any bodies. And he was not at all sure that it was a hopeful sign. There were no signs of life at all. No signs of a battle except the damage to the buildings and fortifications. Surely, he thought, there would be corpses, or at least signs of burial. Frantically he scanned the area for a funeral pyre or a mass grave. Perhaps that mound over there was new.

'What do you see, manling?' Gotrek asked again. There was a note of menace in his voice now.

'The mansion has been attacked,' he said. He was not sure how he managed to keep his voice steady but he did. 'And it looks like everyone has simply vanished.'

'Into thin air?'

'It looks like it.'

'I don't like it,' Gotrek said. 'It smells of a trap.'

Felix was forced to agree with the Slayer's assessment. There was a wrongness about the situation down there that he did not like in the least. On the other hand, he desperately needed to find out what had happened to Ulrika. Let her be alive, he prayed.

The airship moved ever closer to the deserted-looking mansion.

GREY SEER THANQUOL gazed at the approaching airship through the eyepiece of his periscope. As always, he was more impressed than he cared to admit by the dwarfs' creation. That such a massive vessel could fly hinted at a magic greater than his own. Yet he knew it was not magic that kept the huge vessel aloft, but the dwarfs' arcane technology.

He began to chew on some carefully hoarded pieces of powdered warpstone, knowing soon he would need all the sorcerous strength it could grant him. He felt a little weak. Last night his magical duel with the human wizard had taken nearly all his strength. It had almost upset all of his carefully laid plans. Who would have expected the humans to have such a strong mage in their midst? Still, in the end, Thanquol had triumphed, as was only inevitable. The power of a true servant of the Horned Rat would always overcome the feeble magic of mankind, just as the righteous skaven warriors had finally succeeded in taking the human keep. It filled Thanquol's heart with pride to think they had managed it even though they had only outnumbered the humans ten to one. It was a fitting tribute to the genius of his leadership that victory was his in the teeth of such odds.

They had even taken some prisoners, who would doubtless serve as suitable subjects for Clan Moulder's experiments once this expedition was over. It pained Thanquol to think that they had not had enough time yet to really interrogate their captives. There was nothing he found more relaxing than breaking a few terrified humans to his will. In particular he was pleased to have the human wizard in his clutches. The man had been knocked unconscious by magical backlash when attempting to dispel Thanquol's last spell. Once he was conscious and Thanquol had the time, he would torture the man for the secret of his spells.

They had even managed to capture a few breeders, which was an unexpected bonus. The survivors were imprisoned in the cellars except for the youngest and, Thanquol guessed, the most attractive of the breeders whom he thought he might be able to use to lure Felix Jaeger and Gotrek Gurnisson into a trap.

Even the timing of the airship's arrival seemed to favour him. It was getting dark and that would help cover the ambushing troops waiting in the building and the cellars to erupt on the dwarfs. It occurred to Thanquol as he viewed the oncoming airship that Lurk could still be alive, and perhaps he might be able to contact him. That being the case, Thanquol thought, it was worth the attempt. It might prove very useful to have an agent alive and about Thanquol's business up there.

He decided he'd better make the attempt.

LURK'S HEAD WAS splitting. It was not unusual these days. In the recent past he had endured more suffering than any skaven in the history of the world. It was so unfair. He had not asked to stow away on this accursed airship. He had not asked for these changes to come over his body. Doubtless it was the warpstone, he thought, and those lightning bolts that had hit the airship what seemed like an age ago. They had caused the changes. He had heard of similar changes coming over grey seers after prolonged consumption of the stuff, and the Horned Rat alone knew how much warpstone dust he had breathed in since the foolish dwarfs had taken their stupid airship out over the Wastes.

If only he had stayed below in the cupola, where it was safe. Where the air was filtered by screens, there was plenty of food and human and dwarf magic protected you from the effects of Chaos. Alas that had not proved possible. His thirteen-times-be-damned master, Grey Seer Thanquol, had insisted on regular reports and it was impossible for his sorcery to touch his lackey while he was within the protected area. So Lurk had to leave the protection of the gondola to please his accursed master. Thus had Lurk come to be exposed to the mutating dust in the first place. And now, with the cupola full to bursting with stunties, it was all but impossible for Lurk to hide down there. It would only have been a matter of time before he was detected, and he doubted that even a skaven of his prodigious potency could overcome so many dwarf warriors.

He did not know what was worse – the pain in his head or the hunger that burned in his belly. He could not remember ever being so ravenous, not even after battle, when every skaven was most in need of sustenance. The hunger had come on him with the changes in his body. He was huge now, and muscular, in a way he had never been before. He had muscles like a rat-ogre and his tail was like a length of steel cable. His body was probably twice its previous size and his talons were like daggers. Knobs of horn, similar to the ones on Grey Seer Thanquol's cranium, had started to protrude from his skull. Was he becoming a grey seer, Lurk wondered? Or was this a sign of some other blessing from the Horned Rat? Right at this moment, Lurk did not feel particularly blessed. Right now he was feeling tired and hungry and sorry for himself. He was filled with the justifiable caution in the face of his enemies that some mistakenly called fear. And there was this strange buzzing in his head. A buzzing that seemed to take the form of words.

Lurk! You dolt! Is that you?

Lurk wondered whether this was a hallucination brought on by starvation, or whether the horrors he had endured had finally driven him mad. Still, there was something strangely familiar about the voice, an annoying arrogance and a contempt for everyone but its owner.

Lurk! Answer me! I know you are there! I can sense you!

Lurk's paws strayed to the amulet Grey Seer Thanquol had given him. Was it possible, he asked? After all these long days, that Thanquol had managed to re-establish contact?

I can see the airship, you oaf! And I can feel your feeble mind. If you do not answer me, I shall consume your pathetic soul, and feed your festering carcass to Boneripper.

The first faint flicker of rebellion flared in Lurk's brain. Who was Grey Seer Thanquol to speak to him in such a manner after all he had endured? Had Thanquol ever ventured into the Chaos Wastes? Had Thanquol ever travelled so far in such a dangerous and experimental vehicle? Had Thanquol ever been exposed to warpstone dust and mutated in such an uncontrollable fashion? Just let him try and feed me to Boneripper, Lurk thought, as the rage built up in his mind. I will tear the creature limb from limb, consume its flesh, crack its bones for marrow and spit the gristle at you, mighty Grey Seer Thanquol. You see if I don't.

But what he did was reach out and touch the crystal. 'Mightiest of masters,' he chittered. 'Can it really be you? Has your omnipotent sorcery finally succeeded in overcoming the dire obstacles placed in its way by those wicked dwarfs and re-established contact with your faithful Lurk?'

Yes, idiot, it has!

The baleful thought blasted through the ether and lodged itself in Lurk's brain. Lurk was amazed that his mouth and forebrain could mouth such gross and insincere flattery while his hindbrain and entire spirit festered with rebellion. He knew that given a chance he would kill Thanquol, and the world would be none the worse for it. The grey seer was mad and incompetent. He deserved to die and be replaced by someone better. Someone not unlike Lurk, in fact. He knew now that it was not only his body that the warpstone had altered but his mind and spirit. He had become smarter and his eyes had been opened to many things. He knew now he was cleverer than Thanquol, and could lead far better, if given a chance. For the moment though, he decided that prudent skaven caution was the best course.

'Where are you, mightiest of masters?'

I am below you in the human fortress, waiting to spring a trap on those stunted fools. Now report to me! Where have you been? Why have you not responded to my potent spells of communication?

Because they never reached me, you overbearing clod, thought Lurk. 'Perhaps my feeble brain was incapable of encompassing such potent sorceries, most masterful of mages,' he replied.

Report! Are there many dwarfs on the airship? Is it damaged? Where have you been? Do you have many treasures on board?

What is this mad skaven on about? Treasures? What treasures could there possibly be? Grey Seer Thanquol had no idea what had been going on up here, that much was obvious. Did he think that Lurk had the run of the airship? That the dwarfs gave him a cheery greeting and an answer to all his questions? His disrespect for Thanquol increased with every passing moment. His mouth said: 'Which question should I answer first, wisest of leaders?'

Answer as you will but answer quick-quick! We may not have much time before...

'Before what, most perspicacious of potentates?'

Never mind. Just be ready to act when I give the order.

'As always, most commanding of commanders.'

If he closed his eyes, Lurk could visualise Grey Seer Thanquol standing before him, red orbs gleaming with mad knowledge, the froth of the warpstone snuff to which he was addicted clinging to his lips. Lurk wished the grey seer was here right now so that he could reach out and wring his scrawny neck. He flexed his talons in anticipation.

Soon the airship will dock and our trap will be sprung! Prepare to spread as much chaos and confusion among the stunties as you can, but be careful not to damage the airship!

Prepare to get myself killed furthering your crazed schemes, you mean. Lurk had no intention of endangering his life for the greater glory of Grey Seer Thanquol. It occurred to him that he had done this quite often enough already without adding to the tally of misdeeds that Thanquol owed him for. 'Of course, master. I live to obey,' he said.

Good-good! See that you do and you will be well rewarded! Fail me and–

'Say no more, most persuasive of pontificators. I will not fail you.'

Now answer my questions! Are there many dwarfs on board?

Lurk answered the catechism, being careful to overstate the strength of the dwarfs in every respect. It was as well to have your excuses prepared in advance with Grey Seer Thanquol. It was something he had learned from the master himself.

FELIX PEERED DOWN at the mansion. It was as bad as he had feared. There was no sign of life. No! Wait! What was that? Was it movement at the window? He focussed the spyglass on it but by the time he had done so it was gone.

'I suppose we had better go down and investigate,' said Gotrek testily, pulling the sling from his arm and flexing the muscles experimentally.

'What if it's a trap?' Felix asked.

'What's your point, manling? What if it is a trap?'

Felix considered his words carefully. The Slayer was still determined to seek his doom, that much was obvious. But for once Felix was keen to accompany him. He needed to find out what had happened here. He desperately needed to know what had become of Ulrika. And her people, he added as a guilty afterthought, though he admitted to himself there was only one person down there whose fate he really cared about.

'We'll go down together,' Felix said.

'Snorri will come with you,' said Snorri.

'I think the rest of us should stay with the airship,' Borek said. 'No sense in risking everything and everyone at this late stage.'

The old scholar at least had the grace to look embarrassed as he said it. Not that Felix blamed him. If he had been in command of the ship he would have forbade any of the crew except the Slayers to go down. And the only reason he would not have forbade them was because he would have known it was useless to give them orders anyway.

'We'll dock at the tower,' he said. 'And you can make your way down. At least the thing is still standing, and it looks completely undamaged too. That's a stroke of luck.'

'Is it?' Felix asked, drawing his dragon-hilted sword. 'I wonder if luck has anything to do with it.'

GREY SEER THANQUOL chuckled malevolently. It was all coming together perfectly. All the pawns were in position. He had even managed to recontact that imbecile Lurk. Perhaps the little runt might still prove to be of some use, Thanquol thought, though he did not have high hopes. Lurk had not proven to be that great a minion in the past. Still, you could never tell.

He looked at the blond-furred breeder he had ordered brought up from the cellar. He guessed she was attractive by the strange standards of the humans, and you never knew, he might be able to use her as a negotiating chip. Human males were strangely protective of their breeders, the Horned Rat alone knew why.

He showed her his fangs menacingly, and to his surprise she showed neither fear nor awe. Instead she spat on his face. Thanquol licked away the spittle with his long pink tongue and flexed his claws menacingly. Once again, the breeder surprised him. She reached for the hilt of the sword that was no longer scabbarded at her waist, and Thanquol was suddenly glad it was not there. It seemed that this breeder might actually be dangerous.

'Be very quiet!' he chittered softly and menacingly. 'Or your life will be forfeit. Grey Seer Thanquol has spoken.'

If she recognised his name she gave no sign. 'It's always nice to know the name of the rat you intend to kill,' she said.

Thanquol opened his eyes a fraction and let her see the power burning there. This time she did quail a little, as almost anyone would confronted by the supernatural glow.

'Do not be stupid, breeder. Kill me you will not. Live you only at my pleasure. Die you will if you annoy me.'

'You are the skaven sorcerer of whom Felix spoke,' she murmured to herself, so low that Thanquol almost did not hear. Almost.

'Know you the accursed Felix Jaeger?' he demanded.

She seemed to realise her mistake for her mouth snapped shut, and she said nothing more. Thanquol bared his fangs in a grin. 'Interesting. Very-very.'

He turned this knowledge over in his head, wondering what he might do with it, wondering what the nature of the relationship between this breeder and Felix Jaeger was. Had they mated? A possibility. Humans always seemed to be in heat. It was their way. Did they have runts? No. Not enough time. Thanquol cursed. If only he had found this out earlier, he might have been able to do something with the knowledge. Now, he no longer had the time. He needed to prepare his mind for the great spell of binding.

'Boneripper!' he commanded. 'Watch this breeder. Do not let her escape.'

He sensed other eyes on him, and noticed the nearest Moulder clawleader was watching him closely. How much of the exchange between Thanquol and the breeder had he followed, Thanquol wondered? Not that it mattered. There would be time soon enough to get to the bottom of all this. His enemies were almost within his grasp.

* * *

FELIX WATCHED AS the airship nosed into position near the tower. The dwarfs dropped their grapnels then pulled the ship gently into place. The boarding ramp was extended between the tower and the ship. Felix drew his dragon-hilted sword and got ready to make the long descent to the ground below. He was nervous. He sensed evil eyes watching him. Just your imagination, he told himself, but he knew it was not.

'Ready, manling?' Gotrek asked.

'As I'll ever be.'

'Snorri's ready too,' said Snorri Nosebiter.

'Then let's go.'

As they strode across the ramp, Felix was once more uncomfortably aware of how it flexed beneath their weight and how high up they were. The wind whipped his long red cloak and tugged at his hair. It was cold and chill as only a wind from the northern steppes could be.

Gotrek and Snorri would have looked almost comical, swathed as they were in bandages, had they not been so serious. Felix doubted that anybody in his right mind would laugh at two Slayers when this mood was upon them. He did not feel much like laughing himself. He could not help but notice that both Gotrek and Snorri were moving slowly and favouring their wounded sides. He hoped nothing was down there to attack them. When fully fit he knew Gotrek was a match for just about anything that walked on two legs, and nearly anything on four, but right now he was heavily wounded, and that would count sorely against him if there was fighting.

'I'll go first,' Felix said, moving to the ladder. He doubted that the elevator cage would work right now, and anyway he did not want to be caught in it if they were attacked. It was too much like a death trap.

'In your dreams, manling,' Gotrek said.

'Snorri has a doom to find too,' said Snorri. 'Your job is to record it, young Felix.'

'I only agreed to do that for Gotrek,' Felix said touchily.

'Well, if Snorri happens to be there when I find mine, you can surely give me a few lines, manling.'

Felix looked at the ground below. He was fairly certain he saw movement within the windows of the manor. 'Is there anybody alive down there?' he shouted. There was no sense in being subtle. Any enemies would already have seen and heard the *Spirit of Grungni* arrive.

'There certainly is, manling,' Gotrek said. 'I can hear them.'

'Snorri smells skaven,' said Snorri.

'Great,' Felix said. 'That's just what we needed.'

'I'm glad you think so, young Felix,' said Snorri. 'Snorri thinks so too.'

'I have a few scores to settle with those ratmen,' Gotrek said.

'I'm pretty sure they have a few to settle with us, Gotrek,' said Felix. After Nuln, he was sure that the skaven would not be in the slightest disposed to talk with them. That was for sure. He forced himself to keep climbing down.

LURK PADDED THROUGH the great balloon. He knew the airship had come to a halt. He had heard the engine noise fade and die. He had felt the ship shudder as it nudged against something, felt the faint sideways movement as it was tied up. He knew it was time to be about his business. His business, not Grey Seer Thanquol's. He knew that if ever he was to escape from this accursed vessel full of stunties there would never be a better time than during Thanquol's attack. That would keep the crew busy while Lurk made his getaway. There would be time to make his excuses to Thanquol later. Lurk poised himself in readiness to spring into action.

ULRIKA WATCHED THE small figures step out onto the platform above. One of them, she could see, was Felix. Her heart sank. She had not felt this bad since the skaven assault force had swarmed over the walls and began slaughtering her people. She consoled herself with the thought that she had at least killed half a dozen of the scuttling monsters before she was clubbed down from behind.

Not that it had made much difference; there had been just too many of the things. Still, she calculated that her force had taken out a good half of the skaven. She felt sick with worry. All day she had been locked up in the cellars, part of her home turned into a cell, not knowing whether her father or her friends were still alive and now she was being forced to watch while this gloating, horned-headed albino sorcerer stood ready to ambush Felix and his crew. She had no hopes that they could drive off the ratmen. There were not enough of them aboard the airship to withstand the chittering hordes.

She looked around and wished she still had her weapons.

Not that she fancied her chances much against the huge rat-ogre that acted as Grey Seer Thanquol's bodyguard even fully armed but she might have stood some chance. As it was, there was no hope at all. She wished she possessed Max Schreiber's sorcerous powers, then it would not have mattered if she was armed or not. What havoc the mage had wrought last night before being blasted by some spell of the mad ratman before her. Schreiber alone must have killed fifty of the skaven.

Such thoughts were getting her nowhere. If wishes were horses we'd all ride chargers, as her father used to say. There had to be something she could do, some way she could warn Felix and the others and still escape. She thought about it. Even if there was no escape she could still warn them. She was the hard daughter of a hard land. If her life was forfeit then so be it.

She glanced around at the hall and the seething sea of rat-like faces. It was a pity they were the last thing she was going to see in this life, she thought, as she hesitated for a moment, then opened her mouth and prepared to shout a warning.

GREY SEER THANQUOL felt the power surge within him. His moment was almost here. Gurnisson, Jaeger and the beautiful, beautiful airship were almost within his grasp.

He reached into his pouch and found the necessary components. A piece of magnetised warpstone. A sliver of rune-encrusted metal. The thirteen-sided amulet inscribed with the thirteen fatal runes of utter power. He had everything he needed. He was ready to begin. There would be no escape for his enemies this time. He was certain of that.

He flexed his paws, reached out with his spirit, drew power from the winds of magic and prepared to unleash his spell.

TWO

AMBUSH AT
STRAGHOV MANSION

FELIX LOOKED DOWN. He was not happy. Of the many things he hated and feared in this life, skaven came close to the top of the list. He had loathed the vile vermin ever since he and the Slayer had first encountered them in the sewers of Nuln. What was worse, the awful creatures seemed to have dogged their footsteps ever since, even assaulting the Lonely Tower before their expedition to the Chaos Wastes. Who would have thought they would have shown up here, though? The northernmost provinces of Kislev were a long way from anywhere. Was the reach of the Horned Rat so long?

Still, why should he be surprised by anything in this life? It sometimes seemed to him that he and the Slayer were the most unlucky creatures ever to walk the face of the world. Everywhere they went, they encountered the servants of Chaos. Everywhere they went, they met with disaster and destruction. Another, worse, thought pushed that idea from his mind. Was it possible that Ulrika was alive and down there in the clutches of the ratmen? It was something that did not bear thinking about.

'Should we go on down?' Felix asked. They were half way down the ladder, on the fifth platform.

'Why not?' Gotrek replied. 'You wanted to find out what happened to the Kislevites.'

'Under the circumstances, I'm pretty sure I can guess.'

'Guessing isn't good enough, manling. There may be some humans alive down there, and they granted us fire and shelter.'

'Fire and shelter and a bucket of vodka for Snorri,' added Snorri helpfully.

'That settles it then,' Felix said sourly. 'I'll gladly sell my life for a bucket of vodka.'

Felix knew he was just grumbling for the sake of form. Even if the two Slayers had not been there, he liked to think he would continue anyway to find out the fate of Ulrika and her family. Flanked by Gotrek and Snorri there was no turning back. He consoled himself with the thought that if there were skaven down there, a lot of them were going to die.

Unless they have some of those terrible sharpshooters, Felix thought. Or even some with crossbows. Easiest thing in the world to pick us off from a distance. Or maybe not. Not in this light. Not with all these wooden crossbars around. And Snorri and Gotrek were short; they would not make good targets. Of course, that left one obvious target for any sniping. He tried to push the thought from his mind as he put his weight on the rungs of the ladder once more.

A GLOW SURROUNDED Grey Seer Thanquol. For a moment Ulrika stood frozen, wondering what new horror the skaven sorcerer was about to unleash. The aura of power that surrounded the creature was almost overwhelming. The skaven raised two objects it had taken from its pouch and began chanting something in its own high-pitched tongue. All skaven eyes in the room were upon it. The rat-ogre growled as it sensed the gathering of power. Ulrika decided that it did not matter what the skaven was up to. This was her best chance to do something. Whatever wickedness Thanquol was about to commit, she would put a stop to it.

She sprang forward and sent her booted foot crashing into Grey Seer Thanquol's groin. The skaven gave a squeal of pain and bent over double, dropping his sorcerous adjuncts. A strange smell of musk suddenly filled the air. The rat-ogre roared and reached for her. She dived forward, below its outstretched claws. They missed her by inches as she passed between its columnar legs and headed for the door.

The skaven shrieked in confusion. Ulrika threw the bar on the door and dashed into the next chamber. The rat-ogre bellowed its rage behind her. She saw a surprised skaven in front of her. Desperation gave her strength. She punched it on the snout. It shrieked in pain and dropped its sword. Ulrika stamped on its lower paw, and while it hopped away reached down to pick up its scimitar. It wasn't quite what she was used to, but she felt better with a weapon in her hand.

She looked around: to her left were the stairs down into the cellars where her people were imprisoned, to the right was a long corridor full of skaven. No choice as to direction then. With luck she might be able to free a few of her folk. Failing that a narrow corridor was a much better place to make a last stand than an open hallway.

Under the circumstances, she had no choice at all.

'WHAT WAS THAT?' Felix asked, hearing a distant roar that was all too familiar. It came hot on the heels of a high-pitched squeal of pain.

'Sounds like one of those big rat monsters to me,' said Gotrek. 'Whatever it is, it's mine.'

'Can Snorri have one too?' asked Snorri plaintively.

'You can have mine,' Felix said, pausing on the lowest platform and getting ready to fight.

'Thank you, young Felix,' said Snorri. He sounded grateful.

GREY SEER THANQUOL clutched his tender bits and cursed. That foolish breeder would pay for this indignity, he swore. She had dared to lay her filthy paws on the greatest of skaven sorcerers. Worse yet, she had interrupted him just as he was about to unleash his spell, the one that would make the ambush foolproof, a spell of compelling potency that would bind the airship until he released it.

Not to worry, there was still time. The element of surprise was still his.

Only at that moment, as the tears of agony cleared from his eyes, did he realise the full outrageous folly of his underlings. They had mistaken his scream of pain for the signal to attack and had come surging out of the buildings to attack Gotrek Gurnisson, Felix Jaeger and the other Slayer.

Would these minions never learn to follow orders?' Thanquol wailed.

Then he realised that the worst had come to pass. Seeing the horde of ratmen surging towards the base of the tower, the cowardly dwarfs had already cast off. Even as he watched, the airship was gaining height above the battlefield. Perhaps it would escape before he could use his magic. It was an awful thought.

Thanquol swore that the human breeder was really, really going to pay when he got his paws on her. Right now, though, he had another problem. He had to take charge of this attack before it became a complete fiasco.

LURK SNITCHTONGUE FELT the airship suddenly gain altitude. He heard the engines roar. His keen ears could hear the dwarfish bellow of orders through the speaking tubes in the ship. Just for a moment, he wished that he understood that foul guttural tongue, but then he realised that he did not have to. It was quite obvious what had happened. The dwarfs had spotted the ambush Grey Seer Thanquol had set for them, and were busy escaping from it. Just one more proof, if any were needed, of Thanquol's gross incompetence.

Not that it would do Lurk much good. He was still stuck on the ship and his chance of escape was all but gone. He could hear dwarfs clambering up the ladders within the gasbag to reach the turrets mounted on top of the airship. It seemed that they were preparing themselves for a fight.

Unreasoning rage filled Lurk's brain for a moment, threatening to swamp every rational thought. He would clamber up there and tear them limb from limb and then he would feast on their warm bleeding flesh. He would cave in their skulls then scoop out their brains to make a tasty morsel to satisfy his hunger. He would stick his snout in their entrails and suck out their intestines while they squealed in pain.

Just as quickly, prudent skaven caution returned and resumed command. Perhaps it would be better to clamber up and see if there was any way he could take advantage of the situation. Certainly it was pointless going down into the cupola. There were just too many dwarfs down there even for a skaven of Lurk's surpassing might. Even in his tormented state he could remember only too well how deadly Gotrek Gurnisson's axe was.

Quickly he scurried to the ladder and began to pull himself up it.

* * *

'HERE THEY COME,' shouted Gotrek.

There's no need to sound so pleased about it, thought Felix, but he kept the thought to himself. He knew he was soon going to need all his strength for fighting. A mass of tightly packed skaven warriors had erupted from the manor house, swords raised, mouths frothing. It was like something out of a particularly nasty nightmare. Any hopes that he might have had for Ulrika's survival vanished immediately. At least he could avenge her, he thought. A fair number of skaven were going to die in the next few minutes.

The tower shivered. Fearing the worst, Felix looked up. His fears were confirmed. The airship's engines roared to life as it slowly reversed away. Any thought of retreat to the *Spirit of Grungni* could be abandoned.

Thanks, lads, thought Felix. Just what I needed to make my day complete.

'Come on up and die!' Gotrek roared.

'Snorri's got a present for you,' yelled Snorri, brandishing his axe with one hand and his hammer in the other.

Felix settled himself behind one of the support struts, hoping to get some cover from any missile weapons the skaven might care to deploy. The mass of ratmen warriors had reached the foot of the tower now. Some swarmed up the ladder, others clambered up the legs of the structure itself. There were far too many of them to count, and as he watched Felix saw the monstrous form of a rat-ogre emerge from the manor house. Given the number of close calls he had endured with these monsters in the past, the sight did not reassure him.

'Not going to be much of a fight, this,' Gotrek complained.

'Easy,' said Snorri.

Felix wished he shared the confidence of these two maniacs. His stomach churned with the fear he always felt before a fight. He wanted nothing more now than to get to grips with the foe, to end this waiting. Part of him even considered jumping down into the mass of skaven but he knew it would be suicide. The fall was too long and he would be surrounded from all sides and dragged down.

The first furry snout poked up the ladder. Gotrek split it with one stroke of his axe. Black blood splattered his bandages. The skaven dropped down, knocking away the others on the ladder. It started to dawn on Felix that actually, as long as they stayed here, they would have quite a good chance of surviving. Not too many of the skaven could get at them at once, and most of them would be in the uncomfortable position of having to raise themselves onto the platform, leaving themselves vulnerable for vital moments as they did so.

'This is too easy,' Gotrek said.

'Snorri thinks we should climb down and start killing properly,' said Snorri.

Don't you dare, thought Felix, noticing that pink eyes were glaring at him as a skaven pulled itself up the metal strut. He lashed out at it, but in desperation it leapt forward, fangs bared, going right for his throat.

In a heartbeat he was too busy trying to stay alive to think about the precariousness of their situation.

VAREK RACED THROUGH the corridors of the *Spirit of Grungni*. Swiftly he entered the hangar deck. The gyrocopters were waiting. He clambered into a cockpit, and worked the crank of the ignition. The engine roared to life. Wind hit Varek's face as the rotors began to spin. Dwarf engineers were already opening the doors at the back of the gondola. One by one the gyrocopters rumbled forward and dropped into the night. He was glad they had used the time flying over the Chaos Wastes to unpack and assemble the crated flying machines. It looked like they would all be needed now. Varek felt a sick feeling in the pit of his stomach as his own copter dropped away from the airship, then the rotors above him churned the air and he began to gain altitude. He reached down into the satchel beside him and began to fumble for a bomb.

This was almost as exciting as the trip into Karag Dum, he thought.

ULRIKA RACED DOWN the stairs. A skaven turned to look at her, snarling. She split its skull with one stroke of the stolen sword. Its surprised companion growled at her. A strange acrid stink filled the air. She noticed that the creature was venting some sort of musk from glands near its tail. She struck out at it. Sparks flashed as its blade parried her own. There was a screech of metal on metal as she slid her sword down its blade. The guards of the two weapons met. She twisted her sword, disarming her foe. It leapt back, screeching for mercy. She gave it none.

'What's going on out there?' she heard a mighty voice bellow. She almost cried with relief at its familiarity.

'Father – is that you?' She was already throwing the door open.

'Ulrika,' said her father, Ivan, reaching out to grasp her in a fierce hug. His bushy beard tickled her face. She saw a dozen more ragged and beaten looking men in the cellar. 'What's going on?'

'The airship has come back. The skaven are trying to ambush it,' she gasped out.

'How many of the others are left alive?'

'I don't know. I think there are more prisoners down here in the cellars.'

Ivan reached down and picked up the sword of one of the skaven guards. He tossed it to his tall, thin, cadaverous-looking lieutenant, Oleg, and then picked up the sword belonging to the other skaven. His other favourite, Standa, short, burly and high-cheek boned, looked disappointed that there was no blade for him. 'Filthy weapons but they'll have to do.'

'What shall we do?' Ulrika asked.

'Free as many prisoners as we can find. Kill as many skaven as we can. Use the weapons to arm our warriors, then fight or escape depending on the situation.'

'That's a pretty sketchy plan,' she said, smiling.

'Sorry, daughter, but it's the best I can manage under the circumstances.'

'It'll have to do.'

GREY SEER THANQUOL gnawed on his lower lip as he watched his warriors swarming up the tower. He could see that things were not going well. His brave skaven had the advantage in numbers but their foes' position was a strong one. Gotrek Gurnisson held his ground above the ladder, and chopped anything that came at him. The other Slayer and Felix Jaeger roved around the platform killing any ratman who climbed up the outside of the tower. Thanquol was torn between aiding his troops and preventing the *Spirit of Grungni* from escaping.

He stood there undecided for a moment, and then decided to stick as close to the original plan as possible. After all, it was a mighty scheme of his own devising and it should still work despite the incompetence of his lackeys. He opened his mouth and began to chant the words of his spell.

The winds of magic howled in his ears as he drew their energies to him. Pure pleasure surged through him as the power of the warpstone filled him.

FELIX DUCKED A blow from a skaven sword and slashed at the rat-man attacking him. The skaven leapt back, claws scrabbling on the metal surface of the tower as it realised how close to the edge it was. Felix cursed. He had hoped that in its panic the creature would jump straight off. Well, he could always give it some assistance. He sprang forward, barrelling into it with all his weight. The skaven was much lighter than he and was sent tumbling back through the air, over the edge of the platform. And good riddance, thought Felix before he noticed that the thing had managed to grab a support strut with its tail and was dangling there upside down. Smiling nastily Felix chopped at the creature's long hairless tail. The tail parted and the skaven shrieked something in its incomprehensible tongue as it dropped to its doom. Felix had time for one brief snarl of satisfaction before the pitter-patter of paws on metal warned him that another skaven was behind him.

He whirled, sword raised to face his foe.

LURK POKED HIS snout up through the hatchway. He looked around. Dwarfs had taken up position behind the strange-looking guns that filled the rotating turrets on top of the airship. He had seen enough of Clan Skryre's engines to know that those guns would probably rip him apart if he tried to attack them. While he was a mighty and invincible skaven warrior there was no sense in courting needless death. There was nothing for him up here.

There was a roaring sound from below him, and suddenly some sort of flying machine rose into view over the airship. Lurk ducked as it whizzed directly above his head. Here was powerful sorcery, he thought, looking at the small vehicle. If only he had known what it was earlier, maybe he could have stolen it and escaped.

'Oi! What's that?' he heard one of the dwarfs shout.

May the Horned Rat consume their souls, the dwarfs had spotted him! He ducked back out of sight, scuttling down the ladder, wondering what to do next. Perhaps he could go and hide among the nacelles of gas that filled the balloon. No.

Pointless. Sooner or later they would seek him out in sufficient numbers to ensure his death. While this would almost certainly fulfil Grey Seer Thanquol's dictum that he create a distraction on the airship, it would do him no good whatsoever. If he was going to help Thanquol to victory he wanted to be alive to claim his share of the credit for the triumph.

Not that Thanquol would allow anyone to share in that, a small sour part of his brain quibbled.

He kept dropping until he reached the bottom of the gasbag. He saw a dwarf face peering up at him from the hatch that led down into the airship proper. Whichever way he looked there were foes. Nothing for it, then, but to fight. It would not have been his first choice of action but it looked like he had run out of options.

He bared his fangs and reached out with his claws. The terrified dwarf ducked back into the gondola, pulling the hatch shut behind him. A surge of pain passed through Lurk. He realised his tail had been caught in the heavy hatch.

Someone, he decided, was going to pay for that.

ULRIKA FUMBLED HER way through the darkened cellars. The stink of skaven mingled with scents familiar from her childhood, all but overlaying the smell of too many people cramped into too small a space. She was glad though. It meant a lot of her folk were still alive, more than she had dared hope for. They were locked in with the vodka barrels and in the holding cellars from which the hungry skaven horde had emptied the provisions.

She wished she had a lantern. She wished she had more weapons. She pushed those thoughts aside. It was pointless wishing for things she could not have. She was going to have to work with what she did have. She listened. Even through the tightly packed earth she could hear the sounds of fighting. She could hear the roar of the rat-ogre, the squeals of wounded skaven and the sound of something else.

It sounded like explosions. What was going on up there? Had the skaven sorcerer unleashed some foul spell? She gave the door of the last cellar a push and confronted two cowering skaven. They obviously had been set here for a special purpose, and that purpose was immediately obvious. One of them held a knife at the throat of Max Schreiber. Max was unconscious, his beautiful golden robes ripped and filthy. The other skaven, a huge black-furred monster rose to meet her.

'Prepare to die, foolish breeder,' it chittered, in poorly accented Reikspeil.

FELIX SAW THAT things were beginning to turn against them. Despite their best efforts more and more skaven were gaining the platform. Slowed by their wounds, Snorri and Gotrek were not fighting as well as they normally would. With only three of them they could not cover all the possible means of getting on to the platform. There were four pylons, one at each corner of the tower, and the central ladder. While they managed to guard three, two were always clear for the skaven and as more and more of them forced their way onto the platform, they could not even hold those successfully.

He looked around. Wounded or not, the Slayers were wreaking awful havoc. The platform floor was sticky with blood and spilled entrails. It was increasingly hard to keep a firm footing in the mess. He dreaded the fact that at any moment he might lose his balance and go slithering over the edge. Here and there in the dimming light he could see bodies that had literally been broken apart by the Slayers' axes. Bones and lungs and internal organs had all flopped into the light.

In one swift flash of terrible insight it struck Felix that they were differently arranged from human entrails, and that it was a dreadful thing that he had seen enough opened corpses to know this. A flicker of movement sent his peripheral vision to Gotrek. The Slayer stood on top of a pile of mangled bodies. He held one skaven in the air at arm's length, throttling it, while his axe described a huge half-circle holding the skaven's comrades at bay. Black skaven blood soiled Gotrek's bandages. Froth blew from his lips. He howled like a madman, drowning out the frightened chittering war cries and the screams of his opponents. Nearby Snorri lashed out with his two weapons, chopping and smashing like a demented butcher in a hellish abattoir. He smiled as he fought, obviously enjoying the mayhem and uncaring as to the nearness of death.

The stink was abominable. There was the wet fur reek of skaven, the odd musky scent they emitted when frightened, the smell of excrement and torn bodies and blood. At any other time, it would have made Felix want to be sick but right now he found it oddly exhilarating. As always when death was close his senses were almost intolerably keen and he found himself savouring every moment.

A mighty roaring filled his ears. He was suddenly aware of flashes from the base of the tower and the movement of large ominous shadows above him. He risked a glance up and saw a gyrocopter had been catapulted from the airship and was soaring above them. He had a brief glimpse of the mad face of Malakai Makaisson at its controls, as the insane engineer rained bombs down at the foot of the tower. He heard the anguished, fearful screaming of the skaven massed there. The tower itself shook as if kicked by a giant, and Felix had to fight to keep his footing amid the gore. He offered up a prayer to Sigmar that the bombs didn't send the whole towering structure crashing to the earth, burying them all in a chaos of smashed wooden beams.

Did Makaisson have any idea what he was doing, Felix wondered? Did he care? Looking down Felix could see that he was causing terrible casualties among the skaven. Broken ratman bodies were hurled skywards. Some were torn completely to bits by the force of the explosions. Others lay on the ground, limbless, bleeding and shrieking. It was a wonder that the skaven could hold their ground in the teeth of so ferocious an assault. Felix realised that more bombs were cascading down, this time from the airship. One hit the tower near him, fuse spluttering. For a horrible moment, he felt that his time had come, that he was about to be blown into a thousand tiny fragments of flesh. He froze on the spot for an instant but then courage and mobility returned and he kicked the bomb off the platform. He saw it disappear, sparks trailing from its flickering fuse, into the crowd below. A heartbeat later a terrible explosion blasted through the skaven.

That was too close, thought Felix. He shook his fist in the air and shouted, 'Watch what you're doing, you stupid bastard!'

It was all too much for the skaven down below. They scattered in all directions, unable to face the death crashing down on them from above any more. A glow from the door of the mansion attracted Felix's attention. He saw a familiar form illuminated by it. Astonishment almost paralysed him. He recognised the skaven sorcerer. It was Grey Seer Thanquol, who had led the attack on Nuln, and whom Felix had last seen fleeing from the ballroom of the Elector Countess's palace. How had he got here, Felix wondered? Had the creature come all this way simply to get revenge? Was it possible that the grey seer had been behind the attack on the Lonely Tower?

From the swirling energy around the figure he could tell that the grey seer was about to cast a spell.

What new madness was this?

LURK STOOD ON the edge of the cupola. The whole hellish scene was visible below, illuminated by flashes of light from the bombs. He saw his luckless kin torn apart by the violent blasts and felt thoroughly and profoundly glad that he was not down there with them. The relief evaporated when he realised the precariousness of his own position. If he did not get off the airship soon he would be caught by the dwarfs and overwhelmed by their sheer numbers. He needed to get away now but he could see no way to do it.

Except one. The airship was moving close to the tower again. It was just possible that he could leap from the top of the cupola and land on the tower. It was dangerous, and if he mistimed his leap or missed his footing he would be sent plunging to his doom. On the other hand, if he stayed here his death was certain, and any chance was better than no chance at all. Lurk screwed his courage to the sticking point. He felt his muscles tense, his heart rate accelerate, his musk glands tighten.

Any second now he was going to do it.

ULRIKA DUCKED BELOW the black-furred skaven's swipe and slashed back. The creature bounded away from her counterblow and bumped into the skaven with its blade at Schreiber's neck, sending it flying. Ulrika realised that the ratman probably had orders to kill the wizard at the first sign of any trouble. It would make sense. On his own, a conscious Schreiber could wreak as much havoc as a troop of cavalry. Wizards had that kind of power.

She realised that she would have to do her best to save his life, and quickly. She sprang forward while the skaven were still entangled, and split the skull of the huge black beast with one powerful stroke. Its corpse flopped to the earth, trapping its smaller fellow. Taking advantage of the fact, she buried her sword in the still living skaven's throat and then kicked it a couple of times for good measure.

After ensuring both were dead, she turned to Schreiber. He was bruised and his hair and eyebrows looked singed but a quick check told her his heart was still beating, a fact for which she was profoundly thankful. Gently she shook him, knowing it was risky to treat an injured man in such a way, and yet needing him to be awake and helping her. He groaned and mumbled and his eyes flickered open. Slowly she saw consciousness return. He smiled through bruised lips.

'I am too sore to be dead,' he said eventually. 'It's pleasant to re-enter the world of the living and be greeted by such a beautiful face.'

'There's no time for flattery, Max Schreiber. The skaven are still here and upstairs a battle rages. We need your help.'

'Tis always the way,' he grumbled, pulling himself slowly and painfully to his feet. He brushed himself down, disgusted at seeing how soiled his golden robes were. 'No one wants to know a wizard... until they have a problem. Then it's different.'

'Herr Schreiber, have your wounds rendered you insane?'

'No, Ulrika. I'm just attempting to lighten the situation with a joke. You're a lovely woman, but if I may say so your sense of humour is not your strong point.'

'Just get on with it, Max.'

'And thank you for saving me. I owe you for it.'

'You owe me nothing. Just get out there and start casting spells – like you did the other night.'

He nodded and then a sudden serious expression flashed across his face. 'The grey seer is gathering its powers, and they are immense. I have never felt the winds of magic swirl and flow so turbulently. I wonder what new evil it is up to.'

GREY SEER THANQUOL felt the power surging within him. It was like a snake in his belly, in his chest, fighting to get out. He had consumed an enormous amount of warpstone, enough to have caused lesser skaven mages to explode or devolve into primordial ooze but he was Thanquol. He was the greatest of the grey seers, the mightiest of mages, the supreme sorcerer of the skaven people. Nothing was beyond his powers. Nothing.

Control yourself, he thought. Think. *Think*. He knew only too well the feeling of extreme self-confidence that filled the habitual warpstone user at such moments as this. Indeed, he believed that most skaven sorcerers had moments of utter grandiosity mere heartbeats before the warpstone led them to their final doom. He was not going to be one of them. It was true that like all grey seers, he had a healthy regard for his own abilities' but he was not going to allow the potent raw Chaos stuff to drown out his sense of self-preservation. A sense that was, at this very moment, asserting itself and letting him know that he needed to cast the spell and vent the power now, before it consumed him. It was difficult to do so with so much raw sorcerous energy coursing through his veins and the ecstasy of unlimited power bubbling in his brain, but he knew that he must do it or his doom was certain.

Slowly he forced himself to recite the words of the potent incantation he had devised. One by one he reconstructed the intricate maze of paw gestures that would focus the magic. As he moved his arm, streamers of pure magical energy followed his talons, as if he were slashing holes in the very substance of reality, which in a way, he supposed, he was. He moved his arms in ever-wider gestures; he shrieked the potent syllables of the incantation ever louder. As he did so, a nimbus of light played round his body. Raw magical energy began to leak from his eyes, his snout, his muzzle and the lower extremities of his body. He felt the power roiling back and forth in his gut like acid and knew that he was involved in a race against time, that if he did not complete his spell soon, the power would rip him apart. The part of his mind that was not caught up in the complex mystic geometry of the spell swore that never, ever again would he consume so much warpstone.

He rushed through the last potent syllables of the incantation and made the final paw gestures. Slowly at first a writhing mass of green tendrils extended themselves from his body. Then one by one, the filaments reached out and up, seeking the airship. Thanquol felt his whole body tingle with vibrant energy as they did so. His fur stood on end and his tail was fully extended. His whole body was uncannily sensitive. The faintest kiss of air on his fur felt like someone was rubbing him down with a wire brush. It was painful and yet not unpleasant. He forced himself to concentrate once more, to see each tentacle of energy as an extension of himself, a thing that he could control, that he could feel through as if it were his paw tips.

He extended the web of his power. The spell was a giant claw with which he could grasp the airship and immobilise it. Now those foolish dwarfs would learn the folly of opposing Grey Seer Thanquol, mightiest of mages, master of all magics. He would take their puny airship and crush it. He would smash it to pieces and cast it to earth. He would...

No! What was he thinking? That was the warpstone dust speaking. He would merely immobilise the airship and let his minions take it. Yes. That was it. Concentrate, he told himself. Don't lose sight of the goal now that it is almost within your grasp.

His questing fingers of power touched the airship's cupola. Thanquol shrieked. He felt as if he had been scorched. What wickedness was this? What evil sorcery was at work here? He watched the streamers of green light retreat from the airship at his command. Of course, the airship was protected against Chaos magic. It needed to have been since it had flown across the Wastes. Gingerly Thanquol sent the streamers flickering back again. He knew he had time. What seemed like minutes to him in his exalted state were mere heartbeats to others. His questing tendrils played over the cupola and retreated. It was no use trying to grasp the airship there. It was well protected. He extended his reach to the gasbag. Success! It was not shielded. No! Correction. Parts of it were. The bits that held turrets. Suddenly as he ran his power over the lower part of the gasbag he sensed a familiar, and yet somehow subtly changed presence. It was Lurk! He detached one streamer of energy to grasp his wayward minion, catching him in mid-leap. The rest he continued to weave around the unshielded parts of the gasbag, anchoring the airship in place.

No! What was happening! Why was he starting to rise from the ground! This was not supposed to... Wait! He had it. Thanquol alone could not anchor the airship. His weight was insubstantial compared to the mass of the flying ship. A moment's consideration told him exactly what he needed to do to bind himself to the earth.

As quick as thought he created more streamers of warp-stone energy and sent them burrowing deep into the ground, questing downwards like the roots of some sorcerously swift growing plant. Now he was locked in place. Now he had the leverage to pit himself against the airship's engines. He exerted his power once more.

Instantly he felt himself being drawn back to earth again, and the airship with him. This was more like it. He was a giant! He was a god! With his magic he was going to pull the *Spirit of Grungni* right out of the sky. He had it hooked like a fish on a line, and now all he needed to do was reel it in. There was nothing any of those pitiful fools could do to stop him.

Extending his power to the fullest, he slowly but surely began to pull the airship to the ground.

FELIX WATCHED IN astonishment as a mass of shimmering streamers of light surged up from the doorway of the mansion, curling round the tower like serpents until eventually they engulfed the airship. For a moment, the fighting stopped and all eyes were drawn upwards to watch the sorcerous spectacle. For an instant the lights touched the cupola and withdrew, but only for a moment were they thwarted. Almost immediately they encircled the gasbag of the balloon. Felix could see the skin of its surface flex and he wondered whether the skaven intended to rip the bag asunder and destroy the airship.

Seconds later it became apparent that this was not the grey seer's plan. Felix's mouth gaped in astonishment as slowly but surely the *Spirit of Grungni* was drawn downwards towards the ground. The skaven had ceased to retreat, so awe-stricken were they by this display of the grey seer's powers. It looked all too possible that the airship was going to be captured.

It seemed as if the airship, and with it the proceeds of the expedition to Karag Dum, was doomed.

THREE

BATTLE!

ULRIKA AND Max Schreiber raced through the cellars. All around her were the freed prisoners. Some were armed with weapons taken from dead skaven guards, others were arming themselves with cudgels made from broken chairs, old tools and kitchen knives. Ulrika was not reassured.

'How many?' she asked her father.

'About thirty who can fight. About fifty all told.'

'So few?'

'So few.'

'Do you think our patrols will return in time?'

'We must not count on it.'

'What is going on above?'

'You would know better than I, daughter. I have been down here all this time.'

'Mighty magics are being unleashed,' Max Schreiber said. 'I fear the skaven are going to capture the airship. I suspect that may have been their plan all along.'

'They must be stopped.'

'How? We could not stop them last night when we held the walls and had a hundred armed men. How can we do so now?'

'We must find a way, daughter.'

Max Schreiber smiled. 'We have an advantage now that we did not have last night.'

'And what's that?' asked Ulrika.

'They will not be expecting us.'

'By Taal, Max Schreiber, you have a gift for looking on the bright side,' boomed Ivan.

'Let's go up and see what we can do. At least in the confusion there may be a chance to escape.'

'There will be no escape, Max Schreiber. This is my ancestral home. I will not abandon it to some stinking, gods-poxed rat-men.'

'I can see why you get on so well with the dwarfs,' said Max Schreiber. 'You're all as stubborn as hell.'

FELIX JAEGER WATCHED in awe as the grey seer dragged the *Spirit of Grungni* earthwards. One small skaven was engaged in a contest of strength with an enormous vessel and he was winning. The dwarfs were not going to be beaten quietly though. The engines of the airship roared and Felix could tell from the angle of the fins that whoever was at the controls was trying to get the ship up. The streamers of energy left a glittering after-image on his field of vision. It was an incredible display of magical power, one of the greatest he had ever seen.

'Best get down there and kill that skaven magician,' said Gotrek.

'A good plan,' said Snorri.

An idiotic plan, Felix thought. All we have to do is fight our way through a small skaven army and confront a sorcerer who is capable of plucking an airship from the sky. On the other hand, he could think of nothing better himself. The airship represented their best hope of escape and if it were captured or destroyed, they were doomed.

'Let's get on with it then,' Felix said with no great enthusiasm.

NOW IS THE moment of my triumph, thought Grey Seer Thanquol. Now all skaven will bow before my genius. Now the Council of Thirteen must recognise my accomplishments. He felt capable of reaching up and pulling the moons from the sky and the stars from the heavens. Come to think of it, that might not be a bad idea. Morrslieb, the lesser moon, was said to be made of a gigantic chunk of warpstone. If he could grasp it, then...

No. Best stick to the matter at hand. First he would capture the airship then he would seize Morrslieb. And if he could not reach it with his spells perhaps he could fly there in the airship. Fully formed, a plan of awful majesty appeared in Thanquol's mind. He could use the airship to fly to the moon and mine all the warpstone he would ever need. It would be an achievement unsurpassed in all the annals of skavendom, and surely his reward must be a place at the Council table. At the very least. Perhaps the whole Council would bow before him, and recognise him as the greatest of all servants of the Horned Rat. Such was the magnificence of his vision that for a moment, Thanquol was lost in contemplation. Only when he felt the strands of his power slipping away was he drawn back to reality by the realisation that first he would have to land his fish before any of it would be possible. He threw himself back into the struggle with renewed ferocity.

LURK WAS NOT happy. In mid-leap he had been caught by one of those huge streamers of energy and tossed all over the sky in a deranged frenzy of movement. He had long known how potent the grey seer was but never till now had he shown such full evidence of his might. Was this some sort of revenge by Grey Seer Thanquol for his disloyal thoughts? Had Thanquol been aware of Lurk's ideas concerning him all along? Did he plan to end Lurk's torment by dashing him into the ground?

'No-no, master!' he gibbered. 'Spare your loyalest of servants. I will serve you faithfully all of my days. Blast those other foul vermin. They hate you. I do not. I have always done my best for you!'

If Thanquol heard Lurk's earnest prayers, there was no sign. Filled with fear, Lurk watched the ground rise to meet him.

ULRIKA PUT her sword through the back of the skaven cowering in the hall, and went to the window to look at the source of the eerie glow. She had never seen anything like it. The horn-headed skaven mage floated in the air about twenty strides above the ground. It was anchored to the earth by hundreds of streamers of light, and with hundreds of others it was drawing the straining airship down.

Beneath it, hundreds of skaven muzzles pointed at the sky. They stood frozen in awe, watching their master at work. Beside her she heard Max Schreiber mutter, 'By Sigmar, how does it contain all that power and not explode? It must be consuming pure warpstone, and yet it still has not died.'

'What?' she asked.

'That thing out there is filled with the raw stuff of Chaos. It is using it to power its spell. It should not be possible for any mortal thing to be doing this but it is. I have no idea how.'

'Perhaps it would be better if you applied your mind to the idea of killing it,' Ulrika suggested.

'I am not sure I have the strength.'

'Then things do not look good.'

'You have a gift for understatement, my dear.'

FELIX WATCHED GOTREK descend the ladder. With one arm the Slayer held the rungs, with the other he wielded his axe like a club, dropping it down on the skulls of any skaven below him. By sheer ferocity Gotrek managed to reach the bottom and clear a space around the base of the ladder. Moments later Snorri joined him. Seeing no other option, Felix began his own descent.

A roar from above him told him that the gyrocopter had returned for another pass. Felix watched a bomb hurtle towards the hovering grey seer. The fuse timing, always a tricky thing at best, was not good, and the bomb went hurtling past Thanquol to explode amidst the skaven. Once more aware of their peril, they tried frantically to hurl themselves aside only to be blown asunder by the dwarf explosive.

Felix shuddered, thinking just how easy it would be for one of those bombs to go astray and catch himself, Gotrek and Snorri in the blast. It did not bear thinking about. Instead he threw himself forward hacking desperately to right and left, trying his best to smash a path through the massed ranks of skaven to the place where Grey Seer Thanquol hovered. Although what he was going to do when he got there eluded him.

GREY SEER THANQUOL opened his mouth and roared with only slightly crazed laughter. His senses had expanded with his power. He saw himself as a towering giant looking down on the insects below him. His spirit form was as large as the airship with which he grappled. He was a being of awesome proportions. Surely, he thought, this must be how the Horned Rat felt when he gazed down into the world of mortals. Perhaps it was an omen, a harbinger of things to come. Perhaps there would be no limits to Thanquol's destiny. Perhaps he could stride where no skaven had strode before and scale the very peaks of godhood. Certainly at this moment, with the warpstone coursing through his veins, it all seemed possible. There was nothing he could not do.

He was the master of this situation now. Nothing was going to stop him. Not even his accursed nemesis, Gotrek Gurnisson, or his devious henchman, Felix Jaeger. Finally after all these long months of effort he was going to achieve complete victory over them. How sweet that feeling was!

Wait! What was that? He glanced down and saw the gyrocopter flash past. He noticed the bomb that just missed him and exploded among his troops, sending their souls spiralling upwards to join the Horned Rat. How dare they attack the Horned Rat's chosen emissary on earth? He would show them. Quick as thought he reached out with his tentacles of power and swatted the gyrocopter like a man might swat a fly. Unfortunately he was a tad too slow to catch the fast moving craft and his blow missed.

Only incidentally did he become aware of something sticking to one of his tentacles. Of course. It was that rascal, Lurk. Briefly, Thanquol considered smashing his errant henchman into the ground as a punishment for his failures but then, through the psychic link that allowed him to perceive through his energy streams, he became aware of the gratifying way Lurk was swearing eternal obedience to him, and more, he was suddenly aware of the changes that had overtaken his minion, of the warpstone coursing through his body, and the way it had been altered. This was something worth investigating. He took a moment to place Lurk not too gently on the ground and returned to his efforts to swat the gyrocopter.

It proved frustratingly elusive. Still, he thought, the sheer satisfaction of smashing it would be its own reward.

FELIX WATCHED IN horror as streamers of light impacted on the gyrocopter. The small flying machine began to break up, its parts tumbling headlong through the air, to smash into the ground killing more skaven. A huge cloud of steam and smoke erupted from the broken vehicle's engine. It was followed by a massive explosion, the blast of which sent him tumbling headlong. He guessed that the stock of bombs on the gyrocopter had just gone off. Skaven screams told him the dwarf pilot was not the only casualty.

Overhead the other gyrocopters flashed. One down, three to go, thought Felix.

'WHAT DO WE do?' Ulrika asked. 'You're the magician. This is your field.'

'There is no way any mortal form can contain that amount of power for any great length of time. It's possible that its owner will be consumed by it. It's also possible that the power contained within whatever it is he is eating will be exhausted, and he will lose his strength. If he weakens I might be able to disrupt his spell. Other than that...'

'You are saying that we should do nothing?'

'I am saying that we should wait, Ulrika. There is nothing to be gained by attacking the thing headlong. Look at the way it smashed that gyrocopter. It could easily do the same to us.'

AH, THAT WAS good, thought Grey Seer Thanquol. He felt a monstrous surge of pleasure from destroying that dwarf flyer even at the cost of some dozens of his followers' lives. They were after all expendable. Most skaven were. He was simply glad he wasn't one of them.

He shook his head as a new problem struck him. During the moments that he had chased the flyer, he had let go of the *Spirit of Grungni*. It was heading skyward once more at a great rate of knots. Thanquol reached out with his tentacles of power, determined that he would soon put a stop to that.

No sooner had he grasped the airship once more than he became aware of another challenge. Gotrek Gurnisson, Felix Jaeger and that other accursed Slayer were on the ground and moving towards him. Of course, he was in the air above them but even so he was a little worried. Just the proximity of the Slayer was enough to get on Thanquol's sensitive nerves. He hated that vile creature with a passion.

Now he had the means to end that threat once and for all. What he could do with the gyrocopter he could surely do to one solitary Slayer. Grinning daemonically, he prepared to smash Gotrek Gurnisson into the dirt.

* * *

FELIX WATCHED THE wave of power come towards them. Dozens of streamers of greenish energy raced forward like the tide, smashing aside the screaming skaven between Gotrek and Thanquol. Felix had no doubt whatsoever what would happen when that energy reached them, it was going to be the end of him. He almost closed his eyes, knowing that his doom was moments away but at the last second, determined to see the death that was his, he forced himself to watch.

NOW, THOUGHT Grey Seer Thanquol, bringing his powers to bear on Gotrek Gurnisson. *Now you die!*

FELIX SAW THE leading streamers reach Gotrek. As they did so the Slayer brought his axe round in a great arc. The runes on its edges blazed ever brighter where they came into contact with the grey seer's spell. A smell of ozone filled the air. The streamers flew apart in a cloud of sparks, having met with an ancient magic stronger than they. Felix offered up a prayer to Sigmar and whatever other gods might be listening. The remaining streamers withdrew, coiling upwards and backwards away from Gotrek like a cobra about to strike. Felix knew the Slayer had bought them only a moment's respite.

THANQUOL FELT AS if his fingertips were on fire. Of course, it was only the destruction of his spell that he was sensing but the sensation was similar. He cursed the dwarf. He might have guessed that it would not have been so easy to effect his doom. Still, perhaps if the Slayer was invulnerable, his henchman would not prove to be. He could at least destroy Felix Jaeger.

FELIX SAW THE streamers of light part and begin to flow around Gotrek. To his horror he realised that they were aimed at him, and there was nothing he could do about it. The skaven sorcerer obviously intended to see him dead. The spell rushed onwards, a dozen tendrils moving to the right and left of Gotrek, surging directly towards Felix. At least, thought Felix, the skaven mage was killing more of his own warriors. The way they fell to bits as the energy scythed through them did not bode well for his own fate.

* * *

ULRIKA WATCHED WHAT was happening with her heart in her mouth. She saw Gotrek repulse the grey seer's attack and for a moment thought it might be enough. Then she saw that Thanquol intended to attack Felix.

'Can't you do something?' she asked Max Schreiber.

'In a moment I will try a counter spell. I think I understand what the grey seer is doing now and I might be able to pick apart the weave of it.'

'Felix doesn't have a moment,' Ulrika said, knowing it was already too late.

FELIX STEELED HIMSELF to meet death. This was not quite the way he expected it but then it was said that death never came by the route you thought it would. He braced himself, preparing his muscles for one last futile leap to safety. He doubted there was any way he could avoid the spell. It was all over. The tide of dazzling light hurtled towards him. He fought down the urge to scream.

THIS WAS MORE like it, thought Grey Seer Thanquol, certain that this time at least he was about to kill one of his sworn enemies. That would teach Felix Jaeger to oppose the might of Thanquol. But just before he could crush Jaeger like the insect he was, the Slayer struck once more, lashing out quicker than the eye could follow, first to his left, then to his right, severing the energy bands with that awful axe. Thanquol shrieked with pain. It was like having his own tail cut off.

Worse yet, he felt the warpstone-induced power within him start to stutter and fade. Not now, he thought. No. Not now. Not with triumph so close. But unfortunately, it was so. The energy was already starting to drain out of him. It looked as if the airship was going to escape.

Well at least, he thought, my minions will destroy those upstarts, Jaeger and Gurnisson. Even as he thought it a peculiar sinking sensation struck him. Why is the ground coming closer, he wondered?

'NOW,' ULRIKA HEARD Max Schreiber mutter, and then the mage began to move his hands and incant in some language she did not understand. As she watched a complex structure of light began to take shape in the space in front of the magician, and then with a gesture of his hand he sent it spinning out towards the grey seer. When it struck Thanquol the glow around the skaven sorcerer faded and he went tumbling headlong to the earth.

'Now would be a good time to attack,' Max suggested to her. She did not need to be told a second time.

'Let's go!' she shouted and raced out of the mansion, plunging into the surprised skaven from behind. Roaring with battle-lust the Kislevite survivors followed her.

FELIX WATCHED IN surprise as the glow faded around the grey seer and he began to sink to the earth. He ducked the swing of a skaven warrior and gritted his teeth as he parried a second one. The shock of the impact passed up his arm. He braced himself and slashed downwards cleaving the skaven's skull in two, then whirled to strike the other, slashing it across the throat. Ahead of him Gotrek and Snorri hacked a bloody path towards the skaven mage. They were determined that nothing was going to stop them this time. Bombs continued to rain down from above, dropped by the now freed airship and the circling gyrocopters.

Every time a bomb hit the ground Felix flinched. He half expected one of them to go off near him, and for his body to be torn apart. He heard a voice shouting at the stupid dwarfs to stop bombing them, and he was surprised to discover that it was his own. He hoped that some time soon somebody up there would realise what was happening on the ground and cease the barrage. Felix doubted that Gotrek's heroic doom encompassed being torn limb from limb by his comrades' explosives. Still Felix had seen worse and stupider things happen in battle, and right now, all was chaos round about them.

Slashing around him with renewed vigour Felix hacked his way through the skaven force.

IT JUST WASN'T fair, thought Grey Seer Thanquol. Just when victory was within his grasp it had been snatched away by the incompetence of his lackeys, and the inferior quality of warpstone sent to him by those cretins back in Skavenblight. Why was he doomed to be constantly thwarted in this manner? He was a good and faithful servant to the skaven cause. He was devout in his prayers to the Horned Rat. He asked so little. What was the problem?

He lay exhausted on the ground, prostrated by the sudden failure of his warpstone-induced power, and by the unweaving of his spell. Slowly but surely, the full implications of this sunk in. Somewhere out there was a mage potent enough to undo his work, a mage who was undoubtedly fresh and not drained of energy by his selfless efforts to protect his ungrateful minions, a mage who even now might be planning the destruction of Thanquol while he was vulnerable. The thought made Thanquol's glands tighten with the urge to squirt the musk of fear. This was not a fitting reward for his long service to the Horned Rat and the Council of Thirteen, he decided.

Suddenly he became aware of another and even more terrifying threat. Off to his right, he could hear the bestial bellowing of Gotrek Gurnisson, as the Slayer smashed his way through the skaven troops. Doubtless the dwarf had nothing more in his tiny mind than an unjustifiable desire to exterminate Thanquol and rob the world of his genius. And doubtless the dwarf's henchman, Felix Jaeger, would be there to gloat at Thanquol's demise. What was he to do?

As if he did not have enough reasons to focus his mind on departure, Thanquol heard the sounds of human war-cries from behind him. Where had these new forces come from? Had human reinforcements arrived during the fight? Was this some work of the enemy mage? It mattered not. With the terrifying onslaught of bombs from above, the blood-curdling prospect of combat with Gotrek Gurnisson to the fore, and the attack of this massive new force from behind, Thanquol could see only one option open to him. He would heroically elude capture by this overwhelming force of enemies, and return to exact his revenge another day.

Mustering the last remnants of his powers, he muttered the words of the spell of escape. It would only carry him a few hundred strides out of the fray but this would be enough. From there he would begin his tactical withdrawal.

'WHERE HAS THAT accursed mage got to?' Felix heard Gotrek growl. Felix had no answer. They had reached the spot where he would have sworn he had seen the grey seer fall, and there was nothing there except a faint brimstone aroma in the air. Unreasonably annoyed, Gotrek slaughtered two skaven simultaneously with a stroke of his axe and turned around to look at the monstrous form of the rat-ogre as it approached.

'Mine!' he roared.

'Snorri's!' shouted Snorri.

'Race you for it,' answered Gotrek and rushed forward.

Get on with it, thought Felix as he looked around him. There was a sudden lull in the battle. The strange stink that he had come to associate with frightened skaven attacked his nostrils. He supposed he could not blame them. Their leader had vanished. They were being ripped apart by bombs, assaulted by two of the most vicious Slayers in the world, and ambushed from behind simultaneously. Felix could understand their demoralisation. He doubted that any human force would be less afraid.

Still that did not mean that the peril had passed. The skaven still massively outnumbered their foes, and if given time to realise it, they would return to the fray and quite possibly win. Right now was the moment to seize the advantage and hopefully turn the tide of battle.

He looked around and saw the rat-ogre flanked on one side by Gotrek and the other by Snorri go down under a blizzard of blows. It toppled like a falling oak. If the sight of that did not help them rout the skaven force, nothing would. Shouting a battle-cry, he charged forward. Gotrek and Snorri accompanied him.

Suddenly from up ahead he thought he heard the sound of human war-cries, of one familiar voice shouting orders and encouragement to the troops. His heart leapt. Surely he was hallucinating. There was only one way to find out.

LURK STOPPED GNAWING the flesh of the dead skaven. His hunger momentarily assuaged, he could give his attention back to matters at hand. Behind him he could hear the squeal of terrified skaven, the triumphant shouts of the humans, and the berserker roars of dwarf Slayers. He could tell the battle was lost. It was as certain as the ache in his bones from hitting the ground. Of course, he knew that if it were not for the pain of his injuries, he could turn the tide of battle by his intervention. Unfortunately his bruises, and could that possibly be a sprained ankle, prevented it.

From out of the gloom, beams of golden light scythed into the skaven, slashing them down. It looked like their enemies had sorcerous resources too.

Definitely lost, he thought to himself. Definitely time to go. He picked himself up, glanced around to make sure that no one had noticed him, and scuttled off into the night.

MOVING THROUGH THE carnage of the battlefield Felix caught sight of a familiar figure. His heart leapt. Ulrika was alive. Thinking of nothing else, he moved towards her through the mass of skaven. All around him ratmen turned and fled. They had learned to fear his flashing blade and his proximity to the two Slayers. His mere presence at this moment seemed enough to unnerve them. There was little doubt in his mind that the ratmen were beaten. They milled around looking for a way out, their formation broken, their discipline gone. The loss of their leader and the surprise onslaught from their former captives had been enough to rout them. Now it was only a matter of staying alive while they fled.

'Ulrika!' he shouted, but she did not hear him. At that moment, a huge black-furred skaven leapt at her. Terrified that he was about to lose her just when he had found her at last, Felix raced forward to intervene. He need not have bothered. Ulrika parried the ratman's blow, and put a stop-thrust through its heart. Gurgling in pain, the skaven tumbled forward onto its knees, and then sprawled headlong in the dirt, surrounded by a rapidly spreading pool of its own lifeblood.

Ulrika caught sight of something out of the corner of her eye, and whirled ready to attack. For a long tense moment she and Felix faced each other. Neither moved. Neither said anything. Then simultaneously they both smiled, then made to move together. Unable to stop himself, uncaring of the danger, Felix caught her in his arms. Their lips met. Their bodies strained against each other.

Surrounded by the howling madness of battle, they stood like they were the only two people in the world.

MAX SCHREIBER LOOKED around him. He was tired. As much from the magic he had just wrought as from the reaction to the beating he had taken last night. His limbs felt heavy with fatigue. Not even as an apprentice when he had maintained many a days-long vigil in the service of his master had he ever felt so worn out. Still, victory was theirs. The skaven were routed, and even though they still had numerical superiority,

he doubted they would return. They were not by nature courageous creatures and it took them a long time to get over defeats.

Max liked to think of himself as a scholar, not a warrior, but
he felt satisfied with what he had done here. He had taken a
stand against the forces of Chaos and he had helped turn them
back. Part of him found the experience far more satisfying than
casting protective spells on the homes and vehicles of his
clients. He began to understand the thrill of battle he had
always read about. He smiled sourly as he caught sight of Felix
and Ulrika kissing.

It appeared that for a sheltered scholar he was getting a crash
course in all manner of emotional turmoil. He felt jealousy
gnaw away at him, and he knew that not all of his magic could
root it out.

He was more than a little attracted to Ulrika. For the past few
days he had felt himself in the grip of passion. He really should
have left the mansion days ago but had stayed on under the
pretence of waiting for the *Spirit of Grungni's* return. Seeing the
way that Ulrika looked at Felix he guessed that there was little
chance of her responding to his ardour.

Unless, the most unworthy thought struck him, something
were to happen to Felix Jaeger. Surprised at his own savagery he
sent a hail of golden beams slashing into the retreating skaven.

They died in a most gratifying way.

SILENCE CAME SUDDENLY. The battle was over. The dead lay in
piles around the mansion. The *Spirit of Grungni* hovered overhead, nuzzling the docking tower like a horse being hitched to
a post. The skaven were defeated.

IT WAS LATE. Felix felt tired but elated. He held Ulrika's hand as
if he feared she would vanish if he let go of it, and she did not
seem at all inclined to lose his grip. All his forebodings on the
trip back now seemed senseless and futile phantoms. She was
as glad to see him as he was to see her, and he could not begin
to express how happy that made him. Instead he could only
stand and gaze stupidly into her eyes. Words just would not
come. Fortunately, she seemed content with that.

Snorri stomped over. 'Good fight that,' he said. Black blood
crusted his bandages and he bled from dozens of new small
cuts but he seemed happy with his lot.

'Call that a fight?' Gotrek said. 'I've had more dangerous hair-cuts.'

'I wouldn't want to meet your barber,' Felix said.

'Felix made a joke,' said Snorri. 'Snorri thinks it's funny.'

'Let's get some beer,' Gotrek said. 'Nothing like a bit of light exercise to work up a thirst.'

'Snorri wants a bucket of vodka,' said Snorri. 'And Snorri shall have it.'

Dwarfs had started to climb down the docking tower where the *Spirit of Grungni* was moored. Soon a small contingent of them were helping the Kislevites pile up the bodies for burning.

Felix thought this was as good a time as any for he and Ulrika to retire to their chamber. She agreed.

'I NEVER THOUGHT I would see you again,' Ulrika said.

The dawn was beautiful. Golden beams of sunlight slanted down and caught the endless sea of grass around them. Birds sang. It was so calm that if it were not for the faint smell of burned flesh in the air, Felix would have found it difficult to believe that any battle had taken place the previous evening.

'There were times when I thought I would never see you again. A lot of them,' he replied.

'Was it bad?'

'Very.'

'In the Wastes?'

'In the Wastes and in Karag Dum. You would not believe me if I told you what we found there.'

'Try me.'

'All right,' he said, gathering her close in his arms.

'That's not what I meant,' she said, then kissed him.

'It will do for the moment,' he said, pulling her down into the long grass.

'Yes,' she replied.

AFTERWARDS, AS THEY lay naked on his old woollen cloak, she leaned on her elbow and began to tickle his face with an ear of grass. 'What was it like in the Chaos Wastes?'

'Do we really have to talk about it?'

'Not if you don't want to.'

He considered for a time before replying. 'It is a terrible place. Like the dream of insane gods.'

'That's not very specific.'

'More than you would think. It changes seemingly at random. Landscapes shimmer and shift...'

'Sounds like mirages in the desert.'

'Perhaps. But there are things there... Huge idols large as hills, ruined cities that no man has ever heard of, that might just have dropped from the sky. Endless hordes of monsters, and black-armoured men, all of them dedicated to...'

'What is it? Why do you fall silent.'

'They are coming here. We saw them from the airship. A horde of them. More than I could count, and they are merely the outriders of an even vaster host.'

'Why haven't you mentioned this before?'

'Because I was so happy to see you, and because I am sure Borek has told your father by now.'

Ulrika sat up straight and stared at the horizon. It did not escape Felix's notice that she was looking northward, to the mountains beyond which lay the Wastes of Chaos. He sensed a change in her mood, a new watchful quality that had something of fear in it.

'The forces of Darkness have come this way before. We live on their borders. These are the marchlands. We have fought with them and triumphed in the past.'

'Not against the force that is coming. This will be like the great Chaos Incursion of two centuries ago, in the time of Magnus the Pious.'

She frowned. 'You are sure?'

'I have seen it with my own eyes.'

'Why now? Why in our time?' He thought he detected a hint of fear in her voice.

'I am sure Magnus asked himself the same question.'

'That is not an answer, Felix.' Now there was a note of exasperation. A frown marred her brow. A corresponding annoyance welled up in him.

'I am not a prophet, Ulrika, I am just a man. I cannot answer these questions. I only know that it fits with what I have seen in other places...'

'What other places?' Her words were sharp. He did not like her tone.

'In the Empire, the cultists multiply. The worshippers of Chaos are in every city. Beastmen fill the forests. The number of changelings, of mutated ones, is increasing with every month. Wicked magicians prosper. I sometimes think that the doomsayers are right, and that the end of the world is coming.'

'Those are not cheerful words,' she said reaching out and grasping his hand with feverish strength.

'These are not cheerful times.' He reached out and stroked her cheek. 'We should go back soon. Find out what the others have been saying.'

She smiled wanly and bent forward to kiss his brow. 'I'm glad you're here,' she said suddenly.

'Me too,' said Felix.

MAX SCHREIBER LISTENED to what the dwarfs were saying with growing dismay. Their descriptions of the oncoming Chaos horde chilled him to the bone. The pictures they painted in his mind had even managed to drive out the jealousy he had felt this morning when he saw Felix and Ulrika ride off together.

He had read descriptions of such things from the time of the great war against Chaos two hundred years ago. He did not doubt that this was a force of similar size. For a long time now, he had suspected that such a thing would happen. He had studied the ways of Chaos for too long not to know its power was on the increase. He looked at the dwarfs' faces. They might well have been chiselled from stone. The matter-of-fact way in which they told of their descent into Karag Dum and their battle with the thing they had found there made him look on the Slayers with new respect.

And despite his jealousy of Felix Jaeger he had to admit the man was brave as well as lucky. Max did not think he himself could have faced the thing the dwarfs described with quite the equanimity Jaeger had. He could understand why the dwarfs spoke of him with respect. The thing they had fought was obviously a Greater Daemon of Chaos. He wondered if the dwarfs had any idea of how lucky they had been to survive such an encounter. Not that they had actually succeeded in slaying it, Max knew. Such creatures could not be destroyed by mortals. All that they had done was banish its physical form. It would take on another sooner or later, and return to this plane to seek vengeance. If it could not find Gotrek Gurnisson or Felix Jaeger alive it would seek out their descendants and heirs. Such was the manner of the things.

There were times when Max Schreiber wished he had not studied this subject so long and so hard. Being privy to such knowledge often gave him nightmares. Still, it had been his choice; he had set his feet on this path long ago, and he had been given many opportunities to turn back. He had chosen not to. Ever since he had watched his family butchered by beastmen as a child, he had hated Chaos and all its works. He was sworn to oppose it in any way he could, and that meant learning its ways. Long ago when he had first started his studies as a mage he had encountered those who were of like mind. They needed to be warned of what was coming from the north. The world needed to be warned.

Ivan obviously agreed. 'If what you are saying is true–'

'You doubt my word?' Gotrek Gurnisson said.

'It is not that I doubt it my friend, it's just that part of me would rather not believe it. The tide of Chaos you are describing could sweep away the world.'

'Yes,' said Borek. 'It could.'

'Except the dwarfholds,' Gotrek said stoutly.

'Even those would fall in the end,' Borek said. 'Remember Karag Dum.'

Gotrek smiled sourly. 'I don't see how I could forget it.'

'I must send word to the Ice Queen,' said Ivan. 'The Tzarina must be warned. The armies of Kislev must be mustered.'

'Aye,' said Borek. 'But what about you? You cannot remain here. This manor could not resist the massed might of Chaos.'

'I will summon my riders and head south to Praag. That will be where our forces will meet. However, I must ask a boon of you...'

Max Schreiber leaned forward interestedly. 'So must I,' he said. Ivan looked up and indicated that he should speak first. It was a measure of the respect the Kislevite held for him since he had used his magic on their behalf.

'I must ask passage south with you on the airship if that is possible. There are those I must inform about these events.'

'The Elector Count of Middenheim, perhaps?' Borek said.

'Among others. I am sure that in the face of this threat I can prevail upon him to send aid to Kislev. If nothing else the Knights of the White Wolf will respond.'

'The *Spirit of Grungni* is already full almost beyond capacity,' Borek said. Max tilted his head to show he understood.

'That is a pity, old friend,' Ivan said, 'for I too wished to ask the same boon. I want to send a messenger to the Ice Queen and to be sure your craft is faster than the swiftest rider ever could be.'

'I am sure we could find space,' Borek said. 'If need be we can always find space.'

'Good – I wish to send my daughter Ulrika and two body-guards. Oleg and Standa will go with her.'

They all looked at the old boyar. It was plain from the bleak expression on his face that he had a stronger reason for this than merely warning the Ice Queen. It was clear that he wished to send his beloved daughter out of harm's way, at least for a short time. Max was profoundly grateful that the old man cared enough to do this thing.

'It shall be so,' Borek said.

GREY SEER THANQUOL felt dreadful. His head ached. His body felt as if stormvermin had worked it over with clubs – not that any skaven would dare to do such a thing to him, of course. Worst of all was the sense of failure that gnawed at his bow-els. He was not quite sure how they had done it, but he was sure that somehow Gotrek Gurnisson and Felix Jaeger had contrived to thwart him yet again. Their malefic powers some-times seemed unlimited. And of course there was always the worthlessness of his underlings to be considered.

Not that the masters of Clan Moulder were likely to accept this. He was sure he had seen at least one of his clawleaders scurry away in the mad aftermath of the battle. Doubtless he would poison the minds of his stupid kinsfolk with lies about Thanquol. It was true that a small army of Clan Moulder troops had been lost in the attempt to seize the airship, but Thanquol was not to blame for the inferior quality of his troops. And it was equally true that he had failed to capture the airship as he had promised. But only the most biassed of churls could blame Thanquol for the deviousness of the Slayer and his minions. Of course, he suspected that the Moulder skaven possessed exactly the amount of bias required to make these poorly informed judgements, and it was all too possible that if he were to return to Hell Pit an accident might befall him. There were no limits to the wicked-ness of his enemies.

A familiar black depression, the consequence of too much warpstone used too suddenly, settled on him. The enmity of Moulder was only one part of the problem that faced him now. Another was how to get back to friendly skaven territory across a hundred leagues of plain. He knew from bitter experience that Kislevite horse archers were deadly marksmen and it would only take one arrow to end even so brilliant a career as his. What was particularly worrying was that his supply of warpstone was depleted and his sorcerous powers were at a low ebb. In many ways the situation was as dire as any he had ever faced in his long and incredibly successful career as a grey seer.

What could he do? He knew that there must be some skaven survivors out here on the plain but he was not at all sure that seeking them out was a good idea. They were, after all, the house troops of Clan Moulder and it was conceivable that their misguided minds might hold a grudge against him because of the failure of the plan. Certainly there were many problems here, and even a mind as keen as Thanquol's quailed when he contemplated the difficulties which loomed before him.

A strange smell made his whiskers twitch. It was oddly familiar and yet subtly distorted. He heard something massive moving through the long grass. Something that might conceivably be the size of a rat-ogre. Had Boneripper survived? It did not smell like him. Swiftly Thanquol summoned the remnants of his power. Whatever it was it would not find him defenceless.

Suddenly a monstrous apparition loomed over Grey Seer Thanquol. It was as large as a rat-ogre. It had a horned head, and a large spiked tail. For a brief moment, Thanquol feared he might be facing the Horned Rat itself, come to make him give an account of himself. He felt his musk glands tighten as the thing opened its mouth to speak.

'Grey Seer Thanquol, it is I, the humblest of your servants, Lurk.'

'Lurk! What happened to you?'

'It is a long story, mightiest of masters. Perhaps I should tell it to you as we march.'

Lurk's voice had deepened and though his words were respectful, there was a hungry glint in his eye that Thanquol did not like at all.

Not at all.

FOUR

STORM TOSSED

FROM THE REAR observation deck of the *Spirit of Grungni*, Felix watched the mansion fall away behind them. Sadness filled him. Ivan Straghov's house was a place where he had been happy, before he set off for the Chaos Wastes, and now he doubted that he would ever see it again.

Already the Kislevites were assembling to begin the long ride south. A troop of horsemen had arrived as they debated their plans; they had rounded up mounts that had fled from the skaven attack, and managed to provide horses for most of the survivors. It was agreed that a dozen or so scouts would remain at the mansion for as long as possible to tell the other troops what had happened as they arrived. After that, Ivan and the others figured that any troops abroad when the Chaos horde arrived would soon work out what had happened for themselves and would act accordingly. It was not much of a plan, but it was the best they could do under the circumstances.

Felix turned and looked at Ulrika. Her face showed a strange mixture of emotions. She had not been happy to be dispatched south by airship to inform the Tzarina of their plight, while the others had to ride. She had wanted to share the dangers of her clan's warriors. Felix thought it was possible that if he had not been on the airship, she might not have agreed at all. Certainly he felt that he had helped persuade her to come. So had Max Schreiber.

Felix looked over at the magician. He liked Max but recently he had noticed the strange looks the man was giving him when he was with Ulrika. Was it possible he was jealous? It was easy enough to believe. She was very beautiful and Max had been around the mansion while he had been away in the Chaos Wastes. Who knows what might have happened then? Felix smiled sourly. It sounded like he was feeling more than a little jealous himself.

He consoled himself with the thought that the worst was behind them, at least for a while. They had managed to escape from the Wastes with their lives intact, and they had survived the skaven ambush. From here it was a straight run south to the capital of Kislev, and then on to Karaz-a-Karak where Borek intended to present the survivors of Karag Dum and some of its treasures to the High King of the Dwarfs. Felix wondered what Gotrek really thought of that.

As far as Felix knew the Slayer had been banished from the great underground city, never to return. Felix was not sure whether the exile was self-imposed or a penalty for the Slayer's misdeeds. It had never seemed politic to ask. Gotrek insisted on remaining in Kislev and helping against the Chaos hordes. Felix certainly hoped so. Ivan had pointed out that, as a former engineer, he would be more useful helping prepare the defences to resist a siege. They would get off the airship with Ulrika and her bodyguards.

Whatever the reason, Felix was glad. He wanted to stay with Ulrika and he certainly didn't want the Slayer reminding him of the oath he had sworn to follow him and record his doom. There would be time enough for that later, he did not doubt. With that monstrous army heading south, a mighty struggle was in the offing. There would be plenty of opportunity for Gotrek to find his heroic death.

He reached out and took Ulrika's hand and squeezed her fingers. She turned and smiled at him wanly. It was obvious that her thoughts were with those tiny figures slowly receding into the distance below. She turned and gazed back, like someone trying to memorise a scene and remember people she feared she might never see again.

* * *

IN THE WAN northern daylight, Grey Seer Thanquol studied Lurk closely. He hated to admit it but he was both impressed and intimidated. His lackey looked like he could take on a rat-ogre and win. He was more than twice Thanquol's height and possibly ten times his mass. His claws looked strong as steel and the massive knob of horned bone at the end of his tail looked potent as a mace. Right at this moment, Thanquol rather regretted all the insults he had heaped on Lurk in the past. He was not sure that in his current state of depletion he could summon the magical energies needed to destroy Lurk. Under the circumstances, craftiness and diplomacy, two of Thanquol's greatest gifts, seemed like the most appropriate measures.

'Lurk! I am glad you have returned. Good-good! Together we must bring news of the failure of Clan Moulder's ill-conceived attack on the human fort to the attention of the Council of Thirteen.'

Lurk looked at him with reddishly glowing and strangely forbidding eyes. When he opened his mouth to speak he revealed huge sharp tusks. Thanquol fought down the urge to squirt the musk of fear.

'Yes-yes, most majestic of masters,' Lurk growled in a voice much deeper than the one Thanquol remembered. Thanquol almost let out a sigh of relief. On their long march through the night, Lurk had been strangely surly. At least now this huge warpstone-altered skaven seemed tractable. That was good. He would be able to protect Thanquol from many of the dangers on the route. And who knew? It was certainly possible that studying his mutated form might reveal many secrets, including how to create more of his kind. Dissection revealed many things. However, thought Thanquol, shifting uncomfortably before that unblinking stare, such matters could wait until they had escaped the immediate danger.

'These open spaces crawl with horse soldiers,' Thanquol said. 'The traitors of Moulder will also be out in force. We must use intelligence and cunning to escape our enemies and fulfil our mission.'

'As you say, most persuasive of potentates.' Was there a hint of irony in Lurk's voice, Thanquol wondered? Was it possible his lackey was mocking him? Was that a gleam of hunger in his eyes? Thanquol did not like that look at all. Nor did he like the way in which Lurk was sidling closer. It reminded him uncomfortably of a cat stalking its prey. Lurk licked his lips hungrily.

With vast effort, Thanquol mustered his power. A flickering glow appeared around his paw. Lurk stopped his approach and froze on the spot. He bobbed his head servilely. Thanquol looked at him wondering whether it might not be a good idea to blast him on the spot, and get it over with. Had he possessed his full magical energies he would have done so without hesitation but now he was not sure whether it was a good idea. He did not want to use what little power he had unnecessarily. There were too many threats around him. Lurk watched him warily. He gave the impression of being poised to spring at the slightest provocation. Thanquol had seen that look before in other skaven. He knew it only too well.

'We will head northwards first. Towards the mountains. Our enemies will not expect that. Then we will circle round the edge of the plain till we come upon an entrance to the Underway.'

'A good plan, most benevolent of benefactors.'

'Then let us be away. Quick-quick! I will take the leader's place in the rear.'

Lurk did not seem to object. Looking at his broad back, Thanquol continued to wonder whether this was such a good idea. It was a long way to the mountains on foot, and a longer way yet back to the heartlands of skaven civilisation. Would he be better off travelling with Lurk or should he blast the monster in the back right now? As if sensing his thoughts, Lurk cast him a grim look over his shoulder. Thanquol controlled the urge to squirt the musk of fear.

Perhaps it would be best just to wait and see, he thought.

MAX SCHREIBER WALKED through the airship. It was more difficult than he remembered from his journey to Kislev. Every inch of corridor was filled with packing cases shifted from the hold to make room for the refugees from Karag Dum. Crew members were sleeping on bedrolls in the corridor. It could not be pleasant lying on those riveted cast iron floors. There was very little comfort on the whole ship.

Max was uncomfortable from keeping in a semi-crouch the whole time. The airship had been built for dwarfs which meant that for him the ceilings were far too low. Movement sometimes seemed like an excruciating new form of torture. Of course, most of this trip had turned out to be that.

He still ached from the after-effects of the battle, and his heart felt heavy with jealousy over Felix and Ulrika. He had, of course, refused when the dwarfs had placed him in the same cabin as the two lovers. It had been tactless of them to offer, but then he was used to that from the members of the Elder Race. For a people who prided themselves on having been civilised when humanity was still wearing skins, they could be remarkably uncouth when it came to the subtleties of relationships. Not like the elves, Max thought. Of course, it would have been tactless for him to point this out. Most dwarfs hated the Eldest Race with a passion Max found incomprehensible.

Don't be so negative, he told himself. Look on the bright side. You helped win a victory over the skaven the night before last, and you saved some lives with your magic. You even healed Gotrek and Snorri of the worst of their wounds. You have done good work here. You should be proud.

He paused and looked around for a moment. He wondered about the monster the dwarfs claimed to have spotted on the airship during the battle at the village. He did not doubt they had seen something but perhaps it was an illusion or some minor daemon summoned by the skaven seer. The creature was certainly powerful enough to be capable of such magic. Max considered himself very lucky to have survived that particular encounter. Another thing to be grateful for.

It was amazing, he thought. As an apprentice, secure in his ignorant pride, he had thought that nothing could threaten him once he became a mage. It seemed that most of his career in the arcane arts had consisted of discovering that the world was full of beings more potent than himself.

Another set of illusions shattered. How many had there been now? Let's see – one of his idle fantasies as a youth had been the thought that one day he would learn spells that could compel a woman to love him. He did indeed know such spells now, as well as half a dozen others that would command obedience in all but the most strong-willed. Of course now he was bound by the most sacred of oaths not to use such spells except in defence of the Empire and humanity. Such were the responsibilities that came with power.

The world was a more complicated place than he had ever believed as a lad. He knew he would be putting his immortal soul in peril if he ever used such spells now. The road to damnation was paved not with good intentions but with desires gratified by evil means.

Still, there were times when it had crossed his mind that damnation might not be too high a price for the love of a woman like Ulrika. Swiftly he pushed that thought aside. The snares of Chaos are subtle, he thought, and very, very numerous. He was one of those who should know. His secret masters had taught him that. Look on the bright side, he told himself, and stop thinking such dark thoughts.

Despite all his formidable training, he could not.

ULRIKA WONDERED WHAT was going on. All of a sudden her life seemed to have changed utterly. She had returned from Middenheim scant weeks ago and now she had fled her home, perhaps forever. It did not seem possible that things could change so swiftly.

A few days ago she had fervently wished for Felix's return and dreaded it. Now it had happened and it had made her life more complicated than she would have thought possible. Of course, she was glad to see him, too glad in many ways. She knew that the only reason she had allowed herself to be persuaded to board the airship and warn the Ice Queen was because he was aboard, and she could not bear the thought of parting with him so soon after they had been reunited.

And at the same time, it made her feel guilty and angry. She was a warrior of her people, and warriors did not shirk their duties simply because they were smitten. She wished now she had remained with her father. That would have been the right thing to do, and she knew it. Her place was at his side.

These complex emotions were infuriating and she knew they were making her withdrawn and sometimes unpleasant. And there were other complications. She had seen the way Max Schreiber looked at her. Men had looked at her that way before. She did not find it unpleasant, but she knew that though she liked Max she did not want more than friendship from him. She hoped she could make him understand that. If not, things might turn nasty. She knew some men got that way when they were rejected. Just to make things worse, Max was a wizard. Who knew what he was capable of? Well, that was a worry for the future. She pushed it to one side, one of those things that might never come to pass, worthless to consider until it did.

The question right now was the man standing beside her, holding her hand. Now that Felix was back all the other problems had come back to haunt her. He was a landless wanderer and they were going to the court of the Tzarina. He was oath-bound to follow Gotrek and record his doom. And he was different since he had come back from the Wastes. Quieter and grimmer. Perhaps the Wastes could change a man in more subtle ways than mutation.

And how much did she really know about him? She told herself that these were things that should not make a difference to her feelings, but she knew in her secret heart that they did.

In the distance, she watched storm clouds gathering. They looked different from this altitude but no less menacing. There's a storm coming from the north, she thought, from the Chaos Wastes. The thought filled her heart with fear.

SNORRI LOOKED NORTHWARDS at the gathering clouds. Big storm coming, Snorri could tell. Something to do with the size and the blackness of the clouds and the faint flicker of lightning in the distance. Yes. Big storm coming. Not that Snorri cared. Right at this moment, Snorri was drunk. He had consumed more than a bucket of potato vodka and he was feeling a little the worse for it. That was common these days. Snorri knew he was drinking too much. But then again, Snorri told himself, that was not really possible.

Snorri drank to forget. Snorri had become so good at it that he had forgot what he was drinking to forget. Either that or all those blows to the head he had taken during his career as a Slayer had done it. Right now, he should drink more. It would help him to stay forgetful, just in case.

He knew that whatever it was he was trying to forget was bad. He knew that he had done something that he must atone for, suffered a grief or shame so great that the only thing he could do to expunge it was to seek death in a heroic fashion and thus earn back his good name for himself and his clan. He wondered what it was.

In the corner of his mind, images flickered. A wife, children, little ones, all dead. Had he killed them? He did not think so. Was he responsible for their deaths? The stab of pain in his chest told him yes, Snorri probably was. He had been drunk then too? Yes, he had.

He took another swig from his bucket and offered it to Gotrek. Gotrek shook his head. He rubbed his eyepatch with the knuckles of one big fist and kept his gaze fixed on the clouds.

The storm was definitely getting closer. It was coming from the north to overtake the ship, Snorri could feel it in his bones. The thought occurred to him that it might be sent by the Chaos sorcerers as revenge for what they had done at Karag Dum. He shared the idea with Gotrek but Gotrek just grunted.

Snorri wasn't offended. Even by Slayer standards, Gotrek Gurnisson was grim. Snorri knew he had reason to be. He had once known why Gotrek had shaved his head. He felt sure of it. But too much vodka or too many blows to Snorri's head had knocked the knowledge out again. It was the way, he thought.

Snorri felt bone-deep aches. Amazing how well he had healed, all things considered. That human magician's spell was potent. Still, it could not get rid of all the pain. Snorri had taken a lot of punishment in the past few weeks, been in a lot of fights.

But that was all right. He liked fights. More even than vodka, or good dwarf beer, the madness of battle helped him stay forgetful. In combat he could lose sight of who he was and what he once might have been. He knew this was something he shared with Gotrek. He took another swig and watched the wall of blackness coming closer. Worst storm he had ever seen, he supposed. Worse even than the one the airship had endured in the Wastes.

A vision of the *Spirit of Grungni* smashed to the ground by the force of the storm, lying broken and burned out on the ground filled Snorri's mind. He realised he didn't care. He didn't care much about anything any more. He was a walking corpse now. His life had burned out long ago. At this moment, it did not matter whether the doom he found was a heroic one, as long as it was a doom. Even as he thought this, part of Snorri rebelled. It seemed too much like a betrayal of himself, and of his dead. And still part of him felt that way. He wondered if Gotrek ever felt the same.

Snorri knew it was just another of those things he would never ask. He offered the bucket to Gotrek again. This time the other Slayer took it.

Bad storm coming, Snorri thought. Worst Snorri has ever seen.

THE RISING WIND ruffled Lurk's fur. His stomach growled almost as loudly as a rat-ogre. He felt as if a whole nest of runts were in his belly trying to eat their way out of his stomach. He could not ever recall being this hungry.

Overhead, black clouds boiled. Huge strokes of lightning burst through the darkness giving the scene a hellish flickering illumination. The rain drove into his face, almost blinding him. He had lost the scent of Grey Seer Thanquol, and wondered if the mage were still behind him in the darkness.

The high grass rippled and flowed like the waters of a great ocean. The blades slashed at him like soft impotent swords. He did not like this. He did not like this at all. He wanted to be anywhere but here. He wanted to be in some safe burrow of solid stone, not under this roiling turbulent ever-changing sky.

Silently he cursed Thanquol. The grey seer was, and ever had been, the source of all the misery in Lurk's life. He wished he had taken the opportunity to spring on him when he had the chance. He was sure Thanquol's magic could not have been all that potent then. The grey seer had looked exhausted, as if the efforts of the previous evening had drained him of all power. He knew that his new altered form had been more than capable of overwhelming his former master. He would have liked nothing more than to burrow his snout in the grey seer's belly and eat his intestines, preferably while Thanquol lived.

And yet, despite his gnawing hunger, he had not done so. He had to face that fact. He was not entirely sure why. Part of it was simple force of habit, part of it was justifiable skaven caution in the face of Thanquol's magic, and part of it was natural skaven cunning. He knew that if he just bided his time a suitable opportunity would arise to exact his revenge with far less risk to his own precious hide.

After all, with a skaven as cunning as Thanquol, you could never be sure whether he was really as weak as he was pretending. It was better to be safe than sorry.

Or so he had thought. But now this hideous storm had arisen, and it felt like it would blow away their entire world. Worse, he could sense a strange taint to it, the faint mephitic odour of warpstone. This storm was coming straight from the Wastes. Which no doubt accounted for the odd multi-coloured aspect of the lightning. He turned to ask Thanquol what they should do.

The grey seer was just standing there, eyes wide, mouth open, breathing in the storm winds like a skavenslave gulping down fungusberry wine. It was as if this storm had been made for him. Lurk shivered with fear. Perhaps he could put off his revenge a little longer. After all, he had waited long enough. What difference could a few more minutes, or hours, or days, or even weeks make?

If only he were not so damned hungry. He looked at Thanquol, measuring every ounce of his flesh. Thanquol saw his look and a faint flickering aura of power snaked around his claws. Now was not the right moment for vengeance, Lurk thought. But soon, very soon.

FELIX FELT THE airship shake.

'What was that?' Ulrika asked. She didn't sound afraid. She never did but he could feel her body shiver where it lay against his.

'The wind,' he said. The *Spirit of Grungni* suddenly bucked like a ship on a storm-tossed sea. She clutched tight against him. Felix felt his own heart jump into his mouth. This was not a pleasant sensation but he had experienced its like before in the Chaos Wastes. Come to think of it, so had she. There had been a storm on their first flight between Middenheim and Kislev. He reached out to stroke her hair, and touch her warm and naked body.

'It's nothing to worry about. I've been through worse in the Chaos Wastes.'

A keening sound echoed down the corridor and through the chambers. The whole ship vibrated. 'Just the metal of the ship. It's under strain,' he said, trying to remember all the reassuring phrases that Malakai had taught him. He was surprised at how calm he sounded. He only wished he felt that way. The ship shuddered like a live thing. The two lovers held each other in the darkened cabin. Both were waiting for disaster to strike.

MAX SCHREIBER MADE his way onto the control deck. Things did not look good. He could see nothing through the monstrous black clouds ahead of them save the occasional flicker of a lightning flash. The whole ship shivered. The engines howled like lost souls as they strained to propel the *Spirit of Grungni* against the enormous currents of air.

On the bright side, at least Malakai Makaisson was at the controls. Of all the potential pilots of the ship, Max had most faith in him.

'Tisnae as bad as it looks,' Makaisson said. As always his thick guttural accent and odd dialect confused Max. Makaisson was not the easiest of dwarfs to understand.

'I'm glad you are feeling so confident, Herr Makaisson,' said Max. He glanced around. Aside from the Slayer engineer, every other face on the command deck was a picture of worry. Makaisson played with the earflap of his peculiar leather flying helmet, which had been cut at the top to let his Slayer's crest show through. He adjusted the goggles which sat on top of his head then he looked up at Max and grinned. It was not a reassuring grin. Makaisson did not look sane at the best of times, and at the moment he looked positively crazy.

'Nithin tae worry aboot! Ah've got the ship turned oot o' the wind. We'll joost rin afore the storm till it runs oot o' force. Nithin tae it.'

Actually, Makaisson's words sounded suspiciously sensible, as they often did if you listened to them closely. Max pictured the airship running before the wind just like a sailing ship could. The storm would just make it fly faster. As long as the gasbag remained untorn they should be safe. Just as he was feeling slightly reassured the *Spirit of Grungni* leapt upwards like a horse clearing a fence. Max was forced to grab the edge of one of the command seats just to stay upright.

'A wee bit o' turbulence, man. Dinnae cack yer breeks!'

'IS IT JUST me or is the storm dying down?' Ulrika asked. Felix had been wondering that himself for some time. Hours had passed since the storm had overtaken them, and they had been among the longest hours of Felix's life. The *Spirit of Grungni* had never felt quite so unsafe. At any moment he had felt like the whole thing might just break apart, and they would all be sent tumbling to their deaths. Somehow the presence of Ulrika had just made the whole thing worse. The prospect of his own death was not one that he particularly enjoyed, but the thought of the girl in his arms dying at the same time, and there being nothing he could do about, was just awful.

'I think it is,' he said eventually. He was fairly sure he was telling the truth too. The airship seemed to have slowed a little. The rain no longer beat quite so strongly against the windows. The lightning flashes had become less frequent. Perhaps the worst had indeed passed.

Ulrika buried her head on his shoulder. He held her close and offered up a prayer to Sigmar that they would be spared.

MAX SCHREIBER LOOKED at the speed gauge on the control console. The *Spirit of Grungni* was definitely slowin – a sign, according to Makaisson, that the tailwind was less strong. Max wasn't entirely sure what the dwarf meant, but he thought he got the general idea. He was duly grateful that the gods had spared them.

'Ah telt ye, didn't ah?' said Makaisson,' but wud yese listen? Naw! Ah sade this airship can tak far worse than this but ye ah kent better, didn't ye? Aye, well who was right, that's what ah ask ye, noo?'

'You were, Herr Makaisson, no question,' Max said, and he was grateful that the dwarf had been. He was even grateful that the Slayer had known exactly what to do to save his ship. Perhaps his reputation for causing disasters was not entirely deserved. Ahead of them something huge loomed out of the storm dark gloom.

'What's that?' Max asked.

'It's a bloody mountain, ya eedjeet. Help me turn this damn wheel.'

Desperately Max added his weight to Makaisson's as they tried to change course. Slowly, too slowly, the *Spirit of Grungni* began to turn.

SNORRI WOKE UP. His head was sore and he had to admit his hangover was bad. The whole floor seemed to be tilting and that normally was an effect he usually only got when he was very drunk. Then it dawned on him that maybe it wasn't his hangover. He was on an airship, after all. Maybe the whole thing was tilting? And what was that scraping noise? It sounded like the whole cupola was running along rock. Had they landed? If so, why were they bumping along in this atrocious manner? And why were all those voices in the distance screaming? He looked over at Gotrek. The other Slayer was peering grimly out into the gloom.

'I knew that idiot Makaisson was going to get us all killed,' Gotrek said.

Through the rapidly parting storm clouds Snorri could see mountain peaks all around them. The grinding sound continued. He knew they were scraping rock. Under the circumstances there was only one thing to do. He took another long swig of vodka and waited for the end to come.

MAX SCHREIBER FELT the whole hull of the cupola grind against the mountainside. He prayed feverishly that it would stay intact. On the bright side at least the gasbag was still alright. Just a few more moments and they would be clear. If only the airship would hold together a bit longer. He offered up a prayer to all the gods for their aid.

FIVE

AN AERIAL ENCOUNTER

THE GRINDING OF the hull suddenly ceased. Max felt a momentary surge of relief. The airship was aloft again. They were off the side of the mountain. Makaisson shouted into the speaking tube, 'Ah want reports from the ship. What's the damage? Hoo are the enjuns? Ony holes in the cupola or gasbag? An' ah want ye tae jump tae it, ya bamsticks!'

He pulled control levers and the engine noise died. The airship was still moving, propelled by the wind, but its speed had fallen away to almost nothing. It seemed that the storm had passed them by. Max looked at the Slayer engineer. 'What's the problem?'

'Whaur tae start is the problem! Ah think the enjuns might be a wee bit damaged fae bein' dragged alang the mountainside. Joost a theory mind, but ye can see hoo it wood be possible. An' then there's the wee fact that ah hae nae idea whaur we are.'

'We're in the World's Edge Mountains, obviously,' Max said. 'That was the only range in a hundred leagues and we were blown south. I don't see Chaos Wastes below us.'

'Gae the big man a prize!' jeered Malakai. 'Ah ken we're in the World's Edge Mountains. Ah'm a dwarf, am't ah? Ah ken a mountain range when ah see yin. Ah joost don't know whaur exactly we are in it.'

Max looked at Malakai. The dwarf was upset. Malakai Makaisson was the best-tempered Slayer Max had ever met, and such a display of anger was quite unusual for him. Max was starting to wonder if they were in more trouble than he had imagined.

'I don't see how that's such a big problem.'

'Then let me explain. If we've took serious damage then we're no in ony great shape. Daen repairs in the middle oh naewhaur, way nae proper spares is no gannae be easy. So we might be in for a bit o' a wak hame. Can ye see the problem noo?'

Max suddenly understood why Malakai Makaisson was so upset. He was distraught by the prospect of abandoning his beloved airship. Max could understand that. He was not exactly thrilled by the idea himself. The World's Edge Mountains were huge and filled with marauding tribes of orcs and other monstrous creatures, as well as by countless savage beasts.

'I think there might be another problem,' said one of the apprentice engineers tugging at Makaisson's shoulder.

'Great! An' joost whit exactly might that be?'

'That!' said the other dwarf pointing.

Max glanced in the direction of the dwarf's pointing finger. His eyes went wide. His jaw dropped open. His heartbeat sounded like a drum in his ear. 'Gods preserve us,' he breathed.

'Ah dinnae think they can!' said Makaisson. 'No fae that!'

'WELL, WE'RE STILL alive,' said Felix, rising into a crouch and drawing on his britches.

'I'm glad of that,' said Ulrika. Felix smiled, suddenly looking years younger.

'Me too.' He pulled on his boots and shirt and strapped on his sword. 'I'll just go and see what's happening.'

The sound of boots hammering on the metal floor of the corridor was suddenly loud in his ear.

'Manling, get your sword!' he heard Gotrek shout, as a heavy fist banged on the door.

'Snorri thinks that's a good idea too,' he heard Snorri add.

'What in Sigmar's name is going on?' he asked.

'You'll see for yourself in a minute.'

* * *

MAX SCHREIBER LOOKED through the window of the command deck in astonishment. He could not quite believe what he was seeing but that did not stop the sight of it from filling him with terror.

It was a dragon, and not just any dragon, but quite possibly the largest one he had ever heard of. Not that he was an expert on this particular subject. This was the first and, he quite sincerely hoped, the last he would ever see.

At first, when he saw it in the distance, he had thought it was just a particularly large bird. But it flew oddly for a bird, and as it came closer, he began to get some sense of the scale of the thing compared to its surroundings. It was far too big to be any bird he had ever heard of, including the war eagles of the elves which were large enough to carry a full grown warrior on their back. As it came closer he began to see that the shape was wrong for a bird too. It was too long, and the wings were structured like those of a bat, rather than a bird.

As it came closer still, he noted the long-lizard like body, the enormous snake-like tail, the serpentine neck supporting the massive head. He saw the colours were like no bird that had ever flown save perhaps in the Chaos Wastes. The general colouration of the scaly leathery skin was red but there were glowing highlights in it that blazed all the colours of the rainbow. A massive shield of bone surrounded the monstrous head. A double row of razor-sharp spines ran down the long back. On the command deck pandemonium reigned. Malakai Makaisson shouted orders into the speaking trumpet while all the time throwing the control levers forward to the maximum extent. Engines roared like daemons as the airship picked up speed.

'Gunners tae yer stations!' bellowed Makaisson. 'Ah want every gyrocopter oot there, and ah want it noo!'

Max wondered what good they would do. He felt paralysed with fear as the dragon came effortlessly closer. He had never seen such a large living thing. From nose to tail it must have been as long as the gasbag of the airship. It looked like it could lift a bull in each of its claws. This was something to freeze the heart of even a Slayer.

All around him he could hear the sound of running feet as dwarfs raced to obey Makaisson's orders. The ship echoed with panicked exclamations and oaths as the dwarfs began to realise what they were facing. Given the fact that these were the survivors of Karag Dum, long inured to horror, it was a tribute to quite how fearsome the dragon actually was that it could stir terror in their hearts.

VAREK CLAMBERED INTO the cockpit of the gyrocopter. A dragon, he thought, elated as well as terrified. He had seen a dragon, one of the creatures of legend. One of the eldest of beasts. It was another wonder he had witnessed on this trip, another thing to note down in his book. If he survived, he thought, as the engine roared to life, and the gyrocopter made ready for take-off.

MAX FELT ROOTED to the spot. If someone had told him at that moment he must cast a spell or die, he knew he would be dead. His mind was blank. He could not work magic if his life depended on it. The dragon opened its mouth and roared. The sound echoed like thunder through the mountains. Small flames lapped the sword-sized teeth as it did so. As it came ever closer, Max realised one cause of the horror. What he had thought were small jewels inset in its skin and glittering in the sun were in fact tiny shards of warpstone. He shuddered to think what exposure to that dreaded substance must be doing to the dragon. Mutation and madness were its lot at the very least. Perhaps that accounted for the creature's size, and its odd appearance.

At this range he could see long tendrils of flesh surrounded the mouth and long stalk-like antennae protruded from its brows just above the eyes. Here and there massive pustules blistered the scaly hide. The thing had definitely felt the touch of Chaos. Was it possible it had been brought here by the storm, blown all the way from the Wastes by the force of those daemonic winds? He did not know. He licked his dry lips. He did not want to find out.

The dragon was almost alongside them now, flying parallel with the airship like a whale sculling alongside a cargo vessel. It had yet to attack but Max did not doubt that it was hostile. It was toying with them like a cat might toy with a mouse.

This close he could make out the details of its enormous head. Its eyes glowed yellow, the pupils blazing red suns. A malign intelligence glittered in their depths. A cloud of poisonous-looking gas billowed from its nostrils and mouth, where occasionally small flames lapped forth.

Gods, the thing was big enough to swallow a horse in one gulp. Those claws could shred the gasbag like a man might tear a piece of parchment. If it breathed there was every chance that the gasbag might catch fire and who knew what might happen then. Max shuddered when he considered that the engines of the *Spirit of Grungni* were powered by black stuff. It was one of the most inflammable substances known to alchemical science. There were just far too many things that could go wrong here.

He heard more engines roar as gyrocopter after gyrocopter dropped from the hangar decks of the airship. After the battle at the manor house there were only three left. As far as Max was concerned they would probably cause as much trouble to the dragon as gnats would to a wolf. He could not see any way they could survive this encounter.

Even as he watched the first of the gyrocopters curved into view, heading directly at the dragon. A roaring as of a thousand muskets firing at once told him that the organ gun turrets on top of the gasbags and the bottom of the cupola had opened fire. A line of explosions in the dragon's flesh showed where their shots had struck home.

The dragon roared its wrath. Its long snaky neck curved to bring the open jaws directly into line with the airship. Max fought down the urge to shriek as a cloud of flames and warp-stone gas flashed towards them.

THE WIND WHIPPED against Varek's face. He was filled with exultation and a sense of speed. He whooped wildly as the gyrocopter arced around and up towards the dragon. He felt as if he was being pressed into his seat by a giant fist. He had never felt so alive. He thought he understood one of the secrets of the Slayers now, why they constantly sought out death. This was existence on the very edge, and it was sweet. Ahead of him the huge monster loomed ever larger. Fear clutched at Varek's bowels as he felt its burning gaze fall on him. He fought it down, and made ready to attack.

FELIX HEARD THE sound of the turrets opening fire above them. What was it? What could be attacking them here so far above the ground? It had to be something flying, and something that could move fast to overhaul them. At any moment he expected the firing to stop. He had once seen a demonstration of an organ gun being fired by the Imperial military during the Emperor's day parade back in Altdorf. The thing had ripped apart a small wooden fortification. Nothing could possibly resist the concentrated fire of half a dozen of them, could it?

Gotrek and Snorri had already clambered up the ladder and through the hatch of the gondola. Felix pulled himself up, more swiftly than any dwarf. For a brief moment he was on top of the gondola itself, and he caught sight of what was being fired at. He had a flickering impression of a long reptilian shape, large as the airship, winged like a bat, then the acrid smoke of the organ guns billowed into his line of sight and cut off his view. By all the gods, could it be a dragon, he wondered? Had he really just seen what he thought he had? He most sincerely hoped not.

Snorri and Gotrek continued on up the ladder. It was made of flexible metal hawsers and ran all the way through the gasbag to the top of the airship. It was designed to give access to the turrets up there, and to let the crew into the gasbag to effect repairs.

It was cold up here, and the sting of the wind brought tears to Felix's eyes until he pulled himself inside the gasbag. Now all around he could see hundreds of smaller gasbags. He knew Makaisson had designed them so that even if the outer skin of the balloon was pierced not all the lift gas could escape at once. According to the dwarf, over half of these nacelles would have to be burst before the *Spirit of Grungni* would begin to lose altitude.

Suddenly he felt the temperature rise dramatically. He became aware that flames were flickering below him and there was a terrible stench that reminded him of sewage and warpstone. What was happening?

'Dragonbreath!' he heard Gotrek roar.

I am going to die, Felix thought.

MAX ALMOST SCREAMED as the cloud of burning gas enveloped the airship. He pictured the gasbag catching fire and the whole vessel being blown apart in an apocalyptic blast of heat and flame. For one brief moment, he knew that he was dead. He closed his eyes, took a terrified breath and waited for the inevitable burst of agony that would tell him his life was over. A heartbeat passed, then another and he was still alive. He felt the airship tilt, and then knew it was a false reprieve. He reached out to steady himself instinctively, shocked to find he was still alive.

He opened his eyes, looked around and saw Makaisson still furiously tugging at the controls. The airship was heading upwards, climbing steeply. He looked around to see the dragon below them, spreading its wings, beginning a long lazy spiral upwards. Around it the three gyrocopters flitted like mosquitoes.

'We're still alive,' Max said.

'Weel spotted!' said Makaisson. 'Cannae pit much past you, big man, can we?'

'How? Why aren't we burned to death? Why didn't the gasbag catch fire?'

'Taks mare than a brief scorching to heat metal, as ye would ken if ye ever worked iron, so the cupola didnae melt. We were a wee bit luckier wie the gasbag. Had the explodin' problem wi' ma last airship, so this time ah treated the gasbag an' the nacelles wi' a flameproof alchemical mix. Joost as well, really.'

'Makaisson, I don't care what others say about you, I think you're a genius.'

'Thanks, ah think,' Makaisson said. He made a small adjustment to the controls. 'By the way, whit exactly dae others say aboot me? No that ah care, ye ken.'

FELIX EMERGED ON the top of the airship. A metal dorsal spine ran along the top of the gasbag. From it, nets hung over the gasbag itself so that the brave and the foolhardy could climb over. Along the spine were organ gun turrets. A small handrail, set at the right height for dwarfs, ran along the spine. Felix grabbed it and hauled himself into the open. The wind tugged at his hair, and brought tears to his eyes. It roared in his ears when it wasn't drowned out by the thunder of the organ guns. He could see Gotrek and Snorri shout and wave their fists at the dragon but he couldn't hear a word they were saying. Probably just as well, really; it most likely wasn't anything sensible.

He shook his head, knowing that he was deliberately trying to distract himself from the awesome sight below. It was indeed a dragon, rising through the clouds. Beneath it he could see the streams and valleys of what he assumed must be the World's Edge Mountains. Gyrocopters buzzed around the mighty beast.

For a moment, he thought how few men had ever been privileged to witness such a sight, but it dawned on him that right now he would cheerfully swap the privilege to be on the ground and as far away from that huge creature as was humanly possible.

He could see that the gyrocopters were using their steamjets on the dragon, but ineffectually. A creature which burned internally with the fires of Chaos was unlikely to be hurt by a scalding jet of superheated water. Maybe if they tried blasting it directly down the creature's throat it might extinguish the fire but he doubted it. The bombs being lobbed by the pilots were proving just as ineffectual at the moment. Against such a swiftly moving target, it was difficult to judge distances and set the fuse time correctly.

Even as Felix watched he saw bombs explode harmlessly in the air around the dragon. Then with a swift move the dragon turned and breathed on the nearest gyrocopter. It exploded as suddenly and explosively as one of the bombs but on a much more massive scale. Felix offered up a prayer for the soul of the pilot tumbling to the earth in a blazing pyre.

The dragon flexed its wings and began to gain altitude, moving swiftly in pursuit of the *Spirit of Grungni*. There was a lull in the firing as the gunners waited for it to come within range again.

'It's mine,' he heard Gotrek say.

'It's Snorri's,' Snorri replied.

'I think there's enough to go around,' Felix said, reaching for the hilt of his sword. 'No need to fight over... Ow!'

He drew his hand away from the hilt of his blade as if it had been scorched. It hadn't been but when he touched the dragon-headed hilt of the blade he had felt a strange tingling, and a surge of energy the like of which he had never felt before. It was not an unpleasant sensation merely an unexpected one. He reached out to grasp the sword again, half thinking he had imagined the whole thing, but no sooner had he done so than the sensation returned, redoubled.

An odd warmth spread through his hand, up his arm and through his body. He felt good. Any lingering fear he might have had of the dragon vanished. He felt exultation, power and strength pour into him. He found that he was quite looking forward to the dragon getting within striking distance.

The part of him that was an objective observer wondered if he had gone insane. There was nothing good whatsoever about a dragon getting within a hundred leagues of him, nor of this fragile gasbag, and the cupola suspended below it. He knew that some external power must be at work here, some sorcery. Was it possible that Max Schreiber had cast a spell without him knowing it? If so, why had he not noticed any change in Gotrek or Snorri? It made no sense for the magician to cast a spell on him and not the two Slayers, who were a good deal tougher than he.

The dragon swelled in Felix's field of vision, and a sense of expectation filled him. It was definitely coming from the sword, he felt. Holding the blade before him he could see the runes blazing along its length with a strength and a brightness he had never seen before. It was as if they had been inscribed in fire.

He wondered about this. He had never known much about the history of this blade, the one sought by the Templar Aldred all those months ago in the ruins of Karak Eight Peaks. He had always known it was magical. It kept its edge like no blade he had ever known, and had never taken a nick in all his many battles. He had thought that was the limit of the enchantment on it.

Looking at it now, and examining the way it was behaving in the presence of that great dragon below them, it seemed that perhaps the hilt of the sword was more than mere decoration. Perhaps it was expressive of the purpose of the sword. From nowhere but the blade itself, it seemed, came the knowledge he was right.

He joined the Slayers in shouting abuse at the dragon, surprised at his own temerity. Normally, he would never in a million years have dared draw the attention of so powerful a beast to himself in such a way, but it seemed the influence of the sword was affecting him greatly. He could tell by the astonished looks Gotrek and Snorri were giving him that they were just as surprised as he was.

Wings beating the air furiously, the dragon rose to the attack. The gyrocopters rose in its wake, though the part of Felix that was still capable of sane thought wondered what they could do to so baleful a creature.

* * *

THROUGH THE PORTHOLE of the cabin, Ulrika watched the battle below with a growing sense of helplessness. There was nothing she could do to affect the outcome of this struggle. She did not have the skills to man any of the weapons or fly the ship. She doubted that she could nick the fearsome beast even if she could get within striking distance of it. And to make matters worse, they were thousands of strides above the surface of the earth. There was no way to hide or flee even if she wanted to.

No. She refused to sit here and be helpless. There must be something she could do. There was only one thing she could think of, so she did it. She snatched up the short powerful horn bow she used for horseback archery, strapped the quiver of arrows over her shoulder and set off to find a place she could shoot from.

MAX SCHREIBER WAS glad to feel the terror pass. It seemed that the overwhelming power of the dragon to inspire fear in him had been dispelled by something. He was not sure quite what, but somewhere close by he felt a surge of magical energy, pulsing like a beacon. Whatever it was, it was very strong. Was it possible there was another sorcerer on the airship? It did not seem likely. Dwarfs were not known for their proficiency in the magical arts, and he knew that neither Felix nor Ulrika nor either of her two bodyguards were mages. It must be something else.

Whatever it was, he was grateful. His mind was clear, and he felt capable of drawing on the winds of magic once more. He reached deep down into the well of his soul and drew upon his power. In his mind he began to review his most potent spells. Perhaps there was something he could do to affect the outcome of the battle after all. Perhaps.

Looking out of the windows of the command deck at the awesome form of the dragon, he doubted it.

FELIX WATCHED THE dragon come ever closer. He thought he could hear its mighty wing-beats even above the roar of the organ guns. He was impressed by the sheer size of the thing. He did not think he had ever been this close to so large a living creature. It made part of him feel insignificant, puny, despicable.

And another part of him thirsted for it to come within striking distance, to reach a place where he could engage it in

combat. Felix considered this, and realised that whatever it was that
wanted the battle, it wasn't him, it was an external influence. It was
something coming from his sword that was making him brandish his
blade and shout challenges. While he was glad for the relief from fear,
he also resented it. He was the master of his actions, not some ancient
semi-sentient weapon. He forced himself to shut his mouth. By an
effort of will he brought his sword down and held it in the guard position.

It was difficult but he managed it. The blade fought against him,
writhing in his hand like a serpent. In a way he felt like he was drunk,
not quite responsible for his actions. It took all his willpower just to
keep quiet and hold still but he did so, and the more he did so, the
more he felt the strange urges subside. Either he was his own master
again or the sword was conserving its energies for the greater struggle.

'Come taste axeblade,' Gotrek bellowed.

'And have a bit of Snorri's hammer for afters,' shouted Snorri. Felix
watched silently. The creature was almost upon them. He was close
enough to smell the Chaos poison on its breath.

THE WHOLE HULL echoed as if struck by a giant hammer. The force of
the impact almost forced Ulrika from the ladder. She felt the cupola
surge and swing, and she knew that one of those giant claws must
have impacted on the airship. Her heart leapt into her mouth. A vivid
picture of the gondola becoming separated from the gasbag and
plunging earthwards to its doom filled her mind. Quickly she pushed
it away, and resumed her climb. If she was going to die, she wanted
to die fighting.

MAX ROLLED ALONG the floor of the command deck, tossed about like
a child's plaything by the force of the impact. He felt the cupola sway
as the dragon's claws smashed into the side of the airship. The whole
interior of the vessel vibrated like a drum as the huge reptile's wings
beat against it in a flurry of blows. In his mind's eye, he saw the
dragon clutching at the airship like a tiger on the neck of its prey. It
was not a reassuring image.

He looked up and saw Makaisson wrestling with the controls. The
dwarf cursed loudly, 'Bloody overgrown lizard! Tryin' to eat us alive,
so it is. Bloody stupid critter if ye ask me. It cannae eat solid steel. Can
it? Well, can it?'

In his heart, Max was not so sure. He did know that the dragon did
not need to be able to consume them to destroy them. A few more

blows like that would pull the gondola loose and then they would all be dead.

VAREK WAS REALLY excited. He had thought that nothing could top his descent into the bowels of Karag Dum with the Slayers and Felix but this was close to proving him wrong. Aerial combat with a dragon, he thought. What a chapter this would be in his book. He lifted the portable organ gun Makaisson had given him. He decided it was time to get a few good shots at the dragon.

FELIX FELT THE deck sway beneath his feet at the impact. The dragon's claws had smashed into the side of the airship. The sound of shrieking metal filled his ears as the hull gave way under the force of the blow. The dragon's long neck snaked up. It took a bite from the gasbag, lifting away a huge patch of the outer skin. Nacelles exploded in its mouth. Felix shuddered, wondering how much of this punishment the ship could take. A sweep of the enormous tail curled right round the gondola and came down on one of the organ guns, flattening it and the gunner. The wreckage of the turret went plummeting into space, tumbling to earth far far below.

Things were not looking good. The whole hull creaked when the dragon rested its weight on it. The dragon extended its long scaly neck and suddenly its head was looming over Felix.

Gotrek and Snorri rushed forward. Snorri's axe lashed out and bounced from the dragon's hide. His hammer had no discernible effect. Gotrek's axe on the other hand bit home, cleaving the armoured skin and drawing blood. The dragon bellowed with rage. Its enormous head swung round to regard the Slayer balefully. Felix saw the malign intelligence in the creature's eyes and knew that the dragon planned to revenge itself on the tiny creature that had hurt it.

It opened its mouth. The fires of hell burned within its jaws. Felix thought the creature looked almost as if it were smiling. Some strange impulse compelled him to throw himself between Gotrek and the dragon just as it breathed. He fought back the desire to scream as a wall of flame hurtled towards him.

* * *

MAX CHANTED THE words of the spell, drawing more and more magical energy to him. He knew he was only going to get one chance at this and he wanted to make the best use of it. Even if the dragon destroyed them, it gave him slight satisfaction to think that he would hurt it.

As the words tumbled from his mouth, he felt the winds of magic swirl about him. Responding to the arcane properties of the mantra, golden magic was drawn to him. His gestures shaped it, moulded it, the way a potter moulds clay. Beneath his hands and the force of his mind and words, a huge bolt of energy took shape. When the surge of energy was almost too great to hold, he made the final gesture and sent it spiralling towards the dragon.

A massive beam of gold light smashed outwards, passing harmlessly through the crystal of the window, before impacting on the dragon's flesh and boring inwards towards its heart.

ULRIKA PULLED HERSELF out of the hatchway on the top of the gas-bag. She was just in time to see Felix jump between Gotrek and the dragon as it breathed. She knew in that moment that he was going to die.

'No!' she shouted. At the same time, responding without thought, her body was already bringing the bow up to the firing position, nocking the arrow, and bringing it to bear on the dragon's eye.

VAREK PULLED BACK on the control stick with one hand, and blasted away with the portable organ gun with the other. It had very little effect. He could see scales being blasted out of the dragon's hide but it was like using buckshot on a curtain wall. It might be uncomfortable for the dragon, but he was not going to do any real harm. Perhaps his book was going to end here, he thought. Perhaps this was where the story stopped.

FELIX COULD NOT quite believe what happened next. As the flame flashed down at him, he brought the sword up to parry. It was a pointless futile gesture, made more from force of habit than from any hope of being able to save himself. And something happened. The runes on the blade blazed brighter. The blaze of heat and pain did not come. Some sorcerous force protected him.

He felt enormous pressure on him, as if he was pushing against the current of a river. For a moment, he felt as if he was going to be blown right off the top of the gasbag but he braced himself and held his ground. Slowly he forced himself forward, moving to strike the dragon. The blade pulsed brighter in anticipation of the blow.

ULRIKA UNLEASHED THE arrow. It flew straight and true towards the dragon's eye, but at the last second the creature moved and the arrow buried itself in one of the strange tendrils descending from the monster's brow. The creature's roar of hatred was deafening.

THE DRAGON SKJALANDIR was frustrated. This was not going as he had planned. This strange vessel was putting up a fight. There was a sorcerer on board directing spells at him. That dwarf's axe was as potent a weapon as any he had seen in his two thousand years of existence, and as for the sword that puny human was carrying, it almost worried him. It glittered with an ancient malice directed at all of his kind.

Rage and hatred filled him. He was easily angered now. He knew it. He had changed since those two identical albino sorcerers had woken him from his long sleep. He feared he knew why too. The one with the golden staff had driven warpstone charms into his flesh. The one with the ebony staff had wound him round with charms he had been too drowsy to resist. There was something of the memory of their arcane ritual that filled him with fear as well as anger. He remembered the name of a dark god, the Changer, ringing through his lair. He remembered the way the mages had spurned his great hoard. He knew he had been trapped in some sort of spell of their making, and he knew his mind was clouded and there was nothing he could do about it.

The axe bit home again, burying itself in the tendons of his neck. It was like an ant bite to Skjalandir. Painful, irritating, but hardly fatal. The same applied to the spell attacking his flanks, and the stings of those tiny guns. Really there was nothing these little creatures could do that would actually harm him. It was time to end this farce.

Skjalandir considered his options. He could breathe on the gasbag structure above the metal gondola. When he had slashed it, he had detected the thousands of smaller nacelles inside. His draconic mind was quite clever enough to grasp that these were what kept the ship aloft. If they could be made to catch fire...

Would the spell the sword had woven to protect its wielder against his breath protect the inanimate structure? Skjalandir doubted it. He would teach these dwarf interlopers to invade his realm, befoul his hunting grounds with their machines. He would kill them as he had killed all the other dwarfs who had come against him. He would destroy this vessel the way he had destroyed the towns surrounding his lair and there was nothing they could do to stop him.

Or perhaps he should continue to strike at the metal gondola. If he separated it from the gasbag all of those within would plummet to their doom. Then he could pick off the creatures on the gasbag at his leisure. Something within his warpstone-tormented mind preferred the latter option. It was more cruel.

He was aware of the other gyrocopters moving closer. Let them. Their steam breath could not harm him, and their pathetic explosive eggs would barely scratch his armour. That's if they dared use their weapons so close to the airship. They were much more likely to harm their own vessel than to hurt Skjalandir.

MAX FELT THE surge of magical energy above him. A protective spell, he guessed, and not cast by a mortal wizard. All wizards had their own magical signature, as distinctive as a voice. It could be recognised by a fellow worker of the mystic arts unless disguised. A skilled practitioner, like Max, could even tell the race and usually the sex of a caster from it most of the time, but for this one he had no clue. A device or a rune perhaps, and yet there was the hint of some sort of alien intelligence behind it.

Not that he was likely to find out now, Max thought. He had realised moments after he had unleashed his spell that he was fooling himself if he thought he was really going to harm the dragon. He could hurt it, cause it pain, but he could no more kill it than a bee sting could kill an elephant. The creature was too large and powerful and there was too much magic woven into its very nature for Max to be able to really harm it.

Another thing more powerful than I, he thought wryly. I seem to be meeting a lot of them lately.

His mind flickered through the routines of the escape spell, but he doubted it would do much good. It probably couldn't carry him all the way to the ground and even if it could he still would be travelling with all his current velocity in the direction he was currently moving. If he got to earth he would be travelling at the same speed and in the same direction as the *Spirit of Grungni*, and would most likely smash into a rock or a tree or some other obstacle.

And he was not sure he wanted to leave. Ulrika was on this ship and he did not want to abandon her. While she still lived, he wasn't going anywhere.

FELIX LOOKED UP at the dragon. He felt as if it were taunting him. It was flying just out of striking distance and ignoring the challenges roared by Gotrek and Snorri. He knew that it wanted them to know it could destroy them at will. It was toying with them. It appeared that everything he had ever read about the malice and cruelty of dragons was true.

He felt a brief surge of despair. After all this, was it going to end this way? It hardly seemed fair that after all the many adventures he had survived he was going to meet his doom during a chance encounter in the World's Edge Mountains. Then again, who knew when the day of their death would come? Everyone's luck ran out eventually, and recently he had begun to suspect that he had had more than his fair share. He was only sorry that Ulrika was here – and that he was not with her at this final moment.

He glanced over at Gotrek to see how the Slayer was behaving now that his last moments were upon him. Fittingly enough, Felix decided. The dwarf was waving his axe and bellowing threats at the dragon. Snorri was egging him on.

From the corner of his eye, Felix saw something looping upwards to gain height above the dragon and then come crashing down like a swooping hawk.

VAREK GRASPED THE controls of his gyrocopter and gnawed his beard in frustration. He had done his best to slay the dragon but it ignored his organ gun and he could not hit it with his bombs. Now it was about to destroy the *Spirit of Grungni*.

Worse than that, aboard the airship was the lost treasure of Karag Dum and the Hammer of Firebeard, one of the legendary weapons of his people. If the *Spirit of Grungni* was destroyed the hammer might be lost once more, perhaps this time forever. Varek was proud of his part in this expedition, proud of being part of the airship's crew, and prouder yet he had taken part in the expedition that had returned this ancient rune-weapon to his people. If they failed now, he knew that he would have to shave his head and become a Slayer to atone for his failure. He knew he could not live with the knowledge that they had come so far, suffered so much, and yet had failed at the last. He knew it would eat away at him for the rest of his life.

And a heartbeat after that the thought struck him, he knew the answer to his problem. If he became a Slayer he would need to seek his doom in combat against the mightiest of monsters. Before him was one of the mightiest. He would never find another so great, of that he was sure. He had a weapon that might kill it too, although at the cost of his life. Still, it was a mighty deed. A doom that would cause his name to live forever in the annals of his people and bring eternal glory to his clan and his ancestors. With a single action he could become a Dragon Slayer, and save the lives of all his fellows. Not wanting to give himself a chance to reconsider his decision, he acted immediately. He wrenched the control stick of his gyrocopter, jammed the throttle to full and aimed straight for the dragon before him.

The rotor blades hit first biting, great chunks out of the dragon's flesh, then the nose rotors chopped in too. The sudden smashing impact ripped the engine apart, and a massive explosion smashed through Varek's body.

His last regret before darkness took him was that he would never live to complete his book.

FELIX WATCHED THE gyrocopter flash down on the dragon. At the last moment he got a glimpse of a familiar face. Varek, he thought, don't do it! Even if his thought could have influenced Varek's decision it was too late. The gyrocopter smashed into the dragon. Its rotor blades carved out great chunks of dragon flesh. The force of the impact smashed the dragon down and away from the airship. Moments later there was a massive explosion as the gyrocopter and its cargo of explosives ignited. A fireball enveloped the dragon as it fell. Felix could see no way anything could survive. He was wrong.

The dragon tumbled headlong towards the ground's hungry embrace. Felix thought that any second it was going to smash into the ground but it did not. At the last moment, its wings snapped open, and its headlong fall stopped. As Felix watched it began to move upwards once more. At first he feared it was unharmed and coming for them again, but then to his relief he saw that its flight was wobbly and that it was heading off into the distance.

Grief tugged at his heart. He could not believe Varek was gone. The young dwarf had been a companion on one of his most dangerous adventures and suddenly he was just not there any more. Death's claw had reached out and taken him. It was unjust, he decided, looking over at Gotrek and Snorri to see how the Slayers were taking it.

Gotrek wore a look of sorrow and respect and something else that Felix could not quite recognise. 'A good death,' he said slowly and painfully.

'A great death,' said Snorri. 'He will be remembered.'

'He will be avenged,' Gotrek said and Felix knew he meant it.

AGONY COURSING THROUGH his ancient body, Skjalandir dropped away from the airship. In all his long life he had never felt such pain. It was no satisfaction that the creature who had inflicted the wound had died in the moment he struck. This was not good. Best return to his lair and heal. There would be time enough to seek revenge on these accursed creatures.

SIX

A HERO'S WELCOME

FELIX STOOD ON the command deck of the *Spirit of Grungni*. He could tell just by studying the gauges that things were bad. There was no response from about half the dials and the engines. Even from here, just the two remaining motors sounded terrible.

Makaisson limped through the door. Felix had never seen the engineer look so angry.

'Bad?' he asked.

'Ah'll say it bloody is. We're lucky to still be up here. The suspension cables haddin' the gondola tae the gasbag wir near frayed through in three places. Ah hae the lads makin' some repairs but its joost jury-rig stuff. Matter o' time before it ah goes horribly wrang.'

'Doesn't sound good,' Felix said. This seemed to goad Makaisson to further fury.

'Gasbag's ripped! Twa o' the injuns arnae workin' right. Hulls broken in aboot twenty places! We've lost a turret and ah but yin on the gyros. Bloody hell. Ah tell ye. If it's the last thing ah dae, ah'm gannae make that dragon pay for this. It'll rue the day it ever attacked ma airship.'

Felix winced. He was sure that Makaisson meant what he said, but he could not see how he was going to fulfil his vow.

They had hit the dragon with everything they had, and it had still flown away to its lair. Felix was not even sure they had driven it off. He had a feeling that it had let them go because it suited it. They had about as much chance of killing the dragon as Felix had of becoming emperor, he reckoned.

Old Borek limped onto the command deck. He looked more ancient than ever. His stick moved feebly, like that of a blind man, fumbling to find his way. His long beard dragged along the floor. He seemed to be at the end of his strength. The loss of his nephew had hit him hard.

'I'm sorry about Varek,' Felix said. 'He was a fine dwarf.'

Borek looked up at him and smiled sadly.

'He was, Felix Jaeger. He was. I should never have let him come on this expedition. I should never have let him leave the Lonely Tower but he wanted to come so badly...'

Felix remembered Varek's courage in the depths of Karag Dum. His habit of jotting everything down in his great book. His sometimes annoying cheerfulness. His embarrassing hero worship of himself and Gotrek. His short sightedness. His light, slightly pedantic voice. It was difficult to believe that he would never see or hear the young dwarf again. He was surprised. It had been a long time since a death had affected him this badly.

'He was a guid laddie,' Makaisson said. 'Ah probably should-nae hae let him tak me intae teachin' him to fly the gyro.'

'If you hadn't, my friend, I suspect none of us would be here right now.'

'Aye – yer right. The laddie wis a hero.'

'I am the last of my line now,' Borek said. Felix saw two drops of water running down the old dwarf's cheeks. Were they really tears? He looked away to spare the scholar embarrassment.

'Well dinnae you worry! We'll get the basturd that killed him. It's joost gone right to the heid of my very ane list o' grudges.'

Borek just looked away and shook his head in sorrow.

MAX SCHREIBER STOOD on the rear observation deck, looking out through the cracked crystal of the window. It must have been shattered some time during the struggle with the dragon, but he was not sure how or when. The whole airship looked dreadful. Internal fixtures had come loose. The cargo crates and treasure chests had been tossed around during the fight, damaging themselves and anything they had hit. Two of the crew had been crushed to death. Twelve others had needed healing by Max's magic.

He could tell that the airship was badly damaged just from the sick drone of the engines and the lack of headway they were making. Compared to their previous progress this was a snail's pace. He wondered if they would ever get where they needed to go. It seemed that this flight had been dogged by one accident after the other. It was almost as if they were cursed. Perhaps Makaisson's reputation for disaster was not so ill-deserved after all.

He watched the mountain valleys drift by below them. They were following the path of a stream that descended towards the lowlands. He guessed that the torrent of waterfalls would be beautiful if you were down there, but he knew he would never find out. He would probably never see these places again. Enjoy the view, he told himself. Make the most of this while you're here. You will never come this way again. Somehow the cheery teachings of his mentors in the Golden Brotherhood seemed just a little precious in the aftermath of the battle with the dragon. And yet part of him knew that the words were true. He should enjoy the moment and he should be glad. The fight had shown him just how fragile life could be, and just how quickly it could end. Look at poor Varek and the dozen or so other casualties of the fight.

The engines stuttered for a moment, then fell silent. For an instant he felt the *Spirit of Grungni* drift like a rudderless boat on a river. Please, Sigmar, he prayed, aid us. Don't let this happen now. He feared in his heart that the powerless airship might drift into a mountain side or that more of the gas nacelles would burst and they might drop to earth. In the valley below he saw a tiny group of figures moving along at speed. He was not sure but he thought he caught a hint of green.

'Orcs,' he heard Ulrika say from close by. He looked over, surprised.

'Your eyes are better than mine,' he said.

'I've spent my life looking along the shaft of an arrow, not reading books by candlelight,' she said. 'And I long ago learned to recognise orcs at a great distance. Anyone who lives on the plains of Kislev dies swiftly if they do not.'

'Are the greenskins so fearsome then?' he asked. He already knew the answer, he just wanted to hear her voice.

'Bad as Chaos warriors in their own way. Even more savage and they don't know when they're dead. I've seen an orc with two arrows through its heart and half its head cleaved away chop down half a dozen warriors before it died.'

'So have I,' Gotrek Gurnisson said. Max looked over at the Slayer. His massive form filled the hatchway leading into the observation deck. He moved surprisingly quietly for one so massive. Max had not heard him arrive either. 'But a good axe will kill them all in the end.'

Max was relieved to hear the engines start up again. They began to move forward once more.

'Wherever we're going I hope we get there soon,' he said.

'We'll have to wait till night and fix our position by the stars,' Gotrek said. 'Then we'll have a better idea.'

Max wondered if the airship would even make it to nightfall. He had seen some of the ripped hawser cables. It was a miracle they were still here.

'YOU'RE VERY QUIET,' Ulrika said. Felix nodded and drew his cloak tighter about him. It was cold up atop the gasbag and the wind's bite was cruel. They stood on the dorsal spine of the airship watching the two moons rise over the mountains. It was a sight of strange and intense beauty.

'I was thinking about Varek. I never really knew him and now he's gone.'

'Death comes to everyone,' she said. Felix looked at her. He wondered if he'd ever get used to the strong streak of fatalism in her. He supposed being brought up on the plains of North Kislev you got used to death early. He had not quite been so hardened before he set foot on the adventurer's path. Being brought up the son of a rich merchant in Altdorf, the capital of the Empire, had left him quite sheltered. The only death he had really been aware of was that of his mother, when he was nine years old. He had been too young to really understand it.

'I was wondering what he would have done differently today if he had got up knowing this was his last day in the world. To tell the truth, I was wondering what I would have done under the circumstances.'

'Have you come to any conclusions?'

'I might have told you that I loved you.' Felix was surprised to hear himself say the words. He knew he had wanted to say them for a while but had been afraid to. He wasn't sure why. She was silent for a long time. He wondered if she had heard him.

'I might have told you the same thing,' she said eventually. He felt a strange kick in his stomach when she said the words. He turned and looked away into the distance. He felt as close to her at that moment as he ever had to anybody.

'Might?' he asked.

She smiled too and nodded.

'Might.'

They moved a little apart but their hands drifted together and their fingers interlocked. Overhead the stars glittered like specks of ice. The *Spirit of Grungni* ploughed on through the night.

MAX LOOKED THROUGH the spyglass at the stars. 'You're right,' He said. 'That's the polar star, and that is the Fang of the Wolf.'

Makaisson was already making a notation on his chart. He moved the callipers from the point that indicated their position to a red dot. 'Then the nearest place we can seek repairs is Slayer Keep,' he said.

'Slayer Keep?' Max enquired.

'Karak Kadrin. The city of the Slayer King. Tis a grim wee place.'

'With a name like that I wasn't expecting something from a Detlef Sierck comedy.'

'Will dae joost as weel as onywhaur else, so it will.'

'I'm sure it will, Malakai. You're the expert.'

'Aye that ah am.'

Makaisson bellowed orders into the speaking tube. Slowly, like a dying whale, the *Spirit of Grungni* responded, taking a new line through the mountains towards the city of the Slayer King.

FELIX AND ULRIKA stood on the command deck of the *Spirit of Grungni*. Ahead of them, dour and foreboding in the clear light of a mountain morning, lay Slayer Keep. It was a massive fortress carved from the very rock of the mountain peak. Its buildings had not so much been built as carved from the bare rock. Only the outer walls differed. They were built from massive chunks of lichen-encrusted stone. The stonework looked old as the mountains.

Kadrin Peak itself was not the highest of the local mountains by any means, but it stood apart from all its surroundings, dominating a massive valley between two chains of higher, grander mountains. A river ran below it. Borek had told Felix that once a forest had filled the valley, but that it had long ago been chopped down to feed the furnaces of Slayer Keep. Below the city were some of the deepest, darkest and most dangerous mines in all the dwarf realms. There were seams of coal and iron down there that had been worked since before the foundation of the Empire. They provided the raw materials for Kadrin steel, famous through the dwarf realms and the lands of men for making the finest of axe blades. Clouds of dark polluted smoke hung over the city.

Felix did not think he had ever seen a more forbidding place. It was a grim fortress of crudely cut stone. Knowing the pride that dwarfs took in their masonry, Felix could only guess that the crudeness of the architecture was a statement of some sort. Karak Kadrin spoke of squat primitive power. It was a castle designed to be defended. A place meant to endure siege. An outpost in a place of infinite danger. He did not like the look of it particularly.

Already he could see warriors gathering on the walls. Various war engines were being brought to bear upon them. Ballistae, catapults and other things the purpose of which he could only guess were all being swivelled towards them. Even though Borek had insisted on draping rune banners from below the *Spirit of Grungni*, the occupants of Slayer Keep were treating them as a potential threat. Felix could see the sense in that. Had the airship appeared over any city of the Empire it would have caused similar consternation, even if it was flying the colours of Karl Franz himself.

As Felix watched, the last gyrocopter whisked past the airship and sped towards the city. It was a machine that would be recognised by any dwarf, and it carried a message for Ungrimm Ironfist, the Slayer King himself. Makaisson threw the engines of the *Spirit of Grungni* into reverse and they hovered just out of ballista range waiting for permission to land.

'A grim place,' Felix said to Ulrika. She nodded agreement to him. They had been strangely shy of each other since their conversation last night. He could not speak for her, but he was relatively new to all of this. He had felt no strong emotional attachment to anyone since the death of Kirsten at Fort von Diehl.

'As well it might be, Felix Jaeger,' Borek said from his chair. He looked up at Felix with rheumy old eyes, from which all the spark of triumph had vanished. 'If you knew its history, you would understand more. Slayer Keep has endured more sieges than any other dwarfhold, and it is the home of the Cult of Slayers, and the Shrine of Grimnir, who is the most bloodthirsty of all our Ancestor Gods.'

'You say Grimnir is bloodthirsty.' Ulrika asked. 'Does he accept living sacrifices then?'

'Only the lives of his Slayers. He takes their death in payment for their sins. And their hair.'

Borek must have noticed the startled look pass across Felix's face, for he added, 'Most Slayers take their vow before the great altar of Grimnir down there, that is where they shave their heads, then they burn their hair in the great furnace. Outside is the street of skin artists, where they have their first tattoos inked into their flesh.'

'Did Gotrek take his vow there?' Ulrika asked. Felix tilted his head. The question had crossed his mind too.

'I don't believe so. To my knowledge he has never set foot in this city before, though I do not know all of his deeds.'

'Then is he really a Slayer?' asked Ulrika. Borek smiled.

'It does not matter where a dwarf takes the oath and shaves his head. He is a Slayer when it is done. Many choose to take the oath at Grimnir's shrine for the sake of form. They have their names carved on the great pillar in the temple and that way all will know of their passing from life.'

'But they're not yet dead,' Ulrika said.

'Not yet. But to family and friends, to clan and hearth, a dwarf is dead the moment he takes the oath. It may be that Gotrek chose you as a rememberer, Felix Jaeger, because he had not yet had his name carved on the pillar of woe.'

'I don't follow you,' said Felix.

'No one would know of his deed had he fallen in a far place with no dwarfs to witness it. A rememberer would bring word of his doom to us, and see his name carved on the pillar.'

'That is not what he asked me to do.'

Borek smiled sourly. 'The son of Gurni was never conventional even before he became a Slayer. Once he greatly craved renown. I think in a way he still does.'

Felix was about to ask more when he was interrupted by a dull roaring noise from the distance.

'What is that?' he asked. 'Are we being attacked?'

The sour smile widened on Borek's face. 'I would guess that the Slayer King has received word of our quest's success. That is cheering you hear.'

AND INDEED IT was, thought Felix, as the battered airship half-drifted over the dwarf city. Looking down all he could see was a seething ocean of dwarf faces, looking up. He could hear roaring and chanting. Drums beat, mighty horns sounded. Banners and flags were draped from every window of the city. Felix wondered where they found space to house all those dwarfs. The fortress city did not look large enough to be home to all of them. Then he remembered that like the great ice mountains floating in the Sea of Claws, most of a dwarfhold was hidden from sight, leaving only their smallest portion visible on the surface.

Below them he saw an enormous structure, squat and massive, with a massive sculpture of two crossed axes inset in its roof. Strange runes were set on the stonework that reminded Felix of those he had seen blazing on Gotrek's axe. He guessed they held some mystical significance for dwarfs.

He looked at Ulrika and smiled. It was the first time in his life he could ever remember being welcomed as a hero anywhere.

GREY SEER THANQUOL looked at Lurk. Lurk glared back at the magician with loathing in his eyes. Thanquol's magic had brought down a grazing elk. Lurk had consumed most of it before Thanquol had even buried his snout in the flesh. He was not best pleased.

Granted, he needed far less meat than his mutated henchman, and he could not have eaten one hundredth of what Lurk had anyway, but that was not the point. It was the disrespect that galled him. He was a grey seer. Lurk was a lowly warrior even if he was now a huge and powerful mutant. He should have waited till after Thanquol ate his fill before beginning this disgusting orgy of consumption, and he should have asked Thanquol's leave to eat. He was, after all, a mere lackey.

Briefly Thanquol considered pointing this out. Very briefly. Lurk was now far more physically powerful than Thanquol. The seer's full magical power had yet to come back after the battle, and he had only the smallest piece of warpstone left to augment his energies. He wanted to save it for an emergency.

No, he decided. It was merely prudent skaven caution to avoid a confrontation with Lurk at this moment. He knew he was physically no match for the great brute. But then again, he consoled himself, what did that matter? As a feeble and skinny runt he had used his gigantic intellect to exact vengeance on skaven far larger and stronger than he. The same thing would happen here eventually, of that he was certain. Also, the thought had crossed his mind that the more Lurk ate now, the less likely he would be tempted to kill and eat Thanquol later. The grey seer had seen some of the hungry glances his minion had been shooting at him. They were in no sense reassuring.

'Where are we, most knowledgeable of navigators?' Lurk asked. Thanquol wondered if he detected just a hint of irony in Lurk's tone. He dismissed the thought instantly. Lurk was far too stupid to mock his master.

'We are coming ever nearer to our destination,' Thanquol replied with his best oracular vagueness.

'And where exactly is that, most sagacious of seers?'

'Cease this relentless badgering, Lurk. If it was in your best interests to know our whereabouts, reveal them to you I would. Let me worry about such matters. You just continue to eat!'

There, thought Thanquol, that showed Lurk. And it gave him some time to think, which was good. For, if the truth be told, Thanquol had no idea where they were. In the storm they had wandered aimlessly. The driving rain had obscured everything more than a few tail lengths from view. He guessed that they were on course, for the mountains were still ahead of them. Once there it should simply mean following the path south-wards until they came upon a gateway to the Underways. If worst came to worst, Thanquol knew he could always use some of his power to cast a divination spell. Come to think of it, it might be worth telling Lurk that. It might prevent the massive dolt from braining Thanquol while he slept.

Thanquol considered sneaking off while Lurk rested, and making his own way back. Two things prevented it. He suspected that he might be safer with the mutant here on the plains. The Kislevites would doubtless attack the larger of them first on the mistaken assumption that it was the most dangerous. The second reason was that Thanquol suspected Lurk might well be able to track him down. His senses were as keen as any skaven Thanquol had ever known. And in that case sneaking off would only leave Thanquol with the onerous task of explaining his business. For Lurk in his new impudent state might take exception to such behaviour on the grey seer's part. Prudent skaven caution argued for staying with Lurk at least for the moment.

Once this was over, though, Thanquol swore, things would be different. He would exact a vengeance on Lurk that would be spoken of in terrified whispers by future generations. That would teach him to heap such indignities on the head of a grey seer.

ALL EXCEPT THE skeleton crew of the *Spirit of Grungni* were ushered towards the palace of the Slayer King. An honour guard of warriors clashed their axes upon their shields. Hargrim and the other survivors of Karag Dum had looked stunned at the sheer scale of their welcome. They had once believed themselves the only dwarfs left in the world. Now they knew differently. Felix felt proud to be there. The cheers of the crowds still rang in his ears. He could recall dwarf children running into the street to touch the hem of his cloak so that they could tell their descendants they had done so. Until they had pushed their way through the massed cheering throng, Felix had no idea of the scale of their deed or what it really meant to the dwarf people.

His association with Gotrek, characterised as it was mostly by outlawry and failure, had in no way prepared him for this. It was like being a king. Perhaps this is how Emperor Karl Franz felt every time he rode though Altdorf, Felix thought, and turned and beamed at Ulrika. She smiled up at him proudly. It seemed she too had no idea of what the *Spirit of Grungni* had accomplished until this moment.

Looking at his companions, Felix felt happier than he had in a long time. The acclaim even seemed to have raised the spirits of Borek and Makaisson, and since Varek's death these two had looked as thoroughly miserable as any dwarfs Felix had ever seen, which was saying something.

Only Gotrek looked glum. His expression was as sour as that of a man sucking on a lemon. He glared at the crowd from under his bristling brows with his one good eye, and paused only to occasionally spit at an onlooker who came too close to touching his axe.

'Why so gloomy?' Felix asked. Gotrek shot him a glare that would have daunted anybody else. 'I want to know for the telling of your tale,' Felix added.

'Tis of no consequence,' Gotrek said. 'And it would not do to mention it in my death poem.'

'Tell me anyway.'

Gotrek sucked his few remaining teeth, spat on the ground, and worked his thumb into the empty socket below his eyepatch. Felix thought he was not going to reply, but then a shame-faced look passed across the Slayer's face. 'I was thinking that if I had died slaying the daemon, it would have been the mightiest doom ever achieved by a Slayer. A laughable, empty vanity, manling, but it crossed my mind.'

Felix did not know what to say so he kept quiet. Ulrika looked at Gotrek, astonished, as if she had never considered the dwarf capable of such an admission. 'Well, I am glad you're still alive, and that you brought Felix back.'

To Felix's astonishment the Slayer laughed. He looked as if he was going to clap Ulrika on the back but caught himself, and forced himself to look grim once more. He glared at the ground, as if embarrassed. At that moment, Felix caught some indication of how much this approbation really meant to the Slayer, how much it actually meant to him to be cheered by his people, and just how well he was hiding it.

I'm happy for him, thought Felix; he has little enough in his life to give him joy.

THE SLAYER KING was a morose-looking dwarf, squat and powerful like all his race, his hair cut in the distinctive crested fashion favoured by the Cult of Grimnir. His features were massive and his nose was long and beaky. His eyes glittered with a maniacal intelligence. His voice when he spoke was resonant and powerful. 'Greetings, Borek Forkbeard. Greetings, Gotrek, son of Gurni. Greetings Snorri Nosebiter. Greetings Malakai, son of Makai.'

Felix feared the Slayer King was going to greet them all by name, and his fears proved well-founded. He did so.

'You have performed a deed of great renown, all of you. Not in all the long years since I ascended my father's throne have I heard of such heroism. The return of Firebeard's hammer is a blessing beyond measure to the kingdom of the dwarfs, and all the kin of Grungni have cause to thank you this day. If there is any boon I can grant you, you have but to name it and–'

'Aye, there is,' said Makaisson.

The Slayer King paused and eyed Makaisson balefully. He was just getting into his oratorical stride and obviously had not anticipated any interruptions just yet. Felix wondered if all dwarf kings were so long-winded.

'You have but to tell me, and if it's in my power–'

'Ah want a workshop and the service of twenty blacksmiths, and ah want to ken everythin' you can fin oot aboot a big beast o' a dragon that dwells aboot fifty leagues northwest o' here...'

A gasp passed around the room. 'That would be Skjalandir, the ancient firedrake. Why?' enquired the Slayer King, obviously shocked to brevity.

'Ah'm gannae kill the basturd,' Makaisson said. 'Stone deid!'

'And I'm going to help him,' Gotrek said.

'Snorri Nosebiter will too,' said Snorri. A huge roar of applause passed through the chamber.

'Truly you are stalwart examples to Slayers the world over,' said the Slayer King. 'You have no sooner returned from one mighty deed than you show willing to start another...'

Listening to this madness, it struck Felix that there was a larger issue here which should be addressed. While the Slayers were excited about the prospect of facing the dragon once more, a massive Chaos army was on the move. In the great scheme of things he was sure it posed a larger threat to the world than a single dragon ever would. He thought he saw an opportunity here to make a difference, and to help Ulrika's people and his own.

'There is another thing worth mentioning,' Felix spoke up. All eyes in the chamber turned to him. He felt suddenly self-conscious. He was well aware that not all the dwarfs looking at him were pleased that a human was daring to speak in the throne room of their king.

'And what is that, Felix Jaeger?' asked the Slayer King.

'A huge Chaos army approaches from the north.'

'Does it pursue you?' the Slayer King asked. Felix paused for a moment to think about this. It was something he had never considered. Had their deeds in Karag Dum been the start of all this, the pebble that caused the avalanche? He doubted it. The whole idea was too far fetched.

'No. I do not think so.'

'Then why is it a problem? I can see that if–'

'Because soon it will enter Kislev, and if it is not stopped there, it will thrust onwards into the lands of dwarfs and men.'

'Surely that is a bridge that will be crossed when we come to it?'

Felix could see that this was going to be the old, old story. The forces of Darkness were someone else's problem. Men and dwarfs would not unite their forces until after it was too late. The enemy would be dealt with only once it became an immediate threat. In the meantime others could fight and die facing it. Felix realised he was being unfair but he felt a little angry. He had learned enough about dwarfs not to let his anger show. They became unbearably stubborn in any form of conflict.

'I suppose all the glory of facing it will belong to the people of Kislev and their Imperial allies then,' he said calmly. A quiet came over the room, and he knew he had their full undivided attention. 'I mentioned it only because this dwarfhold is known as Slayer Keep, and when the Chaos force arrives there will be many mighty monsters to slay and dreadful foes to face.'

A murmur went around the room. Felix knew that his words would be passed around the city swiftly. Even if the king offered no aid, he felt sure that many Slayers would go to Kislev in the hope of achieving a mighty death. To make his point absolutely clearly, he added,. 'It would be a great and memorable doom to fall in such a battle. After all, who does not remember those heroes who fell in defence of Praag during the last great war against Chaos?'

Ungrimm Ironfist's reply surprised Felix. 'That was but a short time ago as dwarfs reckon such things, Felix Jaeger, but your point is well taken. I will think upon what you have said.'

Of course, Felix thought, dwarfs live longer than men, and their records stretch back further. To them two centuries was not so long ago. Old Borek there had actually been alive during the last great Chaos incursion. Borek's rheumy eyes caught Felix's glance and seemed to be aware of what he was thinking. The old dwarf leaned forward on his staff and spoke.

'Felix Jaeger speaks to good purpose, your majesty. I can indeed recall the last war with Chaos and it was a dreadful thing. If another such conflict is in the offing we had best prepare now, make new alliances and stand by the old ones. For those of us who have but recently been in the Wastes have seen this foe at first hand and know how terrible it is.'

The Slayer King nodded. Borek continued to speak. 'It may be that the Hammer of Firebeard was returned to us at this time by the will of the Ancestor Gods to aid us in the coming battle. Perhaps all of this is part of a greater design than we can comprehend.'

'I will seek guidance at the Temple of Grimnir,' said the Slayer King. 'It may well be that what you say is true.'

Felix felt grateful to the old dwarf for his wisdom and understanding.

'That's aw very weil,' Makaisson said. 'Ah still want that dragon deid. Ah would like to use your engineering shops and your forges. Ah think ah hae an idea o' hoo tae dae it.'

'Whatever you require shall be provided, Malakai Makaisson, and my own personal engineers shall be put at your service.'

Makaisson did not look quite so happy at this, Felix thought. He guessed that the prospect of sharing his new designs with the king's engineers did not thrill him. Like many a dwarf engineer, Makaisson preferred to keep his secrets, Felix guessed. On the other hand, he could not turn down the king's offer with good grace and still expect aid. Makaisson seemed to have come to the same conclusion.

'Aye, weel, that'll dae fine.'

FELIX AND ULRIKA inspected their chamber. It was spartan in the style he had come to expect at Karak Kadrin, but at least the bed and other furnishings were built on a human scale. It was obvious this place was designed for human emissaries and equally obvious that it had not been used in some time. The air smelled a little musty. Instead of blankets a mass of furs covered the bed.

'I thought that was never going to end,' Ulrika said. 'Dwarfs can be very long-winded when they want to be.'

Felix agreed. 'True. Still this was an important thing for them. In some ways I suppose it would be as if one of the Runefangs had been lost and returned to the Empire. Probably more so. Firebeard's hammer appears to have religious significance to them.'

'Everything seems to,' Ulrika said. There was an undertone of antagonism to her words. She seemed to be wanting to disagree with him, and he with her. They had been this way ever since their talk that night on the *Spirit of Grungni*. Felix guessed they were both nervous about what the future held for them. He reached out and stroked her cheek. She caught his hand and turned it palm up to kiss it.

'What is going to happen to us, Felix?' she asked suddenly.

Felix looked at her. He was wondering that himself. All through this long day there had been a strange tension between them, an undertone of anger that he did not quite understand. What was there to be so nervous about? They had survived the trip here, lived through an encounter with a dragon, and the near destruction of the airship. Why were they behaving so now?

He looked down at her beautiful face. She had never seemed so lovely. He searched for an answer to her question within himself. Perhaps it was the very fact that they were safe that was causing them this stress. Now, at least for the moment, there were no external threats to distract them, nothing to keep them from the question that was now being asked. What was to become of them?

Their lives were so uncertain. A massive Chaos army approached from the north. Perhaps it was the harbinger of the end of the world. Somewhere far to the north her father and his riders might even now be facing the oncoming horde. Gotrek, Malakai and Snorri Nosebiter seemed determined to go and face the dragon. Ulrika had been charged with a mission to the Ice Queen. She almost certainly would have no home to go back to. And what could he offer her?

He was not rich. He had been disowned by his family and then rejected their offer of reconciliation. He was merely a landless wanderer bound to record the Slayer's doom. Worse than that, he was starting to suspect that it was his own doom too. He and Gotrek had travelled so far and survived so much that their destinies seemed intertwined. He could almost believe that the Slayer was destined to perform some world-shaking deed and it was his duty to witness it.

He realised that the silence had stretched for many heartbeats and he still had not answered her, that he had no answer to give. 'I do not know,' he said softly, 'and I wish I did.'

'So do I,' she said. 'So do I.'

She leaned forward and kissed him, and they fell entwined onto the bed.

MAX SCHREIBER STALKED the streets of Karak Kadrin, knowing that he had found what he was looking for. Around him the buildings were higher, the doorways taller. In the narrow alleyways, he could hear human voices mingling with the deeper tones of the dwarfs. Men and women of the Empire looked at him from the open fronts of shops. They sat among their goods. Some looked at him speculatively, seeing him for what he was. Others shouted invitations to him to come in and study their wares. Max smiled. Even in these remote mountains, in this citadel of the Elder Race, there was a small human quarter. Men and dwarfs were bound by many ancient ties of faith and alliance, but none were more ancient than the bonds of trade. He had known that even here, in this distant highland city, he would find merchants, and with them a way of communicating with his order and his allies. He reached inside his robes and found the letter he had written and closed with his own rune. He smiled, feeling the magic he had woven into it. No one but a member of his order would be able to open the letter without the script vanishing like mist in the morning sun.

Just in case, though, he had written the message in code which he hoped was readable only to one of his fellows. In the letter he had put all he knew of the *Spirit of Grungni*'s journey and the oncoming Chaos army. He mentioned the increased skaven activity along the border and he described in detail his encounter with the grey seer and the spells that it had unleashed. In this way, he thought, even if something happened to him, those who came after would be better prepared to deal with the ratman threat. In a way it was a testament to his life as well as a report to his superiors in the order of the Golden Hammer. He knew his report was timely. It had been a long time since any member of the ancient society had ventured as far north as Max had, and even knowing what he did about the Powers of Chaos, he had been shocked by what he had seen and heard. The arm of Chaos had grown long, and Kislev itself was threatened. And Kislev was the bulwark of the Empire against the incursions of Chaos. If it fell, then the hordes of Darkness could drive deep into the lands of men.

And he did not doubt that many traitors would rise up to aid them, and the monsters and mutants of the woods would emerge and...

Max knew only too well how frail the Empire was, and how easily it might fall into darkness. It was what his order had been formed to guard against. He knew that he must send a warning. He hoped to deliver it himself in person, but the future was never certain, and who knew what might happen to him? This letter was a safeguard against ill-chance. Even if he were to die, he hoped his warning and his knowledge would find its way into the right hands.

He paused in front of a tavern, bearing the sign of the Emperor's Griffon. He knew that he needed to find traders returning to the lands of men, preferably some who were heading all the way to Middenheim. This was a place he had been told he might find some. He took a deep breath and entered the beery warmth of the tavern's interior.

As he entered the place fell silent. He knew he had been recognised as one of the men who had arrived on the airship. He glanced around and smiled. Immediately someone offered to buy him a drink. He smiled his acceptance and prepared himself to answer a thousand questions.

Hopefully, after that, he would find someone to deliver his message.

FELIX LOOKED OUT of the chamber window. It was small and circular, and covered with thick well-made glass. Through it, he could see a fine view of the mountains opposite. Behind him, he heard Ulrika stir on the bed.

'I must be leaving soon,' she said. Felix nodded, wondering what business she had here in the Slayer King's palace.

'Where are you going?'

'The court of the Ice Queen.' He continued to gaze at the mountain opposite, noticing the crown of clouds around its peak. Suddenly the meaning of her words sank in, and he swung around to look at her.

'Right now?' he asked, his heart sinking.

'Now is as good a time as any. I have a message to deliver to my queen.'

'You can't,' Felix said. Her posture stiffened. Her face became a controlled mask.

'What do you mean by that? Who are you to tell me what I can or cannot do?'

'I am not trying to tell you what to do.' Felix knew that she was right. He had meant to tell her she could not go, he did not want her to, but at the same time he also knew he had no power over her. He searched for a way to retrieve the situation. 'I was just saying you don't know the way.'

'I dare say I can find out. Someone here must know the way back to human lands.' She sounded unreasonably angry. Once again, Felix suspected she was trying to pick a fight. 'The king will know for sure, and there must be libraries with maps. Perhaps he can arrange a guide.'

'Why not wait until the *Spirit of Grungni* is repaired. It will surely get you there much quicker than your own two feet. And a lot more safely.'

'In the way it got us here safely you mean?'

'Yes. No. I mean, once it's repaired it can cross these mountains a hundred times as swiftly as a man or woman on foot.'

'Maybe, but how long will that take? And who says I must go afoot? Surely there must be some horses in this city.'

'Dwarfs are not famous for their cavalry,' he told her.

'There's no need to be sarcastic.'

'I am not being sarcastic. They don't use horses much save to draw carts, and as pit ponies.'

'There are human traders here.'

'We are in the mountains. They most likely use mules, if anything.'

'You have an answer for everything, don't you?'

Where did this anger come from, Felix wondered? Why were they both so prickly? He was confused. This was not like the stories he had read, the plays he had seen. There were emotions here lurking below the surface, like pike in a pond. Emotions that did not seem logically connected with their words or with their relationship, and which he knew were somehow part of it. How could he be attracted to this woman, care for her, and still be so annoyed by her attitude? How could she feel the same way about him? Somewhere he felt there was a gap between his image of love and the reality of it, and it was not something he had been prepared for by books and poems.

'No,' he said eventually, 'I don't. I just don't want anything bad to happen to you.'

He hoped his expression of concern might pacify her a little but it did not. 'Something bad has already happened,' she said. 'It's happening to the entire world.'

Felix could not fault her reasoning there. He felt the same way. He reached out to pull her close, but she backed away. Unreasoningly annoyed, he turned and walked away himself. The door made a satisfying slamming noise behind him, but already he felt weak, and foolish and guilty.

MAX POURED ANOTHER goblet of wine for his newfound companions. If they had noticed that he had slowed his own drinking they did not seem to care. Boris Blackshield and his brother, Hef, were hard drinking men, and weren't too picky about who paid the tab. After all, as Boris was quick to point out, with the Manflayer loose in the mountains, and the dragon burning the vales, who knew whether you would be alive tomorrow? He seemed proud of the fact that he and his brother blew all of their pay as caravan guards as soon as they hit town, and would leave again with nothing in their purses save their fire-making flints. After all, it just meant that any orc that killed them wouldn't make a profit on the transaction.

Max didn't really care. Their caravan master had already retired to his chamber but before he did so he had agreed to deliver Max's message to a certain address in the Ulrikstrasse in Middenheim, on the understanding that he would receive several gold coins for his trouble. Seeing the glint in the merchant's eye, Max did not doubt it would be delivered. The Ulrikstrasse was only two streets away from the market to which the merchant was bound, and two gold pieces was a hefty reward for a short step. Max knew he most likely should have left after concluding the bargain, but when he had heard men discussing the road to the dwarf city he had decided to stay. After all, he might have to walk home, if the *Spirit of Grungni* could not be repaired, and it did no harm to find out a bit about one's route. Unfortunately, what he heard was more than a little discouraging.

'Tell me about this Manflayer again,' he said to Hef.

'You don't want to know.'

'Humour me, and assume I do.'

'Big orc chieftain, he is, and a bad one. Likes to skin his enemies alive and make his tent from their cured flesh. They say he's assembling an army of greenskins in the mountains, and intends to drive the dwarfs out of their cities.'

'That doesn't seem very likely. This is the strongest fortress I have ever seen...'

'Except Middenheim,' Boris said drunkenly.

'Except Middenheim,' Max agreed gently. 'Surely no mere orc warlord could take it.'

'You can never tell with orcs,' said Hef. 'They're sneaky and clever savages and they say this one has a shaman behind him, a shaman with powerful magic.'

Max felt a prickling of professional interest. 'I'd like to hear about this shaman.'

'Don't know much,' Hef said. 'Just heard tales from the survivors of the caravans they attacked.'

'Not that there's many of them,' said Boris. 'And all of them was fast runners. Who takes the word of yellow-bellies?'

'Just tell me what you heard,' Max said persuasively and poured more wine.

'They say he speaks with the old orc gods,' said Boris.

'And that the gods listen,' added Hef.

'The gods listen to everyone who prays to them,' said Max. 'I don't imagine that orc gods are much different from ours.'

'The difference is that the orc gods answer this shaman's prayers. They say he can tumble cliffs with a howl and smash the walls of forts with a wave of his hand.'

'Maybe he'll do it to the walls of this city,' said Hef.

Max doubted it. The dwarfs had worked runes into their walls that were as potent as any defensive spell known to man, and more powerful than most. It would take more than some howling spellshouter to tumble them down. Max was possessed of a great deal of knowledge about defensive magic, and he doubted that he could protect this city any better if he had a hundred good apprentices and twenty years to work in. It wasn't places like Karak Kadrin that were at risk, he knew. It was the small villages and trader towns along the way.

In any case, though, what he was hearing wasn't good. There were dragons in the mountains and orc warbands gathering. In the north, a Chaos horde advanced, and he had seen for himself that the skaven were active once more. It looked like all those seers prophesying dark times a-coming had the right of it. The world was in a bad way, he thought. Maybe he should drink some more wine. He fought down the urge.

'Tell me about the dragon,' he said.

'It's big and it's bad and it's burned most of the villages between here and the eastern lands.'

'That's all you know?'

'It's an old beast or so I've heard, slept for centuries until something woke it.'

'Woke it?'

'Aye. They say two hundred years ago it took up residence in a cave on Dragon Mountain, ravaged the land and then just as suddenly vanished. Some thought it had died. It seems now it was only sleeping. They say dragons can do that. Sleep for centuries.'

'Very old dragons do that,' said Max. 'So I've read.'

'You can read?' asked Boris.

'Aye. Have some more wine.'

The sellswords drank and talked but Max was not listening too closely any more. Could the dragon really have slept for all this time? And if so, what had wakened it? Maybe it's just the coming of Chaos, he thought. Maybe it's just a sign of the times.

Or perhaps it was something else entirely. There was a pattern emerging here, he felt sure of it. He sensed something dark and evil at work.

THE FORGE BLAZED brightly. The heat was sweltering. Felix noticed it as soon as he walked into the chamber. He halted for a moment and took a deep breath. His anger had burned down now and he felt more guilty than ever. Perhaps he should go back and speak to Ulrika and patch things up. Part of him wanted to do that and part of him fought stubbornly against it. The latter part won. Anyway, he had come here to find something out, and he might as well continue.

He glanced around, looking for Makaisson. Amid the heat and fumes, it was difficult to be sure if he was there. There were many dwarfs present working bellows, hammering cherry-hot metal into new shapes, working with odd engines the purpose of which Felix could not even begin to guess at. All of them were moving with the sort of purposefulness that only dwarfs with a mission could muster.

'Where's Makaisson?' he asked, reaching out and grabbing the shoulder of the nearest passing dwarf. The squat muscular figure jerked a thumb in the direction of one of the other doorways and continued on his way.

Felix moved through the workroom and ducked his head as he entered the chamber beyond. Makaisson was there all right, bending low over a table containing plans and schematics marked with what Felix recognised as the runes used by the Engineers Guild. He looked up as the man came in, sucked his teeth and said, 'Aye, weel, whaut can ah dae for ye, young Felix?'

'I was wondering when the *Spirit of Grungni* will be ready to leave.'

'A couple o' weeks maest likely. Plenty o' time to get this stuff sorted oot and gae that bloody dragon a guid seein' tae.'

'You're not serious,' said Felix, although he knew the Slayer Engineer was most likely all too serious. He had hoped the airship would be repaired soon and could carry Ulrika all the way to the court of the Ice Queen. He had hoped that it might take him with her.

'Ah am so. That big lizard damn near smashed ma airship, and he killed pare young Varek. That's a grudge tae its credit that ah'll soon be settlin', believe you me.'

'How? We barely scratched the thing.'

'Aye, well, ah hae a few thoughts aboot that, don't ye worry. There's a few wee engines ah've haud the idea o' for years, and right noo, ah think is as guid a time as ony to be buildin' them.'

'What good can any weapons do against a thing as mighty as Skjalandir?'

'Ah would hae thocht that by noo ye's hae mare faith in ma machines, Felix Jaeger.'

'I do have faith in your skill, Malakai, but–'

'Well, ah don't suppose ah can blame ye. It was a bloody big beastie richt enough. Even so it can still be killed with the right weapon. Any livin' thing can.'

'So what are you building?' Felix asked, glancing over at the plans. Malakai moved between him and the spread sheets of parchment. Like all dwarf engineers, Felix guessed he could be more than a little touchy when it came to sharing his designs with the world. A very secretive people, the dwarfs.

Makaisson looked up at him for a moment then grinned. 'Tak a look if ye want,' he said, stepping aside, 'Though ah doobt ye'll be able to make hade nor tail o' them.'

Felix looked down and saw that the dwarf was right. The blue papers were covered in squiggles. To some of the lines were attached runic symbols, to others there were none. It was like looking at a scroll inscribed by a particularly demented astrologer.

'You're right. I have no idea what these are,' he said. 'What is it?'

Makaisson rubbed his meaty hands together in satisfaction. 'Ye'll find oot soon enough, don't ye worry. Noo, oot ye go, young Felix. Ah hae got a lot o' work tae dae, and no all that much time to dae it in.'

With that he shooed Felix out of the workshop and into the street. Felix trudged back towards the palace. It was time to bring Ulrika the news. Somehow he just knew she wasn't going to be pleased.

SEVEN

PREPARATIONS

FELIX LOOKED AROUND the tavern blearily. He did not care for it. The Iron Door was a haunt of lowlifes – Slayers, tunnel fighters, renegade engineers, outcast mercenaries and others. It had the reputation for being the nastiest hellhole in the city of the Slayer King, which was saying something. For all that, he noticed, the scarred and surly dwarfs were giving their table a wide berth. Felix was quite glad of it. He was now the only human present, and he did not doubt that if he had not been in the company of Gotrek and Snorri, he would have been in deep trouble.

He knew he was drunk. It seemed that in the past few days he had done very little except drink. While Ulrika studied maps and made ready to depart, Borek and Max scoured the libraries for more information on the dragon and Malakai built his machines, he and the Slayers had done little else but throw down ale. And why not? There was nothing else to do. His fights with Ulrika had gotten worse, and the prospect of heading out to the Dragon Mountain did not fill him with good cheer. Why not get drunk? Why not enjoy himself?

Where was Max? The wizard had disappeared again. He had only stayed long enough to drink a few goblets of wine and tell

them what he had found out. The things he had said were
enough to drive any man to drink. Skjalandir was old and powerful. He had awoken a few months ago and in that time he
had already driven most of the dwarfs out of the high valleys
and burned down most of the towns. A force of mercenaries
hired by villagers had never returned nor had any of the many
Slayers who had set out to kill him. It was feared that one day
soon the monster would attack Karak Kadrin. No one had any
idea what would happen then, but they all knew it would be
bad. So why not get drunk? Ulrika might not approve, but so
what? As she had pointed out, he could not tell her what to do
so why should he let her order him about? He would get drunk
if he wanted to, no matter how much she sulked.

And now he was drunk, gloriously so. They all were: Gotrek,
Snorri Nosebiter, and himself. He was perhaps a trifle less inebriated than the others but it was touch and go. He had not
drunk a quarter of what the Slayers had drunk but dwarf ale
was stronger by far than human ale, and he did not have their
tolerance for it.

The tavern was full. All around were the seediest dwarf warriors Felix had seen since they had fought their way through the
halls of Karag Dum. As he considered this, he realised that they
were being watched.

The stranger lurked in a shadowy alcove of the tavern. His
features were in shadow but Felix could see from his outline
that he had the towering crested haircut that was the mark of a
Slayer. He seemed to become aware of Felix's eyes upon him
and a head poked out of the shadows. Felix saw a narrow-fea-
tured dwarf with mean eyes and a close-cropped beard. His
crest was dyed grey and was shorter than Gotrek's. He was lean
and quite skinny for a dwarf and his jaws worked constantly as
if he were chewing something. Tattoos covered his face and
bare arms in odd patterns. He sauntered closer to their table.
Felix could see he had a long dagger strapped to his leg and a
short handled pick slung over his shoulder. His britches and
vest were black, his sleeveless shirt grey.

'Hear you're going looking for a dragon,' the stranger said.
His voice was low, and the words seemed to come out of the
corner of his mouth. He eyed the trio at the table stealthily.

'What of it?' asked Gotrek.

'Dragons have gold.'

'So I've heard. What is it to you?'

'Skjalandir has a big hoard. Should do anyway. That old fire-drake has terrorised these mountains for nigh on a thousand years.'

'It's not its gold I'm interested in, it's its life. I mean to kill the thing or die in the attempt,' Gotrek said.

'Not if Snorri Nosebiter gets there first,' said Snorri.

'Quite so. I understand exactly. And a mighty death it would be for a Slayer too. I mean to try it myself.'

'Can't stop you,' said Gotrek. 'Just don't get in my way.'

'Fair enough. Mind if I sit and sup with you a while?'

'As long as you can pay for your own beer,' said Gotrek.

'I can do that and buy a round for you all too,' said the new-comer.

Gotrek's and Snorri's eyes widened. Felix gathered this was uncharacteristic behaviour for a dwarf.

'Steg, called by some the Light-fingered, at your service.'

'A thief,' Gotrek said tactlessly.

'Once, to my shame,' said Steg. 'But I'm a Slayer now.'

'You got caught!' said Snorri Nosebiter.

'Aye, in the treasure chamber of the Vorgrund clan with the amber necklace in my hands.' The other Slayers looked at him with interest.

'I'm surprised the Vorgrunds didn't cut your knackers off.'

'They intended to. First they threw me into their dungeon but I picked the locks and escaped. There was a hidden pas-sageway out of their citadel. Of course, there was the shame of being caught and unmasked so I became a Slayer.'

'The shame of being caught!' Gotrek spluttered. Felix was not surprised at Gotrek's outrage. He had always contrived to give the impression that dwarfs had higher standards of honesty than humans. Steg seemed to contradict this, although Felix thought the thief seemed a bit odd by dwarf standards. There was an almost boastful quality to the way he spoke, that was completely at odds with the reticence of Gotrek and Snorri. He was not entirely sane, Felix thought. On the other hand, how many Slayers were?

'Aye. Once I was unmasked no one would speak to me, my clan ostracised me, my betrothed disowned me, which seemed particularly unfair because I only wanted the necklace as a mar-riage gift for her.'

Gotrek glared at Steg. Snorri looked on in unabashed amazement. Steg was confessing to the most heinous of all dwarf crimes, shamelessly and in a perfectly reasonable tone of voice. If Steg noticed he did not give any sign. 'So it was off to the Shrine of Grimnir for a haircut and a beard trim.'

'You don't seem particularly ashamed,' Felix said. Steg looked at him.

'Young human, I am a locksmith by trade, and a thief by compulsion. I am ashamed because I brought dishonour on my clan, and because through my lack of skill I was caught. I seek to atone for my crime by death but before I die, I intend restitution to those I have wronged. Since I spent the gold I took I will take my recompense from my share of the dragon's hoard.'

Felix looked at him sidelong. He wondered how sincere Steg was. Perhaps he suffered from gold fever and merely wanted to be near the treasure. Perhaps he was not really a Slayer at all but merely intended to accompany them and steal the treasure. Who could tell? Gotrek seemed a little mollified by Steg's explanation though. He no longer looked as if he wanted to take his axe to the self-confessed thief's skull. Felix found himself interested in Steg's tale.

'You are a locksmith? I have heard dwarf locksmiths are prodigiously skilled.'

'Aye, we are. I think that was another reason I took to crime. The challenge of it. I wanted to prove myself superior to all other locksmiths by overcoming their creations.'

Gotrek snorted. 'There are some things of which it is better not to speak.'

'Snorri thinks he will have another beer.'

'Felix thinks he will be staggering back to the palace,' said Felix.

'Be careful of your purse,' Steg said. Felix smiled and patted his belt – to discover it was not there.

Steg extended a large hand which contained it. 'Sorry,' he said. 'Old habits die hard.'

ULRIKA SAT IN the library of the Slayer King. The lanterns flickered eerily illuminating the rows and rows of shelves and pigeonholes containing scrolls, leather-bound books, maps and other documents. The Slayer King's library was surprisingly well furnished. Most of the books were unreadable to her, being written in dwarf runes, but there was a good selection of human volumes and many, many maps of the mountains. These were executed with far more detail and precision than human maps. Dwarfs, it seemed, were sticklers for detail.

On the low dwarf crafted table in front of her was spread out a map of the mountains, the latest product of the king's scribes, showing the area around the city for all of a hundred leagues. Little pictographs indicated towns and villages and it was easy to understand their meanings. A gold axe indicated a gold mine. A red axe might be coal or iron. A boat indicated a port where rafts or ships might go down river. Major trails were marked in thick red lines, lesser ones in thinner ones. What looked like perilous portage routes through mountains were lines of red dots. Crossed swords indicated a battle site. An orc's head most likely marked the lair of some greenskin tribe.

Looking at the map she could see that Peak Pass ran down to the lowlands of the eastern Empire. The way was clear but from there it was a long circuitous route to the court of the Ice Queen. The fastest way north to Kislev lay along the old High Road to Karak Ungor, and then down the River Urskoy to Kislev city. Unfortunately the dragon symbol lay athwart what had been a major trade route on the older maps, forcing the thick red line to wind a tortuous path through the peaks far longer than it had once been.

It looked as if Felix was right, she thought sourly. It might be quicker to wait until the airship was repaired. Assuming it could get past the dragon, it would be much faster, and judging by the number of orc symbols on the map, possibly much safer. Looking at the map, she could tell the swiftest way would actually be to go with the Slayers along the Karak Ungor High Road.

Perhaps she simply wanted to believe that, so they could stay together for a little bit longer. It was annoying and frustrating – and saddening too. It was one of the things that put such a strain on their relationship. She wanted to be with him, and this desire made her want to shirk her duty to her father and nation. She knew she should take her father's message to Kislev. And yet she resented her duty for taking her away from Felix, just as she resented him for tearing her from her duty.

She was not sure what she felt about him any more. While they had been separated, she had daydreamed about his return constantly, but his return had changed things. He was not a fantasy figure any more but a real person, and one whom she could find quite annoying at times, with his cleverness and air of sophistication. He had grown up in the capital of the civilised world, after all, and she was the daughter of a border noble of a semi-barbarous land. She had not realised what a difference that could make. His allusions to poets and plays and books went right over her head, and made her feel stupid sometimes. He lacked the straightforward honour code of her people, and he had travelled so far and seen so much in his life that it was intimidating. At the court in Middenheim she had felt dowdy and out of place among all the sophisticated ladies. He made her feel that way sometimes too.

More than that, she felt threatened by the intimacy that had grown between them so strongly and so quickly. All of her life she had been in control of her emotions. She had been raised to be a warrior, to fight as well as any man, to be like the son her father had really wanted. That and her position as heir had kept an emotional distance between her and any man. She was not sure whether she wanted that gap closed.

And then there was his drinking. Ulrika had grown up around hard drinking men but in Kislev, it was a thing reserved for festivals and feasts. It was too dangerous a place for anyone to risk sottishness more than a few times in a year. Since they had reached the city Felix had got drunk every day. It was worrying.

She shook her head. This was not like her. This was the first time she had ever felt this way. To worry so about what a man thought about her, and what she thought about a man. In the past, she had taken lovers according to the easy codes of her people's nobility, for evenings of pleasure. She had never felt any deep emotional connection or any unease whatsoever. But then again, she had understood those men, and what she expected of them, and they of her. She was not sure she understood Felix at all. And she was not sure she could see a future for them either.

Not that it mattered anyway, she thought wryly. With the Chaos horde advancing, and the dangers of the road ahead, there most likely would not be a future anyway, so it seemed pointless to worry. She thrust the thoughts aside and returned to her study of the map, looking for the best route towards her goal. It did seem like accompanying the Slayers was the best way.

She heard the door open and footsteps enter the library. The footsteps were human, and not Felix's light tread. She looked up and saw Max. He gazed at her and winked.

'So I am not the only one burning the midnight oil,' he said.

She nodded, wondering what he was thinking. From the look in his eyes it seemed perfectly possible that he had come here because he knew she was here. At her father's mansion house, he had always been bumping into her, as if by accident. There was also a smell of alcohol on his breath.

'What are you doing here, Max?' she asked. His smile widened.

'I am taking this opportunity to study in a dwarf king's library. They preserve many old books, you know, ones that are rare in the Empire. Some translated from dwarfish by human scribes.'

'I never knew that there were humans who could read dwarfish.'

'Reading is not counted a great gift among the Kislevites,' he said. Ulrika could hear the irony in his tone. It reminded her of Felix, and she felt a small surge of anger. Unaware of this, Max continued to speak. 'Among the citizens of the Empire it is different. Some there can not only read, they can read dwarf runes.'

'I thought it was a secret tongue the dwarfs kept to themselves.'

'It is now. It was not always so. Once dwarfs and men were closer, and in the time of Sigmar Heldenhammer, many were taught the dwarf tongue. Dwarf runes may have formed the basis of the first human alphabets. Certainly, according to the Unfinished Book, Sigmar could speak with dwarfs in their native tongue.'

'Sigmar was a god.'

'He took human form, and his first priests could speak dwarfish too. They passed it on to those who came after. It is still used by many scholars of the church.'

'You are saying that there are humans who can speak dwarfish?'

'The ancient version of the tongue, which is not too dissimilar to modern dwarfish. They are a very conservative people, the Elder Race, and not that much has changed in their language over the past two thousand, five hundred years. If you can speak the old version of the tongue, you can make yourself understood in the modern version. And you can most likely read it.'

'How do you know all this?'

'I am a scholar as well as a magician, and like many scholars I studied in the temples when I was young. Also, a magician these days needs a working knowledge of theology and liturgy if he is not to fall foul of witch hunters. The temples are still not fond of us. There are often times when we need to be able to prove that we are god-fearing men.'

Ulrika remembered the superstitions of her own folk and the hatred that many of the followers of Ulric had borne mages when she was in Middenheim. She could see some sense in his words. 'And are you a god-fearing man, Max Schreiber? Or is your soul in peril?'

'I am more godly than you could guess, Ulrika Magdova. I have been an enemy of Chaos all my life, no matter what the witch hunters might think.'

'You do not need to convince me of that, Max. I saw you fight against the skaven.'

He moved closer and sat down opposite her. She could definitely smell the wine on his breath. 'You are contemplating a journey, I see. Going hunting for dragons, are you?'

'No. I am trying to find a way to Kislev, to bring my father's warning to my people. The Tzarina must know about this impending invasion.'

'You are not going with the dwarfs then? Felix is, isn't he?'

'Felix is sworn to accompany Gotrek. I would not ask him to break an oath.'

Ulrika was not quite sure what to make of the expression that moved across Max's face. In the dim light it was hard to tell if he was surprised, pleased, alarmed or a little of all these things. 'I thought you two were inseparable,' he said eventually.

'We are bed companions, nothing more,' Ulrika knew it wasn't true even as she said it, but it was close enough to the reality of the situation so that she did not feel like a liar. Max winced. Was he jealous or was it something else?

'What is it?' she asked.

'It's just that Kislevite women seem a little more forthright on... matters of the heart than men of the Empire are used to.'

'We are honest.'

'No question of that. It just took me by surprise that is all. In the Empire a lady does not talk of such things.'

Ulrika looked at him. 'They certainly do such things, though. I spent quite enough time in the court at Middenheim to see that. At least we Kislevite women are not hypocrites!'

To her surprise Max laughed. 'Yes. It's true. You have a point.'

'There is no need to talk down to me.'

'I am not doing that.' His tone changed. 'How do you intend to get to Kislev? On foot?'

'By horse, if we can find any in this place.'

'How many of you? Will you be hiring bodyguards?'

'I have Oleg and Standa and I have my own good sword. What need have I of any more?'

'The way between here and Kislev is long and hard and full of peril.' He paused for a minute as if considering something. 'Perhaps you could use another sword on the route, and more than a sword, a magician.'

'Are you offering your services?' Ulrika felt suddenly uneasy. She was not at all sure that she wanted Max riding with her, potent mage though he was.

'Yes.'

'I will think on it.'

'You will need me,' he said confidently. 'There are orcs in those mountains, and they have a shaman with them. It takes magic to fight magic.'

'I have said I will think on it,' she said, and rose to leave. Max bowed goodnight to her. As she reached the door, she felt him gazing at her. He opened his mouth to speak.

'I love you,' he said suddenly.

'You're drunk,' she said and swept out of the door. Even as she did so, she heard him say, 'True, but that doesn't make any difference.'

As she walked through the corridor, she realised she had come to a decision. She would travel with Felix and Gotrek along the High Road to the Urskoy turning; assuming they survived the trip she would make her way north with Oleg and Standa. She felt as if a weight had lifted from her shoulders. She looked forward to seeing Felix and to sharing a bed. They had been apart a lot recently, and she felt some responsibility for that. She would try and make things up.

* * *

MAX STOOD IN the library, feeling foolish. The effects of the wine he had taken earlier in the Emperor's Griffon had not worn off, and had left his tongue loose. Part of him was glad he had said what he had, and another part was deeply embarrassed by the rebuff. He realised that a lifetime of studying magic in musty old books had in no way prepared him for dealing with a living woman. He felt like he had said the wrong thing right from the beginning of the conversation.

This was dreadful. He would have to get a grip on himself. He was a master mage of the Golden College and a secret brother of the ancient order of the Golden Hammer. He was not some callow student of the mysteries. He could not afford to lose control of himself in this or any other way. With his powers, disasters could easily happen. He was only too aware of tales of mages who had wreaked terrible havoc whilst drunk. Not that he was going to. He was too clever for that. He would never try using his powers while inebriated. Not for any reason.

It was dark in here, though. Not enough light to see by. He moved his fingers through the familiar intricate pattern and felt the winds of magic answer. A sphere of softly glowing yellowish light sprang into being around his hand. He rolled it off, and left it to hover in mid-air in the centre of the chamber. Its light flickered erratically as if something were affecting his control of the magic. Perhaps it was the old dwarf protective runes. Perhaps it was something else. He was not going to worry about it now.

He shook his head and looked at the map Ulrika had been studying. It was not difficult to see the story it told. The dragon's awakening had certainly stirred things up in this part of the World's Edge Mountains. Orc tribes were everywhere. Towns had been destroyed. Trade routes were being blocked. He could easily imagine the cascade of troubles.

The dragon awakes and begins destroying human and dwarf towns and eating their flocks. This leads to the trade routes and mountain passes being less well-defended. Orcs and other nastier creatures take advantage of the anarchy to increase their own power. The caravan routes lengthen, sellswords increase their hiring price because of the danger. The cost of goods rises here in the mountains and in the human towns of the Ostermark. The ripples of this one event move out across hundreds of leagues, affecting the lives of thousands of people who will never even see a dragon and may even believe it is only a myth.

Max wondered how often similar chains of events affected the human realms. Doubtless far more than he would ever learn of. It seemed all too likely though that enough of them occurring at once might cause the collapse of the Empire. For one thing, looking at this map, it was difficult to see how the dwarfs might move an army quickly through the mountains if the dragon and the orcs decided to oppose them. Even if they wanted to aid the Kislevites against the marching legions of Chaos, they might not be able to.

Of course, there was always the *Spirit of Grungni*. The airship would allow the movement of many warriors very quickly. Perhaps that would be the answer. If the mighty machine could be repaired. Even then, the dragon had almost destroyed it once. Perhaps it might try again and succeed. Max shook his head. He knew he was simply trying to distract himself from his hopeless passion for Ulrika.

Or was it so hopeless? It appeared that all was not well between her and Felix. Perhaps he might get his chance yet, particularly if she and Herr Jaeger were not travelling together, and he was with her. Who knew what might happen then? He allowed the surge of hope to fade. Just because she and Felix might be falling out did not mean that she would go with him. He felt almost like laughing.

Here he was, sworn to oppose Chaos, with the largest incursion of the forces of Darkness in two centuries about to occur, and all he could think about was this one girl. Somehow, he would have to get his sense of proportion back. He walked over to the shelves and studied the books.

There was indeed a fair number of volumes here, including some copies of the Book of Grudges for Karak Kadrin that dated back well over 3,000 years. The earlier entries were in the almost pure ancient dwarfish he had learned as a youth. He flipped through the pages, and was soon slumped in the chair, snoring, with the old tales of treachery, betrayal and gloom slipping from his hand.

FELIX STAGGERED BACK into the room he shared with Ulrika. He was none too steady on his feet and his efforts at moving quietly seemed to be failing horribly. Already he had kicked over a chamber pot, and sent his sword tumbling to the floor with a loud metallic clatter. Despite her stillness on the bed, he knew Ulrika was awake. He wondered how long she had been waiting for him.

'So you're drunk as well,' she said. She sounded angry.

'You've been drinking,' said Felix stupidly. 'I thought you were going to the king's library to plan your route home.'

'No. Max was drinking.'

'You were drinking with Herr Schreiber.' Felix wondered at how much sullen jealousy managed to creep into his voice during that one sentence.

'No. I was in the library and he came in drunk.'

'And what did you do then?'

'We talked.'

'About what?'

'About the dwarfish language, as if it were any of your business.'

'You've suddenly developed an interest in dwarfish?'

'The maps and books in the library are mostly written in it.'

'That makes a certain amount of sense,' said Felix with unsubtle irony. He began to strip off his clothes and get ready for bed.

'You can be a nasty man, Felix Jaeger.'

'Apparently. And Herr Schreiber isn't?'

'At least Max offered to accompany me to Kislev.'

Felix felt his stomach twist. He had not realised that her words could affect him so much. He threw himself down on the bed beside her, and glanced over. In the darkness her expression was impossible to read. Judging by her voice, she sounded upset. He paused to consider what to say. The silence stretched, a vast empty desert that threatened to swallow anything he could say.

'I would go with you to Kislev,' he said eventually.

'What about the dragon?'

'After it is slain...'

'Ah, after it is slain, you will go...'

'I have sworn an oath, and I know what you Kislevites think of oathbreakers.'

The silence stretched once more. She did not say anything more. Felix considered what to say next, but the beer surged through his brain, and the tentacles of alcohol-induced sleep dragged him down into the sea of slumber.

When he awoke in the morning, Ulrika was gone.

FROM THE BATTLEMENTS above the courtyard of the Slayer King's palace, Max watched the morning sun rise over the mountains. His mouth felt dry. His head ached. His stomach churned. He had not gotten drunk like that since he had been a student, many years ago. He felt vaguely embarrassed and ashamed. In part he knew it was simply the effects of the hangover. In part though, it was the knowledge that he had spoken to Ulrika about something that he should have best kept to himself. In part too he was annoyed at himself for getting drunk. It was a bad thing for a master magician to do. He shuddered when he realised he had been using spells, even such simple ones as casting light globes, while being inebriated. Magic was a tricky and dangerous thing at the best of times, without the added complications of booze. He remembered what his old tutor Jared had to say on the subject. A drunken magician is a foolish magician, and a foolish magician is soon a dead magician.

He knew it should not have happened, but he knew also he had his reasons. He was a mage. He was aware of his state of mind. He took a deep breath, and counted silently and slowly to five as he did so. He held the breath in for a count of ten, and then let it out slowly for a count of twenty. As he did so, he sought to empty his mind, as his tutors had taught him.

At first it would not come. The sickness in his stomach and the dizziness in his head prevented him from managing it. Another danger of drinking, he thought. If an enemy were to attack me now, I would have difficulty protecting myself. He cursed, knowing that such thoughts were themselves a sign that he was failing to perform even this elementary magical exercise. He continued, concentrating on his breathing, trying to feel calm and relaxed, trying to let the tension flow from his muscles.

Slowly, the exercise began to take effect. His thoughts became quieter and slower. His pains seemed to fade a little. Tension oozed from him. At the edge of his mind, he became aware of the tug of the currents of magic. Colours began to swirl in his mind, reds and greens and a predominant gold. He became aware of himself as an empty vessel, into which the power was starting to flow. The magic softly soaked his pains away; his mind began to feel cleaner and clearer and filled with a golden light. A sense of renewal filled him. The touch of magic was like the effects of some of the narcotic drugs he had experimented with under the supervision of his masters. It made him feel full of energy and almost euphoric in a low-key way. His senses were keener. He was aware of the wind's gentle caress on his skin, the faint tickling sensation caused by his woollen robes. The heat in the stones under his fingers. He could hear the faint voices of dwarfs in the depths of the castle that he had only been subliminally aware of before. The light was brighter and his vision clearer. Other senses than the five that mankind normally used clicked in. He could sense the flow of magic all around him, and the faint emanations of living things. He could feel the power of the runes that the dwarfs had bound into their buildings, and the way they channelled primal energies in magical defence. He knew that he could reach out in a manner inexplicable to normal mortals and begin to mould those energies to his will. For a moment, he felt utterly and completely alive, and filled with a gladness that he was sure no non-magician would ever understand.

He achieved emptiness and held it for a few moments, and then as he exhaled began to think again, reviewing his life with a new insight and clarity.

He could see now that he had gotten drunk as a response to the way things had been running out of control in his life. He had undergone a lot of things recently that were alien to the normal routine of his quiet scholarly life. He had been involved in a battle, and fought a sorcerous duel with a mage far mightier than himself. He could easily have died both in that duel, and in the battles with the skaven. He had fallen in love, passionately and uncontrollably and much to his own surprise. Perhaps he had been more vulnerable to it, out in the wilds of Kislev, far from his homelands, and waiting tensely for the return of the airship. True, Ulrika was a lovely woman, but he had known lovelier, and not fallen hard for them. Anyway, it did not matter what the reasons were, the simple fact was that it had happened and had affected him. He had been jealous, and desperate and filled with an anger he had only been barely aware of, and it had driven him to behave badly, and feel temptations he had never known before. He knew that the whole business was a threat to his peace of mind, and in some ways to his soul. His desire for the woman had led him to contemplate dark paths that should have remained closed to him and consider things he should never have given thought to. Last night he had even gone so far as to get drunk and use his magic. He was lucky he had been too drunk to work some of the spells he knew, ones that could bind others to his will.

He closed his eyes and considered the secret knowledge he had gained with such cost. Slaanesh, he thought. To the ignorant, he was the dark god of unspeakable pleasures, a master of daemons, whose pleasure-crazed worshippers engaged in orgies of dreadful excess. And such things did happen, as Max well knew. But this was not the only threat Slaanesh represented. He was the god of the temptations of the flesh, subtle and deadly. He could lure even the wisest onto the road of ruin through the urge to gratify their desires. Max knew that Slaanesh could ruin a man in many ways, through the urge to drink, or take drugs or to bed women. He knew that, in a way, what had happened to him last night was something he had to take seriously, for it was the first step on the path to perdition, if he followed up on it.

It was a thing he knew he must not do. He was sworn to oppose Chaos and not to serve it, that was why he had studied so long and so hard. He knew that he must forswear Ulrika and drink and all the other temptations that might lead him astray, or the consequences would be terrible. But even as he resolved this, part of him whispered that it did not want to do it, and his new insight showed him what might be another truth.

Perhaps he had studied the works of Chaos for so long for a less pure reason, not because he hated it, and wished to oppose it, but because he was fascinated by it. Perhaps he had merely been fooling himself all along.

Even as he told himself that this thought too was but one of the snares of Slaanesh, he was all too aware that it was, at least in part, the truth.

FELIX WANDERED OUT into the street. He had no idea where to find Ulrika but according to the sentries she, Oleg and Standa had left the palace earlier in the morning and headed off in the direction of the fairground that had sprung up around the *Spirit of Grungni* in the valley outside the city. This made sense.

She would be looking for horses to continue her journey and the market there would be as good a place as any to buy them.

As he headed downhill, he noticed that a young dwarf of unusual appearance was looking at him. The dwarf was garbed in furs, and his head was covered in a pinkish fuzz that made it look as if it had recently been shaved. He had an axe slung over one shoulder. Noticing Felix was watching him, he began to move forward and fell into step beside him.

'You are Felix Jaeger!' The dwarf's voice was even lower than usual for a dwarf's and boomed out loudly. As Felix looked he saw that on the dwarf's arms were an intricate series of tattoos, depicting huge, bleeding monsters. An inscription in dwarf runes ran under them. Seeing that Felix had noticed them, the dwarf flexed his arms proudly causing the muscle to ripple and the tattoo to expand.

'You've noticed my tattoos, I see! The inscription reads "Born to Die!"'

'Yes. Very impressive,' said Felix. He lengthened his stride, and soon the dwarf was almost running to keep pace. He had no wish to be rude but he was in a hurry to find Ulrika and apologise for his behaviour of the previous evening. If the youth noticed his brusqueness, he gave no sign.

'Ulli, son of Ulli, at your service, and your clan's,' said the dwarf. He tried bowing as he moved and almost tripped.

'Pleased to meet you,' Felix said, hoping the dwarf would take the hint and leave him alone. His hangover was not making him feel sociable.

'You are a comrade of Gotrek Gurnisson's, aren't you? You have held the Hammer of Firebeard in your hand?' There was a note of awe in the youth's voice as he spoke. Felix was not sure whether it was for Gotrek or for the hammer. He stopped and gazed down at Ulli.

'Yes. What of it?'

'I don't like your tone of voice, human! Do you want to fight me?'

Felix looked at the youth. He was muscular in the apish way that dwarfs often were, but he was nowhere near as fearsome as Gotrek or Snorri Nosebiter. Still, there was no sense in getting into a fight for no reason, particularly not with a Slayer. 'No. I do not want to fight you,' Felix said patiently.

'Good! I would not want to soil my axe with human blood!'

'There's no need to shout,' Felix said quietly.

'Do not tell me how to speak!' roared the dwarf. Instinctively Felix's hand went to the hilt of his blade. The young Slayer seemed to flinch back a little.

'I am not telling you how to speak,' Felix said as politely as he could manage. 'I am merely asking you to calm down a little.'

'I am a Slayer! I am not meant to be calm! I am sworn to die in battle against terrible monsters!'

Felix grimaced sourly. He had heard such lines before from Gotrek but somehow they didn't seem quite so convincing coming from Ulli Ullisson. 'You've probably noticed that I am not a terrible monster,' he said.

'Are you mocking me?'

'As if I would.'

'Good! I demand the respect a Slayer deserves from your sort!'

'And what sort would that be?' Felix asked softly. A dangerous edge had entered his voice. He was getting a little tired of being badgered by this boastful lout. Ulli seemed to notice it, and flinched back again.

'Humans! The younger race! The men of the Empire!'

A crowd of dwarfs was gathering to watch the confrontation. He could hear them muttering to each other in dwarfish. Some of the spectators were nudging each other with their elbows and pointing to him. He heard his own name mentioned several times. It seemed he was quite a well-known figure around the town. 'Is there something I can do for you, Ulli Ullisson?'

'Is it true you intend to hunt down the dragon, Skjalandir?'

'Yes. Why do you ask?'

'I seek a glorious death.'

'Join the queue,' Felix said softly.

'What?' roared Ulli.

'That's nothing new,' Felix said. 'Do you intend to accompany us on our quest?'

'I intend to go in search of the dragon with or without you! Still, if you are asking for my protection, I will grant it!'

'I am not. Good morning to you,' said Felix, and turned and strode away. He did not look back but he could hear Ulli blustering loudly behind him.

* * *

'WE ARE LOST, aren't we, most perspicacious of pathfinders?'

Grey Seer Thanquol did not like the way Lurk said this. There was an undertone of menace, combined with a hint of disbelief in Thanquol's abilities that boded ill for future dealings with his henchman. Thanquol's head hurt. He had run out of warpstone snuff two days ago and it was not helping matters. He felt a terrible craving for it. Maybe he could just nibble a little of his stash of warpstone. No! He knew he must preserve the pure stuff for an emergency. He would need its power then.

'Are we lost?' Lurk asked again.

'No! No!' chittered Thanquol with what he hoped was utter confidence. 'Such are my powers of scrying that we are exactly where we need to be!'

'And where exactly is that?'

'Are you questioning me, Lurk Snitchtongue?'

'Expressing an interest I am.'

Thanquol gazed at the horizon. The glittering peaks that marked the border with the Chaos Wastes seemed a lot closer. Was he being betrayed by his desire for warpstone, he wondered? Had the mysterious lure of those lost lands affected his sense of direction? Or was it simply that this constant badgering by Lurk's inane questioning was beginning to affect his judgement? Perhaps a little of both, he decided.

And of course the weather was not helping either. When it was not raining, it was misty. When it was not misty, it was so bright that it hurt their sensitive skaven eyes and forced them to burrow into the earth rather than risk being spotted. Unwilling as he normally was to admit that humans might be superior to skaven in anything, Thanquol had to admit that a man on horseback was much more likely to spot them before they spotted him. There seemed to be no happy medium. The rains were awful. They drove in hard and reduced visibility to almost zero. They left his fur sodden and deadened his sense of smell. It was as if the very elements conspired with his enemies to undermine Thanquol's sanity.

Actually, he was surprised that he had not considered this before. It seemed all too likely that this atrocious weather was the product of some enemy's spell. Thanquol could think of several candidates. One thing was certain, he swore, when he returned to skaven civilisation, he was going to make someone suffer for the discomfort he had endured. And one candidate for his certain vengeance was no more than a few tail lengths away from him.

Lurk had become less and less endurable as their journey progressed. When he was not being insolent, he was hungry and cast alarmingly voracious looks at his rightful master. When he was not doing that he was asking foolish questions, and actually appeared to be implying that he had no faith in the grey seer's judgement. Thanquol would show him whose judgement was faulty soon enough, he vowed. He was not prepared to put up with insolence from underlings forever.

'You have not answered my question, most scintillating of seers,' said Lurk. Thanquol glared at him until he noticed that Lurk was not looking back but instead was staring off over Thanquol's shoulders. Thanquol bared his teeth in a snarl. That was the oldest trick in the book. He was not going to turn around and let Lurk spring on his back. Did Snitchtongue take him for the merest runt?

'What are you looking at?' Thanquol asked.

'Why not use your awesome powers of divination, and find out for yourself?' suggested Lurk. 'Perhaps you could ascertain what that monstrous cloud on the horizon portends and whether it has anything to do with the way the earth shakes beneath our paws.'

At first Thanquol suspected that Lurk was mocking him till he realised that the ground was indeed vibrating. He risked a quick glance over his shoulder and noticed that there was a massive cloud stretching all the way to the horizon, obscuring everything, even the mountain peaks.

'Some strange mystical phenomenon,' he suggested.

'More like an army on the march, it looks to me, mightiest of masters. And a very large one too.' Lurk could not quite keep the fear from his voice. Thanquol could not exactly blame him. If that cloud was indeed being raised by an army, it was the largest one Thanquol had ever heard of.

Thanquol shuddered. There was little they could do except wait and hide.

ULRIKA LOOKED AROUND the fairground that had sprung up around the airship where it lay outside the town walls. Hundreds of dwarfs surrounded the enclosure and looked at the mighty vessel in awe. Fire eaters and jugglers moved through the crowd. Pie vendors sold their wares from trays around their neck. Alemongers carried massive pitchers of foaming beer through the crowd, dispensing the brew to anyone with a few coppers to spare. A dwarf on stilts towered high over her and shouted jokes to the crowd. Ballad singers rumbled out fanciful tales of the great airship's voyage in the common speech.

She was disappointed. The horse market had proven to be nothing of the sort. It sold only pit ponies, mules and nags that no true Kislevite would be seen dead riding, beasts that would never survive the long trip north. It seemed, annoyingly enough, that once more Felix had been proven right. Dwarfs were not famous for their cavalry nor for their knowledge of horseflesh. She gritted her teeth. She was not going to allow the thought of the man to annoy her today. She did not want to give way to her anger. Last night she had been ready to make up with him, until he had proven himself a drunken sot. Now he would have to apologise to her.

She had never seen quite so many dwarfs from so close up before. There must be hundreds, perhaps thousands of them, most of them at least partially inebriated. They were all bent on celebrating in their own dour way. It seemed that the return of the Hammer of Firebeard was an event of great significance to them. Not that it appeared they needed any excuse to get drunk. In this they were like Kislev men. The alesellers were doing good business, but then so were the smiths and weaponsellers. It seemed that the dwarfs liked to haggle, and buy and sell almost as much as they liked to drink.

'You're a pretty lass,' said a deep, rumbling voice close to Ulrika's elbow. She looked down to see a dwarf standing there. He was squat, muscular and repulsively ugly. His nose had been mashed and a huge hairy wart stood on the end of it. His head had been shaved and a tufted crest of dyed hair rose above it. Huge gold rings dangled from his ears.

'And you're a Slayer.'

'As clever as ye are pretty, I see. Do you fancy a turn in the bushes?' The dwarf gestured insinuatingly at the nearest clump of greenery. It took Ulrika a few moments to work out his meaning. When she did she did not know whether to be angry or amused. Oleg and Standa had reached for their blades. She quelled them with a glance. She was quite capable of handling this situation on her own.

'I don't think so.'

'You'll soon change your mind if you do. There's no a lass ever regretted straddling Bjorni Bjornisson.'

This time Ulrika did laugh. If the Slayer was offended, he gave no sign. 'If ye change yer mind, let me know.'

'I'll be sure to do that,' she said, and turned to go.

'You know Gotrek Gurnisson,' said the Slayer. 'And Felix Jaeger?'

That stopped her. 'Yes.'

'They're going hunting for dragons, so I hear.'

'You hear correctly.'

'I might join them I think. We'll be seeing more of each other, bonnie lass.'

The Slayer turned and walked away. Astonished, Ulrika followed him with her gaze. The last she saw of him, he was disappearing into the crowd, arm in arm with two rouged and none-too-young looking human wenches.

'Never seen anything like that before,' Standa said, a look of discomfort showing on his moon face. Oleg tugged his long, drooping moustaches in agreement.

'You'll see a lot stranger things before we're done travelling, I'll warrant,' said Ulrika. 'Now, let's get going. We might as well get back to the palace. We'll find no horses here.'

She was still not sure she believed what she had just seen herself. That was surely the strangest Slayer she had ever encountered.

THE *Spirit of Grungni* lay at rest. Even to Felix's hungover eyes it was an impressive sight. The massive airship lay in an open field beyond Karak Kadrin. The area was roped off to keep the crowd at bay and surrounded by dwarf soldiers to prevent any interlopers getting too close. The gondola actually rested on the ground anchored by ropes held by hooks driven deep into the ground like tentpegs. More ropes arced up and over the gasbag, running through the guardrails that ran along the top of the dirigible and coming down the other side. Even over the voices of the crowd of spectators Felix could hear the ropes creak as the airship shifted slightly. The spectacle reminded Felix of an old story he had once read of a sleeping giant who had been trapped in his slumber, ensnared in a webwork of ropes, pinned to the earth and unable to move.

Felix had been looking for Ulrika, but like everyone else he was getting distracted by the circus surrounding the airship. He smiled to himself. He had become so accustomed to the *Spirit of Grungni* on the quest for Karag Dum that he had forgotten just how impressive the massive airship was. The onlookers had not. They had come to gape at it, the way they might at some captive dragon.

The guards recognised Felix as he forced his way into the roped-off enclosure, and let him pass. He heard his name murmured by the spectators as he moved closer to the *Spirit of Grungni*. It was strange to be recognised.

Dwarfs swarmed over the fuselage of the airship, painting the gasbag with a pitch-like substance which sealed the rips and tears. Felix knew it was made from some alchemical formula known only to Makaisson and his apprentices. Blacksmiths and artificers worked on the engines and the dented cupola, banging away with hammers, twisting nuts into place with huge spanners. The clangour was deafening. Looking through the portholes, he could see more dwarfs inside. It looked like the repairs were proceeding apace. Borek Forkbeard leaned on his stick and watched the work in progress. He looked sadder and older than ever but a smile crossed his face when he noticed Felix approach.

'Have you seen Ulrika?' the young warrior asked

'I thought I saw her and her guards heading back up to the city.'

Felix clamped down on his disappointment. He did not feel like going back to the palace right now. Maybe he should have some ale. It might help his hangover. He considered this briefly and decided against it. It probably wouldn't help, and he'd need his wits about him when he saw Ulrika again.

'How is it going?' Felix asked. Borek nodded his head. An unlit pipe was clenched between his teeth. Felix knew it was there from force of habit. He would not light it so close to the gasbag.

'Slowly. Makaisson was here yesterday and said it may be some weeks before the airship is ready.'

'Why is he not here himself? Surely he should be supervising this.'

'His apprentices know all that is needful or so he claims. The crew were well trained before we set out. We knew he might not be alive to oversee any repairs that were needed.'

From his expression, Felix could tell that the old dwarf was thinking of someone else who was not here to witness this, his nephew. The scholar continued, 'Makaisson is obsessed with slaying the dragon. He gets like that. He has locked himself up in his workshop and is building weapons to kill the beast. He refuses food and drink, and only came to see the repairs being done yesterday because I banged on his door for an hour.'

Felix looked at him. 'Do you think even Makaisson can come up with something that will destroy Skjalandir?'

Borek shrugged. 'If anyone can, he can. He is a genius. In a dozen centuries the dwarf realms have not cast up an engineer as brilliant as he.'

'A pity then that he has become a Slayer.'

'Aye; he might have changed the world otherwise. If his theories had been accepted. If the Engineers Guild had not hounded him. As it is, his name will go down in history anyway. Creating this airship was a deed worthy of the Ancestors. Piloting it to Karag Dum means his name will live forever, even if he does not.'

'Was the deed really so notable?'

'More than you can imagine. Your name will live as long as the mountains too, Felix Jaeger. Your part in the slaying of the daemon, and the recovery of the Hammer of Firebeard will see to that.'

Felix found this a strange thought. He was not sure how he felt about the knowledge that his name would be recalled in centuries to come, in a time long after he was dead. He did not want to think of dying just yet. It was not a thought he found pleasant.

'Where is the hammer now?'

'It is in the shrine of Grimnir. Hurgrim has left it there for the time being.'

A thought struck Felix. Curiosity overcame him.

'One day I would like to see the inside of the shrine.'

'It is not usual for humans to be allowed to view the inside of Grimnir's sanctum.' Borek paused for a moment. 'But you are the Hammerbearer, and the gods have looked on you with favour, so I suppose an exception could be made in your case.'

'I would like that,' said Felix. If he ever was going to write up the tale of Gotrek's adventures, it might be important. Perhaps seeing the inside of the shrine would give him some insight into the dwarf personality.

'Thank you,' Felix said. 'I will go now.'

'May the Ancestor Gods watch over you, Felix Jaeger.'

'And you,' Felix said, striding away.

GREY SEER THANQUOL watched the dust cloud come ever closer. It billowed to the sky. It was as if all the grass of the plain had caught fire and was sending smoke plumes skyward. The ground vibrated. He could feel the thunder of hundreds of hooves against the earth. His nose twitched. He could smell warpstone in small quantities, and cold steel and flesh, human-like and yet not human. His mystical senses told him that powerful magic was present. He and Lurk exchanged scared looks, animosity temporarily fading as they confronted a threat to their common well-being.

Almost. Thanquol briefly considered running and leaving Lurk to face whatever it was that rushed towards them. What held him in place was the knowledge that it would probably be pointless. Instinct told him that there were so many foes coming towards them, that a few of them could overcome Lurk, and others would still have time to seek him out. Being with Lurk at least offered the possibility of some protection. At moments of stress like these, when the urge to squirt the musk of fear filled him, the scent of another ratman reassured even a skaven as independent as Grey Seer Thanquol.

'Horse warriors, most perceptive of potentates?' rumbled Lurk.

Thanquol shook his horned head and bared his fangs. His mouth felt dry. His heart pounded within his chest. He fought the urge to begin stuffing the last of the powdered warpstone into his mouth.

'No. Others. Not humans.'

'From the north? From the Wastes?'

'Yes! Yes! Black-armoured warriors. Altered beasts. Other things.'

'You have seen this? The Horned Rat has granted you a vision?'

Not in the strictest sense, Thanquol thought, but it served no purpose to let Lurk know, so he maintained a significant silence as he peered into the cloud. The dust made his pink eyes water and his nose twitch. His musk glands felt tight and he lashed his tail to try and dispel the tension. Lurk let out a low threatening growl. Thanquol glared into the advancing dust cloud trying to see into it.

Forms moved within the cloud. Massive, dark shapes that emerged slowly from the gloom and resolved themselves into riders. Thanquol had seen many of the mounted warriors the foolish humans called knights when he had served the Council of Thirteen in Bretonnia. The horsemen reminded him of those, save that their armour was made all of black iron with brass rondels. It was more intricate than any human armour Thanquol had ever seen before. Daemonic faces, twisted runes, arcane symbols: all seemed to have been moulded into the steel by some sorcerous technique.

One warrior had a gaping mawed daemonic face set in his chest plate. His helm echoed the daemon's features and glowing red eyes glared out from behind his visor. Another wore armour covered in monstrous spikes and clutched a similarly spiked mace, shaped like a shrieking human head, in one armoured fist. A third's armour glowed with an eerie yellow light, pulsing softly as if in time to his heartbeat. Behind them came other riders garbed in armour just as fantastically elaborate.

Their weapons were also of black steel set with fiery runes. They carried swords and maces, lances and morning stars. Their shields showed the symbol of Tzeentch, the Great Mutator, one of the four Ruinous Powers. The horses were huge, far bigger than normal human steeds. They needed to be to carry their massive armoured riders, and the weight of the impossibly intricate, segmented barding. Like their riders, the steeds' eyes glowed with baleful internal fires. It was as if the gates of Hell had opened and these awful spectres had ridden straight out.

The Chaos warriors were a terrifying sight, and what was even more frightening was the fact that Thanquol knew they were but the outriders of a vast horde. What had those fiends, Felix Jaeger and Gotrek Gurnisson done, Thanquol wondered? He did not doubt for a moment that the onset of this monstrous army was somehow connected with their mission into the Chaos Wastes. It was just like them to stir up a hornets' nest of malefic forces and then run, leaving others in the path. May the Horned Rat devour their souls, Thanquol cursed.

With a terrified howl, Lurk threw himself headlong on the ground and abased himself. Thanquol cursed him too, and fought the urge to repeat Lurk's action himself. His mind raced. If he prostrated himself before these bloodthirsty madmen, they would most likely simply ride over him, trampling the greatest skaven mind of this age into a bloody husk. Thanquol knew that would never do. He needed to keep all his wits about him if he wanted to survive.

Dramatically he threw his arms wide and let a nimbus of power play around his claws. The leading horse reared but its rider kept it under control and dropped his weapon into the attack position. Thanquol desperately controlled his musk glands as they sought to void themselves. He raised his chin high and let them see his horned head, his white fur, his magnificent lashing tail. He felt his power surge within him, and knew that if worst came to the worst he would take a few of these Tzeentch worshippers with him to greet the Horned Rat in the Thirteenth Level of the Abyss.

'Halt!' he shouted in the common tongue of humans in his most impressive oracular voice. 'I bring you greetings from the Council of Thirteen, lordly rulers of all skavendom.'

If the Chaos warriors were impressed, they gave no sign of it. Instead, one of them touched spurs to the flanks of his mount, dropped his lance and thundered forward, obviously intent on skewering the grey seer.

Everything seemed to slow as the armoured warrior advanced. The spearpoint looked very sharp. Thanquol wondered if his last moment had come.

'Wait! Wait!' shrieked Grey Seer Thanquol. 'Don't kill me. You are making a grave error. I bring tidings from the Council of Thirteen. They wish to make obeisance to your all-conquering army!'

Thanquol thought his doom was upon him. He summoned his power to attempt the escape spell that would cast him across the warp. He was not sure he had the time or the energy, but it seemed like his only slim hope. The glittering lance point came ever closer. It looked sharp as Felix Jaeger's sword and ten times as deadly. Just before it pierced his body, the lancer raised his weapon and let out a bellow of mocking malevolent laughter.

'You wish to ally with us?'

'Yes! Yes!'

'Or you wish to surrender to us?'

'Yes! Yes!'

'Which is it? Or is it both?'

'Both!' Thanquol had squirted the musk of fear, but it did not matter right now. What was important was that he preserve his life and his genius for the benefit of the skaven nation. Once he had gotten through the next few difficult moments, he would go about the business of turning the tables on these arrogant dullards. At the moment though preserving his skin took the highest priority.

'Why should we spare you?'

'We have mighty armies! We can aid you in crushing mankind! We have knowledge of the human cities and human dispositions! We know many things!'

'Perhaps you could spare this mutant's life and keep it as a jester!' roared the creature with the daemon's face on its breast-plate. Thanquol forced himself to bob his head in an appeasing manner, although inwardly he seethed and swore vengeance on the speaker as soon as the moment was right. If there was as much warpstone nearby as he suspected that moment would come soon.

'Or maybe we should nail it to our banners as a warning to the rest of its kind. I have met skaven before. I have fought with them. A nasty treacherous bunch they were too.'

'Doubtless they were renegades,' said Thanquol thinking quickly. 'True skaven always keep faith with their allies.'

'That's a good joke,' said daemon face. 'You shall be our jester!'

'This one is a grey seer,' said a Chaos warrior carrying a massive banner depicting a flayed human brandishing a sword. 'It is possible that it does speak for the Thirteen.'

'So?'

'Perhaps we should spare it! Perhaps the warlord or his pet sorcerers should interrogate it!'

Listen to this one, Thanquol prayed. He shows common sense. And doubtless the horde's leader would have the wisdom to negotiate with a grey seer.

'And we can always offer his soul to Tzeentch afterwards. The seers are said to be magicians and our mighty lord might appreciate such a tasty morsel!'

What have I let myself in for, Grey Seer Thanquol asked himself? Perhaps he should have tried the escape spell but before he knew it, the lancer had stopped, snatched him up and thrown him across his saddle like a sack of wheat. The others had surrounded Lurk and were herding him forwards with their weapons.

In heartbeats they were on their way into the heart of the oncoming Chaos horde. Thanquol's heart raced with fear, and his empty musk-glands hurt from the strain of trying to squirt. It was not a reassuring feeling.

FELIX ENTERED THE inner sanctum of the Temple of Grimnir. His fame had obviously proceeded him. The priests had made no fuss about letting him in. They had simply seemed surprised that any man should want to enter the place. It was dark and gloomy in here after the huge fire that burned bright in the entrance hall, and it took his eyes a few moments to adjust to the dimness.

The enormously thick stone walls muffled all sound. The air smelled of incense and the acrid odour of burned hair. This inner sanctum was empty save for a few old dwarfs in plain robes of red. They carried no weapons; their beards were long and bound with clips that showed the sign of two crossed axes. They seemed to do little else but pray and tend the enormous fire that burned constantly in a pit in the antechamber.

Felix looked around. The ceiling would be considered low in a human temple but it was still three times his own height. Enormous stone sarcophagi lined the walls. Each was as tall as a man and carved to represent a dwarf lying flat on his back, a weapon clutched to his chest. These were the tombs of the Slayer Kings, Felix knew. For many generations the royal family of Karak Kadrin had been buried here.

The centre of the room was dominated by a massive altar over which loomed a statue of a mighty dwarf warrior with an axe held in each hand, standing with his foot on the neck of a dragon. The figure depicted was recognisably a Slayer. His beard was short. A massive crest towered over his head. A dwarf knelt before the altar, murmuring quiet prayers.

On the altar rested the Hammer of Firebeard. Just looking at it, Felix felt a spasm of pain pass through his fingers. He could still remember carrying it into battle against the great Bloodthirster of Karag Dum. Mortal man had not been meant to wield such a weapon, and he paid the price for it in agony.

Sometimes, in the still small hours of the night, he wondered about this. Why, of all the men in the world, had the hammer allowed him to wield it? He was no hero. He had not even wanted to be there in Karag Dum, and he could have lived his entire life quite happily without ever seeing a Great Daemon of Chaos, let alone fighting one.

The Slayer rose to his feet and turned from the altar abruptly, not in the way a man would leave a shrine sacred to his god, but in the manner of a warrior who had been given a command by his general and goes at once to carry it out. As he passed, he looked at Felix. His face showed no surprise at seeing a human there in one of the most sacred sites of his people. Looking at him, Felix thought the dwarf possessed the bleakest eyes he had ever seen. His face might have been chiselled from granite. His features had a primitive massiveness to them of the sort sometimes seen in ancient druidical statues. His head had been recently shaved, save for a tiny strip of hair that might one day grow into a crest. His beard had been reduced to mere stubble.

Felix made the sign of the hammer and advanced on the altar. There was no particular sign of the presence of the dwarf god. The altar was a massive structure carved of solid stone. The hammer appeared to be just a massive warhammer whose head bore the same dwarf runes as the altar itself. Had Felix himself not held the hammer and felt its power, he would have thought it only an impressive weapon and not some holy relic.

Once again, he asked himself why he was here. What had he hoped to gain by visiting the shrine? Some insight into the dwarfs, perhaps? A glimpse of the peculiar psychology that caused so many of them to shave their heads and set out to seek their dooms? It was a hard thing for him to understand, and he could not quite picture himself or any other man doing such a thing.

Or perhaps he could. Men did self-destructive things all the time. They drank to excess and performed feats of foolish bravado. They became addicted to witchweed and weirdroot. They joined the cults of the dark gods of Chaos. They fought duels for the most petty and pointless of reasons. Felix sometimes recognised a perverse and self-destructive urge in himself. Perhaps dwarfs just possessed this to a greater degree, and, in typical dwarf fashion, formalised it more. Perhaps here he might look upon their god and understand why they did this.

He advanced to the front of the altar and knelt at the foot of the statue. The statue itself showed all the dwarf genius for stonework. It was carved to a level of detail that no human sculptor would have the patience or the skill to master. Borek had told him that this statue had been laboured over by five generations of master craftsmen, almost a thousand years as humans reckoned time.

Felix inspected it closely, as if it held the key to some great mystery, as if by studying it he might come to understand what drove Slayers to do what they did. If the statue knew the answer to his questions, it kept an obstinate silence about it. Felix smiled sadly, thinking there was nothing here but old stonework. If these walls were permeated with the essence of millennia of sacrifice, as the dwarfs claimed, Felix could get no sense of it. What had he expected? He was a human, and the dwarf gods showed little enough interest in their own race, so why should they pay any attention to him?

Still, he was in a holy place, and it would do no harm to risk a prayer while he was here. He could think of nothing to ask for, save that the old god grant Gotrek the brave doom he sought, and keep Felix alive to record it. For a moment, as his hands instinctively made the sign of the hammer, Felix thought he sensed something. A deepening of the silence in the place, a keenness coming over his senses, a sense of the presence of something ancient, vast and potent. He gazed up on the blank features of Grimnir once more but they were unchanged. The stern but empty eye sockets in the helm still looked out on the world without pity or understanding.

Felix shook his head. Perhaps it all had been in his imagination. Best mention this to no one. He rose to his feet and almost reached out to touch the hammer for one last time, but as he did so his fingers began to tingle and he remembered all too vividly the pain of bearing the weapon. Perhaps that was the sign he waited for, he thought sourly. Or perhaps it was simply given to a man like him to bear a weapon like that only once in his life, and only for the mightiest of purposes. He did not know.

It made him think of his strange experience with the sword and the dragon. He had wanted to talk Max about it, but things had been touchy between himself and the magician. He suspected they were both jealous of each other over Ulrika. Felix resolved that when the opportunity arose he would discuss it.

He did not look back as he left the shrine and stepped out into the street. It was time to get back to the palace. He knew they would be leaving the city soon.

EIGHT

INTO THE MOUNTAINS

FELIX MARCHED WEARILY along the mountain path. His chainmail shirt felt heavy and strange, now that he was wearing it again for the first time in days. He was glad to have it though. There were orcs in these mountains and he wanted all the protection he could get.

Ahead of him were Oleg and Standa. They flanked Ulrika, who was conspicuously ignoring him. She had accepted his apology for his drunkenness but now she was sulking again. Well, at least she had decided to come with him as far as the turn-off to Urskoy. All of the Kislevites wore leather armour and carried bows. They scanned the mountainside warily even though Peak Pass was supposedly safe territory. He guessed that just being in the mountains made them nervous. Their homes were the flat plains of Kislev, after all, and they were more used to being on horseback than afoot.

Walking just behind them, leaning on a heavy oaken staff, was Max Schreiber. Max looked a dapper figure in the new robes of golden and yellow brocade he'd had tailored back in the city. He looked ill at ease here, and kept studying the path as if expecting an ambush any moment. Felix understood his fear all too well. The rumours back in Karak Kadrin spoke not only of the dragon but of orcs and goblins in the mountains. Felix had fought greenskins before and did not relish the prospect of another encounter with them.

He cast a glance back over his shoulder for reassurance. He was astonished to see that they had gathered companions as they had left the city. Four new Slayers had joined the party. Steg had joined them, as he had said he would back in the Iron Door. He had been lurking at the main gate of Karak Kadrin as they left. Ulli, the boastful young Slayer, had fallen in step with them a few hundred strides along the road. A repulsively ugly dwarf called Bjorni Bjornisson had greeted Ulrika with a knowing leer and begged permission to join them. When no one had answered he seemed to take it for granted and tagged along. Half a league later they had overtaken the hammer-wielding dwarf Felix had seen in the Temple of Grimnir. He seemed to know who they were and lengthened his stride to keep up.

Gotrek strode along, scowling grimly. His axe was slung over his shoulder and he appeared to be doing his best to ignore his comrades. Snorri Nosebiter chuckled as Bjorni Bjornisson bawled out the ninety-seventh verse of some bawdy song which involved a Slayer, a troll and a convent full of Shallyite nuns among other things. Bjorni was singing in the common tongue so they might all have the benefit of his humour. Felix was astonished by the imagination he showed. He doubted that half the things the Slayer sang were even physically possible.

Behind them rode Malakai. He drove a cart full of mysterious equipment which he refused to let anybody see. As the cart bounced along the rutted road, Felix could hear the clatter of metal on metal, so he knew that the engineer's days at the forge had produced something, though he had no idea what. Every so often the dwarf flexed the reins and the two small pit ponies pulled the heavy cart a little harder.

Felix smiled sourly. It was his suggestion that the Kislevites should try riding the ponies, the only horseflesh available in the city of the Slayer King, that had put him in the doghouse with Ulrika this time. She had not wanted to see the joke. He guessed that she was already embarrassed enough by having to accompany the Slayers after all, and his comment had been all that it took to goad her to fury. This insight had come rather too late to do him any good.

Behind the wagon came Steg, who Felix occasionally saw sneaking peeks at the wagon whenever they stopped. It was only the presence of the last two Slayers, Ulli and the silent newcomer, that kept him from investigating. Felix did not know which was worse, Bjorni's singing or Ulli's incessant boasting. At least the last dwarf, the nameless one, was quiet. There was that to be thankful for.

He supposed there were other things to be grateful for as well. It was a beautiful day. The mountain air was fresh and pure. The sky was clear and blue with not a cloud in sight. Mountain flowers bloomed along the side of the pass. Had it not been for their eventual destination Felix might almost have enjoyed the walk. In his career as Gotrek's henchman he had been in far less prepossessing places.

Here the Peak Pass was wide and easy to travel. It descended into the plains of the eastern Empire and joined the trade road through the province of Osterland. The path was wide and paved with cracked flagstones that testified to the length of time dwarfs had been using the route. Felix would have liked to follow this path back down into the lands of men, but his oath to follow Gotrek and his desire to be with Ulrika compelled him to do otherwise.

Soon they would turn northwards to take the Old High Road to Karak Ungor, into the valleys haunted by the dragon and by man-hating orcs. He did his best to forget this and concentrate on his surroundings. Copses of pine trees darkened the mountain sides. Smoke rose from where dwarf charcoal burners were at work. Here and there along higher trails herds of goats and sheep were watched over by dwarf shepherds. It was a wonder to Felix to see members of the Elder Race engaged in such mundane professions.

He always thought of them as Slayers and engineers and diggers of tunnels. To him, as to most men, dwarfs were miners, dwellers in deep tunnels, makers of fine weapons. It was hard now, despite the evidence of his own eyes, to dispel that image. Still, he supposed like everyone else, the Elder Race had to eat, and there certainly were dwarf brewers, butchers and bakers. He had seen evidence of this with his own eyes back in Karak Kadrin. He supposed his own experience with dwarfs had up till now been limited to the more exotic types the mountain people produced: Slayers, scholars, engineers, priests. He had never visited a fully functioning dwarf city, only the tiny colony that dwelled amid the ruins of Karag Eight Peaks, and the enormous desolate labyrinth of Karag Dum. The huge industrial complex at the Lonely Tower that had produced the *Spirit of Grungni* was far from typical, he knew. It was a secret kept even from the majority of the Elder Race.

He flexed his shoulders to settle his pack more comfortably. He had considered asking Malakai if he could put it on the cart, but had decided against it for two reasons. The Slayer engineer was touchy enough at the moment, and he wanted to have all his stuff on him if for some reason he got separated from the rest of the party. He had learned enough in his years of adventuring to be prepared for the worst.

He shook his head, realising that he was simply trying to distract himself from thinking about Ulrika. He knew that if she was being unreasonable, he was too, and he was damned if he could find any reason for it. He just seemed unduly sensitive to her behaviour. It was as if everything she did had a magnified effect on it. What, in any other human being, he would have dismissed as a minor foible, somehow became in her a major flaw. Words, which from anyone else would have been simply a joke, became subtle insults and putdowns, to be brooded over and analysed in depth. The fact that Max was walking closer to her than he was became a threat, and made him unreasonably jealous. Part of him knew that this undue sensitivity was because he was in love, and that perhaps her odd behaviour came about for a similar reason. But part of him went ahead and acted on his own unreasonable impulses anyway. This was something the love poets never mentioned, and he felt annoyed by it. Perhaps it meant that he was not really in love with her after all.

Or perhaps the love poets simplified things, to make them neater and to turn them into better stories. And perhaps they were not being dishonest either. Memory played tricks. He remembered his first love Kirsten fondly, had forgotten most of the bad things about their relationship and idolised the good ones. Yet he knew that he and Kirsten had had bad days, and had argued and had simply not wanted to talk to each other. It was only human. And he had cared about her in spite of the bad things that sometimes happened between them. Sometimes he suspected it was easier and more pleasant to live with the memories of a past love than it was to be involved in a new one. After all, he could edit his memories the way he had once edited his poems, selecting the good parts, polishing them till they shone. Reality always had flaws. Bellies rumbled when you made love. Words that should be spoken sometimes never are. Real people were contradictory, annoying and sometimes selfish. Just like he was, he reminded himself.

He knew that Ulrika was being unreasonable. He knew that he was in the right. He knew that he should wait for her to come and apologise. His pride demanded it, and so did this strange near subliminal anger. Yet somehow he found his legs carrying himself forward to her side, and his lips murmuring an apology, and his hand reaching out to take hers and squeeze her fingers.

And just as strangely as everything else, he found that this made him, if not happy, at least content.

THE CAMP FIRE burned. Felix helped himself to another slice of waybread and spiced dwarf sausage. He looked across at Ulrika and smiled. She smiled back. They had made their peace that day, at least for a little while. Max Schreiber was a shadowy form on the far side of the flames. He sat cross-legged on the ground, breathing deeply, seemingly engaged in some mystical exercise. Felix did not know why but he felt certain that despite the fact he appeared to be asleep Max was well aware of all that went on around him. Oleg and Standa kept guard a few paces off, facing out into the darkness so as not to ruin their night vision. Feeling the wine he had drunk earlier go right to his bladder, Felix excused himself and got up to make water.

On his return he paused to observe the dwarfs for a moment. Makaisson sat glaring into the flames, while his fingers toyed idly with the innards of some small clockwork device. Beside the engineer sat Bjorni, Ulli and the silent dwarf. As Felix passed Bjorni summoned up the courage to do what Felix had wanted to do all day.

'What's your name?' he asked the stranger.

'Grimme,' answered the newcomer, and his tone and his features were more than enough to prevent any further questions. Bjorni decided that this just made him a better audience.

'Well, Grimme, you might have heard stories about me and the three elf maidens. It's not true. Well not entirely true. There were only two of them, and only one was elven, well half-elven actually, and I didn't find that out till later, though the pointy ears should have been a giveaway but she was wearing a head scarf you see. And I was drunk, and all cats are grey in the dark and...'

If Grimme heard he gave no sign. He simply continued to stare morosely into the fire. Felix tried to tune Bjorni out. He and Ulli seemed to have become soul mates. They at least provided each other with an audience for their endless boasting. Bjorni had an interminable source of anecdotes about his love life. Ulli talked of nothing except the fights he had been in, and the battles he was going to win.

'...and then I said, bring me a donkey,' Bjorni said. 'You should have seen the look on her face...'

Felix glanced over at the other Slayers to see how they were taking it. Grimme simply glared bleakly into the fire, lost in some inner world of misery and torment. Felix wanted to talk to him but he knew his attentions would not be welcome.

Steg sat beneath the wagon, whittling a piece of wood with his knife, seemingly unaware of the casual glances Makaisson directed at him occasionally. Beyond the wagon, Snorri Nosebiter and Gotrek kept watch. Felix walked over to see how it was going.

'There is a stranger coming,' said Snorri Nosebiter. 'Snorri can smell him.'

Gotrek grunted. 'I have known that for the last five minutes. It is a dwarf that comes and one we'll soon be having words with.'

Felix knew better than to question Gotrek or ask how he knew what he did. Over the years he had developed a tremendous respect for the keenness of the Slayer's senses. In the dark and wild places of the world, the dwarf was at home in a way a man could never be.

Felix glanced over in the direction Gotrek indicated with a jerk of his thumb. There was something moving out there. In the light of the two moons Felix could see two shadowy outlines. As they came closer, he could hear the clip-clop of hooves on stone.

As the stranger approached Felix saw that it was a dwarf leading a mule.

'Greetings, strangers,' he said. 'Can an old prospector share your fire?'

'Aye, you can,' Gotrek said. 'If you tell us your name.'

'I am Malgrim, son of Hurni, of clan Magrest. Who might you be?'

'I am Gotrek, son of Gurni.'

'Snorri Nosebiter.'

The prospector was within sword's reach now. Felix could see he was a typical dwarf, short but broad. He wore some sort of hooded jerkin which covered his head, and his long beard reached almost to his knees. He had a pickaxe in one hand, and by the way he held it Felix guessed he was proficient at using it as a weapon. There was a shovel slung over the pack on the mule's back, along with the sort of mesh pans prospectors used to filter gold from river water. The dwarf's face was seamed and his eyes were wary. They went a trifle wider when he saw that Gotrek and Snorri were Slayers, and wider still when he saw that Felix was a human.

'Two Slayers travelling with a man of the Empire,' he said. 'I am sure there is a tale there.'

Felix accompanied the dwarfs back to the fire. Malgrim looked at the five Slayers and then at Gotrek and Snorri. 'I had not heard the kinfolk mustered for war,' he said. 'No battle-banners have passed among the mountain clans.'

'There is no mustering,' Gotrek said and slumped down beside the fire.

Felix realised that Malgrim thought the only reason so many Slayers could have assembled was to answer a call to battle.

'A pity,' said Malgrim, 'for there is great need. The orcs of the mountains assemble for battle. Ugrek Manflayer has organised all the tribes under his banner.'

Felix shivered. Even in distant Altdorf, he had heard tales of the Manflayer. His name was used to terrify naughty children. He was said to be a gigantic orc who skinned his captives alive and used their hides to make his clothing. Felix had always considered the tale merely a legend, but the prospector sounded convinced of his existence, and he did not seem like a dwarf who merely recounted traveller's tales for the sake of it.

To Felix's surprise it was Max Schreiber who spoke next. 'There are tales of a greenskin shaman in the mountains. He is said to have powerful magic. I heard he too follows the Manflayer.'

'Well, if they get in our way, we'll show them what their innards look like!' bellowed Ulli. 'We are on our way to slay the dragon Skjalandir.'

The prospector glanced around him and slowly nodded his head, as if understanding were dawning. 'I had wondered what would bring seven Slayers into the mountains when no battle-banners fly. It is a mighty death indeed that you seek for the dragon will give you one. Since his reawakening he has scoured the High Valleys and made of the Manling Vales a desolation. Still, I wonder if you will even catch sight of him for the greenskins are numerous and there are human bandits in the hills too.'

'Things are grim in the mountains,' Felix said. If Malgrim heard the irony in his voice he gave no sign.

'Aye. There were always wild hill men but they have been joined by desperate folk driven from their farms by the depredations of the orcs and the firedrake. Life is short and cheap in the heights right now. Even more so than usual.'

'Why does Ungrimm Ironfist not gather his army and restore the peace?' said Felix.

Malgrim's laughter was joined by the other dwarfs. 'It is Ungrimm's duty to keep Peak Pass clear, and prevent the orc hordes of the east from passing through into the lands of men. If he was to desert this vale with his force and the greenskins got word of it, then an orc horde would soon be rampaging through your Empire's eastern provinces.'

'Why is that important to the dwarfs? Why should they care whether Osterland is invaded?'

Malgrim looked shocked. 'There are binding oaths and treaties of friendship between our peoples. Humans may forget the old ties, but the kinfolk do not. As our ancestors swore so shall we do.'

'Aye, tis so!' bellowed Ulli.

'Also,' Malgrim added, 'this pass is ours. We will not allow the greenskins free passage through it.'

Felix could see that all of this was simply a long-winded way of saying that the dwarfs would not send forces to clear out the High Peak Road. As he considered the prospector's words another thought struck him. If the Elder Race felt this way, why would they even consider sending troops to aid the Kislevites? Simple reflection gave him the answer. The threat of Chaos was of an order of magnitude greater than mere greenskin tribes raiding into human and dwarf lands. If the northlands fell before the onslaught of the hordes then all the southlands would fall soon afterwards. At least, he hoped the dwarfs thought this way. There was little hope of help if they did not.

'I say we stop and slaughter some greenskins on our way to face the dragon!' said Ulli.

'You can if ye want tae,' Makaisson said. 'Ah hae business wae that big beastie and it wullnae wait.'

'The greenskins will still be there after the dragon is dealt with. That's if any of us are alive to care,' Bjorni said.

'If any orcs get in our way we will kill them,' Gotrek said. 'Otherwise we go to kill the dragon.'

'Snorri thinks that's a fine plan,' said Snorri Nosebiter, then added wistfully, 'still, Snorri wouldn't mind slaughtering a few greenies.'

'It's late,' Gotrek said. 'Those who aren't on guard should get some sleep.'

The prospector nodded and laid himself down by the fire. Felix returned to where Ulrika and the other humans were sitting.

'What was that all about?' Ulrika asked.

'The Slayers can't decide whether we should cleanse the mountains of orcs or dragons first.'

'Why not do both?' asked Oleg ironically.

'Hush!' Felix said. 'They might hear you.'

ALL AROUND great bonfires blazed. From nearby Thanquol could hear the disquieting roars of beastmen and the thunder of huge drums. He could smell tens of thousands of beastmen nearby and thousands of the black armoured Chaos warriors. He knew then that he was in the encampment of the largest army he had encountered since he himself had commanded the massive skaven force that attacked Nuln. He also suspected that in terms of sheer raw power this monstrous force completely outclassed even that mighty skaven horde. He knew enough of the followers of Chaos to understand that one for one they were more than a match for all but the most puissant of skaven.

All around he could smell warpstone, and his magician's senses told him that the winds of magic blew strong around this army. It was worrying, for he knew that this force possessed not only mere physical might, but a terrible magical potency as well. He knew that even at the peak of his powers he would be hard pressed to overcome the sorcerers gathered here, and he was far from the unassailable height of his awesome abilities.

He could tell just from the flow of energies around him that his captors were approaching the heart of the horde, the nexus around which all this energy flowed. As they came closer he sensed the presence of mighty beings, creatures of a potency he had not encountered since he stood before the Council of Thirteen themselves.

At the heart of the camp was a great gathering of armoured Chaos warriors. Their steeds roamed nearby as the masters squatted beside camp fires that burned yellow and green and other colours that spoke of magical origin. They talked to each other in their debased tongue and Thanquol could tell just from their tone that they were boasting of conquests to come. Just looking at them filled his heart with fear and tightened his musk glands. He glanced around, suddenly grateful that Lurk was there. The presence of another skaven was somehow reassuring even to Grey Seer Thanquol in the centre of this awful force.

Ahead of them, he was sure they would find the war leaders of the horde. He sensed their presence before he saw them, and when they came into view he knew his impressions were correct.

A huge armoured figure lounged in a massive throne of crystal that pulsed with subdued yellows and greens. The throne floated a fingerbreadth over the ground. Using his sorcerer's senses Thanquol could see that both the man and his seat were permeated with the energies of Chaos. Across his knees was a massive two-handed broadsword covered in yellowish glowing runes. Thanquol did not have to be told that the weapon was enwrapped with the mightiest of killing magics. He could see this for himself, just as he could see that the armour was designed to act not merely as a shield against weapons but against sorcery too. The man's armour was golden with greenish rondels and inscribed with runes that Thanquol knew were sacred to Tzeentch.

Flanking the throne were two figures. They were lean and vulturish, unarmoured and swathed in huge cloaks whose folds gave them a resemblance to wings. Their skin had an albino whiteness that was close to the grey seer's own. Looking closely at their thin, hungry features and hellishly glowing eyes Thanquol could see that they were twins, identical in all ways except one. The one on the general's right hand side held a gold sheathed staff in his right hand. The one on the left held a staff of ebony and silver in his left hand. The hand which held the gold-sheathed staff had long talon-like nails of gold. The talons of the left-hand wizard were encased in silver. That the two were potent sorcerers was immediately obvious to Thanquol. Unwilling as he was to concede that any save the Council of Thirteen might be stronger than he in the use of magic, he knew that he would need to consume prodigious amounts of warpstone to overcome either one of these two in sorcerous battle. If they worked together, he feared to consider the powers they might wield.

The Chaos warlord glared balefully down at Thanquol. The grey seer at once prostrated himself, and said, 'I bring greetings, mighty warlord, from the Council of Thirteen.'

'Your masters knew of our coming then, grey seer?' said the warlord. Thanquol thought it better to lie than to admit the truth. He sensed tendrils of mystical energy coming from the two wizards who flanked the warlord. Immediately he masked his thoughts as best he could. Since he was a grey seer, he knew this was very well indeed.

'They sensed a mighty gathering of forces and sent me northwards to investigate.'

Well, it could almost be true, thought Thanquol. 'Alone and unaccompanied. That is most unusual,' said the magus with the gold staff.

'I am accompanied by my bodyguard, Lurk Snitchtongue, and protected by my own mighty magic. What need have I of any other protection?' Thanquol said, a hint of his old arrogance returning.

'What need indeed,' said the sorcerer with the ebony staff. Thanquol noticed the hint of mockery in his voice and vowed that one day he would make the magician pay for it. How dare this hairless ape make light of the greatest sorcerer in skavendom. 'Tis true your bodyguard shows signs of the blessings of our lord Tzeentch. The Great Mutator has touched him. He has the favour of the Changer of the Ways.'

Thanquol glared over at Lurk, who preened himself visibly at these words. Black rage ate at the grey seer's bowels. Thanquol wondered if Lurk had been consorting with the followers of the Chaos Powers while he was in the Wastes. That would explain the changes in him, for sure. If this were the case he would be made to pay for his apostasy to the Horned Rat. Another score to settle, Thanquol told himself. Assuming he survived this encounter, which at the moment looked by no means certain.

'You lead this great host?' Thanquol asked, out of politeness.

'I am Arek Demonheart,' said the Chaos warrior, 'Chosen of Tzeentch. These are Kelmain Blackstaff and Loigor Goldenrod, my spellcrafters.'

'I thank you for this information, mighty one,' Thanquol said diplomatically. 'I am Grey Seer Thanquol and I abase myself a thousand times before you and offer you the alliance of the Council of Thirteen.'

Thanquol knew he was being a little premature here but he was determined to say anything he needed to get himself out of this trap. 'We have no need of alliances, Grey Seer Thanquol. What you see here is but the vanguard of a greater host. The Powers march forth to claim the lands of men once more. Those who do not abase themselves before the Powers of Ruin, and most especially my master Tzeentch, will be destroyed. This world will be cleansed and remade in the image we desire and all the false gods and their followers will be swept away.'

There was something in Arek's voice that compelled belief. His words almost convinced even Thanquol, but the grey seer was too wily a sorcerer and too well schooled in the ways of magic not to recognise a potent spell when he encountered one. He dismissed the hypnotic compulsion in the voice by an effort of will. A glance at Lurk told him that his henchman was making no such effort. He looked at Arek enthralled.

Thanquol could understand why. Lurk was ensnared by the Gift of Tzeentch the warlord was using, and his feeble mind was enthralled by the dark visions of conquest that hovered behind the Chaos warrior's words. He had even raised his head from the dirt the better to hear them. The two sorcerers looked down at him with mocking interest. Thanquol concentrated on matters at hand, deciding he had best find out what was going on, while his enemies seemed in the mood to answer his questions.

'All four of the Powers march then?'

'Aye. Tis the way. When one makes a move, the others must respond, lest they lose some advantage.'

That made sense to a skaven as astute as Thanquol. It was exactly the way the clans of his own race manoeuvred back in Skavenblight. He sensed that he was beginning to understand what was happening here, and might even be able to use it to his advantage. Perhaps he could even see the reason why these Chaos worshippers had spared him.

'There are advantages to be gained in alliances,' he said. 'My own god is mighty and has great powers. My people possess vast armies.'

'Your god is weaker than ours, Grey Seer Thanquol, but his aid might prove useful. Your armies might join our own in time. Certainly, we are the only ones who will make this offer. The followers of Khorne are too brutish. The followers of Nurgle care only for the spreading of their foul plagues, and the followers of Slaanesh are too wrapped up in their own pursuit of pleasure to consider aught but that.'

'I will convey your words to the Council of Thirteen and explain all that you have said to them.' Thanquol mouthed the empty words expertly, still worrying about what had been done to Lurk.

'See that you do, Grey Seer Thanquol, and your rewards will be great.'

'I thank you mighty warlord.' Suddenly a thought struck Thanquol. He doubted that his request would be granted but he could see no harm in asking. 'I sense the substance known as warpstone is carried by your army.'

'It is one of our master's greatest gifts and is used in sorcery and in the making of weapons.'

'We too use it for such purposes, which I take as a sign of our common purpose,' said Thanquol, pleased with his own eloquence.

'Do you wish some?' asked the sorcerer with the golden staff. Thanquol could not quite believe his luck. He licked his lips greedily.

'Yes-yes!' he said.

'Then you shall have it.' The sorcerer flexed his fingers and the air in front of him glowed. Particles of greenish dust flowed together forming a ball the size of Thanquol's fist. With another gesture the mage sent it spinning towards the grey seer. Thanquol knew instantly what it was, and snatched it out of the air. His paw tingled as he closed it around a sphere of the purest warpstone he had ever encountered. Hastily he pushed it into his pouch. He could not believe the fools had just handed him the key to so much power. Some inner instinct, which he had long ago learned to trust, told him to be careful. Perhaps all of this was merely a trap. Still, he could not quite see what the Chaos worshippers had to gain. He was already in their power.

'An enclave of your kind is near,' Arek said. 'The place called Hell Pit. I will instruct my riders to escort you there. See that you bear our words to your rulers, Grey Seer Thanquol, and speak fairly of us.'

'Rest assured I will,' Thanquol said, offering up a silent prayer to the Horned Rat thanking him for his deliverance. It looked like he and Lurk were going to get away from the horde with their lives.

The suspicious part of him, which had kept him alive so long, told him that it wasn't going to be quite that easy.

FELIX WATCHED AS Malgrim rolled up his blankets and placed them in the pack on the mule's back. The dwarf looked at them and then shook his head.

'I'd tell you all to be careful, but it would be daft to say that to seven Slayers and a rememberer, so I'll just thank you for the use of your fire, your food and your company.'

'Have you any news of the road ahead?' Felix asked.

'Aye,' said the prospector. 'About a day's march ahead, you'll find the village of Gelt. It's an odd place, a meeting place for prospectors, and a trading post for the mountain-folk. There's a deep mine there still. And an inn. I suggest you take advantage of it, for you'll be seeing the last friendly faces you're going to see for a while.'

Malgrim paused and considered his next words. 'That's if the orcs haven't razed the place to the ground.'

NINE

AN ORCISH ENCOUNTER

FELIX STRODE DOWN the path into the small valley. He was pleased to see that Gelt still stood. It was a placid enough looking little settlement, if you discounted the high stone walls, topped with a wooden palisade, and the guard towers that loomed above the walls. It had been built on a knob of rock rising in the middle of the valley. From his vantage point on the trail above the village, Felix could see smoke drifting upwards through holes cut in the turf roofed stone cottages. There was a large central structure he took to be the inn. On a ledge above the village was what he first took to be another watchtower and eventually realised was the fortified entrance to the mine. A gravel path ran all the way down the hillside to the gates of the town.

Judging from the size of the place several hundred people lived there, and by the look of the fortifications, it would be a hard place to take by storm. He could see humans and dwarfs walking the stony streets in about equal numbers.

'Looks like a safe enough place,' he said aloud, as much to reassure himself as for the sake of speaking.

'Aye, manling, providing the attackers don't have siege engines,' said Gotrek.

175

'Or powerful sorcery,' said Max Schreiber.

'Or aren't mounted on flying monsters,' added Ulrika.

Felix glanced around at his companions. 'Sorry I spoke,' he said eventually. 'I hate to destroy your cheery mood.'

'Snorri is looking forward to a drop of ale,' said Snorri Nosebiter. 'Old Hargrim said the Broken Pickaxe brews the best ale in the mountains.'

'Then what are we waiting for?' Gotrek said. 'Let's get down there.'

'Don't worry, Felix Jaeger,' Ulli said. 'No orc would dare attack Gelt while I am there.'

'Wonder if they have any bar girls?' Bjorni said. 'I could use a little company.'

'Maybe there'll be a game of chance,' said Steg. 'I brought my own special dice.'

Grimme merely shook his head, sucked his teeth, and marched stolidly down the hill. At the rear, Standa and Oleg glanced over their shoulders. They had their strung bows held ready in their hands, but there was no perceptible threat.

'Go on,' Felix said. 'We should be safe for this evening, at least.'

'If the dragon doesn't come get us,' Oleg said.

'Look on the bright side,' Felix said. Misgivings and forebodings aside, everybody looked a little happier once they were past the dwarf sentries on the gate.

THE BROKEN PICKAXE had a large common room. A roaring fire served to keep out the chill of the mountain night. Felix glanced around at the crowd. Their party was attracting a lot of attention, which wasn't surprising when you considered it. How often did these people see seven Slayers travelling in the company of five humans?

The crowd itself was an unusual one. It seemed to consist of an equal mix of humans and dwarfs. Most of the dwarfs had the pale faces and scrubbed clean look of miners after work. The humans were a more mixed bunch. Some of the tougher looking ones wore the warm leather garments favoured by high mountain prospectors. Others looked like peddlers and shopkeepers. None of them looked exactly prosperous, but none looked starved either.

A silence had spread across the room as the Slayers took up one long table. This close to Karak Kadrin no one was going to be stupid enough to object. All of them knew exactly what the Slayers were and what they were capable of when annoyed. Felix had joined Ulrika, Max and the two bodyguards at the table next to the Slayers. Some semblance of normal business was restored when Gotrek called for ale, an order swiftly seconded by Snorri Nosebiter and Malakai Makaisson.

A fat, prosperous looking dwarf with a balding head, rosy cheeks and a long greying beard brought the ale over himself. Judging by the proprietorial air he cast over the place, he was obviously the owner of the inn.

'You'll be wanting rooms for the night?' he asked.

'The Slayers will sleep in the common room,' Gotrek said. 'The humans might want their own chambers.'

'We do,' said Ulrika, glancing over at Felix. Max noticed this and looked away, adding, 'I'll take a room to myself.'

'Me and Standa will stay in the common room,' Oleg said tugging morosely at his moustache. Standa beamed approval of his comrade's decision. Ulrika agreed.

'I'll see the best rooms are aired and the beds turned out. There's a nip in the air, so you'll be wanting a fire, no doubt?'

Felix could imagine that the bill was increasing with every word, but so what, he thought. This might be his last chance of a comfortable bed in this life, so why stint tonight?

'Why not?'

'And you'll be wanting food too, no doubt?'

'Aye. Bring us the stew we smell, and bread and cheese,' said Ulli.

'And more ale,' added Snorri. 'Snorri has a thirst.'

'And you'll be paying for the rooms and the food now, will you?'

The innkeeper was obviously taking no chances with their absconding without paying, even if they were Slayers. Possibly even because they were Slayers. After all, they were dwarfs who had somehow failed to abide by the normal dwarf code of honour. Malakai Makaisson dug into his purse and gold changed hands. Felix could not see how much but the innkeeper's eyes widened, and he became particularly jovial. It looked like Malakai thought the same way as Felix did about staying in the inn.

'And that'll keep the beers comin' ah nicht,' said Malakai. 'And ah'll be sleeping in the wagon so there's no need to clear me a space in the common room.'

Steg looked a little disgruntled by that, but after a sip of the ale, his expression became slightly more contented.

'That it will,' said the innkeeper and bellowed instructions to his staff. Bjorni's eyes widened as a busty barmaid approached. Within seconds, he was slapping her rump, and whispering in her ear. If the barmaid was offended she gave no sign.

Felix sampled a drop of the ale, and nodded. 'Malgrim was right,' he said. 'This is fine ale.'

'It's not bad,' allowed Gotrek, which for the Slayer was high praise indeed.

Now that he had been paid, the innkeeper seemed more inclined to be sociable. 'And you'll be taking the High Road to Radasdorp then?'

'If it's on the way to the dragon's mountain we will,' bellowed Ulli, obviously taking a great deal of pleasure from the buzz of conversation this started.

'So it's the dragon you're after,' said the innkeeper.

'Aye,' Malakai said. 'We're gannae kill the great big scaly beastie!'

'It's been tried before,' said the innkeeper. Felix looked over, his interest suddenly piqued.

'By whom?' he asked.

'Half a dozen Slayers have passed through here in the past couple of years – not all at once mind,' said the innkeeper. 'None of them ever came back.'

'The orcs probably ate them,' bellowed one of the humans.

'Or skinned them,' added another man ominously.

'Aye,' said an ancient looking miner. 'That'd be likely enough. One of the Slayers was found skinned alive and nailed to a tree by the roadside. They reckon the Manflayer is using his hide for a new pair of boots now.'

'Another's head was found on a spike up near the Mirnek Pass. The crows was pecking his eyes out so they was.'

'And there was one of those human knights, on a big black charger,' said the innkeeper. 'Said he had a magic sword and a dragon-killing lance.'

'He never came back either,' one of the dwarfs said gloomily.

'Most likely the orcs got him too,' said the first man who spoke.

'Or the human bandits. Henrik Richter is a nasty piece of work,' said the innkeeper. Seeing Felix's enquiring glance, he said, 'He's the local bandit chief these days. He's been forging the human bands into a small army. Since the Manflayer came the humans have needed it to survive. They say there'll be war for control of the high country between those two soon. I can believe it.'

'It sounds like the High Road has become very dangerous,' Felix said.

'This was never the safest of places to live,' said the innkeeper. 'But ever since the dragon came back it's got downright dangerous. I reckon it's only a matter of time before it attacks Gelt. It's said to have destroyed all the other towns along the High Road now.'

'You mean we could just wait here and it will come to us?' Felix asked hopefully.

'Aye. Most likely.'

'Ah dinnae hae time tae waste. I want that beastie deid, and ah want it soon.'

'There's more glory in seeking it out!' shouted Ulli. 'And if any greenskin or any human tries to stop us, they'll get a blow from my axe.'

'Och, if any of them try to stop us, ah hae a nasty wee surprise for them,' Malakai said. Felix did not doubt that was true. He had seen ample evidence of the Engineer's genius at devising weapons. Of course, most of Malakai's weapons were experimental and subject to malfunction. Some of them might prove as dangerous to their wielders as to any foe.

'And what might that be?' asked a large burly man who looked more like a mercenary than a prospector.

'Onybody that's interested can attack us and find oot,' said Malakai with a hint of satisfaction. Felix was now really curious about what the engineer had up his sleeve.

'There are plenty here in the mountains will take you up on that,' said the man with a sneer. Felix wondered if this fool was tired of living. It was not wise to sneer at any Slayer, even one as relatively even tempered as Malakai was.

'They're mare than welcome tae,' was all the engineer said in response, and returned to glugging down his beer.

The innkeeper said, 'You pay no attention to Peter. He is a surly chap at the best of times, and these are not the best of times. He used to make a living selling all along the High Road. Now there's damn few left to sell to. The dragon's seen to that.'

'We'll change that!' bellowed Ulli. His boast was met with laughter from the other tables. For some reason, the dwarfs present refused to take the young Slayer as seriously as the others. Ulli did not seem to mind as long as he was the centre of attention.

'You may laugh but you'll see. You won't mock us after the dragon is dead.'

'You'll be dead as well,' shouted someone and the others laughed.

'What of it,' shouted Ulli. 'Everybody dies.'

'Some sooner than others,' said Peter.

Bjorni had the barmaid on his knee now. She was running her fingers through his beard while he looked up at her with a lascivious leer. A moment later the woman was tumbled off his knee by a huge man with a scarred face and massive hands. He was without a doubt one of the bouncers.

'Leave Essie alone,' he said, his voice flat and menacing.

'Let it be, Otto,' said the innkeeper. 'You know this always happens.'

'What is that to you?' asked Bjorni innocently.

'She's my wife.'

Felix groaned aloud. He had seen women like Essie before when he and Gotrek worked the taverns of Nuln. Women married to large violent men who thrived on their jealous attention. He couldn't understand why they did it, but they did. The bouncer looked over at him.

'What are you whining about, boy?' he said. Felix looked up at him. The man was big. Perhaps a head taller than he was, and broad in proportion. His arms looked almost as large as Gotrek's.

'Some ale went down the wrong way.'

'Watch it or I'll take that tankard and stick it up your...'

Felix looked at him, and started to rise from his seat, but it was already too late. Bjorni had taken his fist and whacked Otto between the legs while the bouncer wasn't looking. The big man groaned and bent double, and as he went over Bjorni took his tankard and smacked him hard on the head. Otto's eyes crossed and he slumped forward unconscious.

'Not the first jealous husband I've had to deal with,' said Bjorni tugging lasciviously at the wart on his nose. 'Now, love, what say you and me find a quiet corner and...'

The girl was bent down over Otto and shrieking. 'Otto, what has that brute done to you?'

'He'll be all right in the morning,' Bjorni said. 'Now how about we go behind the woodshed. There's a big gold piece in it for you if...'

'Go to hell,' said Essie.

Bjorni shrugged and sat down again. 'Another ale, landlord. My jar is suddenly empty.'

The innkeeper was looking at the Slayers warily again. Still, with his biggest bouncer down, and the newcomers not seeming about to start any more trouble, he decided it was best to humour them.

'More ale, it is,' he said.

'I'll help you carry him upstairs,' said Steg to Essie, moving over to the slumped body and making as if to pick him up.

'Don't bother,' said the girl. 'I don't need any of your help.'

Steg shrugged and dropped the body once more. Felix wondered if he was the only one to notice that the bouncer's purse was suddenly missing from his belt.

'I think I'll just go for a walk,' said Steg.

'Ah think ah'll go with ye,' Malakai said. 'It's aboot time for me to turn in anyway.'

If Steg was disappointed at missing the opportunity to search Makaisson's wagon, he did not show it.

'Time for bed,' Felix said, looking over at Ulrika to see if she agreed with him. She nodded and they made their way up the stairs.

GRUND HUGENOSE OF the Broken Nose tribe looked down on the village. His orc eyes were much keener than any human's, and even by the dim light of the two moons he could make out all he needed. From his vantage point, he could see the wagon in the courtyard. It told him that someone would be leaving the small fortified outpost soon. That meant manflesh, and steel weapons, and maybe gold and rotgut booze. He slipped back from the cliff edge, and headed up the trail.

There was no need to tell the Manflayer about this, he decided. It was a small party and the spoils would be barely enough for him and the lads. He would get his warband together, and make sure that whatever was on that wagon would be his before the next night's stars shone.

* * *

FELIX AWOKE TO the sound of metal ringing against metal outside the inn. He threw open the shutters and looked out to see what was going on. From the racket he half expected to see half a dozen orcs swordfighting with Templars in the courtyard but the source of the noise was not immediately evident. After a moment or two of looking he noticed that the back of Malakai Makaisson's cart was bouncing up and down, and that the covered wagon was where all the row was coming from.

'What is it, Felix?' Ulrika asked.

'Don't know,' he said, 'but it looks like Malakai is up to something.'

'If it's important we'll find out soon enough. Now come back to bed,' she said. Glancing back at her naked form he did not have to be asked twice.

FELIX'S LEGS ACHED from the strain of the constant uphill walking. His feet were sore from slamming down on the hard rocks of the High Road. He drew his red cloak of Sudenland wool tight around his shoulder, glad of it now. Despite the brightness of the sun, it was chilly in these mountain heights and getting chillier. A cold breeze blew down the valleys, and ruffled his hair with invisible fingers.

He smiled at Ulrika. They were getting on better today, as they usually did after the nights they slept together. She smiled back warmly. Felix could tell she was as tired as he, if not more so, but was determined to show no sign of it. Felix felt a certain sympathy for her. She had grown up on the flat plains of Kislev and had even less experience than he of mountain walking. He at least had travelled among the peaks before he had fallen in with Gotrek. Oleg and Standa were quite visibly faltering. Their breath came in gasps, and every now and again, one or the other would bend over almost double, legs spread wide, hands resting on thighs, heads bowed as they attempted to catch their breaths.

Of all the humans, Max Schreiber showed the least sign of fatigue, which surprised Felix no end. He had gotten used to thinking of the wizard as a sedentary scholar, and yet he had taken to the hills as if born to them. He leaned on his high staff and spoke encouragingly to Oleg then put his hand on the Kislevite's shoulder. Felix could have sworn he saw a spark of energy pass between the two men, and then Oleg rose to his full height, and began to walk with renewed vigour. Perhaps that was Max's secret, Felix decided, maybe he was using his magic to give him strength while they walked, and maybe he had used it to lend some of that strength to Oleg.

Whatever it was, it was effective, Felix thought. Max seemed almost at home here as the dwarfs, and, until today, Felix would have thought that impossible for any human. The dwarfs were unbelievably cheery, considering they were Slayers and bound on a mission that most likely meant their deaths. They strode along tirelessly, taking the steepest of gradients with no apparent effort, sometimes deviating from the path, and scrambling easily up near vertical slopes apparently just for the sheer joy of it.

Only Malakai did not do so. He stayed with his cart at all times, goading his ponies when they balked on the steep inclines, keeping a beady eye on their surroundings and most especially on Steg, whenever the suspected thief strayed close to the cart. Gotrek and Snorri led the way. Felix could see them at the head of the column, cresting the nearest ridge, where the pathway wound ever higher and further up slope.

'It is beautiful, is it not?' said Ulrika. Felix glanced around, knowing what she meant. The mountains had a strange barren loveliness that seemed like a reward for making the effort of walking among them. On either side loomed the great grey flanks of mountains, spotted here and there by the green of woods and scrub brush. High above them glittered the snow-line, and the chill proud peaks. Boulders rose from the mountainside, and occasionally blocked the path. Felix guessed that this was where stones had been dislodged and rolled downslope.

Far below them, he could see Gelt. Through a pass between two nearby mountains the trail wound down to a cold clear lake.

'Yes, it is,' he said. 'Though not nearly as beautiful as you.'

She shook her head. 'You are a shameless flatterer, Felix Jaeger.'

'It is not flattery. It is merely the truth.'

She turned and looked away for a moment, and her smile took on a strange sad quality. 'What am I going to do without you?' she asked.

'What do you mean?'

'I have never met a man who makes me feel like you do.'

Felix knew she meant it as compliment but felt embarrassed nonetheless. 'Is that good or bad?'

'I do not know,' she said. 'I do know it is confusing.'

He struggled for a reply, and could not find exactly the right words to say what he felt. He was almost glad when he heard Gotrek bellow, 'Looks like trouble ahead!'

FELIX AND ULRIKA made their way to the crest of the ridge. The path ran on, descending into a small valley before passing once more over a series of ridges that rose like giant frozen waves to the horizon. Gotrek and Snorri stood on the ridge, silhouetted against the skyline.

A quick glance showed Felix exactly what Gotrek meant. Hurrying along the path towards them were a group of greenskin warriors. Felix tried counting them, but there were too many and they were too tightly packed for him to be very successful in his efforts. He gave up somewhere over twenty.

'There are fifty-four of them,' Ulrika said.

'Your eyes are better than mine.'

'Either that or my counting skills are.' He knew she was attempting a joke but he could hear the strain in her voice.

Oleg and Standa got into position beside them. They had already strung their bows. Ulrika began to ready hers. Max took up a position beside them, leaning on his staff with both hands. 'It seems we are outnumbered,' he said eventually.

'They are only greenskins,' said Snorri. 'No need to worry.'

'They outnumber us more than four to one,' Max said. 'That causes me just a little concern.'

'One dwarf is worth ten orcs!' boomed Ulli.

'Particularly in bed,' Bjorni said with a leer.

'Don't you ever think of anything else?' Felix asked.

'Sometimes I think about fighting,' Bjorni said. 'And I think now is as good a time as any to dwell on that.'

'Aye,' Gotrek said. 'That it is. We'll meet them here, and let them come up at us. I would normally take the battle to them but it would be a pity to fall to an orc scimitar when there's a dragon in these mountains.'

'Sound thinking,' Felix said ironically. Behind him he could hear Malakai Makaisson's cart rumbling slowly up the hill. Felix sincerely hoped that Malakai had the weapons he had been promising and that they worked.

'Snorri thinks we should just charge them,' said Snorri Nosebiter.

'I think Gotrek's plan is better,' Ulli said. Felix wondered if he heard just a little fear in the boastful dwarf's voice. It would not surprise him. Emptiest vessels make the loudest noise, his father had always claimed. And he should know, thought Felix, for his father was a very loud man.

'I wonder if they have any gold,' said Steg. 'You can never tell. If they've just robbed a prospector they might have.' He became aware of the looks the others were giving him and shrugged affably. 'You never know. That's all I'm saying.'

'I'm more concerned as to whether they have any bows,' said Gotrek. 'Being pin-cushioned by greenskin arrows is no death for a Slayer.'

'I might be able to do something about that,' said Max Schreiber. 'If the winds of magic are strong enough, and there's no shaman down there.'

'Doesn't look like there is,' Gotrek said. 'If there was, he would be dancing around and chanting nonsense to his gods.'

The orcs were maybe four hundred paces below them now. Just out of arrow range but closing fast. Felix could hear their savage guttural war-cries. They brandished their weapons menacingly.

'Maybe we could turn back,' Ulli said. Felix glanced over at him. He looked pale, and a little shaken.

'That might not be a bad idea,' Gotrek said. Felix looked at Gotrek curiously. In all their long association, this was the first time he had ever heard the Slayer evince a desire to retreat.

'Why?' he asked.

'Because there are some more greenskins to kill down there.'

Felix looked back in the direction they had come. Orcs and other smaller creatures were pouring down the slopes behind them. It appeared their line of retreat was cut off.

'This is not looking good,' said Felix. He noticed that some of the smaller greenskins were mounted on huge spider-like creatures. Just the sight of those savage steeds made his flesh crawl. They were coming on with terrible speed. He began to think that perhaps the Slayers had been overconfident proceeding into the mountains in such a pitifully small party.

'For them, manling,' Gotrek said. 'For them.'

'I wished I shared your confidence,' Felix said.

'Ah'll deal wae this bunch,' Malakai said. 'You see tae the yins in front o' ye.'

'Are you sure you're up to it?' Felix said.

'Ye can bet on it,' Malakai said. With one hand he pulled a lever and the canvas cover of the wagon dropped away. Revealed was an odd looking multi-barrelled gun, mounted on a tripod. Felix had seen a smaller version of the weapon before, and knew what it was capable of. Malakai pulled the brake lever of the wagon, locking it in position on the far side of the hill.

The spider riders to the rear had begun their advance up the hill. Felix watched as Malakai sighted down the barrel of his weapon and clutched the trigger guards tight. Felix risked a glance at the other side of the hill. The orcs had begun their climb, shouting confidently as they came. Felix knew that if their foes had any idea of what was waiting for them at the top of the hill, they would not be so confident. Still, he wondered, would it be enough?

Ulrika, Standa and Oleg had begun to fire their short composite bows. Arrows whooshed away downhill, and impaled three of the leading orcs. Two went down, one with an arrow through his eye, another with one through his throat. The third kept coming despite the feathered shaft embedded in his breast.

In response to the arrow fire, the greenskins began to spread out so they would not be quite so tightly packed together and not make such good targets. Savage they might be, Felix thought, but they were not stupid. At this moment, he wished he had learned to use a bow. In his youth he had been given some training with duelling pistols, but none in archery. It was not the mark of the gentleman his father had hoped to turn him into. Right at this moment it would have been very useful though. Apparently the orcs agreed, several of them had unslung bows from their backs and begun to string them. It looked like an archery duel was about to break out. All around him, the Slayers bellowed taunts at the greenskins, mocking them, and brandishing their weapons.

Gotrek raised his axe above his head, and bellowed, 'Come on up and die!'

'Snorri wants to fight!' shouted Snorri Nosebiter.

'I slept with your mothers,' Bjorni shouted, then fell quiet, as the other dwarfs all stared at him. 'Well, needs must when daemons drive,' he muttered at last. As the dwarfs hurled insults, Ulrika and the Kislevites kept up a steady stream of arrow fire at the orcs. Three more fell but the rest howled angry war-cries and kept on coming.

Suddenly a sound like thunder erupted behind them. Felix looked back to see that Malakai Makaisson had activated his gun. Flames flickered as flint strikers struck home. The barrels rotated and death roared forth from the weapon. As Felix watched one of the spiders crumpled in the middle, its body torn asunder, its legs twitching feebly. Malakai moved the gun slightly on its tripod and the arc of fire changed. A second spider crumpled and then a third.

Unfortunately, the roar of the gun spooked the ponies. It was either that or the sight of the unnaturally huge spiders coming towards them. They began to rear and buck and lash out with their hind legs, kicking at the cart and wrestling with their harness in a desperate attempt to get free. One of the kicks smashed into the brake lever, knocking the mechanism loose and snapping it in two. Another flurry of blows sent the cart rumbling downslope. Slowly at first, and then moving ever faster, it picked up speed. Felix considered racing after it and trying to stop it, but swiftly realised that it was futile. There was no way a man of ordinary strength could bring the careening vehicle to a halt.

If Malakai Makaisson was dismayed he gave no sign of it. He shouted a dwarf warcry and kept firing, mowing down another spider rider. The last two moved to intercept him.

'Beware, manling,' Felix heard Gotrek say, and twisted his head to look at the oncoming orcs once more. Half a dozen of them had managed to get their bows ready and were returning fire at the hilltop. Felix flinched as arrows blurred towards him, then suddenly Max Schreiber raised his hands and finished whatever spell he had been muttering. A glowing sphere of golden light sprang up around the hilltop. The arrows struck its shimmering translucent surface and caught fire, disintegrating harmlessly in a shower of sparks.

The advancing orcs halted in confusion, dismayed by this display of sorcerous power. The Kislevites kept the stream of arrows coming, taking down two more orcs. Felix guessed that they had taken perhaps ten of the orcs out of the combat now. Still, that left more than enough to overwhelm the hilltop. A crunching sound behind him drew his attention again. He looked back.

Through the shimmering haze he saw that one of the spider riders had got in the way of the cart and had been crushed under its heavy ironshod wheels. The last one was torn to shreds by a burst of fire from the organ gun. Malakai continued to rumble downhill into the horde of goblin troops. Felix could see them looking up at the oncoming Slayer with wide-eyed panic. Malakai continued to bellow and roar challenges as he raced towards the small greenskins.

A shout from the front drew Felix's attention back there. The orcs had overcome their dismay swiftly enough and continued their advance. Realising the futility of their efforts the greenskin archers had put away their bows, drawn their heavy black iron scimitars, and now rushed to join their comrades. Felix hastily judged the distance and readied his own dragon-hilted sword.

'I reckon you've time for one more shot, and then you'd better get your blades out,' he told Ulrika.

A faint smile curved her lips, as she drew the bowstring to her cheek and loosed. 'You don't say,' she said as another orc dropped. From behind them came the sound of explosions. What was Malakai up to, Felix wondered? He dared not look and see the first of the onrushing orcs were almost within striking distance. Ulrika fired once more at almost point blank range, and then hastily dropped her bow and drew her sword. Felix stepped forward, ready to interpose himself between her and anyone who might strike at her before her weapon was out.

The sound of Max's chanting altered, and the sphere of golden light collapsed inwards, tendrils of energy congealing into a far smaller sphere about the size of a man's head that hovered just in front of Max. Another gesture shattered the sphere and sent bolts of golden light raining down onto the orcs. In an instant the whole front row was felled by the blaze of magical energy. Felix saw one orc sink to its knees, the whole front of its chest ripped away, its ribs visible through the smoking hole in its armour.

'Right, lads,' Gotrek said. 'Let's get stuck in!'

It was all the encouragement the Slayers needed. All six of them raced forward at the discouraged orcs who stood gawping at them, the momentum of their charge lost in the face of Max's magical onslaught. Even as Felix watched, Gotrek stormed in amidst the orcs. His axe rose and fell in a bloody arc, smashing through one orc to bury itself in the chest of another. With a brutal twist, the Slayer pulled it free and sliced about him, the mighty mystical blade transformed into a whirlwind of death in his hands.

Snorri raced in behind him, axe and hammer held at the ready. He lashed about him with mighty strokes, uncaring of his own life. Each of his blows downed an orc reducing them to lifeless husks in an instant. The other Slayers joined them, forming a wedge that cleaved through the orcs, like a ship sailing through a sea of green blood. Felix watched in awe at the destruction the dwarfs wreaked. He doubted that a company of knights could have created more havoc than the Slayers had in those few brief instants.

Bjorni head-butted one orc and as it drew back, he lashed out with his axe, severing its head. Laughing like a maniac, he stamped on the foot of another, kneed it in the groin and then drove his axe into its chest before it could recover. Pale-faced Ulli moved alongside him using his own axe two-handed, hewing at his foes like a woodcutter chopping a trunk. Felix could see he was far less skilled than the other dwarfs but his strokes were nonetheless effective, powered as they were by his mighty dwarf muscles.

Steg lurked at the rear, lashing out with his pickaxe at any orc who threatened to get round his comrades. His eyes darted everywhere, as if looking for loot, but not even his greed could get the better of him in the middle of this swirling, turbulent melee. Grimme fought off to the right on his own, and the carnage he created was appalling. He used his huge hammer two-handed but with a speed that rivalled Gotrek's. One mighty blow reduced an orc's skull to jelly. A second sideways stroke knocked a greenskin head clean off, sending it flying a hundred strides down the slope.

A company of men would have routed in instants under the fury of the Slayers' attack, but these orcs were made of sterner stuff. For a moment only they wavered, and then they threw themselves into the fray with a berserker bravery that almost matched their foes'. They swarmed in over the dwarfs, seeking to overcome them with sheer weight of numbers. A few of them, noticing the humans who stood waiting on the hilltop, swept past the Slayers and charged. Felix considered the position for an instant. Would it be better to wait or charge? Here, they had the advantage of position. If they charged they would have the advantage of momentum.

A glance told him that the orcs did not seem to be too winded by their uphill run. He reached his decision instantly.

'Let's go!' he shouted, and ran forward. Ulrika and her bodyguards followed.

'Stay close. Watch each other's backs!' Ulrika cried. Felix was glad she had thought of it. It was the one advantage they might have in the midst of the chaos that surrounded them.

Moving downslope added to his speed. He selected the largest of the onrushing orcs as his target and raised his blade high. At the last second, he brought his blade down, ducked under the orc's stroke and with a backward slice chopped it across the spine. He felt bone crunch and leather give way under the impact of his razor-sharp blade and then the orc dropped, its legs no longer obeying it. Standa kicked it in the head as he passed, and the orc grunted and lay still.

Felix was lost in the madness of battle. He ducked and dodged, parried and struck, thrusting out with his blade into the tightly packed mass of bodies. Sweat almost blinded him, blood splattered his face and arms. The howls and screams of his foes almost deafened him. The shock of each parry almost tore his blade from his numb fingers.

He lashed out to left and right, trying always to keep Ulrika in view, lest a foe strike her down unawares. He saw her fighting with her long Kislevite sword. She moved through the fray like some warrior goddess. If she could not match the orcs for strength, she made up for it in speed. Battle madness seemed to overtake her. Felix had fought her once in play, but had never really witnessed her fight in earnest. Some primordial rage seemed to fill her, and transformed her into an engine of destruction. She danced through the battle like a flame, whirling and cutting, and leaving a trail of death in her wake. Behind her Oleg and Standa fought like men possessed, guarding her flanks. They lacked her skill and speed, but fought with the deadly competence of veterans.

Out of the corner of his eye, Felix caught a flicker of golden light. He glimpsed Max moving through the orcs. His whole body was surrounded by a flicker of yellowish light which seemed to deflect blows. Whenever his staff struck an orc there was a flash of utter brilliance and the smell of burning meat filled the air. Felix knew that the mage's enchanted weapon was burning through whatever it touched. The moment passed. Another orc attacked and Felix was hard pressed to defend himself. He backed away up the hill, frantically trying to keep his balance as he parried, desperately hoping that he would not trip over some unseen obstruction, like a boulder or an orc corpse. His foe was a massive orc, a head taller than he, and half again as broad. Its long ape-like arms gave it greater reach. Its red eyes were filled with hate and bloodlust, and spittle and foam erupted from its mouth, drenching the tusk-like teeth that protruded from its lower jaw. It looked like it fully intended to kill Felix then eat him. It was very strong and very fast, and for a sickening instant Felix doubted his own ability to stop it.

From some dark depth of his mind bubbled up the realisation that if he fell here, he would never get his chance to confront the dragon. As if in answer to this, he felt new strength flow into him from the sword. The tidal wave of energy drove back fatigue and fear. He blocked the orc's blow easily, catching its blade with his own, and holding it with ease, as if the orc did not outweigh him by ten stone. He saw a look of shock twist across the orc's face, as it registered this feat by its relatively puny foe.

Then time seemed to slow for Felix. He moved at normal speed but everything around him moved at half its usual pace. He drew his blade back from the orc and before it had time to respond separated its head from its shoulders. He strode forward into the fray once more, killing as he went.

In an instant the orcs realised they were overmatched. One of them turned to run and, in a heartbeat, all of his surviving brethren came to the same decision. As they chose to flee the dwarfs cut them down. As they ran the Slayers and their human companions followed. The short-legged dwarfs were soon outdistanced but the humans managed to keep up and chop down a few more from behind.

Still, there were too many to overtake and kill them all, and Felix realised that if they kept on the orcs might regroup and overwhelm the humans. He shouted for Ulrika and her bodyguards to halt and reluctantly they obeyed. The orcs kept running.

From behind the ridge top came the sound of another explosion. Felix could see a cloud of black smoke rising skyward. Instantly the thought came to him that Malakai Makaisson was down there somewhere, fighting alone against a horde of goblins.

'We've got to get back and help Malakai,' he said, and saw understanding pass across Ulrika's face. She nodded and turned at once, Standa and Oleg following her. Felix cursed under his breath as the strain of running up hill told on his legs. His clothes were already saturated with sweat and wet with blood. His muscles ached from the strain of the fight. Yet he forced himself to keep up with the Kislevites.

He saw that the Slayers had already turned and were racing across the ridge top in the direction of the other battle. He rushed onwards as they vanished out of sight, feeling confident that as they had vanquished the savage orcs, the goblins were likely to prove far less of a threat. Then the thought of those giant spiders entered his mind, and his feelings of confidence vanished.

Silhouetted on the ridge-line, Max Schreiber raised his staff high. A nimbus of yellowish light flickered around him, but it was less bright than it had been and Felix knew instinctively that Max had exhausted a great deal of his strength. Even so, he swirled his staff around his head, and as he did so, the tip seemed to catch fire. Angry golden light blazed brighter and brighter with each rotation of the staff, as if it were a firebrand catching alight in the motion. Finally, having gathered sufficient power, Max unleashed it, sending a torrent of energy vanishing downslope. The spell was answered by the high-pitched, piping screams of dying goblins.

Felix crested the ridge ahead of Ulrika and her bodyguards, and looked down on a scene of appalling carnage. The Engineer's cart had cut a bloody swathe through the goblin horde's ranks. The huge spiders were crushed or blown apart. Many small goblin bodies lay still on the ground, testament to the terrifying power of the organ gun. Malakai himself stood precariously atop the cart which had crashed to a halt in a depression by the side of the road. He tossed black bombs into the massed goblins.

The greenskins huddled together, kept at bay by the power of the explosives, as they tried to gather their courage and assault the inventor. Now it looked as if Max's spell and the sudden advent of six Slayers was enough to daunt them completely. They turned and fled back the way they came. Seeing their departure, Felix decided that he had had enough of slaughter for one day, and slowed from a run to a walk. Ulrika and the Kislevites swept past him, and moved to join the Slayers below.

Felix let them. He knew they would never catch the greenskins now.

GRUND RAN AS hard as he ever had in his life. He liked a fight as much as the next orc but those stunties had just been too much. He had never seen anyone fight like that dwarf with the magic axe save Ugrek himself. He knew that if he wanted revenge he would have to tell the Manflayer his tale. Ugrek would get the lads together then, and they would all come down and stomp those stunties. Grund hoped the warboss was still camped at Bloody Fist knoll. It was less than a day away., a lot less if Grund kept up this pace. Thinking about the stunty with the axe, he decided that might not be such a bad idea.

FELIX PASSED THE corpse of a goblin. Smoke rose from the body along with the smell of scorched flesh. It looked like the greenskin had died as a result of Max's spell. There was no mark on the body, no hole that would have marked the passage of organ gun shell or shrapnel from a bomb. When he looked closely, he saw that the small humanoid's eyes had exploded in their sockets, splattering jelly across its face. It was not a pretty sight but then again, few corpses ever were.

He walked to another of the creatures that lay sprawled face down in the dirt, and turned it over with his boot. It was not very large. Its body was no bigger than that of a child of ten. Its legs were very short in proportion to the length of its torso and the arms very long. Its head was big for its body. The creature wore a sort of hooded leather tunic, dyed bright yellow, and a sickly green. In death the hood had fallen back to reveal its face.

The features were twisted and malevolent and cunning. The nose was as long and as thin as a carrot, the mouth filled with sharp, rat-like teeth. The thing that struck him most was the creature's hands. They were gnarled and strong, with large knuckles and very long, very dextrous-looking fingers. Something about them made Felix think of stranglers, and he knew that he would not have liked to find those hands wrapped round his throat.

In death, though, the creature looked curiously pathetic. There was something infinitely sad about its small, still form. He mentioned this to Ulrika who stood nearby watching him. She looked at him with blank incomprehension.

'It's dead,' she said. 'And that's good. For it would have killed us if it had got the chance.'

'You're right,' Felix said but still somehow he felt something like shame when he looked down on the small corpse.

FELIX WALKED OVER to where Malakai Makaisson stood atop his cart. The engineer glared down truculently and Felix soon saw why. One of the wagon's wheels had come off, and the buck-board had fallen open spilling the engineer's tools and equipment into the dirt. At least Malakai himself did not look too hurt, although his fingers were black and his face was smudged with soot or oil.

'Are you alright?' Felix asked.

'Aye. Niver better! It'll tak mare than these sleekit wee beasties tae dae fur me, don't you worry. It's ma stuff ah'm worried aboot. Ah hope this crash hisnae damaged it ony.'

'I'll help you gather it up,' Felix offered.

'Dinnae you bother. Ah hae ma ane system fur this. Ah'll sort it oot masel.'

'Suit yourself,' Felix said.

He strode over to where Gotrek and Snorri stood side by side, inspecting the hills into which the goblins had fled.

'Snorri reckons we've seen the last of them,' said Snorri.

Gotrek spat on the ground, and shook his head truculently. 'Then you should leave the thinking to others, Snorri Nosebiter. For they'll be back as soon as they find their brethren. And there will be more of them next time. You can bet gold on it.'

Felix was forced to agree. Some instinct told him that they had not heard the last of the greenskins, not by a long chalk.

Behind him came the sound of hammering, as Malakai Makaisson proceeded to repair his wagon.

'We'll kill them all then,' Ulli said. Felix could see that his face was still pale, and his fingers shook where they gripped his axe. Still, he had acquitted himself well enough in the battle.

'In a brothel in Nuln they had what they claimed were goblin girls,' said Bjorni reflectively. 'They weren't though. They were just human lassies with their faces painted green and their teeth filed.'

'I could have lived my whole life cheerfully without ever finding that out,' Felix said.

'Well you'd be missing something then,' Bjorni said with his repulsive leer.

Felix turned and walked away.

TEN

ENCOUNTERS ON THE ROAD

IT WAS DAWN. The fire was dead, reduced to a black pit of ash and cinders. Stuffing a hunk of rubbery cheese into his mouth, biting on sour dwarf waybread and washing it all down with flat ale, Felix watched as the dwarfs and the Kislevites broke camp.

Ulrika smiled at him. He reached out and squeezed her hand, and was glad to feel the pressure returned. Over Ulrika's shoulder he could see Bjorni giving him a wink. The dwarf leered repulsively then grabbed his left biceps with his right hand and made a pumping gesture. Felix looked away.

Malakai had fixed his wagon, packing away some of his components in wooden crates, leaving a bunch of things that looked suspiciously like weapons within easy reach. The ponies had returned after a couple of hours of wandering the previous evening, and were now standing docile in their harnesses.

The other Slayers had their weapons to hand and their packs over their backs and looked ready for trouble. Oleg and Standa had their bows ready. Only Max Schreiber looked out of sorts. He seemed pale and drawn and more than a little tired. A bemused, somewhat thoughtful expression marked his face.

He stood taller. He had in some subtle way altered, and Felix was not quite sure how.

'Let's go,' shouted Gotrek. 'We're still a long way from the Dragon Vale.'

Malakai jerked the reins. The Slayers fell into marching step. Far off, in the distance, Felix could see small clouds.

MAX SCHREIBER FELT exhausted. He had used a lot of power yesterday in the battle with the greenskins.

He had not slept well. Jealousy gnawed at him while Felix and Ulrika lay together under blankets on the far side of the fire. That and the snoring of the dwarfs had not made for a restful night. Eventually, after hours of staring at the cold glitter of the stars, he had managed to get to sleep. Mere moments later, it seemed, Snorri was kicking him awake. He felt like he had not slept at all. His eyed seemed glued together and he ached. Still, all things considered, he did not feel quite as bad as he had expected, and he wondered why.

He took a deep breath and tested the winds of magic. They blew weakly this day, he knew, but, even so, touching them sent a tingling through his veins, and renewed his energy. He closed his eyes and probed his own being. He felt depleted, and at the same time, curiously elated.

He knew also that the expenditure of power in yesterday's battle had done him good, in some as yet undefined way. Sometimes, he knew, using his arts was the only way to improve them. He had gained no new insights he could think of during the battle yesterday, yet he knew he had gained something. He had managed to handle the flow of the magical winds with more fluency than he ever had before, and he had delved deeper into the well of his soul than at any time in the past. He knew his power was increasing.

In the past few weeks he had been called on several times to use his powers as he never had before. In combat with the skaven, with the dragon and yesterday with the orcs. He had used the power under pressures and stresses, the like of which he rarely encountered before in his scholarly life. It seemed to be having some profound effect on him.

As he grasped at the winds of magic and drew them to himself, he knew he was now a vessel of energies greater than any he had ever held. His senses seemed keener. His grasp of the flows of magic was stronger. His magical vision had grown more perceptive.

He was now aware in a way he had not been before of the play of awesome energies through the runes of Gotrek's axe, and of the less strong, but nonetheless still potent, magic that permeated the blade Felix carried. He sensed that both weapons had been forged with a purpose, and he could almost grasp what those purposes were. He knew Gotrek's axe had been forged to be baneful to Chaos.

And yesterday, when Felix had drawn his blade, he had become briefly aware that it possessed something like sentience. Max wondered whether Felix knew. Most likely, yes. It would be almost impossible to bear a weapon like that for any time, and not be aware of it. Unless of course the weapon itself had concealed its power and its purpose. He decided that it was something he should talk with Felix about when he got the chance.

It was something the young man should be warned about.

GRUND ABASED HIMSELF before Ugrek Manflayer. To be more precise, he abased himself before Ugrek Manflayer's tent. It offended Grund's orcish sensibilities to throw himself on the ground before anyone or anything, but with the Manflayer it paid to be careful. He was very touchy, and his temper was a thing that put fear even into orcs. That and his habit of skinning his enemies and eating bits of them while they still lived.

Ugrek's bodyguards grunted with barely suppressed sniggers at the Broken Nose chieftain's discomfiture. Let them, he thought. He had seen them humiliated often enough by their boss. They silenced themselves instantly when the entrance flap opened and Ugrek emerged from his tent of human skin. Grund shivered. The shaman Ixix was with the big chief and that was never good. The little runt was even madder than Ugrek and claimed to speak with the gods in his dreams. Grund supposed it must be true. Why else would the mighty Manflayer listen to a wizened little runt like the goblin?

'Wot is it?' Ugrek asked. Grund looked up at him. Ugrek was the largest orc in the world, Grund was sure of it. He was nearly a head taller than any other orc in the mountains, and far stronger. In one hand he carried his magical cleaver, in the other he held a big axe. His armour had to be made special-like by the captured human smith that Ugrek kept chained to his tentpole. His helmet had two huge horns protruding from it. His eyes were a healthy red.

Grund quickly explained what had happened. Much to his surprise, Ugrek looked at the shaman and then starting laughing. Ixix began to giggle too. He laughed so hard he had to wipe his nose on his snot-encrusted cloak. Grund didn't think he saw anything funny in the situation but he laughed anyway, just to be on the safe side. It never hurt to humour the big boss. Soon the bodyguards joined in. Once they were all howling with mirth, Ugrek silenced them with a gesture of his fist. He looked down at the shaman.

'It's the dream for sure,' said Ixix. 'The gods spoke true. They are going to kill the dragon and then you are going to kill them. You will have a magic axe to match your magic cleaver, and you'll have all the dragon's treasure too.'

'I will be the greatest orc war leader in the world?' asked Ugrek.

'You will be the greatest orc war leader in the world.'

'Send out word!' Ugrek bellowed. 'Summon the tribes. We go to the Dragon Vale. We've got some stunties to kill.'

Just as everybody ran to obey his orders, Ugrek stopped them again. He was like that. 'And tell every last one of your boys to leave the stunties alone till they get there too. They are mine. I am going to kill them and eat their hearts.'

ULRIKA MARCHED ALONG through the mountains. She was not unhappy, but she was not happy either. She wondered what was happening between her and Felix. There were times when she felt certain that she loved him, and there were times when she felt equally certain that she felt nothing at all. It was odd how the passion came and went. Sometimes, as in the moment last night when they had sat by the fire and held hands, she felt they were connected deeply, as if by strong magic. And there were times, like this morning, as they marched forward under these brooding clouds when his merest glance could goad her to fury, and the look of stupid devotion she sometimes caught in his eye made her want to slap him in the face. At times like that it was almost as if he were a different man from the one who lay beside her in the night, as if he were a stranger who somehow had invaded her life.

She thought about that for a moment, and corrected herself. No. Sometimes, she felt like *she* was a different person, that something within her had changed in a way that she did not understand herself. He was the source of a spectrum of emotions that both enthralled and frightened her in a way no feelings ever had before. She feared to lose him, but she felt like running away from him. Somehow, in some strange way, he had gained power over her life, and she both hated this and wondered at it.

She glanced up at the turbulent clouds and felt that in some ways they reflected her own inner turmoil.

'Best get ready,' Gotrek said from behind her. 'Looks like it's going to rain hard.'

GREY SEER THANQUOL looked up at the gates of Hell Pit. The walls of the monstrous crater loomed above him. Poisonous-looking lichen covered the gnarled rock. Ahead of him, carved to resemble a monstrous rat-like head with gaping jaws, was the entrance to the lair of Clan Moulder. The black iron gates of the portcullis were its teeth and skaven heads peaked out from its eye sockets. In the distance Thanquol could hear the bellowing of beasts and sense the presence of a brain-numbing amount of warpstone. The sky overhead glittered with strange colours, as clouds of chemicals rose from the chimneys within the crater to pollute the air all around.

The thunder of hooves told Thanquol that the riders of Chaos had departed behind him. A tingling of his flesh told him that whatever spell had enwrapped them had departed with them. Thanquol felt certain that the spell was simply one to warp time and enhance their speed, allowing them to cover the distance been the horde and Hell Pit in a quarter of the time it would normally have taken. At least he hoped that was what it was. As far as he could tell, he had suffered no ill-effects from the magic nor had it affected him permanently.

He breathed a prayer to the Horned Rat, almost grateful for his delivery. The followers of Tzeentch had been as good as their word, and delivered him unharmed to this citadel of skavendom. Thanquol paused only for a moment to wonder why. The followers of the Lord of Change were famed for their cunning, not their mercy. Still, he reflected, they most likely had been impressed by his incredible eloquence. Thanquol knew that no matter how cunning they might be, they could not match wits with a grey seer. He knew that once again he had overcome his enemies by the sheer power of his intelligence.

He was uneasy. He wished that they had not brought him here of all places. He would have preferred any other stronghold than Hell Pit. Any port in a storm, Thanquol thought. And at least now he had great tidings to deliver. Surely, in the face of the threat of Chaos, the elders of Clan Moulder would see the sense of making a common cause with Thanquol.

He kicked Lurk up the posterior. 'Rise-rise! Get up lazy beast! Now is no time for resting!'

Lurk glared up at him with hate-filled eyes. Foam frothed around his lips. His chest rose and fell like bellows. He had been hard pressed to keep up with the Chaos steeds that had carried his maste, but, suspecting that to fall behind would mean his death, he had somehow managed to force his battered body to keep up. Whatever spell the Chaos sorcerers had cast had affected him too. He had not been left behind in spite of their supernatural pace.

Thanquol was aware of red skaven eyes glaring down at him from above the huge carved gate. He knew that weapons were being brought to bear on him, and that reinforcements were being hastily summoned to augment the guards within.

From high above a skaven voice chittered: 'Who is there? What is your business with Clan Moulder?'

Thanquol drew himself up to his full height and tilted back his head so that his horns were fully visible. He knew the guard would recognise the mark of the Horned Rat's favour. He gave them a few heartbeats to appreciate it, then boomed out in his most impressive oratorical voice, 'It is Grey Seer Thanquol come bearing important tidings for your masters.'

'Are you Thanquol or Thanquol's ghost?' a tremulous voice came back. 'Grey Seer Thanquol is dead. Killed by the dwarfs and their human allies at the battle of the horse soldiers' burrow.'

Always, always, this idiocy to contend with, thought Thanquol unhappily. 'Do I look dead, foolish vermin? Open this gate and take me to your masters or I will unleash a spell of grievous deadliness to consume your bones!'

He let a glow of pale warpfire build up around his hand to show that he meant what he said. In truth, he was certain that the protective magics woven into the crater's walls would most likely be able to withstand even his most potent sorceries, but how could a mere sentry know this?

'I must consult with my masters. Wait! Wait!' Thanquol was not sure whether the guard skaven meant to stay his spell or simply wait outside the gate. It did not matter. He knew that as soon as someone in authority was summoned he would be allowed inside.

Now all he had to do was consider what he was going to say. He needed to work out what would be advantageous to tell the Moulders and what was needful to keep from them. Such things could wait, he told himself. Suddenly, confidence filled him. He knew that a skaven of his supreme intellect would have no trouble outwitting the dullards of Moulder, just as he had easily out-thought the followers of Tzeentch.

Still, he was troubled. Even for a skaven of his superlative abilities, escaping the clutches of the Chaos horde had seemed a little too easy.

FELIX STARED ALONG the valley. He was amazed by how quickly things changed in the mountains. This morning it had been bright and sunny, clear as a summer's day on the plains of Kislev. Now it was dreary and cold, with a chilliness to the wind that reminded him of snow and winter. The clouds were low and dark. In the distance he could see the flicker of lightning strokes, and hear the faraway boom of thunder.

The mountains themselves had changed appearance just as dramatically. At dawn they had been bright, clean titans, almost hospitable-seeming. Now they loomed large, dark and forbidding in the dreary light. The further peaks were obscured by more cloud. He felt his own mood darkening. The change in the weather had added to the ominous, oppressive atmosphere caused by knowing that they were coming ever closer to the dragon's lair.

Ulrika had moved to the head of the column and was scouting alongside Standa and Oleg. It made a certain amount of sense. She had by far the keenest eyes in the party and would be able to perceive a threat before anyone else. At least, such had been her logic. Felix felt that it was just as much to get away from him. She had become remote and withdrawn again, and ignored all his attempts at conversation. He was fast coming to the conclusion that he would never understand women, or at the very least never understand her.

He became aware that Max Schreiber had fallen into step beside him. The mage's face wore a curious look, at once exalted, yet indrawn. His first impressions this morning had been correct, Felix thought. There was something different about Max now. He looked even more like a sorcerer than ever he had before. Felix tried to tell himself that it was because now he was simply more aware of the power the mage wielded, but he knew it was more than this. A distinct change had come over the magician in the past few days. Now, more than ever, he seemed like a figure of hidden might.

'Felix, may I ask you a few questions about the sword you bear?'

'Why?'

'I am interested in it. It seems to me to be an artifact of considerable power, and it seems to be... awakening.'

'What do you mean?'

'I mean I have sensed changes in it. The weapon harbours some sort of sentience, and it is gaining in strength.'

Felix thought about the burst of power he had received in the battle yesterday, and the way the blade had shielded him from dragonfire on the *Spirit of Grungni*. He had long known the weapon possessed magical qualities but not until recently had it exhibited anything like these powers. In the past it had simply been a blade that never lost its edge, with runes that glowed mysteriously under certain circumstances.

'Do you think that it is dangerous in any way?' he asked nervously. Max shrugged. A frown marred his fine features.

'I do not know. All magical weapons are in some way perilous. They are repositories of power that can sometimes affect their wielders in unpredictable ways. Sentient weapons are the most perilous of all, for they can warp the minds and souls of those who carry them.'

Felix felt his flesh crawl at the magician's words. He did not doubt that they were true. He fought down the instinctive urge to draw the blade and simply cast it away that rose up in him. 'Are you saying that the blade might be able to control me?'

'It is unlikely, unless it is particularly potent, and you are particularly weak-minded, which, I hasten to add, you do not appear to be. It might be able to affect your thinking a little, or take partial control in moments of stress. A weapon of the type I suspect this is could not control you, if you decided not to let it. At least, I hope not.'

'You are starting to worry me, Max.'

'That is not my intention. Could I ask how you came by the weapon?'

Felix considered this for a moment. 'It belonged to the Templar Aldred of the Order of the Fiery Heart. I took it from him after he died.'

Even as he said the words, Felix realised that this was both true and untrue. The blade had belonged to Aldred only for moments, when he had snatched it up from the hoard of the Chaos troll in Karag Eight Peaks. The Templar had come seeking the blade; it had not belonged to him. And yet, it felt like it did, or at least it felt like it belonged to his order. Felix had on many occasions felt as if he were merely the temporary custodian of the blade and he had fully intended to return it when the time was right. He mentioned all of these thoughts to Max. The magician looked thoughtful.

'It seems to me that the blade has been influencing your thoughts for a long time, albeit subtly. It also sounds like you have been unconsciously resisting its influence, which is both normal and instinctive when it comes to magic.'

'Why would this blade be trying to influence me?'

'Perhaps there is a geas attached to it. Or perhaps it is one of those weapons which possesses a single overriding purpose. Maybe it was forged with the destruction of a particular foe or type of foe in mind. Have you ever thought that this might be the case?'

'I suspect you already know the answer.'

'Just looking at the workmanship of the hilt is a clue, I would say. I would guess that the blade started to show changes after we encountered the dragon.'

'You would be right.' Felix told the mage of the way the blade had protected him from dragonfire, and of the way it had intervened in the previous day's battle when he had felt he might not survive to confront the beast. Max listened intently until after Felix had finished then said, 'I think your blade was forged to be a bane to dragons.'

'Do you mean you think it will give me the power to kill Skjalandir?'

'I don't know. I think it could hurt Skjalandir in a way that a normal blade could not but I don't think it will guarantee you could kill him. There are plenty of examples from history of heroes armed with the most potent magical weapons failing to kill the great drakes. Even Sigmar only wounded the Great Wyrm, Abraxas.'

'You are not reassuring me, Max,' Felix said. 'I thought for a moment I was about to become the hero of some mighty tale.'

'Truthfully, Felix, judging by your deeds you and Gotrek are already that. I am a magician, not a prophet or a seer, but I do not think it is entirely by chance that your sword, Gotrek's axe, Malakai's weapons and even my own self are here. I suspect the workings of fate. If I were a more vain and a more devout man, I would see the hand of the gods.'

'I find that difficult to imagine,' Felix said. 'I find it easier to believe that Gotrek and I live under the curse of the gods.'

'You are too cynical, Herr Jaeger.'

'If you had seen what I have seen, you would be cynical too,' said Felix.

Max looked at Felix, as if trying to weigh how serious he was. After a moment, he glanced away.

'Gotrek was right,' he said. 'It's going to rain. Hard.'

THE TRACK DESCENDED into a long valley that might almost have been in the lowlands of the eastern Empire. Trees covered the slopes of the valley sides. Dry-stone walls turned the hills into a patchwork of overgrown fields. Here and there, patches of wild flowers bloomed. Felix caught the distinctive scent of wildberry and summer-thorn roses. Houses were visible among the walls, and at first glance, a stranger might easily have taken the place as inhabited.

A second glance would convince them otherwise, Felix thought. The grey unmortared walls, built like the dykes themselves, were scorched and blackened as if by fire. The sod roofs of many had caved in. Weeds had overgrown the kitchen gardens. There were no signs of domesticated beasts anywhere. Just the occasional dog, gone feral, which looked at them with hungry eyes and then slunk away.

'Dragon work,' Ulli said.

'Or the work of reavers,' Gotrek said, gesturing to a patch of white bones bleaching in the long grass. Felix walked over to them and discovered grass growing through the eye sockets of a human skull. A rusty blade lay near at hand, and by pushing the grass aside, he discovered the rotting remains of a leather cuirass. It looked like it had been chewed, perhaps by hungry dogs.

Even as he studied the remains, he felt cold wetness on his hair and on his face. The dark clouds above had finally made good on their promise of rain.

'We can shelter amid these ruins,' Max said. 'Part of the roof is still intact, and we can rig a tarpaulin over the rest of it.'

'Why not just creep into the back of the wagon?' suggested Steg, with a glint in his eye.

'Over ma deid boadie!' Malakai said. Something in Steg's appearance suggested that he might not be averse to that idea.

'I don't suppose the ruins will be haunted,' boomed Ulli. He looked a little pale and nervous once more.

'You're not afraid of ghosts?' Bjorni asked. 'Are you?'

'I fear nothing!' Ulli said. 'But only a fool tempts the wrath of the spirits of the dead.'

'I suppose that means we should send Snorri in,' Bjorni said nastily.

'Snorri thinks that's a good idea,' said Snorri, oblivious to the insult. 'Snorri isn't afraid of ghosts.'

'There are no ghosts in this place, or if there are they are the ghosts of mewling men, and what need have we to fear them,' Gotrek said and stomped after Snorri.

'Might as well get in out of the rain,' Felix said, and looked around to see if the Kislevites agreed with them.

'Ah'll joost stay wae ma wagon,' said Malakai Makaisson, glaring at Steg from under his beetling brows.

Steg shook his head, and disappeared inside. He was smirking to himself. For the first time it occurred to Felix that Steg might actually enjoy tormenting the engineer – and that in some perverse way, Malakai took pleasure in being tormented. He shrugged. If the Slayers wanted to indulge in such petty bickering it was no business of his.

THE RAIN DRUMMED down on the roof of the cottage. It was a typical peasant dwelling: one large room which had once been inhabited by humans, their dogs and their cattle. Rain puddled in the middle of the packed earth floor under the hole in the roof. Rats scuttled about amid the remains of the furniture. Despite the damp, Snorri had managed to get a fire crackling over by the chimney, and the not unpleasant smell of wood smoke filled the room. More clouds of smoke drifted across the chamber, mingling with the weed fumes from the Slayers' pipes. All of the Slayers save Ulli had produced them, and were puffing away in the morose silence that passed as companionability among dwarfs.

Listening to the rain, Felix found time to be glad that the goblins had not attacked them in the middle of the storm. He wondered how Malakai's gunpowder weapons would have functioned then. Not well, he guessed. He prayed that it was a fine day when they finally confronted the dragon. That made him think of the sword. He drew it from the scabbard and began to inspect the blade, studying it with an intensity he had never used before.

It was a well-made weapon. From the dragon's head on the pommel to the runes on the blade it gave every indication of high quality. The steel of the blade gleamed. The edges were razor sharp despite the fact he had never taken a whetstone to them. The runes caught the firelight, but, at that moment, appeared merely decorative. There was no hint of any sorcerous power lurking within the blade, and, looking at it, Felix found it hard to believe that there could be. The weapon seemed so prosaic that, were it not for his memories of its power, he would have thought it merely another rich man's blade, not some mystical weapon. Then again, Firebeard's hammer had looked the same way back in the Temple of Grimnir, and Felix knew exactly how potent it was.

'You look thoughtful,' Ulrika said. Felix looked up at her. She had been standing in the doorway not moments before, staring out into the rain.

'And you look lovely,' he said.

'Always ready with flattery,' she said, but there was no hostility in her tone. 'What were you thinking about?'

'I was thinking about this sword, and how I found it, and about the dragon.' Without meaning to, he found himself telling her of the quest to Karag Eight Peaks, of how he and Gotrek and Albrecht and the others had fought their way into the dark tunnels beneath the mountains, and had slain the

Chaos troll. He told her of the spirits of the dwarf kings who had appeared before them, and of how they had left the treasures of the lost city in the tomb and he spoke of the eerie grandeur of the ancient dwarf city. It was only when he noticed that silence had fallen over the chamber that he realised that all the dwarfs were listening to him. Suddenly embarrassed, he stopped, but Snorri looked over at him and said, 'Go on, young Felix. Snorri likes a tale as much as the next dwarf and yours is a good one.'

The other dwarfs nodded acquiescence, so Felix spoke on, telling of battles with Chaos warriors in the woods of the Empire, and encounters with evil cultists in the cities of men. He talked of the battle with the skaven amid the blazing buildings of Nuln, and of the long voyage across the Chaos Wastes in search of the lost dwarfhold of Karag Dum. It was dark by the time he finished, and the silence in the chamber had intensified. He realised that at some time during his speech the rain had stopped.

He looked up, and at that moment the smoke cloud whichfilled the room billowed under the impact of the night breeze, the same breeze that parted the storm clouds. Through the gap he caught a glimpse of the cold sky. Two moons hovered there. The larger one shone silver, sending a chill light down to bathe the land. The lesser moon glowed greenishly, and the aura that surrounded it obscured the stars. He was certain that its glow was brighter than ever he had seen it before, brighter even than on that unholy Geheimnisnacht when he and Gotrek had fought with the worshippers of Slaanesh. He knew then, in the innermost recesses of his soul, that the power of Chaos was growing in proportion to the moon's glow, and that however long he lived, that moon was going to grow brighter until its light eclipsed its larger sibling. He was suddenly dreadfully afraid.

If any of the dwarfs noticed they gave no sign. Eventually, Bjorni spoke, 'By Grungni, Grimnir and Valaya, Felix Jaeger, you have seen more of the ancient holy places of the dwarfs than many of the dwarfs. I do not know whether you have been blessed or cursed, but I believe that somehow the gods look on you with favour. Why else would you have been chosen to wield the Hammer of Firebeard?'

All the other dwarfs except Gotrek nodded their agreement. Felix noted that some time during his tale-telling Gotrek had vanished outside. He could hear the Slayer talking to Malakai Makaisson now that he had stopped speaking himself. Bjorni glanced around, a feverish light illuminating his ugly face. He spat into the fire, rubbed his hands and spoke:

'Tis a night for tale-telling so I'll give you a yarn. Some of you may have heard the awful rumours about the night I met two elf maidens in a tavern in Marienberg. I want to tell you that the story is not true. Well, not entirely true. It happened like this...'

The groans and jeers of the other dwarfs threatened for a moment to cut him off but he continued unabashed. Felix looked over at Ulrika. 'Shall we take a walk?' he asked.

She nodded agreement.

THE SMELL OF damp and rain-soaked earth assaulted Felix's nostrils. He looked around warily. They had walked a long way from the cottage and the fire. Perhaps too far for safety in these perilous mountains. Still, he sensed that they had both wanted to be alone, to speak freely, far from the dwarfs. This was the one way they could have some privacy. He was willing to risk the danger, if only for a few minutes.

Ulrika's hand felt warm in his. He noticed that her fingers were calloused from blade-work. Her hair smelled faintly of sweat. As did her clothes. It was not a romantic scent but it was hers, and he liked it. He glanced at her face, admiring the profile. She was most certainly beautiful, and at that moment looked thoughtful.

'Felix, what is to become of us?' she asked.

He considered her question for a moment, knowing he was no closer to an answer than he had been in Karak Kadrin. After a while he spoke.

'I will go with the Slayers to face the dragon. You will go on to Kislev and carry your father's warning to the Ice Queen. If I survive I will seek you out.'

'Then what?'

'Then most likely we will go to Praag or wherever the armies muster to fight the Chaos hordes.' He glanced up at the greenly glowing moon, and shivered. 'And then perhaps we will die.'

'I do not think I want to die,' she said softly. It sounded as if it came as a revelation to her. Perhaps it did. He knew she was born and bred on the plains of northern Kislev, where duty and death were things children were taught as soon as they were old enough to understand their meanings.

'No one does.'

'I have been given a holy trust by my father. I am to bear word of his need to our liege lady. And yet I find myself thinking of... abandoning my duty and running away, of finding a place to hide for a while to laugh and love and live. I find myself thinking this and I am horrified. What would my father think? What would the spirits of my ancestors think?'

'What do *you* think?'

'If I were to run away, would you go with me?'

Felix looked at her. At that moment, he forgot about his oath to Gotrek, about the destiny that Max Schreiber had talked of, about his own dreams and illusions of heroism. 'Yes. Do you want to go?'

She was silent for a long moment, and he could see the struggle written on her face. A tear trickled down her cheek, and he almost reached out to wipe it away. Something kept him from doing it. He felt that at that moment, their two lives were hanging in the balance, and that perhaps she could change their destinies with a single word. He looked into her eyes, and saw a spirit at war, and thought, she truly does love me. He was going to speak, but at that moment she turned away. He did not move his hand. The silence lengthened. 'I do not know,' she said. 'I do not know you and I do not know myself any more. You are a fool, Felix Jaeger, and you have made a fool of me. I will go with you to face the dragon.'

She turned and fled away from him back towards the ruined cottage, running as if all the fiends of Chaos were at her heels. Felix wondered what had happened, and realised that he did not have a clue.

FELIX RETURNED TO find a stranger by the fire. He was a tall, scarred man, garbed in leather. A wide-brimmed leather hat shaded his face. A longsword lay scabbarded by his side. A bundle of cloth, tied to the end of a staff pushed into the earthen floor and the lute the stranger plucked idly with his fingers marked him as a wandering minstrel.

No one was showing the slightest interest, but the stranger did not seem too bothered. He looked only too grateful for the fire, and companions to share it with. Felix wasn't really all that interested in him. He wanted to talk with Ulrika but she had already cast herself down on the far side of the fire, and lay between her bodyguards, seemingly determined to pretend he was not there. Felix felt obscurely hurt. His pride was wounded. If that's what she wants, he thought, then let her get on with it. He wanted some time to think about what she had said anyway.

'Who are you?' he asked the stranger, none too politely. The stranger regarded him pleasantly enough.

'Johan Gatz is my name, friend. What is yours?'

'Felix Jaeger.'

'You are a companion to these Slayers?'

'Yes.'

'It's common enough to see men and dwarfs travelling together in these mountains. It is less common to see three Kislevites, a sorcerer, a man of the Empire and a gang of Slayers journeying as a group. Have you joined together for protection on the road, or is there a tale here I might sing of?'

'That depends on what type of songs you sing,' Felix said.

'All sorts.'

'As I told you earlier, we're going to kill the dragon,' bellowed Ulli boastfully. Johan Gatz winced and raised an eyebrow. 'And you are accompanying these Slayers on their death quest? Your friends here have told me all manner of tales about you and Gotrek there. You've led interesting lives.'

'Apparently so.' Felix did not know why he was offended by the man's curiosity but he was. It was quite common for minstrels to be inquisitive. Their stock in trade was quite often as much news and gossip as it was songs and music. The dwarfs seemed none too bothered by him, but there was something about the man that rubbed Felix the wrong way. He tried telling himself that he was being unfair, that he was just upset by his conversation with Ulrika, but there was something about the man that made him suspicious.

'How came you to be wandering through these mountains?' Felix asked. 'I would have thought this a dangerous region for a man to travel in alone.'

'A minstrel may travel anywhere he pleases. Even the most savage brigand will not slay a penniless player when he can have a song for free.'

'I had not heard orcs and goblins were so appreciative of strolling players.'

'I am a fast runner,' said Johan Gatz with an easy smile. 'Though in truth, I must confess that I am somewhat alarmed by what I have found here.'

'Really?'

'Yes. The last time I passed this way was several years ago. The High Road then was lined with towns and villages where a man could earn his bread and some coin. The region was not so wild and lawless. There were neither orcs nor bandits here then. Had I known what I know now, I would not have come back this way but would have stayed in Ostmark regardless of the competition there.'

'It might have been wiser.'

'Aye, that it might. Hindsight is always wise sight, as my dear old mother used to say.'

'You say that even the most desperate bandits will leave a minstrel alone. Have you met any?'

'I have met some who might have been, though they let me be.'

'Have you heard aught of Henrik Richter? He is said to be the king of the bandits hereabouts.'

Johan Gatz laughed out loud. 'Then he rules a pretty poor kingdom as far as I can see. I have seen no great armies of bandits nor have I heard anything of this bandit king although I confess that now that you mention him, it might be a good idea for a song.'

'I have never met any bandits quite so romantic as the ones you hear about in minstrels' songs,' Felix said. 'None I have ever met robbed from the rich and gave to the poor, or fought unjust landowners for the rights of the downtrodden. The ones I met only wanted to separate my head from my shoulders and my purse from my belt.'

'You have met many bandits then, Herr Jaeger?' asked Johan Gatz with an odd gleam in his eye.

'A few,' replied Felix.

'Then you must be a hardier man than you seem, to still be alive. You do not sound like a mercenary or a swordsman, if I may say so.'

'Hardy enough,' Felix said, sensing a subtle insult in the man's words.

'Felix Jaeger is one of the mightiest men Snorri Nosebiter has ever known,' said Snorri from the far side of the fire. Felix looked over at him in surprise. He had not thought he had made quite such a good impression on the Slayer. Nor had he been aware that the Slayer had been listening quite so closely to the conversation. 'Of course, that is not saying much,' added Snorri quickly to general laughter from the dwarfs.

Felix shrugged and gave his attention back to the minstrel. 'We go to slay the dragon,' he said. 'There should be a song in it, if you care to accompany us.'

'I like living,' said the minstrel. 'But should you survive the experience, seek me out and I will make a song of the tale. It will probably make me famous.'

He paused for a moment, and considered his words. 'Do you honestly think you have a chance of surviving? Can you even make it to the mountain, if what you tell me of orcs and goblins and human bandits is true?'

'We have already put a warband of greenskins to flight,' Felix said, knowing that he was boasting, but needled by the minstrel's tone. Once again Johan Gatz raised an eyebrow.

'Twelve of you did that?'

'One is a wizard. The Slayers are mighty. Malakai Makaisson is an excellent weapons engineer.'

'You use dwarf armaments then, gatling canons and such?'

Felix nodded. The minstrel laughed gleefully.

'It seems you are not going about your dragon-slaying in the orthodox manner then. No white horses, no lances, no magical weapons.'

'We are too,' said Snorri. 'Gotrek's axe is magical. He killed a bloody big daemon with it. Snorri saw him. And Felix's sword is magic too. You can tell by the runes if you look closely.'

Felix wondered if Snorri had been eavesdropping on his conversation with Max Schreiber or whether he really could tell by the runes. In either case, Felix wished he had not said anything about the weapons in front of this inquisitive stranger. He had the feeling that he himself had already said too much. He did not know why but he was starting to trust Johan Gatz less and less, and he had not trusted him very much to begin with.

'It seems I have underestimated you,' said the minstrel. 'Your expedition seems remarkably well-prepared. I can almost pity any bandits you run into.'

'It's late,' Felix said. 'I need to get some sleep.'

'That seems wise,' said the stranger mockingly. 'After all you have a busy few days ahead of you.'

Felix threw himself down on the far side of the fire. He took a last glance at the minstrel, and was not surprised to see the man watching him closely. He was surprised to see Max Schreiber was looking suspiciously at Gatz. It seemed he, too, had his suspicions about the man.

Felix wondered if he would wake up in the night with his throat cut, and then decided that it was unlikely. Anybody who tried it with all the Slayers around was in for a very short life afterwards.

Not that it would be much consolation if he himself were dead, Felix thought, as he dropped into a restless slumber.

JOHAN GATZ CURSED. The gods had spat on him again. When he had noticed the wagon, he had hoped to find a small merchant caravan with maybe a few bodyguards down here. He had not expected a gang of Slayers and this bunch of heavily armed humans. He was particularly annoyed by the presence of the wizard. There was no sense in trying to slip out and give the signal that would bring Henrik and the lads down from the mountainside. The wizard was watching him too closely, and the dwarfs were as suspicious as they were surly.

It was only to be expected, he supposed. Luck had not been with Henrik Richter's gang recently. Things hadn't really gone right since the dragon had arrived, and the orcs moved in along the High Road. Once there had been rich pickings along this trail, at least rich enough for a smallish band of former mercenaries and cut-throats. With all the extra mouths to feed, things were not so good. Johan cursed the necessity of taking in the human refugees from the destroyed villages, but there had been no other way. They had needed extra swords just to hold their own citadel against the orcs.

He supposed he should thank Sigmar for small mercies though. At least none of the travellers had questioned his disguise as a wandering minstrel, although that hard eyed man, Jaeger, had seemed suspicious. Taking this lot out was not going to be an easy proposition, he could tell. It wasn't going to be a case of offering an unsuspecting sentry a drugged drink, slitting his throat, and then summoning the boys with a lantern. These laddies were hard, and he did not want to try anything tricky with a magician watching. Anyway, he had always heard that dwarfs could smell poison and his own experience had confirmed this.

He felt certain that confident as this bunch might be, Henrik Richter and his bandit crew could overcome them. At least they could if Henrik assembled his whole army in one spot. They might even be able to do it with the fifty or so men that Henrik had in the foothills above. 'Might' being the operative word. This gang looked tough, and even if Henrik and the boys could overcome them, they would probably take an unacceptable number of the lads to hell with them. On the whole it would probably be best to leave them alone.

There was not going to be any profit in this night's work, he could tell. On the other hand other possibilities suggested themselves. Perhaps he could offer the Slayers an alliance against the orcs. He knew that the stunties hated the green-skins even more than he did. Probably wouldn't work, he thought. They were Slayers and on their way to fight a dragon, and Johan was familiar enough with the ways of dwarfs to know that getting between a stunty and a hoard of gold was a sure way to get boot prints on your chest.

It was then that the idea struck him. This was a well-equipped expedition. Perhaps the Slayers could kill the dragon. Perhaps not. But there was always the possibility that they could, or wound it badly enough so that it might be slaughtered by an army of men. If that were the case...

Skjalandir had a big hoard of treasure, that was for sure. Dragons always did. That being the case, the way to profit from this might be to follow these maniacs and see what happened. Even if they won, they would most likely be weakened enough by the battle for Henrik and the boys to overcome them. And if they lost, maybe they would weaken the dragon. It was an idea he would put to Henrik tomorrow. He was sure his cousin would grasp its significance at once.

Johan licked his lips at the thought of the dragon's hoard of treasure. He was certain that his share would be more than enough to buy him a little tavern in Nuln and let him leave the dangerous profession of banditry aside. Perhaps things were looking up, he told himself, and drifted into dreams of mountains of gold.

* * *

GREY SEER THANQUOL glared around the great antechamber of the Tower of Moulder. He was furious and he was filled with fear. Since his arrival at Hell Pit he had been kept waiting. Clanrat warriors in the distinctive livery of the Masters had shown him and Lurk to this huge room and then abandoned them there. He wondered why he had been brought here. He had never been allowed into the inner citadel of the Moulders before. Previously all his business with them had been conducted in the cavernous chambers in the crater walls that the clan used for all its business transactions. He was not sure whether it was a good sign or a bad sign that he had been brought here. Being right at the heart of the city made him feel exceedingly nervous. He reached out and touched the winds of magic, just to reassure himself. The power of dark magic was strong here. It was hardly surprising, given how close they were to the Chaos Wastes and how much warpstone dust was in the air, but it was reassuring.

Once again he inspected his surroundings, searching for the hidden peepholes he felt certain were there. It was not in the least likely that any skaven clan would allow a stranger to stand unobserved in the heart of their fortress, and Clan Moulder were possibly the most devious and suspicious of all the ratman clans.

Thanquol wandered over to the window and stared balefully out at the benighted city. It was not made from glass but from some translucent leathery substance whose scent reminded him of flesh. It was a disturbing reminder that the raw material on which Clan Moulder's prowess and fortune was based was nothing less than the stuff of life itself.

He looked down on an eerie cityscape. Huge towers that reminded him of the tusks of some enormous beast dominated the inside of the crater. From their towering tips emerged clouds of glowing smoke: livid green, ruby, cobalt blue and all manner of other toxic shades. The pillars of smoke rose to contribute to the huge cloud of pollution that eternally hovered above the crater and sometimes descended to create thickly obscuring fog. Thanquol could tell from the faint eerie glitter that the smoke contained trapped particles of warpstone. Part of him was outraged by this flagrant waste, part of him was awestruck by the display of sheer wealth. He had no idea what was taking place within those towers but the cacophony of screams, howls and bestial roars told him that it was not pleasant.

Among the towers lay other buildings, constructed in a distinctly un-skavenish manner. The buildings were huge tents of decaying leathery flesh, thrown over massive skeletons of twisted bone. They had an odd look that suggested huge ticks or beetles frozen in place by some strange magic. These were the barracks within which the slaves and soldiers of the clans dwelt. The streets below teemed with skaven, and he realised that it was possible that Hell Pit was a ratman city second only to Skavenblight in population.

Here and there, amid the wide streets, were greenishly glowing lakes of polluted water, reputedly still contaminated by the warpstone starfall that had created the vast crater. Far away, he could see the glitter of thousands of lights, windows in the crater wall. It was rumoured that the whole wall had been burrowed out into an endless labyrinth of tunnels and artificial caves to provide burrows and laboratories for the clan. Even as Thanquol watched, a huge door opened in the crater side, and a massive creature emerged. At this distance, in the dark, Thanquol could not make out all the details, but something about the creature suggested a cave rat grown to the size of a mastodon with a howdah on its back.

Across the night sky flickered forms that Thanquol at first took to be bats, but which he swiftly realised were too big. The simplest explanation was that they were mutant bats grown to massive size, but one of them veered closer to the tower, and he realised that it was a skaven with bat-like membranes under its arms. Part of Thanquol felt horror at this blasphemy. Had not the Horned Rat created the skaven in his own image? Was not tampering with shape of the highest of all creatures the supreme sacrilege? Thanquol had always known the Moulders were mad. He had just never realised quite how insane they really were.

Still, it was a brilliant madness, in its way. Even he had to concede that. In this barren place far from the true centre of skaven civilisation, Clan Moulder had done things that even Thanquol had never dreamed of. He wondered if the Council of Thirteen were aware of quite how much the clan had achieved. Surely, he thought, there must be some way he could use all of this to his advantage.

He glanced around the room once again. Here, too, was evidence of the mad genius of Clan Moulder. The leather-covered thrones and couches appeared to be incredibly torpid living things. Every time Thanquol looked back, they had changed position ever so slightly, in a manner at once maddening and slightly sinister. The grey seer suspected that the whole room was designed to make visitors uneasy and put them off-balance in any confrontation with the builders. Finally, Thanquol found what he was looking for. High above in the ceiling amid the warpstone-powered globes of the chandelier, he saw a cluster of eyes. They swayed slightly as they observed him, and then, reacting to the fact he had noticed them, they withdrew into the ceiling, vanishing from sight.

As if this was a signal the door to the chamber opened like a set of great jaws, and the enormously fat figure of Izak Grottle waddled in. A living table covered in bone bowls and translucent fleshy plates followed him.

'Greetings, in the name of Moulder, Grey Seer Thanquol,' rumbled Grottle in his unnaturally deep voice. 'Greetings indeed. It is good to see you once more.'

Thanquol doubted that his old rival was pleased to see him. Grottle had tried to betray Thanquol many times when the grey seer had led the army against Nuln. There was bad blood between them, and Thanquol had sworn he would one day have vengeance on Grottle. He did not doubt that, if the opportunity arose, the Moulder would try to do away with him. He knew he would have to be careful.

Grottle slumped into one of the thrones. Its leathery fur moulded itself to his shape, expanding outwards to make room for his fat rump, then enfolding him in an unnatural manner. Its legs flexed slightly as if with strain, and Thanquol would have sworn he heard it emit a slight grunt. After a moment, the chair's back started to ripple as if it were massaging its occupant. Grottle leaned forward and helped himself to a small broiled rat from the table which had manoeuvred itself into position in front of him.

'So, Grey Seer Thanquol, you have returned bearing the spoils of your attack on the horse-humans' burrow that you promised my Clanlords. You have come to report success in your acquisition of the dwarf airship and have brought the secrets of its construction to share with my overlords. You have come bearing tidings of the whereabouts of the Moulder troops who accompanied you on your quest.'

Grottle forced the rat whole down his throat and then smiled wickedly. He knew that Thanquol had brought no such pleasant tidings. It occurred to the grey seer that Grottle was enjoying this.

'Not exactly,' Thanquol said, twitching his tail uneasily. Grottle helped himself to another morsel.

'Not exactly,' he muttered to himself, in an almost gloating tone. 'Not exactly. This is not good news, Grey Seer Thanquol. This is not good at all. Clan Moulder lent you the services of several hundred of its finest troops, and many, many of our deadliest beasts, on the understanding that we would share the spoils of your success. At the very least, you will be able to return our warriors and our beasts to us then.'

Thanquol knew that Grottle knew that he could do no such thing. The fat monster was simply toying with him, now that he had the grey seer in his power. He wondered if Grottle would dare do away with him. Thanquol was, after all, one of the chosen of the Horned Rat and a favoured emissary of the Council of Thirteen. Surely, not even this ravenous beast would dare harm him. Considered reflection told Thanquol that this was unfortunately not the case.

At this moment there was nobody save the Moulders and Lurk who knew of his whereabouts. He had set off in utmost secrecy, hoping to acquire the airship for himself and return to present himself in triumph to the Council. If anything happened to him now, it would be as if he had simply vanished from the face of the earth. Thanquol's fur rose at the sheer unfairness of it. He had come here in good faith to warn the Moulders of the peril of the approaching Chaos horde, and they were prepared to assassinate him over some petty debt they felt he owed them. He glared at Grottle, and swore that whatever happened he would make this fat fool pay for his insolence. He was still capable of blasting his enemies into their component atoms. Grottle had entered this chamber at his peril. As if sensing the change in Thanquol's mood Grottle looked up at him and growled. It was a fearsome sound, and Thanquol remembered that, for all his enormous bulk, the Moulder could be alarmingly swift and terrifyingly strong in battle. He let his anger subside a little, but remained prepared to instantly summon his powers in his own defence.

'The troops have not returned?' said Thanquol, affecting surprise.

'A very few,' allowed Grottle, spearing another morsel with one of his claws, transferring it to his mouth and gulping it down. 'They brought confused tales of a battle, and sorcery and a massacre of skaven. There were suggestions of incompetent leadership, Grey Seer Thanquol. Very incompetent leadership.'

'I left command of the military side of the venture to the Moulders,' said Thanquol quickly, knowing that in a sense it was true. It was not his fault that the Moulder leaders were incapable of implementing his brilliant plans. 'I would not presume to judge their efficiency.'

Grottle shook his head, as if Thanquol were a particularly slow runt who had failed to understand his meaning. 'You were in overall command, I believe, Grey Seer Thanquol. You were responsible for the success of the mission. You gave many assurances to the Clanlords of Moulder. They are... disappointed. Most disappointed.'

Thanquol's tail stiffened in outrage. He bared his fangs angrily. A nimbus of light winked into being around his fingers as he prepared to unleash his most destructive spell.

'Before you do anything too hasty, Grey Seer Thanquol, please consider this,' Grottle said. 'After the debacle at Nuln, I do not rank quite so highly within my clan as I once did. You might say I am in disgrace. You might also say that my Clanlords consider me expendable, which is why they have delegated me to have this conversation with you. You might further want to consider that you are in the heart of Clan Moulder's greatest citadel. Within call are thousands upon thousands of clanrat warriors. Not to mention a virtually limitless supply of altered beasts. Anyone so foolish as to attack a member of the clan, and then try to escape from this place, would not get more than a hundred strides. I mention this knowing that you are too wise to attempt any such thing. Far too wise.'

Thanquol ground his teeth in frustration. Grottle's threat was clear. Also implicit in the statement was the fact that no one would care if he took Grottle hostage and tried to negotiate a way out. He was almost embarrassed to admit that he had not even considered trying it. Grottle continued to speak. His deep voice sounded mild, gentle even. 'To tell the truth, I was surprised that you came here. I would not have expected it after the... embarrassment with the airship. Why did you come?'

'I bring appalling tidings, and a warning for the masters of Moulder.'

'And what would that be?' Grottle asked disinterestedly. He sucked something from his extended talon. His claws looked alarmingly sharp, Thanquol noted.

'A Chaos horde, limitless in numbers and boundless in power, makes its way southwards. It seems the servants of the four Powers are leaving the Wastes and coming south as they did generations ago.'

'This is grave news. If true.'

'It is true. I swear it by the Thirteen Secret Names of the Horned Rat. I have seen the host with my own eyes, smelled it with my own snout. Lurk and I barely escaped it with our lives.'

Thanquol thought it best not to mention that the followers of Tzeentch had let him go. He wanted to give Grottle no excuse to think that he might be a spy or a traitor to the skaven cause. He knew there were many jealous ratmen who would be only too keen to give such an interpretation to events, despite the inherent ludicrousness of the idea. Despite the fact that Thanquol's name was a byword for devotion to the skaven cause, he was wise enough to know that he had enemies who would give a twisted interpretation to even his most innocent act. He prayed that Lurk would remember this too.

'This is terrible news then. What do you propose that we should do?'

'Muster your armies, make ready to defend Hell Pit against an invasion by the forces of Chaos. It might happen.'

'And if it does not?'

'Then muster your armies anyway. Surely the horde will sow terror and alarm along its path. In the coming war there will be many opportunities to advance the skaven cause.'

Even as his words carried him away, Thanquol could see they were true. The Chaos horde was going to attack the human kingdom. Whatever the outcome, the struggle would surely weaken even the victorious side. All the skaven had to do was wait and new opportunities would inevitably fall into their outstretched paw. 'The Council of Thirteen must be notified at once.'

Grottle yawned and rose from his chair. 'You may be right, Grey Seer Thanquol. I will report your words to my masters. They will decide what to do next.'

Thanquol could not believe it. He had just handed this fat fool information of the utmost importance, and he could not see the urgency of the situation. Thanquol considered blasting him out of sheer frustration. He restrained himself, knowing that he would have to get word to the Council. Armies would have to be assembled. Plans would have to be made. He knew that there was no one better equipped to lead such a force than himself. In his excitement he almost forgot about the airship. In the coming war there would be countless opportunities to cover himself in glory and advance his position in the eyes of the Thirteen. The Horned Rat had surely blessed him once more. Once again he was in the right place at the right time.

Grottle paused at the entrance to the chamber. 'By the way, Grey Seer Thanquol, until this matter is resolved, you are the guest of my clan. We will see to your safety. We will make sure your needs are met. You are, after all, a very special guest. I am sure you understand my meaning.'

Thanquol's heart sank. He knew exactly what Izak Grottle meant. He knew now, beyond a shadow of a doubt, that he was the prisoner of Clan Moulder.

ELEVEN

INTO THE VALLEY OF DEATH

FELIX LOOKED DOWN on the entrance to the Dragon Vale. He had
not seen a scene of such surpassing bleakness since they left the
Chaos Wastes. Around the shores of a small lake lay a collection of burned out ruins that had once been a town. All the
houses, watchtowers and farms that had once surrounded the
town had been equally devastated. The fields were overgrown,
and here and there what could only be bones glittered whitely
amid the long grass. In some ways this was worse than the
Wastes, for it was obvious that the lands below had once been
as thriving and prosperous as they were now desolate.

At the far end of the valley stood a great barren peak, rising
above the slopes of the foothills. There was something especially horrible about this mountain. It had a sense of presence,
of menace. Just by looking at its greyish sides, you could tell
that there was something dreadful lurking there. Felix tried to
tell himself that it was just his imagination. Supplied with the
knowledge that they were within sight of the dragon's lair, his
mind was working overtime, conjuring up an atmosphere of
gloom and destruction.

Even as he tried to reassure himself he knew he was right.
There was something horrible about this place. No birds sang.

The wind that blew down the valley was mournful. The clouds hung low and oppressive in the sky. At any moment, Felix feared to look up and see a huge winged shape descending out of them.

It had been a long march. Almost three days had passed since their encounter with Johan Gatz, and during that time his suspicions about the supposed minstrel had increased. There had been times when Ulrika had thought she had seen men watching them from the hills. Times when he himself had caught sight of greenskins moving along the high slopes parallel to them. It looked as if they were being watched by at least two factions as they had moved through the mountains.

At least the watchers had proved wary. They had stayed well out of bowshot and vanished as soon as the Slayers made the first signs of pursuit. By the time they got to the spot where the greenskins had been, the orcs had vanished. It seemed that the fate of their earlier attackers had taught any would-be ambushers a lesson. Either that or they were waiting for something. Felix could not guess what. Perhaps now they had entered the Dragon Vale, they would be left alone. Or perhaps the greenskins were simply waiting for the dragon to slay the interlopers, then they would descend and despoil the bodies. If the dragon left anything to despoil. Felix wasn't feeling any too cheerful about the outcome of their quest. It was all too easy to believe that every last one of them would die in this place.

He squared his shoulders and smiled experimentally, hoping this would change his mood. If that were the case, he told himself, at least Gotrek would achieve his long-sought doom. He glanced over at Ulrika and any cheery thoughts evaporated. They had barely spoken on the trip here. Actually, she had spoken more to Max Schreiber than to Felix. It was obvious that she was purposefully avoiding him.

In a way he did not blame her. What future was there for them now? They would most likely die within the next few days. And even if by some miracle they survived the encounter with the dragon, they would soon have to face the horde of Chaos rampaging down into Kislev. He was not even sure how he felt about her himself. He was hurt by the way she treated him, and felt absurdly and exaggeratedly sensitive to her behaviour. At times during the march, he had been more concerned by the way she avoided looking at him, or the way she talked to Max, than he was with the possibility that he might soon be slaughtered by the dragon.

Max, at least, looked cheery. He smiled as he joked with Ulrika. Felix's stomach churned as he saw her smile back. He was jealous and guilty and there was nothing he could do about it.

Oleg and Standa refused to look at him too. He was certain it was nothing personal, they were simply standing by Ulrika as was their duty. They could not take his side even if they wanted to. Felix cursed to himself. Even by the excruciating standards of the treks he had endured with Gotrek, this was a miserable journey.

'There's a dragon about here somewhere!' bellowed Ulli. 'I can smell him.'

The other Slayers looked at the youth with a mixture of contempt, amusement and irritation. 'Does your keen nose tell you how soon we will encounter it?' asked Gotrek sarcastically. Ulli fell silent.

'I reckon we'll be at the dragon mount inside a day,' said Bjorni. 'We'll see it then.'

'I wonder how much treasure it has?' Steg said. Felix looked at him uneasily. He could see the gleam of gold fever in the dwarf's eyes. It was not a reassuring sight. Dwarfs had been known to do many dishonourable things under its influence. It seemed he was not the only one who recognised it.

'Dinnae you worry yersel aboot the dragon's gold,' said Malakai. 'You joost keep thinkin' about the big beastie itself.'

Grimme glared at Steg. Steg looked at his feet. He seemed almost embarrassed.

'There's something else down there,' Gotrek said. 'I can smell it. And it's not a dragon.'

Felix had a lot more faith in Gotrek's nose than he had in Ulli's. 'What is it?' he asked.

'I don't know,' Gotrek said. 'But whatever it is, you can bet it won't be friendly.'

'Now there's a surprise,' muttered Felix.

'WHO BE YE?' asked the madwoman as they entered the ruined town. She stood outside the remains of an inn. Like all the buildings in the town it was built from stone. Now it spoke only of the dragon's capacity for destruction. Its walls were scorched and caked with soot from the burning of its timbers. In places the stones had melted and run, a testimony to the heat of the dragon's breath.

Felix looked at her. Her face was filthy and her clothing reeked. She was garbed in tattered rags. A blackened scarf held her matted hair out of her eyes. More rags were wrapped around her feet. A huge claw-like nail emerged from the cloth bandaged around her left foot. Just from looking into her eyes, Felix could tell that she and sanity had parted company a long time ago.

The dwarfs looked at her warily. Gotrek had warned them they were being watched minutes ago, and they had all readied weapons. It was difficult to see what threat she could be to such a heavily armed party unless she were some sort of witch. Felix glanced over at Max. As if reading his thoughts, the sorcerer looked at the woman and shook his head.

'We are travellers, passing through,' Felix said. 'Who are you?'

'I had a name once. I had a man. I had babies. This was my home.' A wild gesture indicated the burned out shell of the tavern. 'No more. Now I wait. Now you travel and you travel to meet death.'

'What do you mean?'

'Death dwells on your road. He dwells in a cave in the mountains. Death came here and devoured my family, my friends and my children. Death will come again for me soon.'

Felix felt an uncomfortable sympathy for the old woman. She had seen her whole life destroyed by the dragon and had retreated into madness. Here was another of the creature's victims, like poor Varek. 'It was the dragon who killed your loved ones,' he said eventually.

'Death is the dragon. The dragon is death,' she said and let out a high pitched cackling laugh. 'And round here death has many servants and many worshippers. As you shall soon find out. As the others did.'

'What others?'

'Other dwarfs with big axes and bad haircuts. Mighty men mounted on chargers and armed with lances. Men of violence who came seeking death's hoard. All of them bones now, scattered along the road to death's cave.'

Felix knew she was referring to some of the Slayers who had preceded them. He wondered about the knights though, and this troop of mercenaries who had apparently come seeking the dragon's treasure. It seemed Skjalandir had visited destruction on them all.

'Tell me about these mercenaries,' Felix said. 'Who were they?'

'They came seeking death's gold. They had swords and shields and axes. They had great engines of destruction and wizards to cast spells. They climbed death's mountain. Death took them. Death gulped down their flesh and spat out their bones. He let a few of them flee and then hunted them down, flying after them on his leathery pinions. Listening to their screams as the shadow of his mighty wings fell across them. In the end, death took them all, but not before he had made them suffer.'

'The dragon played with them,' Max Schreiber said ominously.

'Death is not kind,' said the woman. 'Death will come for us all. Some he lets live so that they might worship him. Some he punishes for their disobedience of his will. Death is a terrible, angry god. Best you turn back, strangers, while you yet may.'

'Are you saying some of the surviving townspeople worship the dragon? Do you?'

'Some there are who still dwell here, who kill newcomers and offer them up as sacrifices to death. I say they are fools. What need has death of their offerings? Death takes what he wishes, and one day he will take their lives as well.'

Wonderful, thought Felix. Not only do we have the dragon, the greenskins and the bandits to worry about, we have some crazed survivors who worship the beast as a god.

'Thank you for your words. Do you need anything?' Felix asked. 'Food? Water? Money?'

The madwoman shook her head, then turned and limped away into the ruins. Felix felt he ought to do something. Perhaps call her back or offer her their protection, then he realised how ludicrous the idea was. They might well not be able to protect themselves, and the safest place for her to be was well away from them.

'Let her go,' said Max Schreiber.

Felix watched her walk away. Part of him thought he might be safer if he did the same.

* * *

THE ROAD WOUND along the shores of the lake. The waters were calm and still, and reflected the surrounding mountains like a mirror. Occasionally, the wind stirred up some waves and sent them to break on the beach. It was the only sound Felix could hear other than the moaning of the wind, and the creak of the wheels of Malakai's wagon. All around the landscape was bleak and desolate. There were many signs of human habitation – bothies, cottages, shepherds' huts – but all of them looked abandoned or destroyed. Felix tried to imagine what the valley must have been like when it was inhabited. Sheep must have grazed along these hills. Woodcutters must have worked amid the copses of firs. Lovers must have walked hand in hand along the water's edge. Doubtless fishing boats had dragged their nets through the lake. Felix had seen the stone pylons that had once supported the burned out pier back in the town. He had seen the blackened hulks of ships overturned in the water, scorched by dragonfire, holed by dragon claws.

It was cold now. He tugged his red Sudenland wool cloak tight around him to fight off the chill. Bjorni broke out into a raucous and bawdy ballad about a troll and a tavern keeper's daughter. His voice boomed out, disturbing the eerie silence. Felix knew that Bjorni was singing to lighten their gloomy mood, but even so, wished that he would not. It seemed somehow unwise to challenge the brooding silence, to draw attention to themselves in any way. To do so invited destruction to descend on them as it had done on the inhabitants of the valley.

Perhaps, thought Felix, that's what Bjorni wanted. He was a Slayer after all, and heroic death was his avowed goal. As if in answer to Bjorni's song there was a distant roar, low-pitched, bestial and threatening. It echoed through the mountains like thunder. It was unnaturally loud and terrifying, and on hearing it Bjorni fell silent. Felix stared at the horizon, convinced that in moments the dragon would be on them. His hand went to the hilt of his sword, and immediately a tingling warmth passed through him. He looked all around, but there was no sign of the dragon save the echo of its voice.

He looked at Ulrika and then Gotrek and saw an unease written on both their faces that mirrored his own. He exchanged glances with the rest of the party and noticed that they were all pallid and withdrawn. For long moments, the silence dragged on. They held their breaths waiting to see what would happen. After a minute or so, Bjorni began to sing again, very quietly at first but his voice gathering strength with every word. He was not singing a bawdy tale this time, but something else, some old dwarf hymn or warsong that resonated through the valley. Soon Malakai joined in, and then Ulli and then Steg. One by one all the dwarfs save Gotrek and Grimme added their voices, then Max Schreiber did as well. Soon Felix found himself humming along.

There was something reassuring about the singing, as if by doing it, they challenged the dragon and reaffirmed their own courage. As he fell into step with the others, Felix felt his courage return, and he marched along with a lighter heart than he had felt in many a day.

Ahead of him, he could see the place where the path left the road, and wound its way up the side of Dragon Mountain.

THE CLOUDS WERE lower. They billowed through the gaps in the surrounding peaks, extending mist-like tentacles to embrace the Dragon Mountain. Visibility decreased. The air became even more chilly. The sense of oppression deepened.

Out of the mist loomed a small manor house. It looked as if it had once belonged to a wealthy family, perhaps some mountain nobleman. As such, Felix realised, it must have been one of the first places to be destroyed when the dragon awoke from its long sleep. Half the walls were tumbled down. Felix found it all too easy to imagine them being crushed by the weight of the dragon's mighty body ploughing through them.

In his mind's eye, he immediately conjured up a picture of what it must have been like to be inside the building with the mighty beast rampaging outside. He could almost smell the thatched roof on fire, feel the heat crackling in his face, the smoke making his eyes water. In his daydream he heard the ear-shattering bellows, the crunch of claws on stone, the shrieks of the dying, the unanswered prayers for mercy. Then finally, he envisioned the unnatural sight of the wall bulging inward, the stones cracking, toppling, giving way, and, in the last moment before fiery death, a glimpse of the dragon's hideous visage, the glare of its huge eyes.

So vivid was the image and so frightening, that he began to wonder if the dragon's mere presence had cast some sort of wicked spell on the place, cursing any who passed to experience the last moments of its doomed victims. He tried telling himself that it was just the mist, the memory of the dragon's roars, and his own impressionable mind that had conjured up the image. Or, perhaps, the image had been created by the sword, responding to the dragon's presence. Certainly he could feel a trickle of energy passing from the blade into his own body. Somehow that did not reassure him.

His legs ached from the long uphill march. He felt cold and lonely and more than a little depressed. He felt in his heart a certainty of impending death that was only slightly relieved by the magical warmth emanating from his sword. The encounter with the madwoman that morning remained with him, and the memory of her words disturbed him. He did indeed feel the closeness of death at this moment, and he realised that he had retreated into himself to avoid confronting it. The others appeared to have done the same. The singing had ceased the moment they had set foot on the path to the dragon's lair. All of the party of adventurers seemed to want to be alone with their thoughts and their prayers.

Felix considered his life. It seemed likely to be much shorter than he would have wanted it to be. He did not consider it particularly wasted though. In his travels with Gotrek he had seen many things, met many people, and even, perhaps, done some good by combating the forces of darkness. He had done some extraordinary things, like flown in an airship, and seen the Chaos Wastes. He had fought with daemons and monsters, and talked with mages and nobles. He had witnessed rituals of magic and depravity, and feats of heroism. He had known a few good women. He had fought duels.

Still there were things he had not done, and things he wanted to do. He had not completed the tale of Gotrek's deeds, or even fairly begun it. He had not reconciled himself with his father and family. He had not even settled things between himself and Ulrika. Of all of them, that at least was possible at this moment, he thought.

With the shadow of imminent death now hanging well and truly over them, it seemed pointless to be jealous, or to worry about what she had been laughing about with Max, or even whether they would ever truly be lovers again. He felt at that moment that he wanted simply to show her some affection, make some human gesture of trust and understanding, connect for what might be the last time. Even if she rejected him or refused to speak to him, he wanted to at least make the effort.

He lengthened his stride and walked up the trail to overtake her. He fell into step beside her, reached out to touch her shoulder gently and get her attention.

'What?' she said. Her tone was not friendly, but it was not unfriendly either. Suddenly, he was filled with odd emotion, a mixture of anger and need and pity and something else. He knew exactly what he wanted to say, and exactly the words needed to say it, and yet it was difficult just to speak them.

'This might be the last chance we ever have to speak to each other,' he said eventually.

'Yes. So?'

'Why are you making this so difficult?'

'You are the one who wanted to talk to me.'

He took a breath to calm himself, and tried to remember his good intentions of just a few minutes before. Eventually he forced his lips to move.

'I just wanted to say that I loved you.'

She looked at him, but said nothing back. He waited for a response for a moment, slowly feeling the weight of hurt and rejection build up within him. Still she said nothing.

Then, suddenly, the dragon's enormous roar filled the air again. The earth beneath their feet seemed to vibrate with it.

'I think we're getting close,' said Ulli.

THE PATHWAY LED up over the brow of the hill, and then sloped down to the right. Felix could see that they had entered a long, barren valley. The air smelled foul, and an acrid chemical stench mingled with the mist. It smelled more like the outside of a tannery than a mountain valley. Even the grass of the slopes in this place had a scorched yellowish look to it. It was as if the malign presence of the dragon had leaked into the earth itself, corrupting it.

Felix realised that he had seen something like this before, in the Chaos Wastes. It was almost like the effects of warpstone.

Malakai halted his wagon and began to search about within it. One after another he produced a selection of devices which he strapped to his chest. Felix recognised some of them. One was a portable gatling gun of the sort Varek had carried into Karag Dum. Others were large bombs he clipped to his harness. The last was a long hollow tube into which he loaded a large projectile before slinging it over his shoulder.

'Ah'm ready to pay the beastie a wee visit noo,' he said, moving down the slope. Gotrek nodded his agreement and ran his thumb along the blade of his axe, producing a bead of blood.

'Come out, dragon!' he bellowed. 'My axe thirsts.'

'I wish you wouldn't do that,' Felix muttered quietly.

Gotrek walked down the path, shoulder to shoulder with Malakai.

'Snorri thinks this will be a good fight,' said Snorri Nosebiter, and hefting his weapons set off after them.

'I wonder if there are any sheep around here. I could use a little relaxation,' Bjorni said, then shrugged and strode downslope. Grimme went with him. This left only the humans, Steg and Ulli standing at the hilltop.

'I suppose somebody ought to guard the cart,' Ulli said. He looked a little shame-faced. Not that Felix blamed him. He was not too keen to go and face the dragon himself.

'I was thinking the same thing,' Steg said. 'There must be lots of valuable stuff here.'

Ulli and Steg looked at each other. They both looked more and more embarrassed.

'I thought Slayers were supposed to seek a heroic death,' Felix said.

'Me too,' agreed Ulrika.

Ulli gazed at his feet. Steg stared at the sky. Both of them looked very afraid.

Felix shook his head, then he strode into the valley of the dragon. Ulrika and her bodyguards followed, bows held at the ready. Max gave Ulli and Steg a look that was somewhere between sympathy and contempt, and then strode into the valley.

To his horror, Felix realised that something was crunching underfoot. Looking down he could see that he was walking on sticks of something brittle and black. It took him a moment to realise that they were fire-scorched bones.

'Well, I guess we know what happened to the other folks who came here,' he whispered. He wanted to be able to talk loudly and bravely but there was something in the air that compelled him to quietness.

'Yes,' Ulrika said, then added, 'I don't think we always knew.' She sounded as if she thought his comment was idiotic. Which in a way, he supposed, it was. He took a deep breath and tried to remain calm. His fingers tightened on the hilt of his sword, and new strength and determination flowed into him. Felix felt as if he ought to resent the usurpation of his body and his will to the sword's purpose, but actually he was grateful for it. He wondered if he would even have been able to contemplate approaching the great beast if he were not carrying the weapon. He was astounded by the bravery of Ulrika and her henchmen, who did not even have to be here, and who did not have the power of a magical sword to encourage them.

He thought his courage had been tested before in his encounter with the Bloodthirster beneath Karag Dum, but in some ways this was worse. In the ancient dwarf city there had been no possibility of escape. He had been trapped along with the dwarfs. There had been nothing else to do but stand and fight. He did not have to be here.

There was nothing stopping him from running away, or going back to join Ulli and Steg. There was no army of Chaos warriors blocking the way back, as there had been in Karag Dum. He was not entombed deep beneath the earth. He knew that in some ways he was not even bound by his oath to follow Gotrek any more. Only the other night, he had offered to run away with Ulrika in spite of it. And yet, here he was advancing into the mist, marching towards a dragon's lair, apparently of his own free will.

It was not that simple though. He was still bound by a whole complex pattern of events, dependencies and emotions. He did still feel some loyalty to Gotrek. He did not want to look like a coward in front of Ulrika and the others. He did not want to destroy his own image of himself. He knew he despised Ulli and Steg for their cowardice, even though he understood their emotions all too well. He did not want to be like them. He did not want Ulrika and Max and the others thinking of him in the same way.

And there was no easy retreat. The hills were still full of orcs and bandits and there was no way back for one man on his own, even accompanied by two cowardly dwarfs. He wondered if Ulli and Steg had realised this. And he suspected that, beneath all his feelings, the power of the sword he held was at work on him, nudging him in the direction it wanted him to go.

Felix wondered if the others were in a similar quandary, if they too felt the same complex mix of emotions that he did. From their grim expressions, it was hard to tell. Every face was a mask of self-control. Every hand was steady.

Not wanting to, and yet somehow compelled to do it, Felix continued to put one foot in front of the other, certain that every step took him closer to death.

MAX COULD SENSE the dragon up ahead, as surely as he could feel the winds of magic. It was an ominous powerful presence that made him want to quiver with fear. He had read about the aura of dragons, of how they inspired fear in even the boldest heart, and, having experienced it once, he had thought that he was prepared for it. He was wrong.

He felt that at any moment the great beast might spring out and end his life with a snap of its jaws. This must be how a bird feels, when it senses the nearness of a cat, he thought. To distract himself, he reached out his senses and grasped at the winds of magic, preparing himself to lash out with a spell at the smallest warning. He had already woven his subtlest and most potent protective spells upon himself and his comrades. He wondered if they had even noticed.

He was also aware that other powers were at work here. The ominous blade that Felix Jaeger bore was beginning to blaze with power. To Max's wizardly eyes it glowed like a beacon. Max could sense the sentience in it was beginning to activate its own spells. Had he not been absolutely certain that the blade was as determined as they to put an end to the dragon, Max would have woven counter spells.

Even as he thought this Max wondered why he was so certain as to the sword's purpose. Was it possible that the blade was affecting his own mind, and making him believe this? He doubted it. He felt that he would have sensed any such encroachment on his mind. He inspected his own mental defences, searching for a breach, just in case, and found none. Then again, any spell of sufficient subtlety to affect his mind would almost certainly leave him thinking that any way.

He almost laughed. Here he was worrying about a relatively minor possibility when ahead of him he sensed a dragon, with a dragon's magic and a dragon's incredible power. What did it matter what the sword was up to? It was not the only magical weapon here. There was Gotrek's awesome axe, a thing that carried a power within it an order of magnitude greater than Felix's sword, a weapon capable of banishing greater daemons.

The more Max thought about these events the more he believed there was a pattern to them. Malakai Makaisson was here, also armed with the deadliest devices dwarf steel-craft was capable of building, and he was here too, his magic having reached new heights of potency on the journey. Surely such things could not be accidents. Perhaps the benevolent powers who stood guard over the world had brought them here for a reason.

Max found himself smiling quietly. This was a dangerous line of thinking. Warriors and wizards who thought themselves specially protected by the gods usually found themselves in an early grave. Perhaps they died serving the god's purposes, perhaps not. The higher powers were rarely open with their human followers, and not necessarily kind to them, either.

If he was honest, he was here because Ulrika was here, and he wanted to protect her. It was a foolish and romantic notion for a wizard, but it was the truth. If that led to his death, then so be it...

He took another breath. Along with the winds of magic, he sensed rottenness and corruption. This was not the simple stink of evil. It was like the smell of gangrenous flesh he had sometimes scented in a hospice during his apprenticeship in healing magic. A faint hope stirred within him.

Perhaps the dragon had been more badly wounded in its attack on the airship than they had thought. For a moment, his heart lightened then realism reasserted itself. Even if the creature was badly hurt, it was not necessarily a good sign.

Dragons, like most beasts, were always at their most dangerous when wounded.

ULRIKA HELD HER bow ready. She was not sure exactly what a single arrow could do against a monster as mighty as the dragon, but she was determined to at least try. She had already given instructions to Standa and Oleg to do the same as she intended to do: aim for the eyes. No matter how well armoured the creature's body might be, its eyes must still be vulnerable. At least she hoped this was the case. She could not see how they could be armoured.

She clung to this thought for reassurance. This was a dreadful place. It stank of death and illness. The bones of the dragon's previous victims lay all around, wrapped in rusting chainmail and mouldering leather, sightless eye-sockets staring towards the heavens. It seemed like hundreds had tried to kill the beast before them, and none of them had succeeded.

For the hundredth time she wondered why she was here. She could have left the Slayers, and tried to make her way north along the High Road. She could even have left Karak Kadrin by the long westerly route. She had not and there were times when she regretted it. Taking a different route would have meant leaving Felix and she had not been prepared to do that. More fool she.

She felt as if she had deserted her duty to her father and her kinsfolk for a stranger. And for what? She had thought she loved him, but, if this was love, it was not like anything the bards sung of. It was fury and irritation, and an insane sensitivity to the least little thing. It was fear, of loss and of having. It was feeling that you had stopped being yourself and were becoming a stranger to the person you had been. It was this powerful brutish force that made you think about a man even though you would not talk to him and even as you walked into a dragon's lair.

She wished he had not agreed to go with her the other night, and she was glad he had, even if it would make him an oathbreaker. She wondered whether they could have slipped away and made it through the mountains into obscurity and a life together. And she knew it was an illusion. They were not the sort of people who could have done that. She could not, in the end, abandon family and duty.

She looked over and saw that Max was smiling, and wondered what the magician could find here to smile about. He was a strange man, but a good one. He could not help it if the gods had gifted him with strange powers. He seemed to at least want to do his best to use them for good, and he had been a true friend to her and the rest of them. She was certain that the only reason he was here was because of her, and she was touched by that, though she thought it was foolish of him to be taking a path that most likely would lead to his death because of love. On the other hand, he was being no more foolish than she.

Up ahead, she saw the Slayers had stopped. They stood before a huge cave mouth. The stink of rot and putrefaction was stronger here, as if they were coming close to its source. They stood now at the mouth of Skjalandir's lair. Where was the dragon, she wondered?

ULLI WATCHED STEG rummaging through the back of Malakai Makaisson's wagon. A look of shame and embarrassment crossed his face. He tugged his beard. He kicked a stone. He felt dreadful. He had always known he was a coward. He had fled from his first battle and been ostracised by his clan. He had sought to atone for it by becoming a Slayer. He had thought that Grimnir might smile on him, and grant him the courage to find death. The god had not done so. In fact it looked like his shame was going to be increased. Who had ever heard of a Slayer who was a coward?

'Found anything interesting in there?' he asked, just to make conversation.

'Lots of gear. Lots of tools,' Steg said. 'Probably weapons. I don't know how to put them together. Must be worth a fortune but I don't know how to use them.'

He sounded angry and disappointed. Ulli wondered if he had really thought to make his fortune by stealing the engineer's devices. He had been wondering that since the start of the trip. Not that he would have minded right now. The engineer's weapons had certainly routed those goblins. With them, they might have stood a chance of getting back. Without them, they probably did not. He glanced back down slope. To his surprise the mist had started to lift. Through it, he thought he saw humanoid shapes, greenskins, coming ever closer. His heart sank. He knew now there was most likely no escape.

He felt something hardening within him. This was hopeless. There was no way back. Whichever way he looked there was only death. Perhaps Grimnir had answered his prayers after all. He came to a decision and climbed up onto the back of the cart. He saw that in the cases Steg had rummaged through were a collection of the black spherical bombs that Malakai was so fond of. They would do. He picked up a blanket and, using it as a sack, quickly filled it with bombs. Steg meanwhile had noticed the orcs.

'Looks like we've got company,' he said.

'Aye,' said Ulli. 'I'd stay and kill them, but the dragon is bigger. It's a better ending for a Slayer.'

Steg shrugged. 'Aye, you're right. And it most likely has gold too.'

'Let's be away then.'

Together they raced down into the Dragon Vale. Ulli hoped that if they hurried they might catch up with the others. He was not sure exactly why, but he felt it might be better to die in company.

THE MOUTH OF the dragon's cave loomed before them. Felix guessed that the roof must be nearly five times his own height. He peered in, half-expecting to catch a glimpse of a huge reptilian head in the heartbeat before its fiery breath incinerated him. He saw nothing save that the cave extended deep into the earth. In the shadowy gloom, he could make out stalactites and stalagmites. For a moment, the cave itself seemed to be the maw of an enormous monster, but then common sense reasserted itself.

'I can't see any dragon,' he said.

'It's in there. I can smell it,' Gotrek said. 'It's down in the dark, cowering. We'll just have to go in and get it.'

Gotrek's description of the dragon's behaviour struck Felix as being unrealistic. He doubted very much that the dragon felt any fear of them at all. It probably just hadn't noticed them.

'We'll need light,' he said. 'It's too dark to see down there.'

Max gestured and a sphere of golden fire hovered in the air above him. He gestured again and the sphere split into five smaller spheres, one of which moved to hover over each of the humans. Felix gathered that Max already knew the dwarfs did not need nearly as much light to see by as men did.

'I guess we're not going to be sneaking up on the dragon anyway,' Felix said. He looked at the others. 'Let's get this over with.'

* * *

As THEY DESCENDED into the darkness, Felix was glad of the magical light. It hovered just behind his head and gave him enough illumination to see by. It was an absolute necessity in this place. The floor of the cavern was rough, and descended steeply into the gloom. Rocks protruded from the floor at intervals. He did not doubt that if he had tried to feel his way forward in the dark, he might easily have fallen and broken his neck.

The way followed many branching paths but it was always obvious, from the smell, and the trail of slimy blood that lay before them, in which direction they would find the dragon. Felix was glad of the marked trail too. This was not one cave, he realised, but a vast underground labyrinth in which it would be all too easy to get lost.

An enormous roar echoed through the caverns. The winding corridors amplified it to the point where it was almost deafening. Felix's ears rang. He had no idea where the dragon might be. Once, judging from the intensity of the sound, he would have thought it was close, but his experiences in the tunnels of dwarf cities had taught him that noises could be deceptive. In a way this was worse. The uncertainty filled him with dread.

Around him the others were shadowy figures. The humans were outlined by the sorcerous spheres. The dwarfs were near invisible as they moved through the gloom. He could see their silhouettes, and hear their voices, but nothing more. The smell of corruption was getting worse. He put his hand over his mouth and nostrils to keep from gagging.

Behind him, he could hear the noise of running feet. He turned to see Ulli and Steg moving down the corridor. He noticed that Ulli had a huge sack thrown over his shoulder.

'I'm glad you could join us after all,' Felix said sardonically. 'You're not too late for the action.'

'We didn't have much choice,' Ulli said, looking more than somewhat embarrassed. 'A whole tribe of greenskins has shown up outside.'

'The way back is cut off,' added Steg.

'Wonderful,' Felix said. 'Just what I needed to hear.'

'Don't worry,' said Snorri. 'We'll get them on the way out.'

THE CAVE BECAME a long high tunnel. Shadows danced away from the glowing globes. The trail led on deeper into the earth. Somewhere off in the distance they could hear running water. The walls were damp, and covered in slick greenish moss. Suddenly the bellowing stopped.

'Och, the beastie must hae smelled us,' said Malakai. 'Ah dinnae doot it kens we're here.'

'Snorri thinks that's just fine,' said Snorri. 'Snorri wouldn't want to take unfair advantage.'

'The creature must die,' Gotrek said. 'The dwarf folk have a mighty grudge against it.'

'Aye,' Grimme said. 'That they have. So have I.'

Everyone looked at him in surprise. It was the first time he had ever spoken to them. His voice was quiet and sad and sour. He met their gazes evenly. Hatred and sorrow were etched upon his face. 'The beast killed my whole clan. I was in the lands of men trading or I would have died with them. I have come back bearing this grudge. I will either kill the beast, or die expunging the shame of failing to die with my clan.'

'The beastie will die,' Malakai said. 'It owes me for what it did tae ma lovely airship.'

'The dragon must pay for the death of Varek,' said Snorri.

'We'll make it,' Bjorni said.

'Are you going to stand here all day boasting?' Gotrek said. 'I have better things to do.'

'Let's go,' Malakai said.

AHEAD THEY COULD hear the roar of water, and see something glittering.

'Gold,' Steg said, lengthening his stride, apparently unconcerned now with his personal safety.

'Or the glitter of dragon scales,' Max said. 'Be prepared to fight.'

As they moved closer, Felix could see a great cavern looming ahead of them. It was a monstrous chamber, as vast as the interior of the Temple of Sigmar in Altdorf. At one end was a waterfall, which tumbled into a large pool. The wetness of the spray moistened Felix's face, even at this distance. The air stank of rotting flesh.

Around the chamber's edge ran several ledges large enough to hold a man. The tunnel on which they walked ran into a crude ramp, smoothed by the passage of the dragon's massive body over the years. Here and there lay the bones of men and beasts and monsters. There was indeed treasure glittering in the cavern, great mounds of it, silver and copper and gold and jewellery all mingled together. It held the eye for mere moments though before it was drawn to the creature that dominated the huge space.

In the centre of the chamber lay the dragon, the largest living thing Felix had ever seen, or hoped to see.

It was the size of a small hill, an enormous mass of muscle and sinew and scale. Its leathery wings were wrapped tight around its body. Its long tail was tipped with a great razor-edged paddle-blade of flesh. Double rows of serrated spines, each as large as a tall man, ran down its spine. Even as Felix watched the monstrous serpentine neck uncurled as the dragon lifted its head to see who disturbed its slumber. It glanced down at them with baleful, hate-filled eyes. Felix could see pain and madness in the gaze. Part of him wanted to flee, but from the blade in his hand came a flow of strength and calm and courage.

Even the dwarfs were daunted by those evil eyes, Felix could tell. Behind him, he heard Ulli and Bjorni and Steg whimper. Even Snorri let out a groan of despair. Only Gotrek, Malakai and Grimme stood their ground with no show of fear. Felix could sense Max and the Kislevites would turn tail at the slightest provocation. He did not blame them. The dragon was as large as the *Spirit of Grungni*. Its mouth was a massive tooth-filled chasm which could easily swallow a man whole. Flame flickered from its nostrils along with clouds of acrid chemical smoke.

'Hold fast,' Felix said, surprised at how calm he sounded. Once again, he felt the power of the sword at work. 'Ulrika, Oleg, Standa, get up on the ledges and start shooting for the eyes, the throat or any vulnerable spot you can think of. Max, can your magic protect us from the flames?'

'Aye. I hope so. For a time, at least.'

'Then do so!' A note of command entered Felix's voice and he was amazed to see them jump to obey. Something else struck him. The dragon was moving slowly, dragging its left side. Hope surged through Felix. He thought he understood what had happened.

'It's wounded,' he said. 'It still hasn't recovered from Varek crashing the gyrocopter into it.'

The dragon reared unsteadily, spreading its wings for balance. Its huge shadow flowed over the wall behind it, but that was not what held Felix's attention. He could see now that he was right. There was a massive wound in the beast's side, which festered greenly. This was the source of the stink in the air. Varek had hurt the creature far more than he had ever believed possible.

'Try firing arrows at the wound in its side,' Felix shouted. 'The scales have fallen away there.'

Ulrika and the two Kislevite bowmen were already running along the ledges, spreading out and taking cover behind the stalagmites. Max raised his staff and a wave of power flowed out of him, setting the air shimmering.

'Charge!' roared Gotrek. All of the Slayers except Malakai raced forward. Without quite understanding why Felix did the same. The dragon moved to meet them, the earth shaking beneath its ponderous tread. Its roars were deafening. Its head looped forward on its neck and it breathed a sheet of flame. Felix raised his sword to parry it as he had done on the airship but there was no need. The shimmering protective field cast by Max held the flames at bay.

From the corner of his eye, Felix noticed that Steg was not running towards the dragon, but towards the largest pile of loot. He dived into it like a swimmer plunging into water and shrieked, 'Gold! Lovely gold! It's all mine.'

He's mad, Felix thought. Even as the dragon loomed over them, Steg tossed handfuls of coins ecstatically into the air, shouting, 'Mine! All mine!'

From behind Felix came a weird spluttering hissing noise. Something flashed past overhead, trailing fire. It exploded in the dragon's wounded side, sending great chunks of flesh hurtling outwards, and exposing bone and inner organs. The dragon let out a fearsome roar that was somewhere between a bellow and a scream. As he closed with the creature, Felix could hear the air hissing out of the dragon's lungs through the hole in its chest.

The mighty creature reared upwards, its wings flexing as it did so. The movement drove the stench of rotting flesh towards its attackers in an almost overpowering wave. Felix fought to keep from gagging, and looked up in wonder. He did not think he had ever imagined a living thing quite so large. It loomed over him like a walking tower. There was something unnatural about it, as if a building had grown legs and started walking around. It was so tall that its head almost touched the ceiling of the cavern, and that was almost twenty times the height of a man.

How can we possibly overcome this, he thought, as awe threatened to paralyse him? It did not seem possible that human or dwarf valour could prevail against such a thing. It was just too big. They were like mice trying to overcome a grown man. Even as these thoughts surged through Felix's mind, Gotrek reached the dragon's foot.

Felix's numbed mind noted that the talons of the creature's paw were almost the size of the Slayer. If this dismayed Gotrek, he gave no sign of it. His axe flashed through a thunderous arc and bit into the dragon's leg at about the spot the ankle would have been in a human. The mighty blade parted scales and flesh. Greenish blood spurted steaming from the wound. The dragon bellowed its rage and pain once more then bent forward, its head coming down with the speed of a striking serpent, its huge jaws opening and threatening to take Gotrek with one gulp.

Felix wondered if the moment of the Slayer's doom had finally arrived.

DESPERATELY ULRIKA TRIED to get a bead on the dragon's eye. It should not be difficult, she told herself. The orb was larger than the targets she had used for archery practice ever since childhood. Of course, those targets had not moved around at enormous speed, nor had they been attached to something quite as overwhelmingly fearsome as a dragon. Part of her did not want to fire for fear of attracting the creature's attention. And, in archery practice, there was not the distraction of having Felix and the Slayers fighting with the target either.

Stay calm, she told herself. Breathe easily. It does not matter how large the beast is. It does not matter what it is doing. It is just another target. You can hit it easily enough. You have hit birds in flight. This should not be so difficult as that.

Time seemed to slow. Her mind emptied and calmed. She drew back the arrow. With what seemed to her incredible slowness, the dragon's head started to descend. She

compensated for the movement, aimed at where the eye
should be when the arrow reached it, and then released.

The arrow flew straight and true. She prayed to Taal that it
would find its mark.

AN ARROW FLASHED out of nowhere and hit the dragon in the eye,
just before the head reached Gotrek. The Slayer threw himself
to one side, and the dragon's jaws snapped shut on empty air.
The dragon's own motion, and Gotrek's hamstringing blow,
combined to overbalance the creature. It tumbled forward,
headlong. Felix cursed, realising that it was going to land on
him. Screams from Ulli and Steg told him that they, too, were
realised that they, too, were in the path of its descent.

The dragon's wings flapped instinctively, slowing its fall.
Felix felt the wind flutter his cloak and threw himself to one
side. Ulli did the same. For some reason, Steg refused to move.
'You can't have my gold,' he shouted, swinging his pick up to
strike at the dragon, even as the huge body landed on him.
Felix heard the squelch as he only just rolled clear.

Felix saw that Malakai was stuffing something into the metal
tube he carried once more. As the dragon started to rise, he finished the operation and swung the cylinder into position on
his shoulder. The dragon stretched its neck towards him, and as
it did so, Malakai pulled some sort of trigger on the front of the
tube. Sparks flew from the back of the tube and another projectile flashed forth and sped straight towards the dragon's
mouth. It reminded Felix of the fireworks he had seen
unleashed at Altdorf to celebrate the Emperor's birthday. No
firework had ever exploded with quite such violence though.
The force of the explosion loosened several of the dragon's
man-sized fangs, and tore a hole in the top of the creature's
mouth. How could anything survive such punishment, Felix
wondered.

It had its terrible festering wound. It had a huge hole ripped
in its chest. It had an arrow sticking from its eye. It had blood
seeping from its ankle where Gotrek had hamstrung it. And yet
it still refused to die. It lashed around in a frenzy. Its tail
cracked the air like a whip. Its wings drummed like thunder. It
lashed out with a claw that would have flattened Malakai like a
swatted fly, had not the engineer thrown himself flat below it.
As the dragon rose for another blow, Felix saw the flattened

form of Steg was still attached to its chest. His pick was driven between the creature's scales, and even in death his hand still clutched the weapon's shaft. The force of the impact had embedded bits of gold in his skin and armour. In death, he glittered.

Gotrek's warcry rang out and Felix saw that the Slayer was at the dragon's rear, chopping at its tail with the axe. Each blow carved great chunks out of the dragon's flesh. Snorri had joined the fray and battered away with axe and hammer. Felix could not see whether his blows were having any effect.

A flash of gold light told Felix that Max had cast a spell. A bolt of uncanny power flashed at the dragon's other eye. The eyeball sizzled and popped and now the dragon was blinded. Grimme raced forward as its head swooped low, and ran almost into the creature's mouth. His hammer smashed through a great arc, and pulped scale and flesh beneath it.

The dragon breathed, and even from where he stood Felix could feel the heat. Grimme was too close to its source for any protective spell to intervene. His armour and hair caught alight. His crest became a sizzling flame. His flesh blackened and then ran like liquid, so fierce was the heat. He did not even have time to scream, then he was gone. The dragon sprawled forward on all fours once more, emitting the fiery jet at its tormentors.

Outrage flared within Felix's brain at the sight of this horrible death. The flames continued to flicker outwards, scouring the ledges on which the Kislevites stood. Max's magical barrier flickered but held, but Felix could see that it was starting to collapse. He had no idea how much longer the wizard could hold it for. Once the shimmering spell shield went down, Ulrika and Max and the archers would suffer the same fate as Grimme. Just the thought of that happening triggered something within Felix's brain. Power flowed out of the sword. Without even realising what he was doing, he found himself running forward towards the mighty beast. His path took him up a pile of treasure and a flying leap took him right on top of the dragon's skull.

If the blinded dragon felt his presence it gave no sign. He stood upright atop its head. The runes on the blade blazed bright with deadly magic. He summoned all his strength and drove the blade downwards, even as he felt the dragon rear up beneath him.

The deadly spells woven into it by its ancient creators enabled the blade to pass through scale and flesh. There was resistance as the enchanted steel met the bones of the skull. Felix leaned forward with all his weight. The blade twisted in his hands, aiding him. In a moment, the weapon was through and its deadly runes were lodged in the dragon's brain.

The dragon gave one last deadly bellow, and its whole body spasmed reflexively. Felix felt a sickening sense of acceleration as its neck uncoiled and the ground receded below him. He was almost thrown clear. Knowing the drop would kill him, Felix held onto the embedded blade with all his strength. Then the dragon began to topple backwards.

This was not such a good idea, thought Felix, as the ground rose to meet him once more.

TWELVE

THE BATTLE

FELIX FELL. He knew that he had moments to live. There was nothing in his mind save fear and a sick sense of vertigo as he dropped. No noble thoughts. No last memories of life. Just the thought that he had made an error. One strange image burned itself into his brain. The sorcerous sphere still followed him, keeping pace effortlessly. It occurred to him that perhaps he could reach out and grab it. The magic that allowed it to fly might slow his fall.

Desperately he grabbed for it, but it remained out of his reach. His sword fell from his hands. He twisted desperately, straining with every fibre of his being to grab the light but it eluded him. He cursed and then there was the impact.

Death was not quite what he expected. There was pain. There was darkness. There was a sense of air being expelled from his lungs. There was a sense of being pushed downwards by an enormous force. He was not sure though that he should feel quite so wet. Blood, he thought irrationally. His body had split open on impact. That was the wetness he felt. Then the wet stuff filled his mouth and started to trickle down his throat. He could not breathe.

I am not dead yet then, he thought. Maybe my lungs are filling with blood like those poor devils I saw dying of poison gas in Nuln.

Panic filled him. This was worse than a nightmare. It was horrible knowing that these were his last few seconds of life and that there was nothing he could do about it.

Then he noticed there were bubbles all around him. The light was still above him. Was he hallucinating, he wondered? Instinctively he grasped that something important was going on here. He had missed something. Then it came to him. He was not dead. He was in water. He must have been catapulted into the pool at the far end of the cave by the force of the dragon's last spasm. There was still a chance that he might live. He breathed out, expelling the water from his mouth, trying desperately not to breathe any more in.

But it was only a chance, he realised. The force pushing him down was not a product of his imagination. It was the pressure from the tons of water falling into the pool, driving him downwards with enormous force. He tried kicking upwards but it was useless. There was nothing he could do against such power.

For a moment he felt despair. He had merely exchanged one death for another. He was not going to be killed by the monster or by the fall, he was going to drown. His lungs were almost empty. In its need for air, his desperate body sought to betray him. It took a huge effort not to breathe in the water.

Fierce resolution filled him. He had not come so far and survived an encounter with a dragon in order to be killed by a waterfall. There had to be something he could do. He relaxed and let the pressure drive him downwards. His face hit rock. His mouth almost opened reflexively to scream but he held it shut by force of will. His lungs felt like they were bursting.

Be calm, he told himself. Think. He noticed that he was starting to drift to one side. The current had hit the rocky floor of the pool and was being deflected. He allowed it to carry him, and the pressure from above eased.

Darkness hovered at the edge of his vision. He was on the verge of blacking out. Just keep going, he told himself. Don't give up. The worst is past. He struck out for the surface and noticed that the glowing sphere still followed him. That was good; it gave him some light to see by.

His chainmail shirt felt like it was made of lead. The weight of it tugged at him, pulling him down. He considered stopping and trying to pull it off, but knew that he would just be wasting precious time and air. He had to keep going.

Stroke by stroke, with all the effort of a man pulling himself up a mountainside, Felix swam for the surface. His limbs felt like lead. He could barely see. His lungs were about to explode. Still he swam onwards and upwards. Until at last, just as he was certain he could endure no more, his head broke the surface, and he breathed in a lungful of pure fresh air.

He was certain he had never tasted anything so sweet.

FELIX PULLED HIMSELF over the edge of the pool. Water puddled at his feet. His clothes were sodden. He saw that the dwarfs and Ulrika were running towards him. Despite the age he felt he had been underwater, he realised that only moments had passed since he killed the dragon. Its huge corpse lay flopping and twitching on the ground nearby, its movements scattering gold coins everywhere.

Ulrika raced up. Tears streamed down her face. 'I thought you were dead,' she said as she embraced him.

'I feel like I ought to be,' he murmured, pulling her close and feeling the warm weight of her body against his.

The dwarfs gathered round to congratulate him.

'AYE, WELL, WE'RE rich,' said Malakai, looking at the dragon's hoard.

'Except that we can't carry more than a small part of this treasure,' Max said.

'And there's a small army of greenskins outside,' Ulli said. 'What are we going to do about them?'

'Kill them,' Gotrek said. 'Or die trying. We've failed to achieve our dooms here. The gods have provided us with another.'

'I've had enough of seeking death for one day,' Felix said.

'You're a dragon slayer now,' Bjorni said. 'Surely you're not scared of a few greenskins.'

'I would like to live to enjoy my triumph,' Felix said sourly.

He looked around. Oleg and Standa were still with them, and more or less unmarked. Gotrek and Snorri appeared unharmed. Ulli looked almost exultant having survived his encounter with Skjalandir. Bjorni contemplated the dragon's hoard in wonder. Their casualties had been surprisingly few. They had been very lucky. Varek had done them more of a favour than they had ever guessed when he gave his life to drive the dragon off. The wound he had inflicted on it had weakened the monster enough for them to kill it. If anyone deserved the title 'dragon slayer' it was Varek.

He walked over and picked up his sword. It no longer felt particularly magical. All power seemed gone from it. It was just a fine blade once more. No hint of its fell purpose remained. Still, it was a good weapon, and he was used to it. He stuck it back in its scabbard.

Felix wondered if he should suggest burying the dead, but Steg was lost beneath the body of the fallen dragon and Grimme was charred to a crisp. It hardly seemed worth the effort. Particularly since the orcs might soon be arriving. He mentioned this to the others.

'Perhaps we can find another way out,' suggested Max. 'These tunnels must lead somewhere.'

'They might be an endless maze,' Ulrika said. 'We could get lost and wander till we die.'

'No dwarf ever got lost underground,' Bjorni said. The other Slayers nodded their agreement.

'Be that as it may,' Felix said, 'there might not be another way out.'

'The manling has the right of it,' Gotrek said. 'And what's more, no Slayer ever ran from a mass of goblins.'

Thinking of the less than totally courageous behaviour exhibited by some of their company, Felix wondered if that were true. Now did not seem like a good time to air his doubts however. Instead he said, 'What are we going to do?'

'Snorri thinks we should go up to the surface and kill them,' said Snorri Nosebiter.

Are these maniacs really going to talk us all into going up to the surface and getting killed, wondered Felix? It seemed all too likely.

'What if they kill us all?' Max asked. 'Are you really going to leave all this treasure here for them to take?'

Thank you, Max, thought Felix. You just mentioned the only thing that might influence a gang of dwarf Slayers in a situation like this.

'They will not pass us,' said Snorri. 'We shall stand on a wall of corpses and throw them back!'

'Let's just assume you don't,' Max said. 'All of this treasure will go to enrich the orcs. They could use it to buy weapons, and attack dwarf lands.'

'No dwarf would ever sell them weapons.'

'Alas, some humans might,' said Max. The dwarfs nodded their heads sagely at the thought of such human treachery.

'You hae a point,' said Malakai. 'If ah had some blastin' pooder ah could rig this ceiling' tae collapse. But ah dinnae!'

'I brought a sack of your bombs from the cart,' Ulli said.

'Guid lad!' said Malakai beaming broadly. The smile faded just as quickly as the thought of someone fumbling around amongst his treasures occurred to him. Felix could read it on his face.

'It's a bit early to be thinking of such things,' Bjorni said. 'Surely we should head up to the cave mouth and take a look.'

'Best be careful, then,' Max said. 'While they think the dragon is still alive I doubt that they will come in. If they see you up there, they might think we killed it, and come looking for us.'

'But we *did* kill the dragon,' said Snorri, obviously confused.

'We will all head up,' Gotrek said. 'Except Malakai and Ulli. You can stay here and rig the tunnel to blow.'

'Right ye are,' Malakai said cheerfully.

Why do I think this is going to end in disaster, thought Felix, as he squelched back up the tunnel, shivering in his sodden clothes?

FELIX CRAWLED FORWARD to the lip of the cave mouth. Ulrika crawled alongside him. The two of them had been selected since they had the best eyesight. Max had doused his light spell so that it would not attract attention to them.

The stone was wet and cold under his hands. Felix wished he had something dry to wear. The mist had cleared away; a bright sun beamed cheerfully down. Carefully he poked his head forward and gazed down into the valley. One look told him the worst had happened.

Instead of one army, there were two. On one side of the valley was a horde of orcs and goblins. They were drawn up in crude battle formation. Massive orcs stood in the centre armed with crude scimitars and round, spike-bossed shields. Masses of goblin archers scuttled about between the ranks. Off to one side were some orc riders mounted on huge battle boars. Their grunts and squeals were audible up the valley. A strange device had been set up on the brow of the hill. It resembled the catapults that Felix had used as a boy, only it was large enough to throw a boulder rather than a small stone. Beside it were several oddly attired goblins, wearing pointed spiked helmets, flapping odd bat-winged attachments fixed to their arms. Spider riders scuttled along the brow of the hill. On the back of one was mounted what must be some sort of shaman. He brandished a skull-tipped staff in the air and chanted encouragement to his troops. The greenskin force must be almost a thousand strong, Felix realised. He was glad the Slayers had not simply rushed out to meet it. There were too many greenskins down there for them to overcome.

Facing the orcs across the valley were hundreds of armed men. There were ranks of halberdiers, and rows upon rows of cross-bowmen. One or two of the leaders were mounted on horseback. There were some wild highlanders with massive two-handed swords. None of the men were well armoured but they were much better disciplined than the orcs. Even if they were outnumbered they still had a chance. Particularly if they held the high ground, Felix thought, and let the greenskins come at them.

This must be the bandit army of Henrik Richter, Felix realised. What had brought him here? What strange chance had caused these two forces to meet outside the dragon's cave?

He heard Ulrika gasp. 'Look there! To the right of the human army,' she whispered.

Felix instantly saw what she meant. He recognised the figure of Johan Gatz, the minstrel. Felix felt his suspicions had been justi-fied. The man had been a spy for the bandits. They must have followed us. Both armies must have. The orcs probably wanted revenge for the slaughter we wreaked. The men probably came to see if they could hijack the treasure, if we slew the dragon.

But why were they drawn up in battle array now, and what were they waiting for?

JOHAN GATZ CURSED. This was not going according to plan. Henrik had assembled the army and brought it here along the high mountain passes as he had asked. The scouts that always watched for sign of the dragon stirring had seen nothing of it since it had flown back from the north well over a week ago. One of them who had witnessed its arrival had even claimed it looked wounded. That fitted with the story the dwarfs had told him. The same men had seen the dwarfs enter the caves this morning, and they had yet to come out. He wondered if they had actually succeeded in killing the beast. It seemed unlikely – the valley was littered with the bones of those who had tried, but there had been something about that bunch which had compelled him to think they might do it.

Either they were the most convincing braggarts Johan had ever heard, or they were something special. Johan knew himself to be a sound judge of character, and they had convinced him. More than that, the names of Gotrek Gurnisson and Felix Jaeger were not unfamiliar to him. On his travels he had heard tales of a pair answering to their description, and if even a tenth part of those tales were true, they were not people to take lightly. Some of the lads had seen the airship pass over the valleys too, so that had confirmed their story of the *Spirit of Grungni*. All in all, he had judged it worth taking the chance of bringing the whole gang here to rob them of the treasure if they should manage to kill Skjalandir. Henrik had thought it worth the risk too.

What they had not counted on was the orcs coming up with the same plan, and being there as well. The idea had been to lie low and wait and see whether the dwarfs came out of the caves. That had gone out the window when the greenskins were spotted. The troops had mustered in plain sight. There was too much bad blood between men and orcs for either side to do differently. It was sheerest stupidity and bad luck, Johan thought.

If they had known the orcs were going to do this, they could have let the greenskins attack the Slayers and then ambushed them afterwards. But all they had gotten were reports of orcs shadowing the Slayers en route, and they did that to every caravan they spotted going through the mountains. Who would have guessed they would assemble their whole force? Now they all stood in the open like idiots, neither side willing to back down in front of the other. Johan shuddered to think of what might happen if the dwarfs did not kill the dragon, and it emerged from the cave. Maybe there were enough warriors assembled here to kill the beast. Even if there were, the casualties would be appalling. Johan considered legging it, but there was no way he could slip away without being noticed.

What could have gotten the greenskins so stirred up, he wondered?

* * *

UGREK MANFLAYER GLARED across at the hated human foes. For the hundredth time he considered ordering his warriors to charge. It would be good to feel human blood flow and human flesh part under his blade. It would be good to break bones and crack skulls. It would be good to kill, he thought. The need to give in to his violent nature was almost overwhelming. Almost.

Ugrek had not risen to be boss of all the orc tribes of the Big Mountains by giving way to his impulses. By orc standards he possessed a great deal of patience and so much cunning that some suspected him of having goblin blood. If anyone still harboured those suspicions they no longer grunted them; he had killed and eaten all those who had muttered such things. He pushed the distracting memories to the back of his mind. He needed to think. There was always the possibility that the shaman's dreams were wrong, and the dwarfs might not succeed in killing the beast. He knew that if the dragon emerged from its lair, it would not do for his lads and the pinkskins to be rucking. That would make them all easy meat for the monster, and Ugrek had no intention of providing anybody with a meal any time soon.

And if the shaman was right, then the dwarf with the big axe would soon come out. Ever since he had heard Grund's tales of the slaughter the dwarf had wreaked with that blade, Ugrek had known it must be his. With such a weapon, and the dragon's treasure, he could forge a horde that would sweep through the human lands like an avalanche. Orcs would muster from across the land to follow him, and kill and loot in his name.

It annoyed him that these humans had got in the way of his destiny. It annoyed him so much that he almost gave the order to attack anyway. Just bad luck that they were here, he thought. Their bad luck. More meat for his troops, he thought. That made him wonder what dragonflesh tasted like. He guessed he would find out soon enough if the shaman's dreams were true.

They always had been in the past. Why not this time?

'WHAT ARE WE going to do?' asked Felix. His explanation of the situation outside had not been well received. The Slayers were silent. Max looked thoughtful. The Kislevites looked worried.

'If we wait there will be a battle,' Max said. 'I don't see how it can be avoided.'

'Maybe they'll send scouts to investigate the caves,' suggested Ulrika. 'It's only a matter of time before one side or the other plucks up the courage to investigate.'

'In either case, our goose is cooked,' Felix said. 'There doesn't seem to be any way out, unless we wait for the battle and try to sneak away then.'

'I will not sneak away, manling,' Gotrek said.

'If there's a battle, Snorri wants to be part of it,' added Snorri Nosebiter.

'I suspect you'll get your wish,' Felix said.

'Everybody has to die sometime,' said Ulli. He seemed to have acquired the proper Slayer attitude of brute stubborn stupidity since the fight with the dragon. Either that or he was in shock.

'I was hoping to die a long time from now in my bed,' Felix said.

'I wanted to die in bed once too. Identical twins it was,' said Bjorni. 'I thought nothing could improve on that.'

The other dwarfs looked at him in disgust. 'You're all just jealous,' he said eventually.

'Enough of this,' Gotrek said. 'It's time for an ending.'

He strode up to the mouth of the cave and raised his axe above his head, holding the shaft in both hands.

'We've killed the dragon!' he shouted. 'If you want its treasure, you're going to have to get it over my dead body.'

For a moment, all was silence then there was a roar of voices. A moment after that Gotrek leapt back as a hail of arrows rained down where he stood. Felix noticed that some were black-fletched, some white. He wondered which had been fired by humans, which by orcs.

'I suppose being pin-cushioned with arrows is no death for a Slayer,' Felix said. Gotrek glared at him.

'You'll see what is a suitable death for a Slayer soon enough, manling.'

'I fear you are correct,' Felix said and readied his blade.

'THAT'S TORN IT,' muttered Johan Gatz, perching himself on one of the boulders strewn across the hillside. The dwarf's appearance had thrown the orcs into turmoil. The leading ranks obviously didn't understand a word of what Gotrek had said, but had correctly assumed their hereditary enemy was taunting them.

They wouldn't have been orcs if they had stood for this. The nearest greenskin archers opened fire on the Slayer. The closest unit of orcs began to lumber up the hill.

What surprised Johan the most was that some of the humans had fired as well. That was a waste of arrows. He supposed the lads must be on edge from waiting. A shout from the front ranks of the humans told him exactly how on edge they were. A group of halberdiers had rushed forward to take the orcs moving towards the cave in the flank.

It was the pebble that started an avalanche. The boar riders charged straight at the nearest unit of men. Hooves churned the thin mountain soil. Enormous droppings spurted from their rear as the creatures grew excited. The mountain clan's men, never the most disciplined of warriors and always eager to prove their bravery, rushed downslope. As they did so, some sort of drug-crazed goblin, using a chain to swing a massive iron ball almost as large as it was, broke out of the greenskin ranks and ploughed through them. In less than a minute all was a chaos of hacking, chopping, howling warriors.

Johan Gatz watched them, thinking that as soon as the opportunity arose, he was out of here.

FELIX HEARD THE crash of weapon on weapon, the screams of dying men, the guttural chanting of the orcs, the howled war cries of men. 'What in the name of Sigmar is going on down there?' he asked.

'Sounds like a battle,' Max said sardonically.

'Your powers of observation astonish me.'

Felix crept cautiously forward to take a look, mindful of the arrows that had almost skewered Gotrek earlier. He looked down and saw that the valley had erupted into a maelstrom of combat. Man and orc and goblin were locked in battle. Most of the human units had managed to restrain themselves from charging and held the higher ground against the more numerous orcs and goblins. As he watched he saw a rank of halberdiers repulse a charge by a gang of hulking green-skinned warriors. Both sides were taking awful casualties. The humans pursued the retreating orcs and were themselves caught in the flanks by a gang of crazed goblin warriors. Even as Felix watched the men vanished beneath a tide of tiny humanoids only half their size.

A strange twanging noise attracted his attention and he glanced over to see one of the oddly garbed goblins clambering onto the giant catapult. The cable was drawn back by a team of sweating lackeys, and then suddenly unleashed. The goblin was ejected into the air and went swooping off towards the human position. It moved its be-winged arms, as if believing it could somehow control its flight, and screamed ecstatically as it flew. Perhaps it did manage to control its direction, for it descended on top of one of the human leaders, impaling him with the spike of its helmet. The impact must have broken its neck, for it did not rise after that. It was an impressive tribute to either its fanaticism or its stupidity that it would give its life like that.

Suddenly other matters urgently required Felix's attention. One group of orcs had broken out of the general ruck and were racing up the hill towards him. He rose into a crouch and backed into the cave.

'They're coming,' he shouted.

UGREK SPAT ON the corpse of his dead foe. So much for waiting, he thought. So much for patience. So much for planning. One shout from that accursed dwarf and those stupid Broken Nose bastards had charged in like orc boys at their first battle. He would crack a few heads and eat few brains for that once this battle was done. By the great green-skinned gods, he would. He glanced around. It wasn't all bad tidings. He thought that his lads could rout these humans easily enough. And then he would have the axe and the dragon's treasure. It wasn't going to be such a bad day after all. He shouted to his bodyguard and began to make his way across the battlefield towards the mouth of the dragon's cave.

He was going to take the axe from the stunty's cold dead hands, he thought. And then he was going to eat his fingers.

JOHAN COULD SEE the battle was finely balanced. The greenskins had the numbers, and their odd weapons and tactics were taking a toll. Those ball-wielding drugged crazed fanatics left a path of red ruin behind them until they collapsed from exhaustion or got entangled in their chains. The flyers had killed more than one brave horseman. The sheer strength and ferocity of the orcs was amazing to watch. He saw one that had to be literally hacked to pieces before it stopped fighting. They did not seem to feel pain as men did.

On the other hand, the humans were better disciplined. They had mostly managed to keep to their ranks and hold the higher ground. The crossbowmen were taking a heavy toll on the lightly armoured orcs and goblins. Even a few of those horrid giant spiders had fallen to them. If only they had a few cannon or even one of those organ guns. Or a squadron of heavy cavalry. With one charge they could have broken the orc ranks. Might as well wish for Sigmar to arrive with the host of the righteous dead, Johan thought. They did not have any knights. They were just going to have to win with what they had.

He wasn't certain this was possible. At least some of the orcs were distracted by attempting to get at the dwarfs in the cave. And it looked like the orc chieftain, the great Ugrek himself, was trying to cut his way up there. Johan decided that he wouldn't want to be up there when the Manflayer arrived. Not for all the gold in the dragon's hoard.

FELIX CHOPPED DOWN the last orc. He was breathing hard, and blood mingled with the water that saturated his clothes. Some of it was his own. He glanced around the cave mouth. Dead orcs lay everywhere. Gotrek and Snorri had done their usual bloody work. Between them they must have put paid to at least ten of the greenskins. Five lay blasted and smoking, a testimony to the deadliness of Max Schreiber's magic. Three more lay with arrows sprouting from their breasts. Felix himself had accounted for three. He guessed the others had killed about a dozen.

They had taken casualties themselves. Standa was dead, his skull split by an orc scimitar. Bjorni had taken a nasty wound. Felix watched Max mutter some kind of healing spell that knitted the flesh together, then wrap a torn piece of his cloak around it. Bjorni looked as pale as a corpse; he had lost a lot of blood. Ulrika and Oleg moved among the bodies, retrieving arrows to replenish their quivers.

About thirty dead orcs, he estimated. It wasn't enough. There were hundreds more greenskins out there, and almost as many desperate men, all of whom would doubtless want their share of the dragon's treasure. Maybe that was the answer. Maybe they should offer to split it with the humans in return for their assistance. Good idea, he thought. Now all he had to do was get it to the human leader. And then wait for the inevitable treachery if they survived the fight.

Footsteps sounded from behind them. He saw Malakai and Ulli coming up the corridor. The engineer was bent almost double. In one hand he held a black bomb. He was dribbling powder from it onto the ground. Felix knew what he was doing. A spark would ignite that powder. The powder would act as a fuse. The fuse would detonate whatever cache of explosives they had left back there.

'It's din,' said Malakai. 'Black powder's in place. If it looks like the orcs are going to over-run us, ah'll set fire tae this pooder, an' boom the whole tunnel comes doon. Then let's see them get the dragon's treasure wie a whole mountain o' rock on tap o' it.'

Felix shivered. He hoped it would not come to this. If it did, it would mean that he and Ulrika would be dead along with all the rest of them. It was not a reassuring thought. He walked over to the woman. It was time for them to talk.

UGREK CHOPPED DOWN another human, thumped one of his own bodyguards who had accidentally blundered into him, and continued to hew his way up the hill. His mighty blade dripped with blood. His axe was smeared with gore. He bellowed instructions and encouragement to his followers, certain that victory would soon be his. Heartened by his presence the lads fought on with redoubled fury, cutting down the pinkskins by the dozen. Ugrek could smell victory.

JOHAN DUCKED BACK behind the rock. A random arrow had come close to ending his life and he did not feel like exposing himself to death at the moment. He glanced up and to his astonishment saw a tiny goblin, his eyes glazed in some sort of trance, go flying overhead. From its arms extended some sort of bat-like artificial wings. On its head was a sharp spiked helmet. Johan could have sworn it was shouting: 'Wheee!'

This was madness, he thought. The orcs were mad, the goblins were mad, his comrades were mad and he was mad for staying here when he could be running. Unfortunately he found the whole scene dreadfully fascinating.

Off at the valley mouth two units of orcs had blundered into each other in their eagerness to get at the men. Now they fought each other with the same ferocious savagery they had wanted to vent on their human foes. Maybe they were from different tribes or clans, Johan thought. Or maybe it was true what he had heard: when an orc's battle lust was up, it would fight with anyone.

A change rippled over the battlefield. He sensed arcane powers at work. His hair stood on end. Something drew his eye to
the goblin shaman the way iron filings were drawn to a magnet.

The shaman's cloak billowed behind him. His spider had
reared, raising its four forelegs as if in salute. A yellow glow
blazed from the goblin's eyes. A swirling green light flickered on
the end of its staff. Streamers of greenish ectoplasm swirled outwards from its tip. When the magic energy touched an orc or a
goblin, the recipient's eyes glowed reddishly, their muscles
swelled like great cables, foam erupted from their mouth and
they fought like berserkers. At each point this happened the battle started to turn against the humans.

Perhaps the shaman's uncanny powers would turn the tide,
Johan thought.

'MAGIC IS BEING unleashed on the battlefield,' Max said. 'I think
the shaman has invoked the power of the orc gods.'

'I wish the gods would aid us,' muttered Felix, surveying the
rent in his chainmail and the agonising red cut on his side the
wizard was healing. Golden light flowed from the mage's hand,
and where it touched his body the area first went extremely hot
and then numbingly cold. It took all Felix's willpower to keep
from screaming. After a moment, the chill passed and sank to a
dull ache. He looked down and saw the flap of skin peeled away
by an orc scimitar blow had knitted together. He could still
remember the agonising pain and the satisfied look on the face
of the orc who had chopped at him. He had turned just too late
to parry the stroke. His own blow had beheaded his attacker. It
had given him a certain satisfaction knowing that he had killed
the brute he thought had killed him. It was a miracle he had not
been killed. He had managed to keep fighting until the greenskins were repelled and Max could heal him.

'The gods gave us courage to stand our ground, manling, and
weapons to cleave our foes. What else do we need?' Gotrek said.

'An army of Sigmarite Templars would be good,' Felix said. 'I
prefer my divine aid to take tangible form.'

Gotrek merely grunted and returned his attention to the cave
mouth. Snorri stood at the edge gazing down.

'Good fight coming,' he said. 'Some big orcs and a shaman
on a spider. The spider is Snorri's.'

'You can have him,' Gotrek said. 'The chieftain is mine.'

Bjorni shook his head. 'I heard somewhere that female spiders eat their partners when mating. I've met some women who did that too.'

'Don't you ever think of anything else?' Ulli asked.

'Only when I'm fighting,' Bjorni said. 'And sometimes not even then.'

Max finished his spell. Felix thanked him and stood up.

'You'll feel real pain in a few hours, but the spell should keep you going till then. You won't be up for much fighting though. Unless...'

Felix knew what Max was thinking. Unless the orcs swarm in, and I'll have to fight anyway. In a few hours it wouldn't matter since they would be dead anyway. The last wave had left Oleg dying slowly from a stomach wound that not even Max's magic could cure. That could so easily have been me, he thought. If the orc's blow had slightly more power behind it. If my mail had not deflected it just enough.

The man's groans and prayers filled the chamber, and worked on Felix's nerves like poison. It would be a mercy to kill him, he thought, and a mercy to the rest of us to silence him.

He shivered. He was becoming as bad as Gotrek and the rest of the dwarfs. Worse. None of them would have suggested such a thing.

Painfully he went over to where Ulrika sat beside the dying man, holding his hand. He noticed that both of them were silent now. Oleg's skin looked waxy. His moustache drooped. A small amount of blood trickled from the corner of his mouth.

'Is there anything I can do?' he asked.

'Nothing,' she said softly. 'He is dead.'

Suddenly Felix felt terribly guilty.

UGREK LED THE lads right up the hill. He chopped down a few of the Broken Noses that were in his way, just to teach them not to do it again, and halted twenty strides away from the cave mouth. He turned for a moment to look back, and saw with some satisfaction that his lads were about to win the battle. The shaman's magic had helped. Filled with the spirit of the gods, his warriors were fighting as if possessed.

The spider had borne its mystic master all the way to where Ugrek stood. No one had interfered with it. It regarded Ugrek with beady intelligent malign eyes, and the warboss wondered whether it was true, and Ixix had bound the spirit of his former shamanic master into it. Not that it mattered. If he gave Ugrek any lip, he would die like anyone else. The shaman was gibbering and pointing at something excitedly. Ugrek looked to see what it was.

In the distance he saw a small dot approaching. From its size, he would have thought it was the dragon, but the dwarfs claimed to have killed it. It would be just like a stunty to lie about such a thing, and let the dragon escape by another exit. It was too late to worry about such things now, he decided.

'Right, lads,' he bellowed. 'Into the cave. Kill the stunties. Grab the treasure. Leave the axe for me!'

Having explained his plan, he implemented it instantly.

FELIX WATCHED THE inexorable tide of greenskins roll up the hill and knew he was going to die. These were the largest, fiercest orcs he had ever seen, and their leader made them look weak and mild-mannered. He was huge, half again as big as a normal orc, and he bore a cleaver in one hand, and an axe in the other. His cloak of manskin billowed behind him. His tusks dripped with saliva. His voice boomed out over the battle. Felix noticed that he was looking back at something and looked to see what it was.

From beside him, he heard Ulrika gasp.

'It looks like we might be saved.'

'Aye, if we can hold on long enough,' he said sourly.

'Who said anything about holding on?' Gotrek asked. 'I say we charge!'

'Snorri agrees,' said Snorri Nosebiter. 'Snorri is going to kill that spider.'

The Slayers plunged downhill to meet the astonished orcs. There was a mighty crash as weapons met and the killing became fast and furious.

JOHAN FELT A shadow fall on him, and looked up. Was this more goblin sorcery, he wondered, seeing the vast shape that filled the sky overhead? No. It did not look like greenskin work although there was certainly powerful magic here. To tell the truth, it looked more like dwarf work. It had runes on the side and it flew the banners of the Slayer King.

This must be the airship the Slayers had told him about, Johan realised. It was certainly impressive. Even as he watched, spluttering black bombs began to fall into the middle of the battle. The explosions tore through greenskin and human ranks indiscriminately. Judging from the way they fell, the dwarfs were trying to aim for the orcs and goblins, but not very hard. It was an impossible task anyway. The two sides were too intermingled for any sort of precision shooting.

A roaring noise announced the entry of another dwarf weapon into the battle. From turrets on the underside of the cupola, gatling cannon roared to life. Shells ripped man and goblin apart with ease. Johan had seen enough. It was time to be going. Maybe he could grab a horse.

THE SOUND OF explosions and the roar of gatling cannons told Felix that the *Spirit of Grungni* was doing its bloody work. His prayer had been answered, it seemed. The dwarfs must have finished repairing the airship and come looking for them. Judging by the new weapons bristling on its sides, they had come prepared to fight the dragon too. Felix knew that even if he died here, he would be avenged.

Screams from nearby drew his attention back to the melee. He watched as Gotrek tore through Ugrek Manflayer's bodyguard. The dwarf killed a foe with every stroke. Snorri was right beside him. True to his word he was aiming for the spider and its rider. Felix wanted to rush down into the melee and aid them, but he was tired and the pain of his wound would make it impossible to fight. No, he would stay here and record Gotrek's doom if it came to him, and hope that the airship arrived in time.

Snorri had reached the spider now. It came for him, huge mandibles dripping poison. Snorri ducked its bite, rolled under its belly, and chopped upwards. Felix heard the spider's evil scream and watched it sag in the middle. Snorri rolled out from behind it and lashed out at its rider, but the shaman leapt from his seat to avoid the blow, and scuttled away. Powerful he might be, but he did not have the nerve to face the Slayer.

Ulrika calmed nocked her bow and fired, nocked her bow and fired. With every shot an orc fell. The death of her bodyguards seemed to have goaded her into a calm, silent killing rage. Malakai stood next to her, his rocket tube over his shoulder. He took careful aim and pulled the trigger. Sparks flew from the rear of the tube and the rocket whizzed forth tearing through the orc ranks, killing half a dozen. Malakai threw down his weapon.

'Last rocket,' he explained, unslinging his portable gatling cannon and starting to blaze away. Bjorni and Ulli fought back to back against the huge orcs. They used their opponents' size against them expertly, ducking between legs, moving through the press of bodies, hacking and chopping as they went. Felix felt useless and wished he could join in.

Then he saw that Gotrek had fought his way to the orc chieftain.

UGREK CONFRONTED THE dwarf with the axe. Good. It saved him hunting the stunty down and killing him. He bellowed a challenge and glared down at the dwarf. Surprisingly the Slayer did not flinch, which was unusual. Ugrek had never met anything on two legs that did not back away when confronted by his massive form. This made him slightly uneasy. Still it did not matter. He was twice the dwarf's size and three times his weight. He was the toughest orc who had ever lived. He was going to kill this stunty.

He lashed out with his cleaver. Surprisingly, the dwarf wasn't there. That was unusual too. Ugrek knew he was fast for an orc. No one had ever been able to match his eye-blurring speed before. The dwarf struck back. That was good too. Ugrek liked it when his food put up a bit of a fight. It made things more interesting.

Sparks flashed as their blades met. The power of the Slayer's blow took Ugrek off guard. He was driven back by the force of the impact. The dwarf was strong. That was good too. Ugrek would gain some of that strength when he ate his heart. He lashed out with his axe. The dwarf ducked beneath it and aimed a counter blow at Ugrek's legs. Ugrek leapt above it, and brought both weapons down at once, knowing there was no way the dwarf could avoid them both.

The dwarf did not try. Instead, he used his axe two-handed and caught both blows in the haft of the weapon. The force of the impact drove him to his knees. He rolled backwards and away, coming to his feet easily. Ugrek was enjoying this. Already the dwarf had lasted longer than any foe Ugrek had ever faced, and he was showing no signs of running out of fight. Ugrek had always

believed that you could measure an orc by the strength of his enemies, and when he killed this Slayer, all orcs would know that
Ugrek was mighty indeed. The thought gave him some satisfaction.

The dwarf came at him, beard bristling, a mad light in his eyes.
He unleashed a hail of blows at Ugrek, each faster and more powerful than the last. It slowly dawned on Ugrek as he parried
desperately that the dwarf had not really been trying before. Being
knocked down by Ugrek had goaded him to make a mighty effort.
Ugrek was forced to admit that the Slayer was almost as mighty as
he was. This was even better. More than ever Ugrek looked forward
to eating his heart.

His arms ached a little from parrying the dwarf's blows. It felt
like his hand had been nicked. This was unusual. He had never
met a foe that had done that before. The Slayer aimed another
blow at him and Ugrek raised his cleaver to parry. At the last
moment, he realised his cleaver wasn't there. In fact, his hand was-
n't there either. The pain he had felt was it being separated from his
wrist. By the gods, that axe was sharp. He must have it, he thought.

It was the last thought to pass through his brain before the axe
descended, bringing eternal darkness with it.

Felix watched Gotrek finish the orc chieftain. The bodyguards
looked panicky, their morale already undermined by the flight of
the shaman, the havoc wreaked by the dwarfs, and the screaming
of their comrades behind them. A few turned and looked back to
see the airship. It was the last straw. They must have thought the
dwarf gods had come to punish them. First one then another
turned and began to flee. Felix looked down to see that the battle
had turned into a general rout. Orcs and goblins and humans all
intermixed, and no longer fighting, streamed out of the valley in
all directions. The relentless death toll inflicted by the *Spirit of
Grungni* was too much for them.

'I do believe we might survive this,' Felix said to Ulrika, then
wondered at the look of horror on her face. He turned to see what
she was pointing at. A stream of fire was already receding into the
depths of the mountain. Malakai's rocket tube lay near at hand.
Instantly Felix realised what had happened. A spark from the
weapon had ignited the detonating powder.

Could they possibly get down there and put it out, Felix
asked himself? He knew he would not be able to, not in his

wounded condition. And he would not ask Max or Ulrika to try something he was not willing to do. He had no idea how powerful the explosives down there were, or what the possible consequences of an explosion might be.

'We'd best get out of here,' he said and tried to move forward only to discover his legs weren't working properly. He fell forward onto his face. His wound must have been worse than he thought.

'Go!' he shouted. 'Save yourselves!'

He felt himself being lifted up by Ulrika and Max and they carried him down the slope towards the dwarfs.

'Prepare yourselves,' he heard Max say. 'The tunnel's about to go up!'

As one the dwarfs threw themselves flat on the ground. Felix felt the earth shake. There was a great blast of fire and heat from behind him, and the sound of rocks collapsing and stone grinding against stone.

'There goes a king's ransom,' he heard Ulli mutter, then the sound of dwarf cursing filled the air.

EPILOGUE

FELIX OPENED HIS eyes and saw the steel ceiling of the *Spirit of Grungni*. Borek and Ulrika stooped over him. He could tell by the rocking of the chamber that the airship was in motion.

'I'm alive, then,' he said.

'Only just,' Borek said. The wrinkles of his ancient face crinkled benevolently as he smiled. 'There was some infection in your wounds. I am surprised that you are alive at all, with what Ulrika here has told me of your adventures. Slaying a dragon is not something most men live through.'

Felix felt embarrassed as well as pleased. 'I am glad to see you. I see you managed to repair the airship.'

'Malakai left very specific instructions.'

'Is he well?'

'He and all the others. Although they are all disappointed about the treasure.'

'Is it lost then?'

'Nothing buried below the earth is ever lost to dwarfs,' said Borek. 'It will take years to excavate all of the rock but we will get it eventually.'

Felix fell silent for a moment, thinking of the bodies of Steg and Grimme. They had received a more thorough burial than anything he could ever have given them. It was an alarming thought that he could have all too easily been buried with them. He reached out and took Ulrika's hand.

'Don't worry,' she said. 'Max says you'll be up and about by the time we reach our destination.'

'Where are we going?' Felix asked, fearing he already knew.

'Praag,' she said simply.

He shivered, knowing the greatest Chaos army assembled in two centuries would soon be there too.

ABOUT THE AUTHOR

William King was born in Stranraer, Scotland, in 1959. His short stories have appeared in *The Year's Best SF, Zenith, White Dwarf* and *Interzone*. He is also the author of three previous Gotrek & Felix novels: *Trollslayer, Skavenslayer* and *Daemonslayer*, and two volumes chronicling the adventures of a Space Marine warrior, Ragnar: *Space Wolf* and *Ragnar's Claw*. He has travelled extensively throughout Europe and Asia, but he currently lives in Prague, where he is hard at work finishing the fifth Gotrek & Felix adventure, *Beastslayer*!

COMING SOON

**More awesome Warhammer
action in THE WINE OF DREAMS,
brand new fantasy from Brian Craig.**

**Here is a short preview
of the mayhem in store...**

From

THE WINE OF DREAMS

SIGURD WAS BUSY now and could not keep Reinmar from looking out on to the river's foaming surface.

The first boom had been breached, so the crowded company of boats had moved forty yards downriver, but its vanguard had been caught and held by the second barrier. The men and beastmen in the boats were able to shoot and thrust at the men defending the storehouses to either side of them, but by virtue of being trapped in crossfire – and directly beneath the crossbows positioned in the upper storeys – they were taking very heavy casualties indeed.

Reinmar immediately saw, and fully understood, that beastmen were in the majority here, and that this was no measured move of a kind that mercenaries might have calculated and executed. The creatures on the boats were hurling missiles in every direction, howling insanely as they did so, leaping at the ledges like mad dogs – but these were far less like dogs than the wolf-like beastmen surprised by Godrich's runaway wagon. These were even more nightmarish than the bodies that had been laid out in the marketplace, with horned heads and blazing eyes, and claws instead of hands.

The contrast between this fight and the one that Reinmar had just helped to win was so striking that a lump rose in his throat, making it impossible for him to swallow. There was nothing useful he could do, as yet, because the long-handled pikes were still doing more than adequate damage in the hands of men who had the strength and skill to wield them – and Sigurd was doing as much damage as any of Vaedecker's veterans, by virtue of his reach and power.

The crossbowmen had done the bulk of their work and they were now conserving their bolts, although they remained ready to pick off selected targets. Most of the pikemen, Reinmar saw, were using their weapons as much to push as to cut, tumbling the beastmen into the water rather than striking deep into their skulls and torsos. Sigurd was the only one who was using the blade of his pike almost as if it were an elongated battle-axe, slashing at faces and limbs.

Reinmar presumed that the regulars knew what they were doing, but he could not help feeling direly anxious when he saw that in spite of their crazy anatomy, the beastmen were able to swim. Those which had been thrust into the water were in considerable danger of being crushed by the jostling boats, but those which could avoid being caught were able to tread water well enough. They were waiting impatiently, but they were waiting nevertheless for an opportunity to rejoin the fight to some effect, and in the meantime others of their kind were working away at the second barrier.

Reinmar could see that the nets had already been sliced up by the beastmen's curiously dextrous claws, and he judged that the boom could not last more than a few minutes. He gripped his sword tightly, in anticipation of its further employment.

'Ready, lad?' Sigurd shouted above the din, audible only because Reinmar was fast by his side.

By way of answer Reinmar raised the bloodstained tip of his sword. He was ready – and he knew that he had to be, because the fight was about to become much fiercer. Once the enemy was able to use the river as a way into the heart of the town, another incursion like the one that had battered down the warehouse doors would not be as easily turned back, because there would be no reinforcements ready to rush forward. Once the river was open, every man in the town would be in the thick of the action. Then, and only then, would the relative strength of the two companies become clear. Then, and only then, would the defenders discover exactly what kind of monsters the enemy would employ to take advantage of the inroads made by its shock troops.

Reinmar rested the tip of his sword on the ground, conserving the muscles of his arm. He could see that even Sigurd's arms were beginning to falter now. Pikes were most useful when their hind ends could be embedded in soil and their heads directed forward like a wall of giant thorns at charging cavalry. They were not meant to be wielded like glorified spears, and Sigurd was paying the price of his unorthodoxy. Reinmar could not see another pikeman who did not have the butt of his weapon grounded, nor could he see a single one whose brow was not covered by the sweat of extended effort. Even so, the beastmen were fighting at closer quarters than they had been a few moments before. They were dying in considerable numbers, but they were still coming relentlessly for more. Not only were they coming, but they were beginning to make good headway.

Two in three pikes had now been grasped by clawed arms stronger than the tired limbs of their owners. Beastmen were actually using the weapons deployed against them as levers and ladders. There were defenders in the water now as well as attackers, and the attackers had the advantage there – whether the swimmers were townsfolk or Vaedecker's regulars they had no expertise at all in fighting in the water, and the sheer animal fury of their adversaries would have been decisive even if they had not been so heavily outnumbered.

More and more beastmen were scrabbling at the ledges of the unloading-bays now, and there were too few blades available to thrust them all back. Sigurd was the last man to drop his pike, but drop it he did, then turned to snatch up his staff – the weapon to which he was most accustomed. 'Now! Now! Now!' he was shouting, at Reinmar and everyone else around him, although none of them could have been in the least doubt that the utmost effort was called for, and that the battle for the storehouse would be won or lost within a quarter of an hour.

Then the second boom broke, and the third almost immediately afterwards. Reinmar knew that the greater battle for the fate of Eilhart passed into its second and deadlier phase – but so had the lesser conflict which was his part in it. From now on, there would be no let up until the battle was decided.

Reinmar had to focus absolutely on the matter of survival.

Vaedecker's infantrymen were already trying to form a defensive line so that the enemy might be confronted with an uninterrupted series of blades, but they had taken casualties and some of their number were still out of place, having been sent to defend the doors on the other side of the building.

The earlier skirmish had been easily won, but it had taken its toll on the organisation, deployment and readiness of the trained soldiers. Now the townspeople had to show what they could do against creatures out of their nightmares. Reinmar and Sigurd placed themselves in the line, and were immediately engaged in furious action.

Reinmar stuck very fast to Sigurd's left-hand side, not merely for his own protection but because the giant needed a blade to assist the work of his staff. Because it had no heavy metal head Sigurd's weapon was less effective than it might have been at cracking skulls, but the advantage of its relative lightness meant that the big man could move it with lightning speed.

Tired though his arms were by their exertions with the pike, Sigurd's reflexes were unimpaired, and as the monsters clambered up out of the water he struck them hard, two or even three at a time. Some fell back into the river, while any that did not sprawled on the stone floor, wide open to the thrusts of Reinmar's blade. Reinmar thrust and thrust and thrust again, but the targets kept re-presenting themselves, and every target had arms and claws, and legs and claws, and a brutal head with horns that might be as long as a man's arm.

Swordplay had always seemed reasonably easy to Reinmar while in training, when thrusts were only intended to demonstrate the possibility of harm. He had thought then that he had an aptitude for this kind of work, but he realised now that an 'aptitude' was not much use in a real fight, where raw power and endurance were the most decisive factors. Reinmar had already discovered that actually doing harm was far more awkward and bruising than merely demonstrating a capacity, and the beastmen climbing out of the bloody water rammed that lesson home.

It had been bad enough trying to cut the squat subhumans or the wolfheads, but the kinds of beastmen that faced Reinmar now were far more difficult to hurt. Not one of them wore artificial armour, but that was because they did not seem to need it. Their clawed arms, in particular, were encased in impenetrable shells, and the horns atop their heads were not merely decorative, always moving this way and that to parry blows of every sort with stubborn solidity.

Reinmar tried at first to aim for the softer parts of the beastmen – their bellies and their throats – but such thrusts were too easily turned aside and ineffectual even when they drew blood. He realised that if he were to strike disabling blows he had to find a weakness that was more easily exploitable. When his sword had bounced off clawed limbs three or four times, though, he realised that there was a disadvantage in the kind of integral armour that the beastmen had. The limbs of such creatures were not nearly as clever as human limbs, because they were too rigidly articulated – and the joints were their most vulnerable points. No fatal wounds could be inflicted by thrusting at what the beastmen had instead of elbows and wrists, but once their claws became unusable they became dead weights, worse than useless.

Reinmar shouted this advice at the top of his voice to anyone who might be listening, but there was no way of knowing whether anyone could hear or understand him. For his own part, he continued thrusting, left then right, then left again, as Sigurd's busy staff set up targets for him and deflected any weapon aimed at his head or heart. Reinmar had to look out for his own feet, but he was a great deal nimbler than beastmen of these cumbersome kinds, and he felt fully entitled to consider himself an aggressor, in command of the manner and tempo of the fight.

That changed. By slow and gradual degrees their situation was transformed, and not to their advantage. He and Sigurd were driven back from the water's edge, one step at a time. As they were driven back they were parted from the swordsmen and spearmen who had tried to form a line with them, and who were also being driven back now that gaps had appeared where men had fallen.

Reinmar knew that he and Sigurd had to delay for as long as possible in the eventuality that they would be forced to stand back to back, isolated from all other support and devoid of further choices. If that time came, he knew their little fraction of the battle would be all but lost – but in trying to force exactly that situation, their enemies were taking substantial losses. The beastmen who were lunging at them refused to die, but now they seemed to have very little, save for their own awful mass, with which to threaten the defenders. Reinmar, Sigurd and their immediate companions had rendered too many claws completely useless with heavy blows and pricking wounds, and the bloated eyes of the foul creatures were becoming very vulnerable as their horns became less adept.

Had the bull-horned beastmen been the last wave of the enemy force that was attempting to storm the storehouse, the battle to defend it would probably have been won within a few more minutes – but they were only second-line forces, little more than human battering-rams intended to sow confusion and gain space. It was impossible to read expressions in their unhuman faces and horrid eyes, but they fought more like automata than men, with dour purpose but no real fervour.

The creatures that came after them were very different, far more frightening and vastly more dangerous.

The Wine of Dreams
– coming soon from
the Black Library

Also from the Black Library

TROLLSLAYER

A Gotrek & Felix novel
by William King

HIGH ON THE HILL the scorched walled castle stood, a stone spider clutching the hilltop with blasted stone feet. Before the gaping maw of its broken gate hanged men dangled on gibbets, flies caught in its single-strand web.

'Time for some bloodletting,' Gotrek said. He ran his left hand through the massive red crest of hair that rose above his shaven tattooed skull. His nose chain tinkled gently, a strange counterpoint to his mad rumbling laughter.

'I am a slayer, manling. Born to die in battle. Fear has no place in my life.'

TROLLSLAYER IS THE first part of the death saga of Gotrek Gurnisson, as retold by his travelling companion Felix Jaeger. Set in the darkly gothic world of Warhammer, Trollslayer is an episodic novel featuring some of the most extraordinary adventures of this deadly pair of heroes. Monsters, daemons, sorcerers, mutants, orcs, beastmen and worse are to be found as Gotrek strives to achieve a noble death in battle. Felix, of course, only has to survive to tell the tale.

Also from the Black Library

SKAVENSLAYER
A Gotrek & Felix novel
by William King

'BEWARE! SKAVEN!' Felix shouted and saw them all reach for their weapons. In moments, swords glittered in the half-light of the burning city. From inside the tavern a number of armoured figures spilled out into the gloom. Felix was relieved to see the massive squat figure of Gotrek among them. There was something enormously reassuring about the immense axe clutched in the dwarf's hands.

'I see you found our scuttling little friends, manling,' Gotrek said, running his thumb along the blade of his axe until a bright red bead of blood appeared.

'Yes,' Felix gasped, struggling to get his breath back before the combat began.

'Good. Let's get killing then!'

SET IN THE MIGHTY city of Nuln, Gotrek and Felix are back in SKAVENSLAYER, the second novel in this epic saga. Seeking to undermine the very fabric of the Empire with their arcane warp-sorcery, the skaven, twisted Chaos rat-men, are at large in the reeking sewers beneath the ancient city. Led by Grey Seer Thanquol, the servants of the Horned Rat are determined to overthrow this bastion of humanity. Against such forces, what possible threat can just two hard-bitten adventurers pose?

Also from the Black Library

DAEMONSLAYER
A Gotrek & Felix novel
by William King

THE ROAR WAS so loud and so terrifying that Felix almost dropped his blade. He looked up and fought the urge to soil his britches. The most frightening thing he had ever seen had entered the hall and behind it he could see the leering heads of beastmen.

As he gazed on the creature in wonder and terror, Felix thought: this is the incarnate nightmare which has bedevilled my people since time began.

'Just remember,' Gotrek said from beside him, 'the daemon is mine!'

FRESH FROM THEIR adventures battling the foul servants of the rat-god in Nuln, Gotrek and Felix are now ready to join an expedition northwards in search of the long-lost dwarf hall of Karag Dum. Setting forth for the hideous Realms of Chaos in an experimental dwarf airship, Gotrek and Felix are sworn to succeed or die in the attempt. But greater and more sinister energies are coming into play, as a daemonic power is awoken to fulfil its ancient, deadly promise.

Also from the Black Library

SPACE WOLF
A Warhammer 40,000 novel
by William King

Ragnar leapt up from his hiding place, bolt pistol spitting death. The nightgangers could not help but notice where he was, and with a mighty roar of frenzied rage they raced towards him. Ragnar answered their war cry with a wolfish howl of his own, and was reassured to hear it echoed back from the throats of the surrounding Blood Claws. He pulled the trigger again and again as the frenzied mass of mutants approached, sending bolter shell after bolter shell rocketing into his targets. Ragnar laughed aloud, feeling the full battle rage come upon him. The beast roared within his soul, demanding to be unleashed.

IN THE GRIM future of Warhammer 40,000, the Space Marines of the Adeptus Astartes are humanity's last hope. On the planet Fenris, young Ragnar is chosen to be inducted into the noble yet savage Space Wolves chapter. But with his ancient primal instincts unleashed by the implanting of the sacred Canis Helix, Ragnar must learn to control the beast within and fight for the greater good of the wolf pack.

Also from the Black Library

RAGNAR'S CLAW
A Warhammer 40,000 novel
by William King

One of the enemy oficers, wearing the peaked cap and
greatcoat of a lieutenant, dared to stick his head above the
parapet. Without breaking stride, Ragnar raised his bolt
pistol and put a shell through the man's head. It exploded
like a melon hit with a sledgehammer. Shouts of
confusion echoed from behind the wall of sandbags, then
a few heretics, braver and more experienced than the rest,
stuck their heads up in order to take a shot at their
attackers. Another mistake: a wave of withering fire from
the Space Marines behind Ragnar scythed through them,
sending their corpses tumbling back amongst their
comrades.

*FROM THE DEATH-WORLD of Fenris come the Space Wolves, the
most savage of the Emperor's Space Marines. Ragnar's Claw
explores the bloody beginnings of Space Wolf Ragnar's first
mission as a young Blood Claw warrior. From the jungle hell
of Galt to the polluted cities of Hive World Venam, Ragnar's
mission takes him on an epic trek across the galaxy to face
the very heart of Evil itself.*

Also from the Black Library

FIRST & ONLY
A Gaunt's Ghosts novel
by Dan Abnett

'THE TANITH ARE strong fighters, general, so I have heard.' The scar tissue of his cheek pinched and twitched slightly, as it often did when he was tense. 'Gaunt is said to be a resourceful leader.'

'You know him?' The general looked up, questioningly.

'I know *of* him, sir. In the main by reputation.'

GAUNT GOT TO his feet, wet with blood and Chaos pus. His Ghosts were moving up the ramp to secure the position. Above them, at the top of the elevator shaft, were over a million Shriven, secure in their bunker batteries. Gaunt's expeditionary force was inside, right at the heart of the enemy stronghold. Commissar Ibram Gaunt smiled.

IT IS THE nightmare future of Warhammer 40,000, and mankind teeters on the brink of extinction. The galaxy-spanning Imperium is riven with dangers, and in the Chaos-infested Sabbat system, Imperial Commissar Gaunt must lead his men through as much in-fighting amongst rival regiments as against the forces of Chaos. FIRST AND ONLY is an epic saga of planetary conquest, grand ambition, treachery and honour.

Also from the Black Library

GHOSTMAKER
A Gaunt's Ghosts novel
by Dan Abnett

THEY WERE A good two hours into the dark, black-trunked forests, tracks churning the filthy ooze and the roar of their engines resonating from the sickly canopy of leaves above, when Colonel Ortiz saw death.

It wore red, and stood in the trees to the right of the track, in plain sight, unmoving, watching his column of Basilisks as they passed along the trackway. It was the lack of movement that chilled Ortiz.

Almost twice a man's height, frighteningly broad, armour the colour of rusty blood, crested by recurve brass antlers. The face was a graven death's head. Daemon. Chaos Warrior. *World Eater!*

IN THE NIGHTMARE future of Warhammer 40,000, mankind teeters on the brink of extinction. The Imperial Guard are humanity's first line of defence against the remorseless assaults of the enemy. For the men of the Tanith First-and-Only and their fearless commander, Commissar Ibram Gaunt, it is a war in which they must be prepared to lay down, not just their bodies, but their very souls.

Also from the Black Library

REALM OF CHAOS
An anthology of Warhammer stories
edited by Marc Gascoigne & Andy Jones

'Markus was confused; the stranger's words were baffling his pain-numbed mind. "Just who are you, foul spawned deviant?"

The warrior laughed again, slapping his hands on his knees. "I am called Estebar. My followers know me as the Master of Slaughter. And I have come for your soul."'
– **The Faithful Servant,** *by Gav Thorpe*

'The wolves are running again. I can haear them panting in the darkness. I race through the forest, trying to outpace them. Behind the wolves I sense another presence, something evil. I am in the place of blood again.' – **Dark Heart,** *by Jonathan Green*

IN THE DARK and gothic world of Warhammer, the ravaging armies of the Ruinous Powers sweep down from the savage north to assail the lands of men. REALM OF CHAOS is a searing collection of a dozen all-action fantasy short stories set in these desperate times.

Also from the Black Library

INTO THE MAELSTROM

An anthology of Warhammer 40,000 stories, edited by Marc Gascoigne & Andy Jones

'THE CHAOS ARMY had travelled from every continent, every shattered city, every ruined sector of Illium to gather on this patch of desert that had once been the control centre of the Imperial Garrison. The sand beneath their feet had been scorched, melted and fused by a final, futile act of suicidal defiance: the detonation of the garrison's remaining nuclear stockpile.' – **Hell in a Bottle** by *Simon Jowett*

'HOARSE SCREAMS and the screech of tortured hot metal filled the air. Massive laser blasts were punching into the spaceship. They superheated the air that men breathed, set fire to everything that could burn and sent fireballs exploding through the crowded passageways.' – **Children of the Emperor** by *Barrington J. Bayley*

IN THE GRIM and gothic nightmare future of Warhammer 40,000, mankind teeters on the brink of extinction. INTO THE MAELSTROM is a storming collection of a dozen action-packed science fiction short stories set in this dark and brooding universe.

Also from the Black Library

STATUS: DEADZONE

An anthology of Necromunda stories, edited by Marc Gascoigne & Andy Jones

'Knife-Edge Liz closed on Terrak Ran'Lo. The old man was moving for cover, crouching behind a side-table. She fell upon him, dragging him to the ground. His breath was wine-rancid, his eyes glazed with age. He looked at the woman, her face sprayed with the blood of the inquisitor, and his eyes span.

"A message from the Underhive," Liz spat and pulled the trigger.' – **Rat in the Walls** by Alex Hammond

'Outside the Last Gasp Saloon, Nathan Creed examined the scrap of parchment. If the map was genuine, Toxic Sump's dome was built directly on top of another, much older settlement. Who knew what ancient treasures lay buried beneath the ash? Creed took the cheroot from his mouth and spat into the dust. The prospector had known. Now he was dead.' – **Bad Spirits** by Jonathan Green

ON THE SAVAGE *factory world of Necromunda, renegade gangs struggle for survival in the shattered tunnels and domes beneath the teeming hive-cities. STATUS: DEADZONE is an awesome anthology of dark science fiction short stories from the devastated urban hell of Necromunda.*